Chance of a Lifetime

Center Point
Large Print

Also by Jodi Thomas and available from
Center Point Large Print:

Just Down the Road
The Comforts of Home
Texas Blue
The Lone Texan
The Tender Texan

**This Large Print Book carries the
Seal of Approval of N.A.V.H.**

Chance of
a Lifetime

JODI THOMAS

CENTER POINT LARGE PRINT
THORNDIKE, MAINE

This Center Point Large Print edition is published in the year 2013 by arrangement with The Berkley Publishing Group, a member of Penguin Group (USA) Inc.

The text of this Large Print edition is unabridged.
In other aspects, this book may
vary from the original edition.
Printed in the United States of America
on permanent paper.
Set in 16-point Times New Roman type.

ISBN: 978-1-61173-661-8

Library of Congress Cataloging-in-Publication Data

Thomas, Jodi.
 Chance of a lifetime : a Harmony novel / Jodi Thomas. — Center Point Large Print edition.
 pages cm
 ISBN 978-1-61173-661-8 (Library binding : alk. paper)
 1. Public librarians—Texas—Harmony—Fiction.
 2. Family secrets—Fiction. 3. Lawyers—Texas—Harmony—Fiction.
 4. Attempted murder—Fiction. 5. Texas—Fiction.
 6. Large type books. I. Title.
PS3570.H5643C43 2013
813'.54—dc23
                                                    2012046425

Chance of a Lifetime

❧ *Chapter 1* ❧

February 3, 2012
Harmony County Library

Hundred-year-old elms cast spiderweb shadows from a dry creek bed to the brick corners of Harmony County Library as Emily Tomlinson closed the blinds over the back window of her office. Night was coming. Time for her to move to the front desk. Grabbing the black sweater, which always hung on a hook beside her desk, she pulled it over her plain cotton blouse and charcoal trousers.

From now until closing, she'd feel wind blow in every time the library doors opened. It would stir her curly brown hair and scatter papers across the main desk, but she didn't mind. Emily loved every hour of her time at work, even the last one on Friday night. Her short curls could take the wind and she welcomed everyone who dropped by.

Before she could settle, winter's frosty breath reached her. For once, she didn't look up. Though she wondered who might be coming in just before closing, she didn't want to see the night beyond the doors. She might be in her early thirties, but the child in her still feared that the night just might look back.

Sam Perkins leaned on his broom and whispered, "You didn't make it out before dark, Miss Tomlinson. You want me to walk you to your car when you lock up? Ain't no other staff here tonight and that wind is liable to carry a slim little thing like you away."

The janitor's voice sounded rusty in daylight, but at night it turned haunting. Sam Perkins had missed his calling as a narrator for ghost tales on a midnight radio show.

Emily didn't like the possibility that everyone who worked in the Harmony County Library knew of her fears, even the janitor. "No, I'll be fine. Who just came in? I was too busy to notice."

Sam shrugged. "Some guy in muddy boots and a cowboy hat worn low."

Emily laughed. "That describes half the men in this town."

The janitor moved on, having used up his ration of conversation for the evening. He wasn't friendly, smelled of cigars most of the time, and had never read a single book as far as she knew, but he was the best janitor/handyman they'd had in the ten years since she'd accepted the post of head librarian. The others had been drifters or drunks, staying only long enough to collect a few weeks' wages to move on, but Sam never missed a day's work.

Emily closed her log and locked the cash drawer for the night. She had a pretty good idea who the cowboy with dirty boots was—he'd come in on Fridays for as long as she could remember. Most of the time he didn't say a word to anyone but her.

Walking around the worn mahogany desk, she crossed to the beautiful old curved staircase that climbed the north wall. Cradled beneath the arch of the stairs were all the new magazines and day-old newspapers from big towns across the state.

Emily had bought comfortable leather chairs from an estate sale so the area looked inviting, even though few visited. Most days, the wall of computers drew all the attention.

Sure enough, Tannon Parker was there. His big frame filled the chair and his long legs blocked half the walk space. His worn gray Stetson was pushed back atop black hair in need of cutting.

"Evening, Tannon," Emily said with a grin. "How's your mother?"

"About the same," he said as he looked up slowly. "She didn't know me. She called me by my dad's name tonight."

For a second, she remembered him as a little boy and not the man before her. He'd been quite like her, an only child with a love for books since birth. The boy she knew seemed a long way from the powerful man before her. He ran a successful business and some say breathed work.

Emily didn't see that man now. He might be a

9

tall man in his prime, but he seemed to carry the weight of the world tonight. She was tempted to reach out and touch his shoulder in comfort.

But she couldn't touch him. They weren't friends anymore—not the way they'd once been. She'd known him all her life, could name every member of his family, but one mistake one night had passed between them years ago and neither knew how to build a bridge over it. He'd told her he would be there and he hadn't been. She'd said she would wait and she didn't.

"I'm sorry," Emily managed to whisper, "about your mom. I'll never forget those great cookies she used to make." A memory of fifteen years past drifted back to her. She and Tannon had both been juniors on the high school newspaper staff. The night before the paper came out everyone always worked late. Tannon's mother would tap on the school window and hold up a tray of cookies. Kids knocked each other down to open the door for her.

"Yeah." Tannon looked toward the front desk as if he didn't know what else to say.

Or maybe he was remembering something else neither would ever forget. A memory that had more to do with pain and blood than cookies.

She straightened, feeling a little like she'd been dismissed. "We'll be closing in twenty minutes. I'll let you know when I have to lock up."

She moved away and began collecting books

left scattered on tables. When she climbed the stairs to where walls in a once huge old home had been removed to allow for long aisles of books, she saw a shadow leaning against the corner window.

"Franky, you still here?"

A girl's giggle reached her before a boy of about fifteen stepped out tugging his partner-in-crime by the hand. "Is my dad here for me?" the kid asked.

Emily noticed the girl had pink lipstick smeared across her mouth. She was staring at Franky like he was a rock star.

"If you two want to check out anything, you need to hurry."

"Yes, ma'am." Franky winked at the girl. "We've already checked out."

The girl giggled and ran down the stairs, joining her friends who were clustered around one of the computers. When she was too far away to hear, Emily whispered to Franky, "How long until you get a car?"

"Fourteen more months," he said with a grin. "I can't wait."

"Me neither." She laughed. "Did you get your homework done?"

"It's Friday, Miss Tomlinson. No one ever does homework on Friday. What if the end of the world came or something and you'd wasted your last few hours doing math or English. Monday morning I could be out fighting zombies or aliens for the last food on the planet and I'd be thinking, Great! At least I got my homework done."

Emily saw his logic. "I hadn't considered that," she said as she walked with him down the stairs.

"Don't people like you worry about that kind of stuff?"

"People like me?"

"You know, older people." Franky shook his shaggy hair. "You should. Tomorrow you could just open your front door and find yourself in a fight for your life." He looked around. "Come to think of it, nobody would probably come in here. No food or weapons or medicine. That's what we'll all be fighting over when the end comes."

She played along. To the boy, she must seem as old as this building. "Zombies don't read?"

He shook his head as if she was beyond dumb. "Miss Tomlinson, I fear you're a goner. Zombies don't do nothing but run around looking for live people to eat. They'll rip your arm off, beat you to death, and then have you for dinner. Maybe you should think about getting a gun or a man to protect you."

When they reached the desk, she handed him a book on the life and works of Hemingway. "Thanks for the advice, Franky. Here's a book that might help with that English assignment that's due Monday. Just in case the world doesn't end."

He looked at her with raised eyebrows. "How'd you know about that?"

Emily winked. "A zombie told me."

Before he could ask more, a horn honked and he darted for the door. "Thanks," he yelled back. "That's my dad."

The girls over by the computer wall all giggled and waved at him. Then, like a gaggle of geese, they all hurried out.

The library was suddenly silent. Emily began turning off the computers and closing doors. It had been a long twelve-hour day, but she had nowhere else to be. Friday nights were like every night for her. She'd go home, eat supper, and read until ten, and then, as if the clock lost all time, she'd open a spiral notebook she kept hidden away and write a few lines. In her mind, scenes would come to her like blinks of lightning in a dark sky. Not a book. Not even a story. But short little plays covering sometimes only moments.

People would be surprised, maybe even shocked, to know her secret hobby, but certain moments had changed her life in the real world, and now she collected fictional ones to piece together for her dreams.

As she tugged on her coat and reached for her keys, she noticed Tannon Parker waiting.

He held the door for her and she thanked him as he checked to make sure the lock clicked solid. She thought of walking on to her car but waited. He might not be much for company, but Tannon was steady and safe. Whatever waited in the darkness wouldn't appear if he was beside her.

For once, he broke the silence. "The zombies wouldn't come after you if the end came like the kid said. They'd go straight to the bakery across the street. The Edison sisters would keep them in food for weeks. Last month I heard they had to move the counter out a foot because the sisters could no longer get behind it to wait on customers."

Emily laughed. "That's not a nice thing to say."

"Just stating a fact. By the time the zombies finished with the third sister, they'd all be diabetic."

"Then they'd cross the street to the library and eat me. Maybe I should buy a gun to fight them off."

"I'd come get you long before then if there were trouble."

She glanced up at him, remembering a time when she had been in trouble and he had not been there. With a quick nervous move, she pulled her car door open and jumped in. Her thank-you was lost in the slam of her door.

A few seconds later, she looked back at him in her rearview mirror. He was standing in the empty parking lot. He looked solid as an oak with his feet wide apart and his hands shoved deep into his western-cut leather jacket. The stoplight caught her at the corner. She watched him as he turned and walked across the street to where he'd parked his pickup in front of the bakery.

It was Friday night and Tannon Parker was headed the same place she was.

Home alone.

Emily smiled, knowing that after ten o'clock she'd write a moment when Tannon would reach for her hand and smile. It would never happen in real life, but she'd collect it anyway for her journal.

❦ *Chapter 2* ❦

A few blocks away from the Harmony Library, Beau Yates finished the last song in his first set at Buffalo Bar and Grill. He ended with an old Gordon Lightfoot song from the seventies called "Sundown."

Beau didn't know why he loved the song. Some of it didn't even make sense to him, but it had a special kind of magic that made folks who heard it stop and sing along. When he finished the final chord, the crowd went wild with applause.

"You did it again." His partner in the band, Border Biggs, laughed. "I swear, man, you're getting better and better and all these drunks know it."

Beau shook his head letting a few strands of his dark hair escape the tie that held it. He couldn't see the gift everyone kept telling him he had. He just followed where the music took him. He knew he was good and liked to perform, but in truth, he played more for himself than the people beyond the cage. Border, on the other hand, played for the fun of it.

Six months ago, when his dad heard that he was playing at a bar, the old man waited in the parking lot one night and preached at full volume about how his only son was wasting his life and shaming his upbringing. At one point he even thanked the Lord for taking Beau's mother so early so she wouldn't feel the humiliation.

Beau might have cared if he'd remembered his mother. He wasn't even sure she was dead, she could have just left. His dad had a way of stating wishes as if they were facts. But Beau just stood there, as he had all his life, and listened to the preaching like his old man was a carnival barker pulling souls in for the next show.

Border Biggs, true friend that he was, had stood beside Beau until his old man got tired and drove off. Then, as if they'd just been delayed a minute, Border said, "How about one of them steaks at the truck stop? I've been hungry for so long my stomach is starting to gnaw on my ribs. Now that my brother is spending all his time over at his girlfriend's house, we may starve to death." He patted his stomach just to prove he was two hundred pounds of hollow.

"Maybe Big thinks we should feed ourselves."

Beau grinned remembering how Border's huge older brother had been complaining about just that for months. "Maybe we should even buy the food. After all, we're old enough to vote and at least you'll be old enough to drink next week. Think about it, Border, your brother's got a right to his own life and his own food. We can't keep waiting until he goes to sleep, then clean out the refrigerator."

Border shook his shaved head. "I was afraid something like this would happen if he ever found a female who smiled at him. I knew it wasn't likely, but I guess I'd better get used to the idea that at least one woman on the planet finds three hundred pounds of dumb muscle cuddly. She's got him not even thinking straight. Last time he came home, all he brought was a gallon of milk and Froot Loops. I hate Froot Loops. If you ask me only clowns should eat them things."

Beau yelled over his shoulder as he led Border to the car. "I love Froot Loops. It's like a Hawaiian vacation for your mouth."

"You must have loved them. You ate them while you watched me starve."

"All right, I'll buy the steaks." They stored the equipment. "But you got to look at the bright side of your brother finding a woman. If Big could find one, maybe you got a chance."

Border nodded. "I'm thinking of getting my next tattoo to say 'I've had my shots. Take me home.' "

Beau saw his partner's arm clearly in the parking lot light. A full sleeve of tats covered it from wrist to shoulder. "You know, Border, I don't understand it. I think you're downright beautiful. I'm shocked girls don't ask to spend the night just so they can admire you while you sleep."

"I know it," Border agreed. "I'm surprised someone doesn't try to shoot me, skin me, and frame me on a wall."

A car backfired a half block away, and both boys ducked behind the car, then laughed. Neither had much in the way of family, but they had each other.

They'd driven to the interstate that night and ordered steaks to celebrate the raise they'd gotten an hour before his father's public lecture. Neither mentioned Beau's dad's screaming. Maybe Border thought the lecture was nothing compared to how his own stepdad used to beat him and his big brother. Maybe he thought Preacher Yates was simply warming up for the next sermon. Either way, Beau was glad he'd had Border beside him then and now.

Tonight memories drifted with the music. Beau hadn't seen his dad for months. The old man was probably telling folks that his son was dead. Beau didn't care. He'd gone from hating the man to feeling sorry for him, but either way Beau had scratched his own name off the family tree.

Harley, the bar's owner, tapped on the cage door with the corner of the tray he carried.

"Food." Border set down his bass guitar. As he opened the door to what Harley called the stage, he asked, "Any chance we could get a beer to go with our burgers, Harley? I think it might improve my playing."

"It probably would, Border, but it ain't happening." The owner swore. "You boys are lucky the sheriff lets you play in this place. I swear if she caught me giving you beer we'd be locked up until you both turn twenty-one."

Beau took his hamburger and leaned back in his chair as he watched the crowd. In the months they'd been playing here, he didn't know Harley Moreland any better than he had when he walked in the bar and asked for a chance to play. Harley was a hard man interested mostly in the bottom line of his business. He was fair but rarely offered a compliment. In fact, his vocabulary consisted mostly of swear words held together by a noun now and then.

Border was half finished with his burger before Beau got his unwrapped.

"You know," Border said as he chewed, "I think there shouldn't be a drinking age. I think it should go by weight. Anyone over two hundred pounds can drink. You ask me, those skinny girls who drink half a beer and make fools of themselves do a lot more damage than I ever would."

"You got a point," Beau said, playing along. "Then, instead of carding people, there could just be a scale at the door. I'm guessing the women wouldn't mind that one bit. I read once that a woman would rather pose nude than tell the truth about her weight."

"Maybe I should start asking every girl I meet her weight. Who knows, one might start stripping." Border was lost in thought.

A beer bottle hit the chicken wire of the cage making Beau jump. "It's going to be a wild night, partner. Not even ten o'clock and the natives are already restless."

Border finished off his dinner. "I don't care, for two hundred dollars a night they can yell and fight all they like."

While Border tested the sound on his bass, Beau looked out at the people crammed into the bar. In the twinkling lights, he usually just saw bodies, not faces, but tonight he tried to find anyone in the crowd he recognized.

He barely remembered the people he'd gone to high school with two years ago. The folks from the church where his daddy preached weren't likely to be in the bar. Ronny Logan, who lived next door to Border and his brother, had said she would come in if she could. She was ten years older than he was, but Beau called the shy woman a friend. All she did was study and cook, but now, between semesters, she needed to have a little fun.

"You see Ronny?" he asked Border.

"She was just being nice by saying she might come. Why should she come? She hears us practicing every day."

Beau continued to look. "I'm making a New Year's resolution."

"You're a month late," Border reminded him.

"I don't care. This year I'm going to find a girlfriend. A real one."

"Yeah, I'm getting a little tired of the imaginary one I got too."

Beau looked at him, trying to figure out what Border was talking about. As usual, he gave up. "I mean a girl who likes me. The women who come in here are all older than us and have been around the dance floor too many times. I want someone my age. Someone smart that I can talk to. Someone pretty without being all made up. Someone who's not flirting with me because she's drunk or has just dumped her boyfriend."

"Well, you shouldn't have much problem with the age or finding someone smarter. With the black hat and boots making you even taller, I'd say you got that lean outlaw look about you women wouldn't mind cuddling up to. Only trouble I see you having is talking to her long enough to ask her out. Every time a pretty girl comes within ten feet of this cage, you start stuttering."

"I plan to work on that. I think I would be all

right if we could just start at the third or fourth date. It's that first one or two that make me nervous."

"How about I put a sack over each of your heads? Then you won't know she's pretty and she won't know she's on a date." Another beer bottle hit the cage. "Third time I put you two together, I'll take the sacks off and, bingo, you're on your third date."

"It's time to go to work," Beau said as he began playing a fast piece that he knew Border would eventually remember and join in. Under his breath, he said to himself, "I'm going to get out there and live so I'll have something to sing about. An artist has to suffer to make what he writes real."

Couples moved to the dance floor. It was time for the boot scooting to begin.

❧ *Chapter 3* ❧

Saturday
Harmony Library

Emily Tomlinson loved Saturday mornings in the library. Families came in together creating a holiday atmosphere. It was almost as if the walls welcomed the noises like a fond old memory from a time when the big house had once been a home.

When she'd been in grade school, her mother always brought her to the library on Saturdays. They'd sit by big windows and read as if there was nothing more important to do in the world, and then they'd take an afternoon break and walk over to the Blue Moon Diner for floats and chili fries. Her mother might know nothing of fashion or etiquette, but Shelley Tomlinson knew books. A dozen times she'd reread a book while Emily read it for the first time. Chapter by chapter, they'd talk about where the story might go.

The library wasn't as full now as it had been then. Families seemed too busy with other things on weekends, but Emily, dressed in her tailored trousers and white blouse, remained the same. Except for the different colors of sweaters and scarves, she almost had a uniform. Dark-rimmed glasses and curly hair, cut short, almost made her look exactly as she had ten years ago when she'd walked in as head librarian.

Since her first week at the job, she liked coming early and getting everything ready before she opened the door as if she were preparing for a party. Walking the stairs, she made sure all the books in the shelves built against the wall were in place.

She noticed one of the books of The Secrets of Comeback Bay series had been pulled from its order and placed on top of the twenty-volume set. No one ever read these old books, which someone had donated over fifty years ago, but now and then people would pull one book to look at the beautiful leather tooling.

Pamela Sue, one of the library's volunteers, called them "staging books" as if they were merely props put there along the stair shelves by some decorator. She said people always put books in show homes they were hoping to sell so potential buyers would think intelligent people lived there.

But this one series of books held a secret all its own. Emily had found it the first month she'd returned to Harmony to take the job. After finishing school and looking for work for four months, this offer seemed to have come out of nowhere, and she'd wanted to prove she could be the best librarian Harmony ever had. So, just after dawn each morning before the library reopened, she'd slipped in and studied the books as she dusted a year of dust away. By the time she officially reopened, she knew the shelves and she'd found the secret.

Now, as Emily remembered that day, she sat down on the stairs and cradled the volume in her hand. In the first of the series, someone had written just below the title in pencil so light she could barely make out the words, *To my secret girlfriend. I'm yours*. The admirer had signed simply *answer V3P11* in the handwriting of someone who might be still in grade school.

24

The note had puzzled Emily for a month before she took the time to check again and on a whim turned to volume three, page eleven. There, written near the fold in another's hand, was *I like you too. Promise you'll never tell anyone and you can be my secret boyfriend. V7P53.*

In volume seven, she'd found the same bold handwriting she'd first seen, only the handwriting was smoother, more polished: *Someday, when I'm rich and famous, I'll come for you. I promise. Write me in V11P7.*

She crossed to the next note. *Sorry it took me so long to answer. I don't come to the library much. I have a boyfriend now, but you can still be my secret one.*

Three more notes had been written into the pages of the stories, then no more. Emily had no idea if they'd been put there fifty years ago, or ten years ago, or the week before the library closed when the former librarian died. Each note talked of the girl dating and the boy waiting.

Months passed before she checked again, reading through the short phrases just as she had before. To her surprise, one more note had been added in the bold hand of an adult. *I've missed you through an eternity and back. Can we start writing again? V3P50.*

Emily flipped through the pages realizing the young lovers had found their secret way of communicating, but she had no idea how long between the writings. It must have been years.

Almost a year passed before the next note. This time she was sure it was from the woman.

I'm glad you're still my secret admirer. At my age one admirer means the world. V8P143.

Emily checked every day for a week, and finally the reply came. *You will always matter to me and you'll always be as beautiful as you were at fifteen. V9P17.*

Weeks went by and Emily finally stopped checking. Finally, just after Christmas, she discovered another note.

I've always remembered you. When you walk past my place, I put my hand on the window pane, wishing I could touch your cheek. Though men have come and gone from my life, I've had no other secret admirer. V12P32.

A few months later, in volume twelve, she found another note written in the bolder hand. *I force myself never to look toward your house. If I did, and saw you, I'm not sure I could walk away, but know that I feel your touch. If not on my cheek, on my heart. V3P99.*

Emily closed her eyes, fighting back tears before she finally pulled the third volume and flipped to page ninety-nine.

Nothing. The couple had started writing when very young and now as adults, maybe even older ones, they'd picked back up their secret code and wrote again.

She found nothing for a year. Emily felt as if she were an audience of one waiting for the next act of a play. She never checked the books unless she was alone, but she caught herself watching people as they climbed the stairs, hoping to see someone pause at the bank of mysteries tucked neatly on a shelf halfway up.

When another note appeared about the time she marked her third year as librarian, Emily felt as if she were now watching old friends. Some- times the notes were short: *Missing you with every breath.* Sometimes they were longer, describing the beauty of the other and ending with *I'll think of you with my last thought and cross over into death waiting for you to join me.*

A month later, she found this simple note: *Wait. When our time comes, it will be so sweet, but for now we must remain as always a secret.*

Before Christmas a new note appeared. *Our fingers touched beneath a book. Heaven comes in small gifts.*

Emily began studying the people, but none looked like they carried such a longing as the two lovers talked about. In truth, most people waited impatiently for her to check out their books. They didn't seem like the type who'd wait one minute, much less a lifetime, for someone.

Before opening, Emily checked for another entry in one of the volumes of The Secrets of Comeback Bay. None this month. Then, she hurried down the stairs to let in Pamela Sue.

The volunteer rushed in protecting her newest hairstyle like it were a work of art. Her long, overbleached hair had been tied atop her head by what looked like a bungee cord.

As always, Emily complimented the latest creation while Pamela Sue set down her many bags of yarn and crafts.

The slender middle-aged lady bragged that she loved reading, but Emily had never seen her check out a single book that didn't come from the craft section.

On the bright side, Pamela Sue was always punctual. Which in the land of volunteers made her perfect. The other Saturday volunteer, Wes Derwood, Emily always thought looked like he might have been a descendant from some line of the rodent family. He came every Saturday as well as Tuesday and Thursday afternoons. He never made it on time and would disappear for hours, claiming he'd been "lost in the stacks" as if the small library were the Amazon. He liked to shelve books and was happy to leave Pamela Sue tethered to the main desk by her knitting yarn.

The part-time secretary and a children's librarian in her eighties who worked weekday mornings called Wes "the finder" because he loved to be given the title and number of a lost book.

The last member of the staff was the library cat

everyone called "Old Gray." He wasn't friendly. He slept on the top shelf in reference and ate all the snacks Wes didn't get to first.

Emily suspected the janitor, Sam Perkins, sometimes misplaced books just to see the excitement on Derwood's face when he found the missing book.

At exactly ten o'clock, Emily waved to Pamela Sue and walked out for her morning break. The cold wind hurried her across the street to the Three Sisters' Bakery.

Tiny, the largest and oldest of the sisters, was manning the counter. "Morning, Miss Librarian, how's business?"

"Business is slow." Tiny always made Emily smile. "Got any chocolate chip muffins left, Tiny?"

Tiny handed her one already in a bag. "I saved you the last one. I put in a sausage ball for that old gray cat."

She circled the counter, fixed her own coffee, and joined Emily by the window.

The baker didn't beat around the bush. "I read the paper this morning about the town council's agenda next week. Appears library budget is on the list."

Emily nodded. "This time it might not go my way."

Both women were silent till Tiny said, "Thirty years ago when my sisters and I started this bakery, we thought we'd only do cakes and cookies. Business wasn't good with two other bakeries and a hundred Girl Scouts in town. We tried everything, including dropping off samples. We increased business to four or five cakes a week, but it wasn't enough to pay the bills. Then, one cold day my sister Geraldine got the idea to sell breakfast baked goods, opening at six in the morning. My father knocked a hole in the wall so people could drive up and get coffee and breakfast on the run. We started showing a profit."

Emily smiled, knowing there had to be a point to Tiny's story. "You're suggesting I open a bakery inside the library or maybe have a drive-through check-out desk?"

"No, dear, but sometimes it doesn't hurt to serve more than one thing."

"We tried having a few college classes."

Tiny nodded. "What about community classes?"

"On what?"

"How about on writing? You could start one of those writers' critique groups where people could come read their work. I'd even furnish the refreshments if you'd let my sister Geraldine in it. She's been saying she wanted to write a book since she could talk. It would look good to have a dozen people meeting regularly. Darn near fill up the parking lot."

"Do you think there are a dozen people who want to write in this town?" Emily couldn't help but think of her moments book she wrote in.

She could never see herself reading it to anyone.

"Sure. If you ask me, half the people in this town spend more time in fiction than reality. Make up a poster and see who you get."

Emily forgot about her muffin and hurried back to work. Within an hour, she had posters up announcing Harmony's first writing club. By two o'clock, three people had already called to sign up: Martha Q Patterson, who owned Winter's Inn Bed-and-Breakfast; the owner of the used bookstore, George Hatcher; and Tiny's sister, Geraldine.

By closing time, Emily was beginning to think the writers' group just might work. As she locked away the cash drawer, a man who looked to be homeless stepped through the door. He had oil stains on both elbows, what looked like tobacco drippings that dotted the lapel of a patched coat, and glasses so thick his eyes reminded her of fly eyes.

"Miss," he said politely, "is it too late for me to sign up for the writers' group?"

"Oh no." She managed a polite smile.

"Then I'd like to be in the group. I've always considered myself a pre-writer. Zack Hunter's my name." He grinned. "And fiction is my game."

"I'll sign you up and look forward to seeing you next Friday, Mr. Hunter."

Zack bobbed his head. "I'll be here." He backed away, bumping into Tannon Parker on his way out.

Emily was still smiling when she met Tannon's gaze. He never came in except on Fridays when the library was open late. "I was just closing up, Tannon," she said formally as she tugged off her glasses. She wasn't vain, but sometimes she felt like she looked out at the world over the rims of her reading glasses.

"I know." He removed his hat. "I came to ask a favor."

"Of course. If I can." She began cataloging what he might ask. A ride home. A few minutes to look up something. The use of a phone.

"I was wondering if you'd have a few minutes to come over and see my mother. We moved her to the assisted living unit of the nursing home a few nights ago. It's not far."

"I . . ." She'd never been to the nursing home. In a town where five generations filled several rows in churches, Emily was an exception. She had no living relatives. But her mother and Tannon's mom had been good friends. At least they had been before what her mother used to call "the accident" happened during Emily's junior year of high school. After that, the mothers still spoke, but they slipped into being more acquaintances than friends.

She needed to remember that "the accident" was fifteen years ago when they were more kids than adults. Tannon was asking for a favor now.

"I wouldn't ask"—he rushed on as if he could

read her thoughts—"but she's been asking for your mother all day. The doc said your mom must have meant a great deal to her when she was young. I figured you look so much like your mother maybe it would calm her down just to see you. Once she gets in a rage, it takes days, sometimes weeks, to calm her down."

When she hesitated, he added, "I'll be right there with you. If it doesn't work, we'll be in and out of her room in five minutes."

"If she doesn't know you, she won't know me." Emily didn't want to see Mrs. Parker. Her parents died while in a car with Paulette and Ted Parker. Tannon's parents were in the backseat and, though hurt, had survived. Emily's parents, both in the front seat, hadn't been so lucky.

"They're trying out some new drugs on her. You might help. A memory coming back spotty like this is worse than no memory at all. She quits cooperating with the staff and all hell breaks loose."

"All right, I'll go visit her, but only for a bit." She picked up her coat, wondering what she would say to a woman she hadn't seen in years.

"I'll drive you over. They're building a new wing, so parking is tricky." He held the door for her.

"Okay, if you'll follow me home first. I don't want to leave my car here."

He nodded, probably guessing she didn't want

to have to return to the parking lot after dark.

As she drove to her apartment building, she couldn't help but think about how Tannon's and her lives crossed back and forth over the years. They'd taken their first swimming lessons together with their mothers watching. They'd pestered each other at cookouts and Christmas parties before they started school and traded books from the time they both began to read. She even remembered being the first person to ride in his car when he'd gotten his license three months before her. He'd taken her for an ice cream, after which they'd circled around the town square a dozen times before he drove her home.

Emily smiled remembering that the ice-cream date had been one of her first memories she'd written in her book of moments.

She parked in her spot in the underground garage and walked out to his pickup, wishing she could remember the hundred fun times and forget the one bad memory when he hadn't been there for her.

They didn't talk as he drove to the nursing home. He parked on a dirt lot that had been roped off for temporary parking and cut the engine. Neither made any effort to open the door. "Emily, I know this is a big favor. If you don't want to do it, I'll understand. You don't owe me this."

"I know," she answered, "but if I can help, I will. My mother would have wanted me to. Though my mom and yours were an unlikely pair, they were best friends." *So were we,* she thought. "The night my folks were killed, I think your mom and mine were getting close again. Mom had written me that week telling me how excited she was that all four of them were going to a Cowboys game in Dallas. I'd talked to her that morning and she told me she'd bought her and dad Cowboys jerseys to wear. I remember laughing thinking how funny they would look sitting next to your parents. I never saw your father without a suit on, and your mother would wear fur to the game.

"If a drunk driver hadn't ended it all, I think Mom would be at your mother's side now."

"Probably so." Tannon didn't sound convinced.

Silently they walked into the nursing home. Tannon held the door for her and they slipped into his mother's room.

The room was lovely, done in pale yellow with flowers on every table, but the sight of Mrs. Parker, curled in the fetal position, broke Emily's heart. She'd withered to frail, and her black hair was snow white. She held a pillow against her as if it were all she had in the world to hang on to.

"Mother," Tannon said as he moved to her side. "Mother? Can you hear me?"

Paulette Parker didn't open her eyes.

Tannon knelt beside the bed and lightly touched her arm. "Mother. I've brought someone to see you. Do you remember Shelley Tomlinson's daughter?"

Emily stood just behind him having no idea what to do. Paulette had been her idea of a perfect lady when she'd been a child. She was always laughing, always the center of attention and drew people to her everywhere she went. She had suits to wear to church with hats and gloves to match. She even owned fur coats, which she wore when her husband took her to plays in New York City. The Parkers weren't any richer than the Tomlinsons, but they seemed to be with Paulette's little touches around the house and her wild stories of their ordinary vacations.

Tannon looked back at Emily. "She's not asleep. She's just closing us out of her world. She does that when she doesn't want to talk to anyone."

Emily knelt beside the bed and whispered to the shell of a woman who'd defined class to a small shy child. "Paulette, it's nice to see you. I was just thinking of how you once taught me how to set the table for high tea. You even had a cover for the teapot you said came all the way from England."

Gray eyes slowly opened. "It did, Shelley, you know it did."

Emily smiled. "Yes, I knew because you always reminded me."

Paulette's thin lips pulled to a smile. "We did have a laugh about that, didn't we? I never told

Ted that it was sent to me by an exchange student we met at the state fair in Dallas. He would have had a fit. I wrote the fellow all through our senior year, and when he said he was sending me a surprise, you and I spent hours trying to guess what it was. A teapot cozy wasn't even on the list."

Emily grinned. "I'd forgotten that." Her mother had died during Emily's junior year in college with what seemed a million things left unsaid between them. She'd never known that her mother even went to a state fair. It seemed far too wild a thing for Shelley Tomlinson to do. After all, she played the piano in church and married before she was twenty. "Do you remember what you and Shelley did at the fair, Paulette?"

"Of course." Tannon's mother straightened, shifting onto her pillow as she tugged up her covers. "We told our parents we had to stay a day longer at the state FHA convention, but we went to the fair. You ate so much fried food you got sick. While we were sitting in the shade, waiting for you to recover, we met these two boys from England. I swear they looked like they could have been the Beatles' brothers. Or at least the one who liked me could have. Yours was redheaded and had a habit of making fun of the way everyone talked, like we were the ones talking funny and not him. Remember how bored we got with him?"

Tannon offered Emily a chair as his mother told a story Emily felt sure no one in either family had ever heard. Paulette swore she fell madly in love with her date for the day, but Shelley had her feet firmly planted on the ground as always and wouldn't give the redheaded Englishman a second glance.

"We ran the park like wild children, sneaking into places and eating food we'd never tried. Just before it got dark, we walked along the back of the fair grounds where people were camped out like gypsies. There was a radio playing music like we'd never heard and little kids with sparklers dancing around in the dark. An old lady read our palms for free."

When the nurse came in, Paulette didn't fight the medicine. She introduced Emily as her best friend, Shelley. "I begged her to go away to college with me," Paulette told the nurse, "but she was determined to marry and now I'm back after a year of higher learning and I can't believe how she's changed."

For a moment, Emily saw the woman Paulette had once been. Her words might not make any sense, but her manner still had polish. She was living somewhere in her late teens when plans could climb to any height and needed no roots.

The medicine began to take effect. When Paulette lay back in her bed, Emily brushed her white hair away from her cheek and kissed her gently. "Good night, dear. Sleep tight and we'll talk again."

"Tomorrow," Paulette whispered and closed her eyes. "We might go swimming. I've got a new two-piece."

Emily watched her for a while remembering how her mother had always said Paulette Parker was fragile, like fine china. Sometime in the years since she'd seen her mother's best friend, the woman had broken and Emily had a feeling all the medicine in the world wouldn't fix her.

As soon as they were in the hallway, she asked Tannon, "How long has your mom been like this?"

He shrugged. "I have a hard time remembering when she wasn't like this. Dad used to just say she needed her rest. Even when I was little, there were days she didn't get out of bed. She used to say that she was given to depression, but she hid it from everyone outside the house. When your folks died and my dad was hurt so badly he was in a wheelchair for almost a year, she couldn't handle it. I came home from college and took over the business for Dad and he tried to get well while he took care of her." Tannon ran his hand through his midnight hair. "My dad's insides were slowly shutting down, and it was still all about Mom."

"I didn't know." She'd really never thought about what had happened to the Parkers after the car wreck. She knew they'd survived it, and her parents had not. She'd come home for the funeral and stayed a week to close up the house and then gone back to college. At college she could pretend that nothing had changed until holidays and breaks with nowhere to go.

Then she'd been offered the library job and had returned to Harmony for the first time since her parents' death. As she'd driven into town, she'd stopped at the cemetery and went to stand at her parents' grave. "I'm home," she'd said with a smile.

It had been almost a dozen years since then and she'd never known about Paulette's condition. Tannon had always kept his answers simple: "She's fine" or "She's better." He had never shared his troubles. Not until tonight.

"Did your dad ever go back to work?"

"No. Once he could walk, he took care of Mom until he died. Then, because I had to run the business, I hired a live-in nurse and a housekeeper for Mom."

Tannon opened the door for her and offered his hand as she climbed into his pickup. He didn't look like he wanted to talk about his mother anymore, so they drove silently back to Emily's apartment.

"Thanks for coming," he said when he'd stopped. "I haven't seen her that happy in a long time. Maybe next time you could ask her what the fortune-teller said."

Emily didn't know what to say. She didn't think there would be a next time. Part of her wanted to remind Tannon that they were no longer friends. They hadn't been for years. He'd hate knowing that she felt sorry for him, but she couldn't help but see the weight he carried. His shoulders were broad, but even strong men sometimes break and she didn't want to think of that happening. She knew how it felt to be broken.

"You want to come in for supper? I left ribs cooking in the slow cooker. They should be falling off the bone by now."

He waited so long to answer that she wished she could take back the offer. She didn't actually want to spend time with him, not really, and she certainly didn't want to hear his made-up reason why he couldn't come in.

"You sure you got enough?" he finally said. "I'm starving."

"Yes. I always cook for the week on Saturday and Sunday." She opened the door and climbed out of the truck. Without another word, she pushed the four-digit code to the main door and walked into the lobby.

He followed.

At the elevator, he waited as she punched the fourth-floor button. She wouldn't have been surprised if he'd bolted.

Once inside her place, he looked around appreciatively. "Nice," he finally said.

"It's not much," she admitted, thinking that she probably should have moved to a larger apartment, but she liked the top floor. "I kind of just collected the furniture over the years. Some of it was tossed away and I rescued it."

He touched an old Bentwood rocker that was next to a Victorian tea table. "It all seems to go together." He glanced up at the bookshelf circling seven inches below the ceiling. "If the library ever needs books you could loan them a few hundred."

Emily laughed. "I've never been able to say good-bye to books. I thought of having someone come in and steal a dozen a month until I notice the space in the shelves."

"Might be a good idea," he agreed.

After he toured her other two rooms, she handed him a plate of ribs.

"This looks great." He remained standing until she joined him.

They were halfway through the meal before she remembered drinks. "All I have is water and a few diet root beers."

"I'll take the water," he answered.

When she jumped up to get the drinks, he asked without looking at her, "Why didn't you move back to your parents' house? I've driven past it a few times over the years. It's all boarded up."

"I guess because I've closed that door." She lined up three chocolate kisses above his plate. "For dessert." She smiled.

"You're pretty good at closing doors," he said more to himself than her. "I kind of have the opposite problem. Every door I ever walked through in my life seemed to be revolving."

They finished the meal in silence. He took his plate to the sink, picked up his hat. "Thank you for the meal and for what you did for my mother tonight."

"You're welcome." She watched him closely, thinking there was little of the boy she'd once known. The man before her was far more stranger than friend.

He shifted, widening his stance as if preparing for a blow. "I'd like to return the favor. Maybe I could buy you dinner so you don't come out a day short on food this week."

"Maybe," she said, the only thing she could think of that wouldn't be a yes or a no.

As she watched Tannon Parker walk toward his pickup, she tried to decide if she should let him back into her life. She'd spent years living in Harmony without having to face her past, but if she let him into even a small part of her world, she might not be able to close the door again.

It was well after ten when she pulled her spiral journal out and wrote a moment of Tannon smiling with a touch of barbecue sauce on his cheek. She'd almost reached over to brush it away.

❦ *Chapter 4* ❦

Tannon Parker drove back to his place. Most folks in town thought he still lived in the big rambling house his dad had built for his mother forty years ago. Ted Parker had been almost twenty years older than Paulette and no one mattered to him except her, not even his only son.

Without turning on a light, Tannon climbed the stairs to his quarters above the Parker Trucking offices, his company and home since he'd left college his junior year. The old man hadn't even bothered to clean out his desk—he'd just turned everything over after the car wreck. "Run the company and pay the bills, boy. I'm going home to your mother."

That first year Tannon had worked night and day learning the trucking business. He'd made mistakes and more than once had to drive a load himself because a driver didn't like taking orders from a kid. He'd learned to be fair and hard. He'd learned to be the boss. He'd learned to stand alone.

Somewhere in the chaos of those first few months, he'd finished out the second-floor loft and moved in. He told the staff it was just a spare room to use when he worked late, but Tannon never spent a night in his parents' home once it was finished, and he doubted either of his parents had missed him.

When his dad died, Tannon hired round-the-clock care for his mother. He stopped by every day to check on her. Sometimes she didn't feel like talking to him. Sometimes she wanted all his attention. Whatever he gave or did was never enough. He couldn't seem to measure up to his father in the undying devotion department, and Paulette wasn't used to settling.

As he flipped on a lamp tonight, the warm colors of his place greeted him. Emily had decorated in the same earthy browns and dark greens. His might be mostly comfortable over-stuffed leather and hers with too many frills and clutter, but they'd used the same palette. Where his place was clean lines and cold in the way of a high-end hotel room, hers was homey. It made him want to settle in at her place and never leave.

She had no idea how closely he'd kept up with her over the years after her parents died. When she'd graduated from Texas Tech, he'd been there. He'd driven to Lubbock and watched her walk the stage in the United Spirit Arena. When families flooded the gym floor after graduation, he'd stood in the stands and watched her standing alone with her diploma in her hand. He'd wanted to go to her, but an ocean of people and memories stood between them, then and now.

After pouring a drink, Tannon walked across the hardwood floor that echoed around his open loft. He might be only thirty-two years old, but tonight he felt like a hundred. He'd asked Emily to talk to his mother because he hoped to calm Paulette down, but once they were at the nursing home, he knew he'd wanted the favor more for his sake. Tannon needed normal in his life, if only for an hour.

He lit the fireplace and relaxed back in his favorite chair. For a while tonight, he'd almost had normal. He would have been happy with just being with Emily at the nursing home, driving there, driving back to her place. Only she'd given him far more. She'd invited him in for dinner, having no idea what a rare gift she'd handed him.

Emily Tomlinson was the last person in Harmony he'd expected to be kind to him. When he'd first taken over the business, he'd learned to be rigid if he wanted to survive. From the drivers to the stockyard owners, the men he worked with would have spotted weakness and eaten him alive. The few people who did offer friendship eventually went away when he rarely returned their calls. He told himself he liked the way he lived. It left him not having to answer to anyone. It left him time to work. It left him alone.

The ringing of the phone ended the silence of his night.

"Parker," Tannon answered as he always did whether at work or home. His trucks were on the road twenty-four hours, seven days a week and every driver knew to call in if there was a problem.

"Mr. Parker, I'm calling with a message from your mother's doctor. He just made night rounds and wanted to thank you for whatever you did tonight. Paulette is resting calmly. She even agreed to eat her dinner. We've guarded hope for improvement."

"I'm glad," Tannon answered, thinking his mood was improving also, but no one cared about him.

No one ever had.

"Well," the nurse said, "I'll call you if there is any change."

When he put the phone down, he flipped off the overhead lights and looked out the long windows running along the south wall of his apartment. He could see the four-story apartment building where Emily lived. What he guessed were the lights from her apartment were still on. He wondered if she was reading or watching TV, or maybe washing up the dishes. If he were there, he'd help her clean up, or probably talk through whatever program she tried to watch, or sit silently beside her while they both read.

It would be heaven to have someone to just be with. Not do anything. Maybe not even think. Just be.

"If wishes were horses," he said aloud, "beggars would ride."

❦ *Chapter 5* ❦

Sunday morning

Beau Yates and his friend Border Biggs spent an hour organizing their meal plan. Ronny, who had the duplex next to the Biggs boys, could be counted on for at least one meal a week and sweets delivered now and then. Border's grandmother always made dinner for the boys on Sunday night at the bed-and-breakfast where she worked. It went unsaid that Beau would be invited. The meal was great, but they'd have to put up with Martha Q Patterson, the owner. Harley fed them on the nights they played at Buffalo's and sometimes on the nights they just went in to rehearse. Only problem there was all he served was hamburgers and wings.

So if they ate cereal for breakfast, snacked on whatever leftovers they found, supplemented with PB&J sandwiches, that meant they only had to buy two meals a week. Border thought they should go to the all-you-can-eat buffet on

Wednesdays at the truck stop. The downside to that was most of the food was left out until someone ate it. The second plan was to order two big meals, eat half, and bring home the leftovers for another meal.

This plan had one flaw. Border always ate all his meal and usually claimed he ate Beau's leftovers in his sleep.

So they went to the third plan. Eat at the Blue Moon Diner. The nightly specials were cheap, and the food good.

The boys split their earnings down the middle. Border was saving for a bigger bike. Beau simply wanted to save all he could. "For a rainy day," he'd said. " 'Cause it's been raining most of my life."

They were full and in good moods when they got back from their Sunday meal at the bed-and-breakfast with Grandma Biggs. She'd made a chocolate cake in a square pan and iced it with white frosting. When they'd fought over it, she'd sliced it down the middle and served each half. Border ate his half, but Beau added most of his cake to the stack of take-out boxes Mrs. Biggs always packed.

While Border went in to put up the leftovers, Beau sat down on the porch of the duplex and began to play. Like they always did, the words to a song seemed to dance in time with the music. He'd been working on the beginning of a song about living through the rainy times and learning to dance in the storm.

Last night, when he played the beginning for the Biggs brothers and Ronny, she cried and said it was the most beautiful song she'd ever heard so Beau figured he'd finish it. Tonight her half of the duplex was dark, which was unusual. Most nights her desk light would be shining, telling them that she was studying.

"Wonder where Ronny is." Border voiced Beau's question. "I noticed her car is parked out back so wherever she went, she walked."

Beau looked out into the street. He'd seen her walk at night sometimes when the nights were warm, but tonight was cold. As he watched, a boat of an old Dodge drove by so slowly they should have tried to charge it for parking. "Well," Beau whispered, "we know she's not visiting her mother. The old bag is circling the place."

Border laughed. "I swear she circles nightly. She's disowned Ronny, but she's still trying to keep up with her like Ronny's a girl and not a full-grown woman." He waved and the Dodge sped up. "Go home, Dallas Logan, and pester someone else."

Beau went back to his song. Border listened for a while and then went inside, complaining about the cold.

When Border yelled good night, Beau wasn't in the mood to crawl under his blanket on the couch. He decided to walk. Maybe Ronny Logan was right, maybe tonight was a good night for a walk.

He liked Harmony best when the town was asleep. He loved to go down to the old town square. There, time seemed to have stood still. It could just as easily have been 1950 as 2012. Nothing much had changed. In the sounds of the night he could hear music. A melody that only belonged to Harmony. Beau hadn't traveled much, but he had a feeling every place had its own beat, only this was his home. This beat kept time with his heart.

He slowed when he saw the sheriff's car pulling alongside him.

"You all right, Beau?" Sheriff Alexandra Matheson asked.

"I'm fine. Just listening to the night." If he'd been anywhere but here, the law officer might have thought him crazy.

"You want a ride home?" she asked.

"No. I'm home." He smiled, proud of himself for not stuttering.

"All right." She understood and pulled slowly away.

Before he made it back to the duplex, another song was already dancing in his mind, but he didn't pick up his guitar when he slipped back into the apartment. He was too busy thinking about how he should change his life and learn to do some hard living like country songs always talked about.

Funny thing, he thought, how he had nothing much. He could pack all he owned in the trunk of a car and he couldn't even afford an apartment, but tonight, with the music in his head, he felt rich.

❧ *Chapter 6* ❧

On weekends Rick Matheson usually worked late at his office across the street from the courthouse. Or at least he tried to work. He'd been a lawyer for over a year and so far he'd yet to defend anyone he believed to be innocent.

Pacing the small office above a used bookstore, he stopped long enough to watch Beau Yates walk the deserted streets below. The kid had more talent than anyone Rick had ever known, but he wasn't sure if it was a gift or a curse. He'd heard once that the German word for "poison" is *gift*. Maybe the gifted in the world aren't all that lucky.

There was a sadness that shadowed Beau Yates like a broken aura, yet when he played, people felt his music all the way to their souls. The whole town was rooting for him to make it big. Well, everyone except his old man, who preached against Beau to anyone who would listen. Brother Yates was a fire-and-brimstone preacher, taking out what he saw as his son's failure on the whole town. If his congregation got any smaller, they could meet at a picnic table in the park.

Rick had to give the kid credit. "Beau Yates has something he believes in," he whispered to himself, "which is more than I have right now."

When he'd first decided to go into law, he'd thought he'd be fighting for the wrongly accused. He'd fight for rights. He'd fight for truth. But, as it turned out, the ones who needed all that couldn't seem to find his door. His cousin Liz Matheson had married Gabe Leary, a graphic artist hermit, and pretty much left Rick her small office. Now she worked mostly from home. Most weeks Rick felt he could scratch one of the Matheson names off the sign outside. He was alone, not sure of what he was doing, and broke.

Rick found plenty of crooks caught red-handed who wanted to plead innocent. People who wanted to sue anyone they could find as their get-rich-quick scheme and couples who insisted on beating each other to death in court over scraps from a broken marriage.

Forcing himself to go back to his desk, he stared down at the case file from yesterday's latest waste of time. A guy, who went by Mouse, had cut his arm climbing out of a house he'd forgotten to make sure wasn't occupied before he robbed. The police had evidence of his blood on the glass, and they had his fingerprints on all the stuff he dropped when he ran. The old couple, who lived in the place, were easily able to ID Mouse as the robber. To make matters worse for Mouse, his car, parked out front of the crime scene, wouldn't start. The sheriff picked him up and found him bleeding from the cut and with his pockets full of evidence.

Rick got assigned to the case. To his shock, Mouse insisted on pleading not guilty. The jury took forty-five minutes to make up their minds. Rick figured it would have been less, but the bailiff made a fresh pot of coffee and set out leftover cookies from an office party down the hall.

Of course, Mouse blamed Rick and demanded that the court appoint another lawyer. On his way out in cuffs, Mouse whispered the same good-bye most of Rick's clients used. Mouse warned him to watch out for accidents, because it he ever got out, Mouse planned to make sure Rick found a few.

Rick lifted the file and tossed it in the drawer with the other losers. He'd worked two jobs to pay his own way through law school, and for what? To listen to threats. To feel like he needed a shower every time he talked to a client. To make half the money his brother, who'd skipped college, made mowing lawns.

At twenty-eight, Rick should be having the time of his life. He knew he wasn't bad-looking, was educated, came from a good family, but with the overhead of the office and the cost of keeping up the appearance of being a successful lawyer, he didn't have enough money for a drink at Buffalo's, much less to spend on a date.

Flipping off the light, he grabbed his empty briefcase and headed home. Once he was in the hallway, he locked his office, checked to make sure his cousin's office next door was locked, and walked toward the back exit where he'd parked his car. The place had been silent since the bookstore downstairs closed an hour ago. During the day he could almost believe he was in the center of things—after all, his wall of windows faced the courthouse, but Rick had always thought the building, with its rattling windows and clanging pipes, was creepy at night.

When he stepped out the exit to a small landing, he turned his collar up against the cold and wished he had his coat. But his winter coat was at the cleaners and money would have to be coming in before he could get it out. The sports jacket would have to do for now.

As the door closed, what light there had been in the back of the building disappeared. The one bulb on a pole at the bottom of the steps was out again. No surprise. The building was falling apart. It took him a minute for his eyes to adjust to the night, but then he began down the old back stairs toward his car. Metal steps had been replaced along the way with wooden ones slightly thicker, giving the stairs an uneven stride. He'd walked it in the dark a hundred times before. He knew the way.

Only tonight the third step was made of air. Rick braced himself realizing a board must have broken. His free hand reached for the railing as his foot readied for the fourth step. It was missing also. Just as he began to fall through the hole in the stairs, his hand clamped around the railing and the wood gave.

His long frame tumbled, bumping into poles a few times before he landed with a thud on a broken slab of concrete below that had once been the steps to the bookstore's back door.

Thoughts tumbled with him. He could be hurt, or die here in the dark. Someone had cut the steps away. He still held his briefcase. A moment later, reality hit along with the pain. He couldn't breathe! He couldn't move!

Rick heard the clock tower begin to chime the hour as if ticking away the seconds he had left of consciousness. He tried to shift away from something stabbing in his back. Concentrating, he fought to stand. Opening his mouth, he struggled to yell. Nothing worked. All he could feel or think about was the pain.

Finally, he managed to pull his phone from his belt with one bloody hand. He held down the number one praying that he'd be able to hold it long enough before he passed out. In the low glow of the phone he thought he saw a shadow of a man dart into the alley thirty feet away.

"Nine-one-one. What is your emergency?"

Rick closed his eyes and let the phone slip from his fingers as pain won the battle.

He drifted in the night, trying to find the way back to the world. In the distance, he heard a siren. Then what seemed much later, someone called his name. Finally, light danced across the darkness like a ball.

"Rick," a woman yelled. "Rick!" She was moving closer. "Oh my God, Rick!"

Someone had found him. He tried to call out but couldn't.

"Phil, call an ambulance," the woman snapped orders as her hand touched Rick's throat. "Then call the hospital and tell them we're bringing Rick Matheson in. They'd better be ready. Looks like a head injury, back injuries, and maybe broken bones in legs."

The light moved closer to his face. "Rick," a woman said again. "Can you hear me? It's Alex." Her badge flashed in the light of others moving in. "We're not moving you until the EMTs get here, but don't worry, I'm with you." He could hear clicking on a phone, then her hushed words. "Dispatch, call Hank and tell him I've found his cousin. He's hurt bad. The ambulance has been called, but he can get here first." She paused for a few seconds, then added, "Back of used bookstore."

She knelt close, shining the light on his face. "Rick, hang on. Hank's on his way. We'll get you some help."

"Thanks for coming," he tried to say, but he wasn't sure the words came out right. A coldness crossed over him and he drifted into a place where there was no thought, no pain.

When he pulled back to the world again, he was surrounded by light so bright it hurt his eyes. For a second he thought he might be in heaven, but the sound of two women arguing almost made him wish for the blackness again.

He managed to open one eye a slit. Dr. Addison Spencer was yelling at his cousin's wife, Alex Matheson, the sheriff.

"I'm taking him in to examine him, Sheriff," the slim blond doctor yelled. "As soon as I know he's not bleeding internally, I'll let you question him."

Alex wasn't giving an inch. "I have to know who did this. The steps were cut, Doc. Don't you understand? Someone tried to kill him."

Dr. Spencer wasn't slowing down. "Get out of my way or I'll have you kicked out of my hospital."

Alex looked like she might argue. She closed her mouth so tight white lines formed around her lips as she nodded once. "All right. Take care of him first, and then I'll find out who did this."

The doc gave a signal to move the bed, then turned back to Alex. "I'll make sure you get to ask those questions as soon as possible."

"In the meantime I'm posting a guard." The sheriff's words ended with the closing of a door and people in masks rushing toward Rick like vultures at a fresh kill.

He lay perfectly still, but he felt like the six-foot buffet at the Golden Corral with everyone poking on him. Slowly, the pain eased enough for him to take a deep breath, but he didn't want to look at what they were doing. Someone was cutting his clothes off, needles were stuck in his arm and someone had taped something cold to his chest. He guessed he was lying nude for a viewing. In his shattered thoughts, he got the idea that if he didn't open his eyes maybe no one could see him if he couldn't see them.

Another breath and the pain eased a fraction more, but the poking and twisting of his body continued.

About the time he fell asleep, someone patted his cheek to wake him up to tell him that it was almost over.

He felt his entire body being lifted and shifted onto another cold surface. His mind decided to drift off and the next thing he felt was a warm blanket being spread over him.

"Rick?" Dr. Spencer said. "Rick, you're going to be all right. Just try not to move. Rick, are you awake?"

"Yes," he said, and the word almost sounded believable.

"The sheriff wants to ask you a few questions. Are you up for it?"

"Yes." He sounded better. At least the word made sense.

"Good." The kind doctor patted his arm as if he were a child. "We'll talk later, but you are a very lucky man to have survived such a fall."

He didn't feel very lucky.

He decided to risk opening his eyes. Sheriff Alex Matheson was standing over him with her husband Hank at her side. She looked worried, but his cousin looked angry.

"What happened?" Rick said, looking straight at Hank. The rancher might be a few years older than he was, and he'd never known Hank Matheson to lie about anything. If the Matheson clan in Harmony had a head, it would be this one strong man. Hank not only ran one of the biggest ranches around, he also served as the volunteer fire chief.

Alex answered for Hank. "We think someone tried to hurt, maybe even kill, you tonight. The stairs were in good shape around four when Liz dropped off some papers. It's pretty dark out there now, but my deputy had no trouble seeing that a couple of the steps had been sawed out. You took a twenty-foot fall."

She leaned close. "Did you hear anything?"

Rick shook his head. "George is always banging around downstairs. I didn't hear anything unusual."

Hank's frown deepened. "You know anyone who would want to kill you?"

Rick tried to smile. "Yeah, most of the people I've represented. One mentioned yesterday that I should watch out for accidents, but he didn't do this. He's locked up and I'd be real surprised if Mouse had a friend who'd help him carry out his threat."

"Anyone else? We think you might have been robbed." Alex pulled out her pad and pen. "Your briefcase was empty."

"It's always empty unless I'm heading into court." Rick didn't want to say that he had nothing besides his lunch to put into it most days. "I thought I saw a shadow of a man moving away, but I can't be sure."

Alex nodded. "Whoever did this could have stayed around to make sure you fell. Could you identify him from a lineup?"

"No. He was little more than a shadow. I didn't get a good look at him."

"How tall?"

"I don't know." Rick knew the drill. "Baseball hat, maybe. Dark jacket. I didn't see or hear anything else except the chiming of the clock."

Rick forgot about the doc's warning and grabbed for his billfold. If the plan was robbery, the guy went to a lot of trouble for seven dollars. A machine above his head immediately started making all kinds of noises.

Dr. Spencer was back. "That's it for tonight, Sheriff. Rick needs to rest." She moved around Rick, checking him as if he were a broken clock that had fallen off the wall and she needed to know he was still ticking.

"All right." Alex smiled at the doc, then took Hank's hand. "Sorry about earlier. I was just trying to do my job."

"Me too," the doc admitted. "We're all worried about him, Alex. Me, you, the whole town. Half the nurses already have a crush on this Matheson." She glanced from Hank to Rick. "They're all so good-looking, but this one is single."

"Which half of the nurses?" Rick asked just before he fell asleep, too exhausted to wait for the answer.

❧ *Chapter 7* ❧

Sunshine sliced into the hospital room through the blinds when Rick finally woke. He vaguely remembered talking to the doc before dawn. She'd gone through all the things wrong with him, including a mild concussion, two cracked ribs, and a gash in his back that needed stitches. Both his legs were badly bruised but no broken bones. Then, with a smile that would have made him fall in love on the spot if she wasn't already attached to a rancher named Tinch Turner, Addison told him to rest a day, then get out of her hospital. They needed the beds.

Rick had drifted off to sleep when she'd left, but the hospital staff had been waking him up every hour since. One wanted his blood. One wanted to feed him and the last one wanted to bathe him. He said no to them all. He'd keep his blood. He wasn't hungry and he'd take a bath when they got all these tubes out of him.

Only this time the staff hadn't wakened him, a smell had. The warm, wonderful smell of his mother's sausage-cheese balls. He took a deep breath and knew they had to be in the room with him. "Mom?"

"Morning, Rick," Marian Matheson said. "It's about time you woke up. These won't be hot much longer. I had to make them before I came because I knew you wouldn't eat the hospital breakfast. How I managed to spoil all my kids rotten is beyond me."

Rick smiled up at his mother. Her hair had turned white in her forties after being widowed, but she still looked young to him.

She put her hand against the side of his face. "That sweet doctor told me not to worry, but I had to come up and see for myself. I don't care how old you get or how tall, you're still my boy."

Rick tried to smile. "I'm all right, Mom. Just an accident."

She nodded and moved away so he wouldn't

see her tear up. His mom cried at weddings, funerals, holidays, and birthdays. Sometimes she cried at sappy movies and cute things her grandchildren said, but not one of her five children ever doubted for a minute that she loved them. Rick didn't doubt it now.

"Roll me up, Mom. I can't wait to eat a few of those sausage balls. I think they may be the cure I've been waiting for."

She laughed. "I knew they'd make you feel better. Hospital food is nothing more than school cafeteria food without the salt. You don't eat right as it is so you might not have the strength to resist the meals here." Now she was back to being the busy, bossy mom he loved. She raised up his bed, got him a towel to serve as a napkin, moved the basket within reach, and hurried out to get juice.

By the time he'd finished off half the basket, the room had filled with his relatives. His mother's three sisters all came with their knitting and sat in the corner by the window. They were the stock for all Matheson mixes, be it wedding or funeral. They kept a sewing bag hospital-ready at all times. Everyone else stood around asking him the same questions over and over: "How you feeling?" "How'd such a thing happen?" "What can we do to help?"

Mathesons in Harmony were like fleas on a dog. No one knew how many there were, but everyone knew they were there.

Over a hundred years ago, when the old man who founded Harmony hired three men, Truman, Matheson, and McAllen, to help him, he probably never dreamed that one, Matheson, would multiply so rapidly. The Trumans had died out except for Reagan Truman, who'd left them last month to go study on an apple farm in Georgia. She was small, but like her old uncle, no one crossed her unless they were ready to fight.

The McAllen family, like the sheriff, Alex, had mostly married into the other families. Rick thought of the McAllens as warriors, and warriors die out. Alex's older brother, Warren, had been a highway patrolman killed in the line of duty and her little brother, Noah, rode bulls for a living.

But the Mathesons produced tall, lean men born to survive in this country. They were mostly ranchers and farmers, and one lawyer, Rick, who was thought to be missing that rugged survival gene his relatives seemed to have.

His three sisters and one brother were scattered around the Texas and Oklahoma panhandles but were keeping his mother busy calling and texting to monitor his condition. With all the cousins dropping by, the place was starting to look like a family reunion.

Rick was relieved when the sheriff came by and politely asked everyone to leave. They all stood their ground, even his aunt May, who was deaf as a post, until Hank said the cafeteria served free coffee and rolls from ten to eleven.

The Matheson gang marched out, leaving Rick alone with the sheriff and Hank.

"Is your head clear?" Alex asked as she pulled out a notepad.

"I think so. I told the doc I didn't want any painkillers except the over-the-counter kind. That other stuff messes with my mind. One of the nurses came in last night to ask me how my leg felt and I told her the two on the right were fine, but the three on the left hurt like hell."

Alex smiled. "You're sane. We need to talk."

Hank stood next to his wife as Alex walked Rick through every detail he could remember about last night. She asked questions now and then, but Rick knew what she wanted and didn't leave out a thing that might be helpful.

When he finished, she said simply, "Someone tried to kill you, Rick. We have to face that fact."

"Yeah, but it doesn't make sense. Most lawyers practice for fifty years without anyone ever coming after them. Why me? I haven't handled anything big. Most of the men I've represented are looking at five or ten years of hard time. Hardly enough to kill the lawyer."

"What about someone else?" Hank asked. "Old girlfriends. Husbands of a lover you had." He grinned. "I've seen you, Rick, women flock to you. Maybe it's that little-lost-puppy-dog look you got going."

Rick shook his head. "All my old girlfriends were glad to get rid of me. I guess they didn't want to housebreak me. And, as far as I know, I've never dated a married woman."

"What about now?"

He shook his head. "I haven't had a date in six months unless you count Martha Q Patterson taking me to lunch now and then. She tells everyone I'm her new boyfriend, but it's just her way of joking."

"Martha Q doesn't count. She just feels sorry for starving lawyers. Some folks feed pigeons; she feeds lawyers. Before you, she used to take Liz out to lunch."

Rick frowned and continued, "I meet a girl my age now and then and think she's perfect. She takes me home, but after a few months she's driving me crazy keeping up with every detail of my life. Then she figures out I'm not that fascinating guy she met. We usually end up with one of us saying, 'Let's be friends.' " Rick winked at Hank. "Unlike you, I've never met a girl that knocked me off my feet."

Hank put his arm around the sheriff's shoulder. He didn't have to say a word. Everyone in town knew how much he loved Alex. Every time she took the night shift at the sheriff's office, Hank was right across the street at the volunteer fire department waiting. He'd built her a house that sat half on McAllen land and half on his ranch. They watched the sun rise over McAllen acres and the sun set over Matheson property.

Alex straightened back into her job. "The point is, Rick, someone tried to kill you and they might try again. I had one of the deputies go by your apartment. The back door lock had been broken and the place was a wreck. Any way you look at it, someone was planning to get to you last night."

"Did they rob me?" Rick wanted to swear. Bad luck was piling up.

"Did you have anything of value in the apartment?"

"No."

"Well, the nothing of value was still there. Dirty clothes, empty pizza boxes, and a jar of pennies you used as a door stop. My guess is they broke the lock so they could get in quick in case the stair trap didn't work. The deputy said the phone line had been cut and every bulb inside was missing from every light fixture."

Rick closed his eyes. His life was shaping up to be a bad mystery novel.

Hank pulled him out of his pity party. "While you're at work or at the courthouse, you're probably safe as long as you park in front and stay where folks can see you. We need to get you somewhere safer than that little apartment you're in when you leave the hospital. How about coming out to the ranch with me? Mom's got a few empty bedrooms at the main house."

Rick shook his head. He liked his privacy too much. He had moved out of the dorm in college before he'd ever had a room to himself. Every summer he'd worked two jobs just to make sure he could afford a place alone when he went back to school.

"Your mom's place might be safer," Hank continued. "It's small, but her condo complex has security."

Rick shook his head. He didn't want to put her in danger. "Don't tell her any of this, would you guys? If she thinks something's wrong, she'll stay home to help and miss her vacation to visit all her grandkids. It's probably nothing, but if trouble is heading my way, I'd feel better knowing Mom is out of danger. I've got to convince her to leave."

Hank agreed.

"I've made a list of our relatives who have places where you'd be safer. Whoever did this is not likely to come onto a farm or ranch, and with all the Matheson farms and ranches around, someone would notice a stranger hanging around long before he could find where you'd gone."

"No." Rick knew he sounded stubborn. "I like staying in town." He knew he couldn't afford a better place with security, even for a few months, but he'd go mad laid up on some farm. "I'll not let some bully run me out of town."

"Well," Alex said with a shrug, "there's always the jail. We could rent you a room."

"Maybe I could just double my locks. The apartment will have to do."

The door bumped suddenly, and a round ball of fake green fur waddled into the room. Nearing her sixties, she'd reached that "who cares" stage about everything in her life from her dress to her manners.

Martha Q Patterson made no pretense that she hadn't been listening to every word they'd said. "I've got your problem solved, Sheriff," she said in a voice raspy from years of smoking. "My lawyer can stay at my place. Winter's Inn Bed-and-Breakfast is within walking distance to his work and I've got a first-rate security system, so he'll be safe."

"Thanks for the offer, Mrs. Patterson, but I can't afford . . ." Rick knew the only reason Martha Q thought he was her lawyer was simply because she took him to lunch once a month. Martha Q didn't need a lawyer, but she did very much want company.

"I'm not giving it to you." She straightened. "I'm asking if you'd consider watching over the place for me. I've decided to go to Dallas for a little work on Saturday, and Mrs. Biggs, my cook, says she won't stay in the house alone because those grandsons of hers have convinced her that the place is haunted. I've no guests coming in for the next few weeks. By then you"—she pointed at Alex—"should be able to find out who's trying to kill my lawyer."

She stared at Rick. "I've got a yard man, a cook, and a housekeeper, and you can stay in a first-floor bedroom, but I'm not paying but a hundred a day, so don't think about charging those lawyer rates on me. One hundred a day to run the place plus room and board seems fair." She raised one eyebrow and looked him up and down. "From the looks of you, you're not running at full speed so maybe I should only pay seventy-five a day."

Rick had always thought Martha Q crazy, but in her own way she was kind. She was also right to have someone watch the old place while she was in Dallas. He figured he could either become a housesitter for a few weeks or defend the bums who'd try to break into Winter's Inn Bed-and-Breakfast when they heard she was gone.

"Any other duties? This sounds almost too easy."

She thought for a moment, then added, "If you're up to it, I'd like you to try and make the writers' group meeting at the library. Way I figure, I'll only miss one, maybe two, sessions while I'm in Dallas. If you'll take notes, I won't get behind."

"I'd be happy to do that." Sitting in on the writers' group might bring him some new clients. If they were anything like the groups he sat in during college, they were mostly women. "You've got yourself a deal. Go ahead with your plans."

Rick smiled, thinking Martha Q could use a lot more work than a face-lift. Her entire body seemed to be moving south. "Your business will be in good hands." He offered his scraped hand. "Thanks for the offer."

"Don't thank me until the job is over. Running a B&B, even an empty one, is not easy. I'll expect you to let the cat in and out. Which is a constant problem. You'll have to wake the housekeeper up and tell her to go home every afternoon, and my house is a hundred years old, so something is constantly breaking, leaking, stopping up, or cracking. I'll leave numbers of who to call when problems come up and they'll know to bill me." She took his hand carefully. "I'll expect you tomorrow. Your room will be ready."

Without another word, she waddled out.

"I don't know about this," Hank whispered just in case she'd stopped on the other side of the door to listen.

"What could go wrong?" Rick answered. "I'll watch over her house, have a security system, be able to walk to work, and have Mrs. Biggs to cook me breakfast. This deal was almost worth the fall."

Hank frowned. "On the downside, you're in an old house and you're barely mobile. Mrs. Biggs won't be any help if trouble comes, and the place is haunted, according to the bookstore owner downtown."

Rick grinned. "I'll be fine. Look at the bright side, all I have to do is call and Alex or one of her deputies can be at the bed-and-breakfast door in five minutes."

❧ *Chapter 8* ☙

Monday

Emily Tomlinson walked into the nursing home feeling like she was doing something wrong. Tannon asking her to come visit his mother was one thing, but Emily just deciding to go was another. Before Saturday night, she'd said nothing to the woman in more than ten years. That didn't exactly make her a close friend, but she couldn't shake the feeling that the visit was something she should do.

Maybe now was the time to start the friendship over. Monday was her only early day off and three o'clock seemed like a good time to pay a visit. She knew deep down she wasn't there to visit Paulette Parker so much as to visit the memory of her mother.

With all her family gone, Emily had no one who could answer her questions. Paulette Parker might be half out of her mind, but she was the only person who would know what her mother had truly been like. Emily had her childhood memories, but they were scattered and disconnected like random toys tucked away in an attic box.

She remembered summer mornings in the garden working beside her parents. Her mother's easy laugh. Her father's gentle smile. Late-night movies with her parents cuddling. Shopping at farmers' markets. Vacations to historic sites. Her mother was always there, always dear in those growing-up years. Emily felt like she knew her mother, but she didn't know Shelley Tomlinson, the girl, the young woman, the dreamer.

She took a deep breath and pushed Paulette's door open hoping to see one more glimpse today of the way her mother had once been.

The thin woman sat in a wheelchair by the window staring out at nothing but a garden wall. Someone had dressed her, with little care, in a plain cotton blouse and dull brown pants. Her collar was turned up on one end and one of her socks caught the leg of her pants. The Paulette that Emily remembered would never have looked so unkempt. She dressed in colorful outfits to garden, and everything about her matched.

"Morning, Mrs. Parker, are you feeling up for a visitor?"

Paulette turned toward her, and for a few seconds her eyes were dull, unseeing, but then she smiled. "You do look like your mother, child. I see her kind brown eyes in your gaze."

Emily pulled up a chair close enough to almost touch knees with the older woman. "I've heard people say that, but I don't see it." She put her hand over Paulette's wrinkled fingers. "Is it all right if I'm here? I don't want to bother you while you're resting."

"It's fine. I've had my lunch and my nap. Now it's sit-up time until supper. My days seem to move around meals and bowel movements. I think I've figured out why people die in places like this . . . boredom. I was thinking about planning my escape, but now that you're here, I think I'll stay until dinner."

Emily smiled. Paulette had always been one of those rare people who said the unexpected, only now she couldn't tell if Tannon's mother were kidding or being deadly serious. She decided to play along. "I'll smuggle in a map of the grounds for you, if you like. With all the construction, I had to walk around a pile of lumber and a mountain of dirt. I had to drop leftover French fries so I'd be able to find my way back to the lot where I parked."

Paulette laughed. "You're a dear. That's just what your mother would have done. People always wondered why we were friends, me so outgoing and her so quiet and shy, but they didn't see the real her. She was always whispering funny things in my ear. I used to tell her I lived big on the outside and she lived big on the inside."

"You two were friends," Emily agreed, remembering pictures of them standing side by side since they'd been in grade school.

"More than that. We accepted each other just the way we were. I remember back when we were young, Shelley's mother was always badgering her to take bigger bites out of life, be braver, take a risk now and then. Shelley hated that. She said once that she was a nibbler at life's banquet and liked it that way."

"You knew my grandmother?"

"Of course. She used to say she wished she had me for a daughter and not Shelley, but I didn't want her for a mother any more than Shelley did most days. Your momma was a good momma, but she sure didn't learn it from any example."

Emily asked questions about her grandparents. Paulette filled in where she could, but she said she rarely went over to Shelley's house, and when she married so young her parents got so mad they moved up north somewhere. "They wouldn't even come to your mother's wedding, so I told her I'd be her mom for the day. I even had an usher walk me in and seat me in the first row."

Emily smiled realizing she'd got that little bit of information she'd hoped for. One glance of her mother's life. "I never knew they didn't make the wedding. My grandparents would have changed their minds if they'd seen how happy my parents were. They were sweethearts."

Paulette agreed and filled in any details she could.

Shelley's mother died of cancer when Emily was a baby. Shelley wasn't able to make it to the funeral, but she heard her father married three months later. As far as Paulette knew, he never made any effort to contact his only daughter or anyone else in Harmony.

"He's dead by now," Paulette said, without any caring in her tone. "No loss. He was pretty much invisible even when we were kids. Never came to any of your mother's school events. If I remember right, he sold farm equipment and was gone a lot."

Emily listened. In her mind, when she'd been a child, she'd imagined grandparents who loved her dearly living far away, but she knew it was only a dream. No cards, no presents, not even phone calls. She could never get her mother to talk about them. Apparently they hadn't been bad parents or good parents—they'd simply faded away.

A nurse stopped in and seemed delighted to see a visitor in the room. "If you'd like, you can wheel her through the main hallway and around to the north door. The grounds outside haven't been torn up there. It's not so windy right now, though the temperature seems to be dropping. This may be the last warm afternoon we have for a while. I hear a cold front is heading our way."

Emily stood. "Are you up for a stroll, Mrs. Parker?"

"Of course. I need to learn where the hole in the fence is."

The nurse tucked a blanket around her while Emily straightened her white blouse and wrapped her own silk scarf around Paulette's neck to add a touch of class.

"Thank you, dear," Paulette said. "You're very kind. My son brought a few clothes, but I'm afraid he's never heard of the word 'accessory.' "

They circled the grounds twice talking mostly of what should be done with the flower beds this time of year and how gray the day seemed. When they came back inside, Emily noticed a nice sitting area off the main entrance and asked if they could take tea in the empty room.

One of the staff nodded. "I think Mrs. Parker might like that. I'll fix it up for you."

By the time they were settled into the colorful room, tea on a tray was delivered. The cups and saucers might have been thick and white, but a colorful napkin covered the brown cafeteria tray. They had hot water in silver cream pitchers and several tea bags along with little cookies that resembled fat goldfish.

Emily couldn't stop smiling. From the time she'd been three or four, Mrs. Parker had kept a tea set just for her in the Parkers' formal living room. While her mother and Paulette talked, Emily would have tea with her dolls. When she'd finished, she'd run off searching through the house for Tannon. He'd always offer to play a game with her or watch TV, but he never joined her for tea and it never occurred to her to ask why.

"This is lovely," Paulette said as she puffed up her scarf. "The tea and the visit are also lovely, dear. I hope you'll come again."

"I'm always off on Monday afternoons. We could make it a regular date until you go home."

"That would be perfect. I'll have Tannon pick up proper tea cookies. These will never do, but I don't want to hurt the staff's feelings. They try so hard to make me happy, you know."

Rain tapping on the window reminded Emily that it was getting late. "I'll see you to your room before I go. I'd better be getting home."

The storm had gotten worse by the time Paulette settled back in her bed. She looked frightened when thunder rattled the windows. "I've always hated storms since the wreck. It was raining that night your parents died, you know. I remember looking up front and seeing that truck coming at us out of the storm like a devil running from hell straight toward us."

Emily sat on the side of the bed and held Paulette's hand. Paulette's big eyes were almost childlike in the growing shadows as she told Emily of that night. She spoke of how happy the four of them had been to be traveling together and how they'd laughed and talked all at once.

"Are you all right, Mrs. Parker?" Emily whispered when Paulette finally fell silent.

"Stay with me a little longer, will you, dear? Just till the storm passes."

"Of course." Emily wasn't sure if she was truly needed or just being manipulated. She remembered how Paulette always seemed to get her way. Once, her mother had said that if the end of the world came and Paulette Parker wasn't ready, the Lord would just have to postpone his plans.

Staff brought dinner, but Paulette didn't eat more than a few bites. She took her pills without much protest and begged Emily to hold her hand until she fell asleep.

Since it was already dark outside, Emily didn't see that it mattered much. Though Emily liked to be in her apartment by dusk, this was an exception.

After a few minutes, Paulette fell asleep. Emily tucked her in as if she were a child and tiptoed out of the room.

Halfway down the hallway, she saw Tannon Parker storming toward her. In his rain slicker and boots, he looked like a giant.

"What are you doing here?" he snapped when he was five feet away. "What's wrong?"

"Nothing." She felt as if she'd been caught doing something wrong. She circled past Tannon and headed for the door.

But he caught up to her. "How is she?" he asked more calmly.

"She's fine. She's asleep."

He kept walking beside her until they reached the first of two doors.

"What are you doing?" Emily asked. "Aren't you going to stop in and check on her?"

"You've already done that. I've got my hands full of problems tonight. She won't know if I'm there or not."

Emily hesitated as she glanced out at the stormy night. "She asked me to stay and hold her hand. She's so afraid of storms. It was raining the night of the wreck, you know. A terrible storm, she told me."

Tannon swore under his breath. "No, it wasn't. I drove up from Denton. I had to drive right by the wreck to get home. My folks and yours were already gone, but I saw the car. The flares were still burning on the road. It hadn't been raining."

She started to argue. He'd been in shock. He probably hadn't noticed.

Tannon's arm circled her waist. "I'll run with you to your car. This rain isn't letting up for a while."

"No, that's—" was all she got out before he shoved the door open and they were running. The mountain of dirt by the construction site seemed to be melting across the temporary boardwalks. His arm held her solid against his side.

When they reached her car, she dropped her keys. As they both knelt to pick them up, he noticed the flat tire.

"I'm not changing that in this weather." He shoved her car key in his pocket. "I'll take you home, then come back and take care of this when the rain stops. I'm guessing it was probably a nail with all this construction going on."

"It's not your problem," she shouted over the rain. "I'll call someone."

He opened the door to his truck parked beside her. "I'm already out in this mess and wet. I'll take you home, Emily."

She wanted to argue, but in truth she had no idea who she'd call for help. The few staff at the library were older and didn't need to be out on a night like this. Pamela Sue would probably never find her and she didn't know her neighbors' phone numbers.

She climbed in, more mad at herself for being so helpless than at him for being so bossy. She was already shivering by the time he walked around to his side and started the engine.

"It'll be warm in a sec," he said. "I can hear your teeth rattling."

They sat listening to the pounding outside, and then he put the truck in reverse.

"Your mom was happy this afternoon. She seemed happy and funny almost like I remembered her."

"Great." He didn't sound like she'd just given him good news.

"What's wrong?"

"Mom lives in a mountain range, Emily. For every high, there is a low." He took a deep breath. "Thanks for visiting and making her day bright. Maybe she'll be on the road to recovery."

"Is it all right if I visit her again?"

"Of course. Just don't get caught up in her moods." He shook his wet hair. "Speaking of moods, I was in a bad one when I yelled at you back there. I'm sorry. It's turning out to be one hell of a night."

"And now you have to deal with me."

"You're the only bright spot, believe me." He pulled into her apartment's underground parking garage and parked by the elevator. Pulling a card off his sun visor, he offered it to her. "If you ever need anything, call me. No matter where you are, I'll come get you."

She wondered if he could tell she was trying to think of a friend who could help, or maybe he was just reading her mind again. "Thanks for the ride." She didn't take the card. He wasn't that close of a friend. If she let him too close, she might let long-hidden memories see light. "Don't worry about my flat tire. I'll call someone to fix it tomorrow and I can walk to the library in the morning."

He didn't say a word as she opened the door and jumped out. He just watched her as she ran for the elevator being held open by one of her neighbors. When she stepped inside and pushed the top floor, he was still sitting in his pickup watching.

The next morning, her car was parked in the garage. The keys were in the seat along with one of his cards. She didn't know whether to be glad or angry that he'd helped her when she hadn't asked for it.

❧ *Chapter 9* ❧

Rick Matheson moved into Winter's Inn Bed-and-Breakfast without going back to his apartment. Hank had packed up a few bags of clothes and loaded them in his truck when he circled by to get Rick in front of the hospital. Anything remaining in his apartment could wait until he was well enough to go back home.

Dr. Addison Spencer waited with him, keeping up a steady lecture on what he could and couldn't do. Mostly what Rick heard was, rest for a few days, get the back wound checked by the end of the week, and don't do anything strenuous.

Rick assured her lawyers rarely do anything strenuous, but he promised to take no more exercise than walking to work until his body stopped aching. Even knowing someone was out there wishing him harm didn't frighten Rick. The town was full of people who were related to him by either blood or marriage. No matter where he went there would be someone watching over him . . . as long as he stayed away from back stairs. Martha Q had been right about the bed-and-breakfast having a fine alarm system, so he wasn't worried about being able to sleep at night.

Alex told him to keep where he was staying a secret, but he had to tell his mother and she'd tell her sisters and of course they'd tell their children. Rick grinned. If he hadn't had to worry about being killed, he might find it interesting that he was probably the most talked-about person in Harmony this week.

Several of the nurses left him their numbers and offered to drop by and check on him, but the last thing Rick needed was women problems on top of all else.

Hank drove him to Winter's Inn and helped him up the front porch stairs. Rick had bruises all along his back, making the muscles tight.

Mrs. Biggs opened the door before they reached the porch. She had his room ready for him and had made a light supper for whenever he was ready. She also explained that Martha Q had gone to Amarillo for a few days of shopping. She planned to be back on Friday for a meeting, and then on Saturday morning she would head to Dallas for her face-lift. Mrs. Biggs said the stress of being beautiful was taking a toll on poor Martha Q's nerves.

Rick limped inside as Hank went back for the luggage. He'd made it to the middle of the entryway when Hank handed over his two bags and said good-bye.

Mrs. Biggs took over helping him to his room.

"Are you single?" Rick asked when he saw the cozy room, mountains of pillows, fireplace going in the hearth below a big-screen TV with basketball playing. "This is heaven."

"I'm widowed, Mr. Matheson," she said simply. "And don't try that Matheson charm on me."

An hour later he asked her to marry him again when she brought him shepherd's pie and apple cobbler.

"Now, Mr. Matheson, you can't keep asking me that. I've got grandsons almost your age."

"I know, but they don't make women like you anymore, Mrs. Biggs. Most of the girls I've dated use the oven to store supplies. Half cuss more than any man I know and none of them wear anything like that sweet perfume you have on."

"It's cinnamon, Mr. Matheson. You're still under the effects of drugs." She picked up a book that had fallen from his bed. "I wanted to let you know that one or both of my grandsons will be by every night to check on me. They both said they're glad you're staying at the house, but my boys worry about me." She hid her smile behind her fingertips. "My Border says Martha Q is tough enough to frighten any trouble away, but he's not so sure about you."

Rick laughed. The big grandsons weren't

exactly boys. Brandon "Big" Biggs was at least six foot six and probably weighed three hundred pounds. His little brother wasn't far behind. Border Biggs shaved his head so all his tattoos would show and the last Rick heard he was playing in a band. "I'm glad they're coming by. If anyone was planning to break in here, they'll think we have a security team walking the grounds."

Mrs. Biggs smiled with pride. "I don't want to brag, but my boys would thump anyone a good one if they messed with me." She moved toward the door. "They usually have dinner with Martha Q and me on Sunday night. Should we continue in her absence?"

"Sounds like a good plan, if I'm invited."

"Of course."

Just before she left, Rick added, "Starting tomorrow morning, I'll have breakfast in the kitchen. I may only work an hour tomorrow, but I plan to work."

She nodded and closed the door. He let his body melt back into the pillows. It had cost him to act as if he wasn't in pain, but Rick didn't want anyone worrying about him. He'd morphed from hurting to being mad. The first thing he planned to do when he got to his office was to go over the list of every person who'd walked in since he started practicing. If he didn't find a name there he'd go through each trial. Not just defendants, but witnesses, families, friends, victims. Somewhere in the list was one name. One person who'd walked away hating him enough to wish him dead.

No, not wish him dead. Rick had to find someone who hated him enough to make it happen.

He leaned back forcing his body to relax. Forty-eight hours ago he'd been leaving his office feeling like he was floating without a direction. A few missing steps had changed all that. Rick now had a mission.

❧ *Chapter 10* ❧

Tuesday

It was almost noon on Tuesday before Tannon Parker made it back to his loft apartment over Parker Trucking's offices. He'd spent the night dealing with a rig that had jackknifed on a windy road in the Oklahoma panhandle, and then he'd driven back to Harmony.

Shedding his clothes as he walked, he headed for the kitchen, needing food even more than he needed sleep.

Nothing.

He called his secretary downstairs and told her to order him the usual groceries. Bread, milk, sandwich meat, canned soup, cereal, frozen pizza, and beer. She knew the brand names without having to ask.

"Oh," he added, "a couple of six-packs of diet root beer."

"I didn't know you liked root beer." She sounded more curious than interested.

"I don't," Tannon said, seeing no need to explain.

She took the hint. "I'll have your order delivered in twenty minutes, Mr. Parker."

"Good. Leave it outside the elevator door. I'll be in the shower. Call me if we have any other problems." He'd stood on the highway most of the night making sure the wreck was clean, but they were still waiting for the mechanic to call in a total on the engine's damage.

A half hour later he'd downed a mixing bowl of cereal and decided he needed sleep more than the office needed him. But when he fell into bed, he didn't relax. The long night played out in his mind. The truck would cost him thousands, but thankfully the driver wasn't hurt.

He hated stormy nights in the trucking business almost as much as he hated snow.

Emily crossed his mind. She thought it had rained the night her parents had been killed. He'd seen the tears in her eyes when she'd told him. She wore her emotions close to the surface and he could always see everything she felt in her big brown eyes.

He took a deep breath and forgot about rainy nights. Emily was all that was on his mind as he drifted into sleep. The memory of how her eyes had sparkled when she'd rationed out her chocolate kisses for dessert was his last thought.

❦ *Chapter 11* ❦

Music filled the bar as Beau played from the cage in the corner. Few folks were in the place tonight and most of them came to eat, not dance, but it didn't matter to Beau. He'd come to play. He'd tied his black hair back as always and wore his cowboy hat low so that he could almost believe he was alone in the bar.

Border had gone with his brother over to the Truman farm to check on the place. Reagan Truman and the Biggs brothers were an odd pairing of friends, but she must trust them because folks said she let very few on her place and she'd given Big the key. The brothers planned to stop for catfish at a shack out that direction when they headed back.

Beau would rather play than eat tonight. He'd been thinking about how he'd never be a star if he didn't start collecting "hard times."

He'd spent his childhood being afraid to do anything. His father used to make him hit his knees and pray for forgiveness for things he thought about doing wrong. Only problem was Beau hadn't really thought about anything, and by the time those evil ideas climbed in his dreams, he sure didn't want to mention his thoughts to God for fear the Lord would take them from him.

"I like your music." A woman's voice pulled him out of his thoughts.

Beau looked up. She was about his height and had on red cowboy boots pulled over her skin-tight jeans. Unlike most of the women who trolled the bar every night, she didn't look old enough to walk in the door. Fake ID, he thought, but he didn't plan to mention it to Harley if the owner hadn't noticed. Blond hair, big blue eyes that twinkled with laughter.

"Th-thanks," he managed, and liked the way she giggled with a bit of nervousness.

"Would you play something for me?" she asked.

"I-if I know it." He didn't dare look down at her body again. As long as he kept his gaze on her eyes, he had a chance of being able to talk without stuttering. "W-what would you like?"

"Anything. I'd just like to know you're playing it for me."

Beau played an old Lee Ann Womack song called "I Hope You Dance."

She sat at the nearest table and didn't move until he'd finished, and then she thanked him and walked away. The fringe on her western vest brushed her hips as if she planned it that way just to tease the boys. Her hair was sandy blond and tied up in a ponytail with a blue satin ribbon. She was Sunday morning beautiful even in the smoky lights.

He couldn't see where she went, but when he packed up and walked out the back door, she was sitting on an old Ford Mustang convertible that someone had restored to better than new.

"Want to go for a ride?" she asked as she opened the passenger's door.

Without a word, he stored his gear inside the kitchen and climbed in. It was cold, too cold for a midnight ride with the top down, but Beau didn't care. He felt like he was living some kind of wild dream with his eyes wide open.

They drove out of town until she found a lonely stretch of blacktop that looked like ink flowing across gray earth. She raced through the night with the radio playing and her hair dancing in the wind. He had no idea where he was going and didn't care.

When they could see no lights from town, she stopped and asked him if he wanted to drive. He nodded and they ran around the car switching seats, but she didn't stay on her side. She slid across the console where a blanket padded the space between bucket seats and cuddled against him for warmth.

Beau drove slowly, wishing the night would last forever. He didn't even know her name, and for some strange reason it didn't seem to matter. He figured sometime later, when this dream was over, he'd realize that a girl like her would never have anything to do with a guy like him, but tonight he planned to enjoy the perfection of one moment.

After a half hour they switched drivers again and she pulled back onto a main road. She slowed to the speed limit and headed toward Harmony. "You don't have to talk, Beau, but could you move over so I could feel your warmth next to me?"

He moved against her side putting his arm along the back of her shoulder. The frosty night air blew his hair, but he didn't seem to feel the cold with the radio on and her so close.

When there were no cars coming, she slowed, tugged his hand from her shoulder, and moved it inside her jacket until his palm rested over one of her small breasts.

"Don't say anything," she whispered. "Just feel me."

He thought of stuttering out that he wasn't sure he could talk, but it didn't seem necessary. He took his time feeling of her breast and decided he liked small breasts just as much as he liked big ones. Not that he'd felt enough to form a clear opinion.

When the lights of town came into view, she moved his hand to her shoulder and drove back to the bar.

The place had closed, but there was enough light

for him to see his junker of a car sitting alone in the lot. When he climbed out, she handed him the ribbon she'd pulled from her ponytail. He laced it between his fingers. She nodded once and drove away.

Beau stood there in the cold for a long time trying to figure out if he'd just had a very real one of those dreams he should be asking forgiveness for or if the girl had really been there in her 1965 write-me-a-ticket red convertible.

The next night he asked the bartender and Harley if they'd seen her and no one remembered a girl like her alone in the bar. Harley said he always carded ponytails twice. Any woman wearing a ponytail was either too dumb to know she looked like a kid or older than she wanted folks to think she was. Either way, he wanted to know the truth.

Later, when he told Border about the girl, Border said it was probably one of his dreams. He had so many about biker chicks and cheerleaders that one was bound to drop out of his head sometime. Beau just happened to pick it up.

Beau caught himself looking for the Ford convertible in every parking lot and watching women with blond hair. He tried to picture each one dressed as she'd been, but none fit. Finally, he decided it was good that he didn't find her again. He wouldn't know what to say anyway and even if he did, he'd never get the words out.

She had changed his life, though. Before he was just nervous around girls his age who were big-breasted; now it was pretty much every female on the planet.

Border asked him a few times to repeat what happened and each time he did the memory became more dream and less real. Details were being airbrushed out with words. The girl had been right. It was best he didn't talk about it. Then, maybe he could keep it real for just a little while longer. But he tried to remember every detail. The girl, the car, the night.

He tied the blue satin ribbon to his guitar and thought of her as he played and wished it had been his songs she'd heard on the radio. When he did make it big he wondered if she'd hear him and think of the night they raced the wind on a moonbeam road to nowhere.

That night as he slept on the Biggs brothers' couch, when all was still, she came to him in his dreams. They rode through the cold air keeping warm as they pressed against each other. He'd whisper to her without stuttering in his dreams. He'd tell her how she'd changed his world.

He crawled out of bed before dawn and wrote a song about needing the closeness of another's body more than he needed words. Someday, he thought, long after I make it big, she'll hear the song on the radio and know I was thinking of her when I wrote it.

❧ *Chapter 12* ❧

Wednesday

Rick crawled out of bed about ten o'clock feeling like he'd have to get better to die. Every muscle and bone in his body hurt. He moved slowly to the bathroom. Taking a shower or a bath was out of the question with all the gauze wrapped around his ribs and back, but he did manage to shave and did his best to wash. He pulled on a T-shirt and old pair of jeans Mrs. Biggs must have washed from the pile in his bag of dirty clothes. She'd left them on a shelf in the bathroom along with a stack of fresh towels.

Walking out of the bath, he moved like an old man to the kitchen. Day three after the accident didn't look any brighter than days one and two had. At this rate, he'd spend the rest of his youth holding on to door frames and accompanying every step with a groan.

Mrs. Biggs smiled at him, but didn't say a word as she went about getting his breakfast ready.

"I don't want much," he said as he lowered to the chair.

"Just eat what you can. The cat will eat the rest." She smiled at a fat tabby cat sitting in the window. "Martha Q calls him Mr. Dolittle but I refuse to address him so formally, so I just call him Cat."

By the time Rick had finished his first cup of coffee, Hank, his cousin, had arrived. Mrs. Biggs poured the rancher a cup and left the room as if she knew the babysitter had arrived.

"I don't think you should go in for a few days, Rick," Hank began. "You need rest."

"I'm fine. I can make it a few hours." Rick remembered his years in high school football when he'd felt terrible after a game. His mother had always made him go to school the next morning, promising him she'd come get him if he didn't feel better by lunch. A dozen times he'd told himself he could make it to lunch, and by then, he'd decide he could survive the rest of the day.

This seemed like one of those days.

He looked at Hank. "You're not worried about me resting. You're worried about me going out, right?"

Hank leaned forward. "The steps were sawed, Rick. Maybe it was some kind of sick joke, maybe it wasn't meant for you, but I've got to think that the guy who did it couldn't have been thinking of anyone else. Someone out there meant to harm you, maybe even kill you. We fixed the steps, but we haven't fixed the problem."

"I can't just hide." Rick shrugged, then groaned. "Sooner or later, I have to step out that door and get some answers."

"All right, but I'm going with you."

"Fine, then you can help me get dressed."

By the time Rick was dressed he was swearing and Hank was laughing. He claimed it would have been easier to put a tux on a cow than put clothes on Rick.

They walked out to Hank's truck with Hank still laughing and Rick still hurting.

By the time they were parked in front of his office, Rick was exhausted. He leaned back and tried to think why he'd been so determined to get out of bed this morning.

"Want to go home?" Hank asked. "I can turn around."

Rick had made it this far. He wouldn't turn back now. "I'll stay a few hours. My car's still parked out back, I might as well drive it over to the B&B. Martha Q told me I could put it in her garage."

"Sounds good. While you're working, I'll take Alex to lunch." Hank helped him out and followed him up the stairs one at a time, then left as soon as Rick was inside his office. He wanted to be helpful, not mothering. "I'll be driving back by here if you want me to help you down the front stairs. It might not be a bad idea."

"I think I can make it." Rick didn't even sound too sure to himself. "But I'd appreciate some help with a few boxes. I'm taking files home. I'll be ready by the time you finish lunch."

Hank nodded and left without another word.

Rick closed the door and slowly lowered himself to the old couch he'd borrowed from the office next door months ago. It took him several minutes, but he finally relaxed enough to breathe normally. In the shadowy room he stared out at the old town square and tried to think of one person in town who wanted him dead.

After a while he decided he'd lived a pitiful life. He'd never loved anyone passionately or hated anyone or anything enough to fight. All he'd ever done was go to school and date people as shallow as himself. He was good to his mother like every decent Southern boy. He went to church now and then. Tried to be polite and kind to folks, but he'd never fought for a cause or marched for what was right.

Maybe someone saw him and just decided he was a waste of air and thought they'd just take him out with a few missing steps.

Rick reasoned he wasn't even a good lawyer. Maybe he should try the back stairs one more time. He might get lucky and land on his head.

The door opened and the portly bookstore owner from downstairs walked in. He rarely climbed the stairs except to complain about Rick making too much noise. "Morning, Counselor." George Hatcher made a slight bow. "I didn't hear anything after you climbed the stairs and decided to come up and see if you'd expired."

"Nope." Rick smiled, deciding George belonged

in a fifties mystery movie. All muted plaid and wrinkled. "I'm just taking my morning nap. How are you today, Mr. Hatcher?"

"I've been busy all morning. I'm not sure if there has been a sudden mass craving for rare books or if it's the curiosity of the crime scene, but people wander through my store and then ask if they can leave out the back door. I hope you've no objection, but I point out the bloodstain you left on the broken concrete. Your blood made a nice-size puddle. One woman almost fainted when she saw it."

"I don't mind. Glad I can offer a boost to your business." Rick almost added that at least he was good for something.

The old guy smiled. "I only wish the sheriff had drawn an outline of where your body landed, you know like they do in the movies. I even thought of drawing one myself, but she might consider that tampering with evidence or something. Would have made a nice addition, though."

"I could go down and model for you."

"Oh no, no." He waved his beefy hands in front of him.

Rick rested his head back on the couch arm. "Well, thanks for checking on me. Let me know if I can be of any help with the tourists."

George Hatcher didn't seem in any hurry to leave. He leaned against the desk. "You know, Rick, before you moved in, this place had been empty for ten years. I've had many a customer in the bookstore swear she heard movement from up here, footsteps, talking, that kind of thing."

"It was probably from Liz's office next door."

"Oh no. Once, a lady traveling through town heard about it and came up asking if she could see this office. She was a friend of the woman who reads palms in my place on Wednesdays. Her stepsister, I think, but that's neither here nor there. Anyway, the woman claimed she could smell ghosts haunting a place. She had me get a key and show her this office a year before you moved in."

"Did you tell Liz this?"

George shook his head. "I didn't want to scare her and I figured it didn't matter since she rented the office next door, but when she talked you into opening, I knew I'd get around to telling you sooner or later. I'm so sorry it was later."

Rick sat up. "Are you telling me that you think a ghost sawed those steps because I rented his place?"

George bobbed his head. "Strange things have happened, and that lady, the friend of my palm reader, swore she smelled visitors from the hereafter right in this very room."

"No way," Rick said.

The bookstore owner didn't look offended. "The woman smelled brimstone and cheap cigars, so we all know what kind of ghost haunted this place. If I were you, I'd think about relocating."

"I think I'll hang around just to irritate the ghosts for a while." Rick got the feeling that this conversation they were having would be repeated to everyone who walked into the bookstore.

"Suit yourself, but if you're ever in trouble, stomp three times and I'll come running. This place is built so poorly I swear I can hear a mouse cross your office."

Rick thanked the bookstore owner and said he'd be down to talk if he ever saw any sightings.

By the time Hank made it back, Rick had managed to make it to his desk and pull out a few files. As he packed his reading for the night, he found a letter amid the scattered mail on the corner of his desk. Rick slit it open, hoping one of his overdue accounts had sent a payment on work already done.

A single word was glued together from scraps of newspaper pasted on a blank piece of paper. *Leave,* was all it said.

Rick handed it to Hank. "I think it's from a cigar-smoking ghost." When Hank raised an eyebrow, he told him all about the bookstore owner's theory.

Hank carefully slid the note and envelope in a folder and said he'd take it over to the sheriff's office. "Alex will know what to do with this," he said.

"It's not really a threat, just a hint at a

direction." Rick didn't even think it was a bad idea. Maybe he should leave and go to work for some big law firm in Dallas or Houston. Only problem was he'd never wanted to live anywhere but Harmony.

They were halfway down the stairs when Hank's cell and the fire alarms in the bookstore went off at the same time.

Rick motioned for him to go on as he continued his slow progress down the steps. A fire would be far more exciting than watching him move down the stairs.

Hank took the steps two at a time, dropped the box of files in the bed of his truck, and ran toward the bookstore.

By the time Rick made it to the ground, he could hear a fire truck blaring toward him and see smoke coming from behind the building. He moved cautiously into the bookstore. The place looked deserted. No fire, but he could smell something burning.

Three steps later, Rick saw flames beyond the open back door. He was halfway through the store before he realized that the dump of trash that was burning was his car.

❧ *Chapter 13* ❧

Friday

Emily worried about the first meeting of the writers' group as if it were a grand reception. Tiny brought the cookies over at noon when the bakery closed. She talked on and on about how excited her sister was to be part of a writing group. Tiny thought they should invite the paper to come out and take a picture. "After all," she'd said, "this is history in the making."

The alcove in the back of the second floor was circled with stained-glass windows and tucked far enough out of the way to seem private. An old rug covered most of the floor in the little room that Emily always thought might have been a lady's morning room. There was plenty of space for ten chairs, but she only set up six. She put the cookies on one table and a stack of books on writing on the other.

At exactly seven o'clock, the would-be writers started arriving. First came Zack Hunter, in probably the cleanest of his stained clothes. He carried a battered old briefcase that appeared to stretch his arm with the weight of paper stuffed into it. After saying hello, he sat down next to the table of cookies.

Next Martha Q Patterson and George Hatcher rushed in out of the cold. They must have met in the parking lot, and by the time they reached the second floor, Martha Q was telling him her life story. "I've thought of writing my memoirs. At first I planned to make each one of my husbands a chapter, but after some thought, I may make each a volume in a series, except, of course, my fourth husband. He'd be more a short story, if you know what I mean."

George Hatcher, the used-bookstore owner, didn't even look like he was listening to the owner of Harmony's bed-and-breakfast. He waited until Martha Q took a seat and then sat as far away as possible. She didn't take offense but simply talked louder. In her bright red jogging suit and rhinestone-studded tennis shoes she would have been hard to miss in a crowd of hundreds.

"I can't stay long tonight," she yelled. "I have to get to bed early so I can make the drive to Dallas tomorrow. I sure don't want to miss anything being gone a few weeks so I asked my lawyer to sit in for me and take notes."

"We'll save you copies," Zack offered. "I got a copy machine right next to my cash register at my store."

Geraldine Edison rushed in, apologizing for being late as she joined the conversation. "I wanted to run copies in case we read our work tonight, but when I turned on the bakery lights some man drove by the window looking for doughnut holes. When I told him we didn't open until seven a.m., he said he'd wait."

Zack Hunter licked the icing off a cookie and commented, "Some folks are addicted to sweets. Especially those powdered-sugar doughnut holes. I started out one summer with a dozen a morning habit and before I knew it I was buying grocery bags full. I even kept them in the freezer just in case morning didn't come soon enough."

Martha Q looked at Zack like he just admitted to being on drugs. She gathered her things and moved over one chair so the baker could have the seat next to Zack.

Geraldine took a deep breath, wiggled into the open place between Zack and Martha Q, and apologized again.

Everyone nodded as if voting to excuse her. Zack Hunter finished off his third cookie and told her how fine he thought they were. Geraldine's round apple cheeks blushed.

Next came a man in his late twenties who introduced himself only as Peter. He was tall and thin, with the look of an English major about him. He asked if he could sit in.

When Emily said yes, he asked if he could smoke his pipe.

She said no, but he kept it in his hand. She decided he was the only one of them who looked like a writer.

Emily stood and welcomed everyone, then began with what she thought would be solid ground rules to set. "Anyone can read as many as ten pages of their work. All comments are to be positive and helpful. No one has to read to stay in the group."

When everyone agreed to the rules, she added, "The rest we'll make up as we go along." She tried to smile. "Now, who would like to read first?"

Peter raised his hand and the group began.

His story was about a dog that had been orphaned during the World War II bombings in London. The dog roamed the streets cussing at God for the horror he saw. It was a dissertation on social unrest.

When Peter finished, Emily asked if there were any comments.

Geraldine said she loved it and that she could almost believe she was there. Zack agreed, though he wasn't sure he understood the true depth of the work. George said it reminded him of a great work about a roach in New York City, then took a moment to pass out ten-percent-off coupons for his bookstore. Martha Q said she didn't think dogs talked, but if they did, they wouldn't cuss. "But cats"—here she straightened like an expert—"they do cuss, so you might want to consider changing the dog to a cat, and while you've got the eraser handy, maybe the Wars of the Roses would be better."

No one agreed or disagreed with her, so after a long pause, Peter politely responded, "I'll think about your suggestions."

This seemed to make everyone happy, and to Emily's surprise, they all began talking at once about which war would be best. No one mentioned the cat/dog conflict and she thought that was for the best.

Everyone took a break for coffee and cookies while Emily stepped out to check on how things were going downstairs. She'd asked Pamela Sue to come in to cover the desk. Though the library had two employees, Emily didn't feel like it would be fair to ask them to work at night since, after all, they never had.

As she reached the bottom of the stairs, she saw Pamela Sue knitting at the desk. Only a few of the usual Friday night crowd were around. All looked quiet.

"How's it going?" A voice from behind her made her jump.

Emily turned to see Tannon sitting in his usual chair by the newspapers. "Fine. Good, actually." She almost added that he was early. He rarely made it in before eight thirty. "Is something wrong?"

"No. I just thought after you finish I could take you out for supper. You could tell me all about the writers' group."

"That would be fine, but you don't need to worry about me," she said, wishing she could think of a reason not to go, but in truth it might be nice to talk about the meeting.

"I'll be here when you're finished." To her surprise, he frowned and lied. "I can't wait to hear what everyone's writing."

She laughed. "I'd better get back." Then, just to torture him, she added, "I'll tell you every detail over dinner."

The second person to read was Geraldine. She was writing a romance set in Washington, D.C., right after the Civil War. "There's no hidden meaning or at least I haven't found it. I just wanted to write a love story and thought the Civil War would make a good setting. It begins the day after Lincoln died."

With that she passed out copies and began. By the third page, her heroine was in bed with one of Grant's captains and she had no idea how her character's undergarments got off her lovely, well-rounded body.

When she finished, Martha Q slapped the woman on the back and proclaimed her writing grand. "Only, honey," she added, "underwear never just disappears—we just wish it would. You did a good job of the writing. I could believe I was right there in the sheets with the handsome captain."

Peter said it was interesting and Zack Hunter asked if she had any pages that they could take home and read ahead.

Since they'd all now lived through a war and love scene together, the group seemed to relax. They talked about writing as if they'd all been hidden away writing for years and thought they were the only ones in town doing so.

The odd mix of people bonded. When Zack read the first chapter of his mystery, everyone joined in to help him with the plot. He had a body at a train station but no clues. For a few minutes, clues were flying around the room like popcorn at a G-rated movie.

At nine, Emily broke up the group. Zack shoved the last two cookies into his pocket and everyone hurried downstairs still talking.

When she reached the desk, she saw Tannon smiling. "It went well?"

"It went well," she confirmed, then realized Tannon was behind the desk and not in front of it. "Where's Pamela Sue?"

"Her cat sitter called and said one of Pamela Sue's cats ate an earring. Pamela Sue had to run home. Since it was a matter of life or death, I offered to take over. It was me, the janitor, or that kissing kid upstairs. Sam said he wouldn't do it because he used to date Martha Q in high school and he didn't want to see her when she came down. I couldn't ask the kid, so that left me no option."

"Thanks." Emily smiled as she began turning off lights. "I should tell Sam not to worry about

Martha Q. Half the town used to date her from what I understand."

Tannon followed her. "No, you don't understand, Emily. I think the old guy still has a crush on her. I watched him stand out of sight and watch her leave before he left. I think he's still sweet on her."

Emily laughed. "You sound like Pamela Sue. She's always thinking people are daydreaming about lives they wish they had."

"Speaking of Pamela Sue"—here he furrowed his brow—"you should fire her. If I hadn't been here, I think she would have simply left."

"She's a volunteer."

"In her case, you got what you paid for." He waited for Emily to collect the grocery bag she carried as a briefcase. "Can we go? I'm starving."

"Of course. Where are we going?"

"We could drive out to the mall and try one of the fast-food places, or over to the highway for the truck stop, or we could go to the diner. It's open for another hour or so."

"The diner." She smiled. "I haven't been there in years. Do they still have chili fries with cheese?"

"Of course." As they locked up, he added, "Where do you usually go?"

"I never eat out. When I was in college, money was tight and I got in the habit of cooking. My only eating out is the bakery for a muffin." She didn't add that people always gave her sad looks

111

when they saw her eating alone. Men could ask for a table for one and have a meal in peace, but the public seemed to think women should travel in groups.

"You live a wild life, Emily Tomlinson," Tanner commented as they walked out. "You want me to follow you home?"

"Would you mind?"

"Not at all."

A half hour later, they were walking into the Blue Moon Diner.

They found a table by the windows and he held her chair for her as if they were in a fancy restaurant that had starched white tablecloths. When they ordered, she noticed he didn't even glance at the menu.

"You've been here before."

"A few times."

He looked happier than she'd ever seen him.

When he ordered a cup of coffee she reminded him that it was late for caffeine.

"You worried about my sleeping habits, Emily?" he asked.

"No," she answered, thinking that it had been so long since she'd had a date she didn't know how to have a conversation with a man. Only this wasn't a date. It was simple payback for a meal.

The waitress returned with their drinks and took their orders. Emily tried to settle into conversation with Tannon, but it didn't come easy. At one point she felt more like she was giving an accounting of how the meeting went than simply discussing it. To her surprise, he seemed interested in every detail.

When the food arrived, they ate in silence. When they finished, he ordered another cup of coffee. Apparently he wasn't in as much hurry for the evening to be over as she was.

She'd run out of anything to say. She wanted to ask about his mother, but she thought she'd let him bring it up first.

Through the window they saw the sheriff's car pass by, and Tannon told her that the diner had been robbed a few mornings ago. Someone must have been hiding in the place. Cass had come in, opened the diner, then stepped out back to dump some trash. When he came back inside he saw a man running for the front door with his cash drawer.

"How much did the guy get?"

Tannon shrugged. "Not much. A few hundred. Cass is mad because he's going to have to buy a new drawer."

When they left the diner, Tannon rested his hand on the small of her back. It seemed a little thing but it was all she thought about as they hurried to the truck. Tannon was almost a head taller than she was and his touch felt comforting and solid.

He turned on the engine but didn't put the truck in gear. Instead, he sat there for a moment, waiting for the heater to warm the air between them. They watched the lights go out in the diner, and then he turned slightly toward her.

"Emily. Thanks for having dinner with me. I don't get out much with people. I guess I'm not great company. I usually stop by and pick up something on the way home."

She watched him knowing his words didn't come easy. "You were fine." She looked away, relieved that they were both in shadows. "I'm surprised you're not married with a couple of kids by now. Most of the people we graduated with are." She thought of adding that he wasn't bad-looking. She'd heard two women in the bakery talking about him once. One said he was walking, breathing sex appeal, but he was hard to work for. He expected everyone in the office to put in forty hours of work a week and everyone knows that no one in an office works every minute. The other added that receptionists didn't stay around long once they learned there would be no sleeping with the boss, but he kept hiring lookers for the front desk.

"I guess your business takes up a lot of time." She couldn't help but wonder if the gossip she'd heard was true. Folks said he was a workaholic who never took a day off. The shy boy she'd known had morphed into a machine.

"Yeah." He shrugged. "Not much time for dating."

"Me neither," she admitted. "In truth, I was never any good at it anyway."

"Me neither. I gave it my best effort in college, but not one girl I took out felt right." He spread his arm over the seat back, almost touching her shoulder.

She didn't move. He was closer than anyone had been to her in a long time, but Tannon didn't make her uncomfortable.

"I used to have a group of friends I'd run with now and then after I was settled back here. We'd play poker and go out to the deer blinds and drink beer without bothering to even try to shoot anything. We even went down to the Fort Worth Stockyards for a rodeo a few years. I thought we were having some great times. Then, one by one, they were roped and dragged off to the altar."

She grinned. "You don't have a very high opinion of marriage."

"It's like selling yourself into slavery. I don't think I ever want to be responsible for making someone else happy. Hell, most days I can't even make myself happy."

"You made me happy tonight." She managed a slight smile. "I haven't had chili cheese fries in years."

He straightened up and got to work backing up the truck. "Then we'll have to do it again."

She sat in silence as they drove back to her place. Part of her didn't want to be friends. There was too much between them neither could talk about. The few weeks after she'd been attacked in the school parking lot all those years ago, she'd cried, wishing he'd come up to the hospital. If he'd just said he was sorry or explained why he hadn't been there, she might have forgiven him. Only now it was too late. She'd finished high school at home and gone off to college without ever seeing Tannon Parker again until he'd started dropping by the library after she took the job. He'd probably been in a dozen times before she ever spoke to him.

She knew the attack in the parking lot that night hadn't been his fault, but every time she thought about it, she remembered. He wasn't there. He hadn't shown up as he'd promised to.

He parked his truck in front of her apartment and walked around to open her door.

"You don't need—"

"I'll walk you to your door," he answered before she could finish.

She punched the code and the security door opened. Neither one of them had anything to say on the way up to her apartment. When she turned the key and pushed her door open, she looked up at him. "Thank you for dinner."

"You're welcome. I know I might not have acted like it, but I enjoyed tonight."

"Me too," she said uncertainly.

After he left, she crossed into her apartment already bright with light from timers plugged into every outlet. She moved to the window and watched him striding toward his truck. The memory of their friendship when they were young floated back to her. He'd never been unkind or rude. He treated her more like a kid sister than a girl his age.

She smiled, thinking about the summer before they entered high school. She'd made him let her practice kissing on him. He'd been more interested in baseball than girls, but he'd agreed. After she'd spent thirty minutes practicing, he'd wanted to continue, but she'd said she'd learned enough.

She knew she'd hurt his feelings by stopping. When he'd walked away that day, he swore that she'd make some man miserable someday and it wouldn't be him.

Emily watched Tannon drive away now. Maybe she owed him one. She might not ever call him friend again, but it wouldn't hurt to go out to eat with him now and then.

❧ *Chapter 14* ❧

Saturday

Rick glared across the table in the sheriff's office at the dozen relatives who'd decided to hold an intervention on his behalf. "I love you all," he began, trying to sound calm, "but I repeat: I am not going to have a bodyguard following me around. I'm related to half the people in this town—that should be enough watching over me." Just for Alex's benefit, he added, "No safe house, no off-the-map farm, no disappearing. I've got work to do." He did have two cases to get ready for even if they were over a month away.

No one in the room looked like they wanted to hear his argument.

Alex, the town sheriff, and Liz, his law partner, had presented all the evidence. One letter, two sawed boards formerly from the stairs, and a picture of the remains of a car he'd driven since his freshman year in college.

Hank showed him a report from an arson expert who said there was no doubt the fire in the car had been set after the backseat had been stuffed with trash.

His mother had even cried, but Rick didn't budge. Deep down, he felt he had to figure this out himself and he had no intention of someone bunking in with him until the crimes were solved. He'd played football through college and no one had taken hits for him then. He wasn't about to let them stand in the way of trouble now.

Finally, the meeting ended with him promising to stay at the bed-and-breakfast. Martha Q had made it plain when she left at six that morning that he'd better do his job.

Since he no longer had a car, he wasn't likely to be traveling far. Under threat of torture from his sister, Rick promised to let one of his cousins know when he left Winter's Inn for work or a date or, of course, the next writers' group meeting at the library. He planned to continue to at least look like he was working, but a date wasn't likely. Not many women wanted to date a homeless, carless lawyer, who apparently had a contract out on his life. With his luck, even the county library wouldn't be safe.

Rick knew he was hurting them by not letting them stand guard over him, but the fear that whoever was after him might go through them frightened him more than being alone. He also wasn't convinced someone wanted to kill him. There was the possibility that whoever sawed the steps and lit the fire in his car might just be trying to take him out of the game. He had two trials coming up. Maybe this was some druggie who wanted the court date delayed.

When the meeting was over, Gabe Leary, Liz's husband, looked at him as if he thought Rick was an idiot. Alex frowned at him as if she were considering locking him up. The rest of the family hugged him as they fought back tears. Rick felt like he was attending his own wake.

Hank drove him back to Winter's Inn with a never-ending list of precautions Rick should take. He didn't get out, since Rick no longer needed help walking, but he waited to leave until Rick stepped inside and closed the door.

Leaning against the frame, Rick wondered how long this nightmare would last. Tomorrow it would be a week since the accident. His body was healing, but he felt like his mind was shattering piece by piece.

"Mr. Matheson?" Mrs. Biggs whispered. "Are you all right?"

"Don't ask," he whispered back, as if saying anything out loud might be the last straw to shatter his reason.

"All right, sir." Mrs. Biggs moved closer and lowered her voice even more. "But we got a problem."

"I'll be glad to help. That's why I'm here, so no matter what's come up, I'll handle it." Stepping into his innkeeper role cheered him for a moment.

He was thinking the problem would involve a call to the plumber, moving some furniture, or changing a lightbulb. It would feel good to do something physical.

"The problem is not an it, sir. It's a woman. She says she's Mrs. Patterson's niece, but I never heard Martha Q mention her. I asked her to wait in the parlor until you came back. I told her you were in charge until Martha Q got back."

"Have you tried to call Martha Q?"

"No, sir. She left her phone with me, saying she didn't want to be bothered. Whatever came up, I was to go to you with the problem."

He should have known a free room and a hundred a day would come with some strings. "I'll take care of it, Mrs. Biggs. Don't worry."

The old lady looked relieved. "I'll bring in some tea," she said, as if that were her assignment in the campaign.

Rick straightened and walked into the parlor obviously decorated when a craft store exploded. He could see a shadow leaning against one of the long parlor windows, but the sun obscured his view. "May I help you?" he said, sliding into his new role.

"I'd like to see my aunt." The long form moved away from the window. She was tall, almost six feet and slim built with the movements of an athlete. "I'm Trace Adams."

When she offered her hand, Rick was surprised by the grip. As she moved away from the sun against her back, her full beauty hit him. Her midnight hair was parted in the middle and woven into a braid that hung past her waist. Intelligent green eyes studied him with caution from a face that was flawless and without makeup as near as he could tell.

"I'm the interim innkeeper, Rick Matheson," he managed as he took her in like a man seeing his first true work of art. She wasn't like any woman he'd ever met. There was something strong and controlled about her reminding him of a warrior. She wasn't a woman any man would call "little lady" or "sweetie." "I'm sorry, but your aunt isn't here. She should be back in a few weeks."

Trace Adams raised a doubting eyebrow as if she was considering the possibility that he'd bumped off old Martha Q and buried her in the basement. "She told me that if I was ever in the area, I'd have a place to hide out for a while. Does the offer stand?"

She was direct. He liked that. Most of the time he listened to females he was wondering what they meant or when they'd get around to the point.

"It does," he answered. "Provided you're not running from the law."

She smiled. "I don't run from anything, mister, never have, but there's a storm coming off the Rockies and headed this way. I thought I'd stop by here and ride it out."

She pointed with her head and he saw the

Harley-Davidson parked in the drive. He finally looked away from her eyes and down her body. Leather. She was dressed totally in black leather, molded to her body like a second skin. She could have stepped straight out of a James Bond movie. How could she possibly be standing in Harmony, Texas?

He walked to the window as if interested in her bike. Like her, it was beautiful and probably cost more than most of the new cars in town. "Are you close to your aunt?"

"No. A few phone calls a year." She slapped her gloves against her palm. "Look, Mr. Matheson, I'm looking more for a quiet place to stay than a long visit. We weren't that close even when she was married to my uncle, husband number four for her, I think. I didn't much care for him so when they divorced, I took Martha Q in the settlement. We've claimed each other ever since, but if there is a problem with me staying here, tell me now so I can make Dallas by dark, because I don't intend to stand around taking a test until you make up your mind."

That directness again, he thought. Surprising, shocking, intriguing. "I'm sorry. I'll get you a key." He had a feeling if he asked one more question she'd be out the door.

"I'll take the attic room." She walked around the desk tucked in the corner of the parlor and took a key from the center drawer as if she already knew where everything was. "Any problem with my putting my bike in the garage?"

"No, please, help yourself." She obviously knew her way around. "My car burned a few days ago so I've no use for the garage."

She looked up at him as if he were drooling again. Information she didn't need, but Rick couldn't seem to stop himself. "I guess you should know, Miss Adams, the sheriff seems to think someone is trying to kill me."

She picked up a bag and walked toward the stairs. "Not my problem, Mr. Matheson, unless your screaming wakes me."

He watched her disappear up the stairs and wasn't surprised when Mrs. Biggs poked her head around the corner to watch also. "Friendly, isn't she?" Mrs. Biggs laughed. "I can see why Martha Q loves her so."

"How come you don't know her, but she seems to know her way around?"

"Martha Q had the place open for a while before I got here. She could have visited then, but I've never seen so much as a Christmas card from family. Then, with family like that, cards might not be a priority."

"You think she's really Martha Q's niece?"

"She's strange enough to be. Martha Q told me once that one of her husbands was so wild his wolf pack of a family wouldn't even claim him. She said he ran full throttle all day and most of the night. Once, he caught her napping and gave her such a hard time about it, she left him. She claimed he was great in bed, but if she'd been married to him another six months she would have been dead from exhaustion." Mrs. Biggs glanced up the stairs. "This one looks like she could be from that branch of the family."

Mrs. Biggs looked him up and down. "If I were you I'd stay away from her. A woman like her would kill you."

Rick was getting tired of everyone thinking he couldn't take care of himself, but in this case the old lady was probably right. A night with Trace Adams might be his last.

Rick laughed. "She's sure going to make it interesting around here. You know, I think I feel better than I have all week."

He spent the rest of the day watching for the lady in leather. Now and then he'd hear a door close or footsteps above, but she did not appear. A half hour before dusk he saw her running down the drive wearing a black jogging suit with a hood. Her movements were long and fast like a seasoned runner.

Strange, he hadn't heard her coming down the stairs.

When she returned it was full dark. She stopped on the porch to stretch. Rick couldn't resist grabbing his jacket and stepping outside. "You have a good run?" he asked.

She glared at him for a moment, then turned away.

He fought to keep from rattling off his entire life's résumé. He wanted to tell her that he had been a football star in high school and played all four years in college. She might like that. He was a lawyer. Women always thought he was handsome. He could never remember being turned down for a date.

Rick forced his mind to stop listing things that probably wouldn't impress her anyway. He suspected that even if he smiled big enough to show his dimple, she'd just walk around him. So he settled for the basics. "What time would you like breakfast?"

"I don't . . ."

"We are a bed-and-breakfast," he reminded her.

"All right. How about seven?"

He'd thought more like nine or ten. "It *is* Sunday tomorrow, you know."

"I know. That's why I thought I'd sleep in and wait until seven."

Was she teasing him? Somehow he doubted it. "Seven it is. I'll tell Mrs. Biggs."

She walked past him.

"Good night," he said when she was halfway up the stairs.

He went into the sitting room on the second floor where he'd set up his office. He needed to get his mind off the woman upstairs and work on finding the man who had it in for him.

Whoever he was, he'd taken the time to saw the steps. He'd rounded up trash, mostly packing material and dead wood, and stuffed it into his car. He'd mailed a note: *Leave.*

Rick wrote down *premeditated* on a legal pad. This wasn't a crime of anger or rage. Whoever did this must have been watching him for a while. The guy knew where Rick parked his car, what time he left the office, and that he was the only one who used the back stairs after dark.

Rick added *logical* to his list. ⟶

The law office was in the center of town. Whoever set the fire had to be able to move around during the daylight without anyone noticing him. Even if he'd filled the car at night, he'd lit the fire during daylight hours when it would draw the most attention. When Rick would see it.

He wrote down George Hatcher's name on the paper, then scratched it out. He was certainly close enough to have sparked the fire and saw the steps, but the bookstore owner had no motive.

At ten o'clock, Rick stood and stretched. It was time to call it a night. In his stocking feet, he passed the stairs on the way to his room and decided to climb. After all, he was paid to watch over the house. He might as well make sure everything was locked up. With great care, he slowly moved up each step testing his muscles.

The attic widened at the top of the stairs. The top floor was big enough for two small rooms with a bath in between. One door was closed. Trace Adams had picked that one, he guessed. The bathroom door was open and so was the other bedroom.

Without a sound, he moved into the darkened bedroom and walked to where the windows opened out with a grand view of Harmony sleeping.

For a few minutes he looked out and took it all in, thinking about how much he loved this town. No one was going to run him out. He planned to live his life and be buried with generations of his family here. Until the staircase accident it had never seemed so important. Someday, if he ever got where he could afford it, he'd travel the world on vacation, but he'd always return home to Harmony.

The light from the other window drew him. For a moment, he didn't see her sitting just outside the glow from her room. She was on the roof with just enough moonlight to outline her form. She was sitting as still as stone with her knees pulled up to her chin. Her black hair was free of its braid. The ends were dancing in the wind, but she didn't seem to notice.

He thought of opening the window and yelling for her to get inside. The fall would kill her if she slipped. As he watched her, he realized she was in no danger. She'd done exactly this on rooftops before. The beautiful, strong young woman was in her element.

Suddenly, he didn't want to tell her about himself; he wanted to know about her. Most women tell you everything about themselves by the time the main course arrives at dinner, but not this one. Rick sensed she didn't believe in sharing. She couldn't be out of her twenties, but he suspected that she'd spent her life alone.

As he watched, she stood and lowered herself back into the window of her bedroom with the ease of one who'd done so dozens of times. A moment later, her light blinked out and he heard a door close. A few moments later, the shower came on.

Rick moved out of the room and headed back down to his room.

❧ *Chapter 15* ❧

As he played to a Saturday night crowd, Beau Yates found himself watching people more than usual. If his mystery blond girl showed up once at Buffalo's, she might again. Over the week since he'd seen her, she'd become more dream than memory.

About midnight, it began to rain. The tapping on the tin roof made the music take on a blend of old western songs, so he played some of the tunes he'd listened to at his grandfather's place in the summers. The old man would play one record after another letting the music spread out off his front porch and move through the trees. He lived along the breaks where flat land turned rocky. He'd said once that he built his house at the end of the world and when Beau was little he believed his father's father.

Beau loved his summers with his grandfather best when it rained and he could hear the music splashing against the water as rain poured in sheets off the roof. The old man lived alone, but he claimed he never felt alone when he listened to his records because they held all the good memories of his life. Once in a while he'd say his wife used to rock babies to this one or he'd heard that song when he came home from the war and all the protests were going on.

With his father and stepmother doing mission trips in the summer, Beau learned to breathe in music until it stayed in his lungs all winter long. The last summer, the old man gave him his guitar. Beau played the Gibson so much that his father threatened to break it. After that, he only played when his father was gone. His stepmom never said she liked his music, but she never complained to his dad.

Tonight, he played for his grandpa, hoping he could hear it all the way from heaven. Border would play bass on the songs he knew, but he didn't seem to mind when Beau played alone. For Border, this was the life. For Beau, it was just the beginning.

During the break, Border's big brother came in and told them he was moving in with his girlfriend and they could have the duplex. The place was owned by Martha Q Patterson, their grandmother's boss, and no one thought she'd mind as long as the rent was paid.

Beau and Border couldn't wait to get home and redecorate their new place. For the first time in over a year, Beau would have a bedroom to sleep in and not just a blanket on a broken-down couch. Big had said he was leaving the furniture but taking the rest of his stuff.

"We can drive over to Bailey to the all-night Walmart and get us sheets. You don't have any and mine are so ripped up I feel like a mummy when I wake up after rolling around in them," Border said as they packed up after closing time.

"Any of the towels yours?" Beau asked.

"No. I'm guessing Big will take all three so we might want to buy us some. And soap. I'm tired of washing with them little bars we steal every time we stay at the crummy motels."

"And food. Real food like fruit and frozen dinners. Your brother won't be coming by dropping off cereal and chips for us. You think he left the bowls and silverware?"

"Don't know. We better pick up plastic of everything. That way we won't have to wash up." Border hooted. "Hell, Beau, we sound like we're getting married."

Within an hour, they'd filled two grocery carts. Sheets, mattress pads, new blankets, towels, food, paper goods, cola, milk, and toilet paper. On the way through the clothing racks, they both picked out black T-shirts to wear when they played.

When the total went over two hundred dollars, Border claimed he'd never be able to afford to get married. Beau didn't care. For the first time since he'd walked out of his father's house, he felt like he was on his own.

On the way back to Harmony, they talked about some of the things they could do to decorate. Harley would give them old beer crates. If they could rig up something that looked like a table, they could use the crates as chairs and have somewhere to eat besides the couch or the porch.

"Since we're fixing the place up," Border said soberly, "we might want to think about fixing the lock. We're almost to the level that we could have something worth stealing."

Beau agreed. He'd already been putting away money for a good computer. If he had that, he could take a few classes online, maybe even go into Clifton Creek and take one on finance. One of these days he would be making big money and he didn't plan on handing it over to anyone to manage.

Sometimes he thought he must be a fool for dreaming so big, but then other times he knew he'd be a fool if he didn't. When he made money, big money, he already had plans of what he wanted to do with it.

That night, in the room that had been Border's big brother's, Beau organized his things. He didn't have much, not even enough to fill the four-drawer chest, but it felt good to have a place. The bed was good, or at least it had been. Now it sloped in the middle, but Beau didn't mind.

As they did every Saturday night, he and Border split their wages for playing in half. Border was saving for a tattoo and a new kickstand for his bike, but Beau was just saving. Since they'd started, he managed to put over a thousand dollars inside the lining of his shaving kit.

He flipped to the back of the spiral book where he wrote his songs and started a list of things he needed to do. Open a bank account. Buy new boots. Learn to cook something. He didn't much care what. It would just be nice, now that he had his own place, to be able to say he could cook. Ronny, next door, was a good cook. Maybe he'd ask her to show him how to make French toast.

As he drifted off to sleep, he wondered where the girl with the blond ponytail was tonight and if she was thinking of him. She knew where he worked. She would have to find him there if she wanted to see him again because he'd never be able to find her.

Next time maybe he'd ask her name before they drove off in her old restored Mustang. Maybe he'd kiss her a few times as they crossed through the night. Maybe he'd even bring her back here to his place at dawn and make her French toast.

❧ *Chapter 16* ❧

Sunday

A storm blew through Texas early Sunday morning as if it had avalanched down from the North Pole and met with no resistance. The howling wind woke Rick Matheson before dawn, and by first light he was standing in front of the bay windows off the second-floor sitting room, watching winter turn the world white.

By noon, everything in town stopped moving. Churches and cafés closed their doors. Beyond the old cottonwoods and elms that ran behind the bed-and-breakfast, the whole town looked asleep. The stoplights were blinking, muted by falling snow, and the old clock tower had a hat of white. Rick had a feeling it was going to be a hot chocolate and fireplace-blazing kind of day.

Which was fine with him. He'd had all the excitement he wanted for a while.

The only movement on the streets were four-wheel drives taking hospital and emergency staff to work. The snowplow would be wasting time between snow still falling and snow blowing. Somehow the stillness of it all made Rick feel safe for the first time since he'd taken the fall.

Alex and Hank both texted that they were working if he needed them, but the feeling seemed to be that not even a killer would venture out in this weather.

Rick stood watching a cloudy horizon and listening to the big house creak with the storm as the old heater in the basement clicked on and off. The one guest at Winter's Inn must have decided to sleep in because he hadn't heard movement from the floor above him all morning.

Rick missed Trace Adams at breakfast. She'd made it to the kitchen before him, talked Mrs. Biggs into a tray, and was gone when he walked in for his first cup of coffee. The only noise he'd heard inside the house all morning was Mrs. Biggs baking. She claimed not even the weather would keep her grandsons away for supper. Her oldest grandson was off on Sundays, unless he was needed as a volunteer at the fire department. Her youngest usually slept until dinnertime since he played in a band on Saturday night.

As the snow piled up outside, Rick tried to

forget that directly one floor above him was a very sexy stranger, probably dressed in black. He had no doubt that if she wore a nightgown, it would be midnight black just like her hair.

After a huge breakfast, he'd gone back to bed for a while, tried watching TV and reading, but still couldn't get her out of his mind. There was something about her that drew him. He'd never met a woman who didn't smile at him.

By midmorning, when she still hadn't shown up, he wandered back downstairs and decided it was time to pull the bandages off his back and take a real shower. He'd tried a few baths after wrapping up in plastic wrap to keep the wound dry, he'd washed his hair in the sink every morning, but he didn't feel clean. Since he could remember, he'd been a shower man, and baths just didn't cut it.

Carefully, he tugged the bandage off his back and looked at his wound in the bathroom mirror. One side of his body was bruised from shoulder to hip. The cut, where jagged concrete had ripped into his shoulder, was puffy but healing. If he could wash off some of the dried blood and bandage adhesive, it wouldn't look nearly as menacing.

Rick turned the water as hot as he could stand it and stepped in the shower Martha Q must have thought would be funny to decorate like a circus tent. Lowering his head, he braced his hands on either side of the shower head and let the water run over his back.

It felt so good to be clean. Still moving slowly, he soaped up, then just stood in the steady stream wondering how long he had before the hot water would run out in the entire place.

A thump at the door brought him back from paradise.

He stood very still listening.

The thump came again. Harder.

Rick glanced around for a weapon. Nothing.

The door gave with the third thump and Rick reached for a towel.

The fat cat wiggled around the door, looking bothered that the air was all steamed up. Walking across the room, the cat sat just outside the shower as if waiting for him to step out.

It took a minute for Rick's heart to stop pounding. He turned the water off, wrapped the towel around his waist, and stepped onto the bath mat.

The cat jumped in for his turn, licking the water from the shower floor.

Rick laughed. "Water in your bowl in the kitchen not good enough for you?"

The tabby paid him no mind.

He grabbed another towel and scrubbed his head, then dropped it over his shoulders and reached for his shaving gear.

A softer thump hit the door. "Leaving already?"

he said, without looking at the cat. "I thought you'd stay in here a while and keep me company."

"I haven't been in," a woman's voice answered. "And I've no wish to keep you company."

Rick looked up into green eyes watching him from the opening. To his surprise, she was smiling. He reached down to ensure the towel around his waist was secure, then added, "I thought you were the cat."

She just stared at him as if he were dumber than lint. Her gaze moved down his body to his feet where the cat had decided to share the small bath mat.

"You always shower with Martha Q's cat?"

"Always," he said, trying to act like he barely noticed her watching him shave. She was wearing a white T-shirt today that fit like a second skin. The black jacket over her shoulders looked like it might have belonged to a biker in the fifties. He wouldn't have been surprised if there were a Hell's Angels patch on the back.

"You need medical attention," she finally said in a low voice.

"I'm fine. I just took a fall last week." To his shock, she shoved the door open and walked in.

Without comment, she tugged the towel across his shoulders and held a red spot up for his inspection. Blood.

"I'm bleeding?" he said in surprise, and she gave him that now familiar you're-an-idiot look again.

"Turn around so I can see. It looks like one of the stitches didn't hold." Her cool hand was already moving over his shoulder. "Didn't your doctor tell you to be careful? This wound should still have antiseptic on it and a bandage to keep it clean."

"It did until I got in the shower."

"It needs care," she pushed. "You should have it seen to immediately."

"Of course. It's no problem. I'll just go get the doc to stitch it back."

"How you planning to get to the hospital? You have no car and I can't take you on my bike."

She was right. The few people who were out in this storm were helping in emergencies. No one would want to come over so he could go get one stitch fixed. Mrs. Biggs didn't own a car and it was too far to walk.

He met her green-eyed stare and they came to the same conclusion.

"Sit down," she ordered reluctantly. "I'll tape it together."

He did as he was told and she collected all she'd need from the medicine kit the hospital had sent home with him.

"You've done this before," he said more as a statement than a question.

"A few times." When he seemed to be waiting for more of an answer, she added, "You know, Girl Scouts."

Rick didn't believe her. She somehow wasn't the Girl Scout type, but he didn't know her well enough to ask for more information.

The bathroom seemed to be getting smaller and he could think of nothing else to say to Trace Adams. If he moved, or complained, she'd probably cuss him out. She did have a gentle touch, though.

Finally, she patted his shoulder. "That should hold until you can see a doc." She moved to the door. "You got a nice body, Matheson. It's a shame to see it so bruised. You're lucky you didn't break half your bones in that fall."

"Yeah." He set his jaw. "Real lucky."

She closed the door and was gone. When he dressed, he decided to go looking for her. He hadn't even said thanks for her help. And, after all, since they were trapped in a house together, they might as well talk.

He found her in his favorite room, the upstairs sitting room. Bookshelves lined the interior and a huge bay window framed out the rest. Great old reading chairs were turned so that whoever sat in them could see both the window and the fireplace. From the size of the blaze, she must have just added logs to the fire.

She was sitting cross-legged in one of the chairs near the windows. A watery sun was trying to make an appearance since he'd been here earlier. The few rays that slipped through the clouds turned the snow to diamonds in places.

Trace Adams was going through an old album with little interest except to pass time. She glanced up at him as if he were no more than a passing stranger.

"Yours?" He pointed to the picture album.

"No. I found it on the bookshelf. You think these are Martha Q's relatives?" She turned one page toward him. The tintype looked like a group of poor relations from the *Gone With the Wind* era.

He shrugged. "I doubt it. From the way she moved around from marriage to marriage, I wouldn't think of her as a collector of much. More likely it came with the house when she bought it."

Trace flipped a page to another picture of young people sitting on a bluff beside a dirt road. Across the bottom, someone had printed, *Moving west*.

Trace looked up at him. "It's strange. Someone must have collected these pictures for years, for generations. There are soldiers in Civil War uniforms in here. Then, somewhere in the fifties, it just stopped. It's like someone stuffed the album on a shelf and forgot about it. Like the past no longer mattered."

Rick sat in the chair across from her. "Maybe the last of the family died. I heard this house passed from owner to owner for several years before Martha Q bought it."

"Or maybe the descendants don't know about

this book. Maybe it was just put on the shelf with the other books and no one remembered to take it when they sold the old house."

"Maybe." He grinned. "You like a mystery, Miss Adams?"

She closed the book. "I guess. I like pieces to fit together."

"Want me to tell you mine? How I got hurt? Why I'm here?"

She relaxed back in the chair. "Normally I'd say no, but since there's nothing else to do and I seem trapped with a guy who shares his showers with a cat, sure, go ahead, tell me."

Mrs. Biggs brought in a tray of coffee and banana nut bread. They both thanked her. Half the bread vanished before Rick stood and began his story. Because Trace was at least mildly interested, he included every detail he could remember. He also made note that her questions were worded as if she came from a law enforcement background, or, he considered, she had a criminal mind-set.

As he talked, he paced in front of the windows as if presenting evidence to the jury.

She was asking questions when he saw her face change suddenly into shock.

Before he could understand what was happening, Trace lunged at him, knocking him backward into the chair he'd been sitting in earlier.

Just as his wounded shoulder slammed into the chair, he heard the shattering of glass and a ball the size of a cannon hit the bookshelf, sending books raining down on them.

"Stay down!" she yelled as she jumped off him and ran to the corner of the window.

Rick wasn't sure he could move. "What happened?" he said far more calmly than he felt.

"Someone tried to hit you, but they've vanished, and with this wind, even the tracks will be gone by the time I can get down there."

She rushed to the bookshelf and dug through the scattered books.

Rick moved to the edge of his chair as she stood and carried something toward him. She held two broken pieces of metal out for him to inspect.

He took the offering and put the pieces together. "It's one of Martha Q's garden statues. If you hadn't knocked me out of the way, I might have been killed by a garden elf." He leaned back in the chair. "If I weren't so mad, I'd think this was funny."

Mrs. Biggs ran into the room and screamed at the sight of the beautiful window shattered across the floor, then looked at both of them. "Are you all right? What happened?"

Trace took charge. "Help me find something to block up this window and then we should call the sheriff and report this. Whoever threw that statue wasn't some kid out playing in the snow. They must have seen you in the window and meant to do you harm."

Mrs. Biggs shook her head. "Maybe it was an accident, or the wind."

No one in the room believed her, but she was still rattling off possibilities when she left.

Trace turned to Rick. "Are you all right?"

He lied and nodded.

"I think I should check that shoulder wound once we get the window blocked, and it might be a good idea to pull all drapes and blinds so no one can see in. Whoever did this might be out there waiting for another chance."

He agreed. "We won't have to call the sheriff. An alarm is going off at the station now. I just hope someone is there to answer it."

Mrs. Biggs showed up with a card table and duct tape. Before they could get it secure, a deputy from the sheriff's department was pounding on the door.

Rick sat watching as Deputy Gentry and Trace boarded up the window. He could feel blood running down his back, but he didn't say a word. In the fall, more stitches must have broken open, but if she hadn't hit him hard enough to knock him down, he might be dead or blind from shattering glass, or . . .

He didn't want to think of any more ors. This strange woman who acted like she didn't care about him at all had just saved his life and she'd done so with far more skills than any Girl Scout had.

When Trace finished with the window, she draped a quilt over Rick and said to the deputy, "We need to get him to the hospital."

Deputy Gentry didn't argue, but Rick looked directly at her. "You coming along?"

She shrugged. "Might as well. Unless you want me to call your mother, Matheson?"

"No, don't call anyone. Let's go." He pulled the quilt around him knowing it would be soaked with blood by the time he got to the hospital. "I'd rather have you, Adams, if you're willing, than all my relatives out on these roads." She wasn't exactly Florence Nightingale, but she'd do.

To his surprise, she circled his waist and moved with him to the side entrance where Gentry had pulled the cruiser.

He ignored the pain and tried to smile. "You worried about me?"

"You're looking a little pale," she said as she climbed in the back next to him.

He leaned his head back as all that had just happened began to register along with the pain of bruises mounting all along his back. "In case I pass out, I want to say thanks right now."

"You're welcome," she answered. "Now be still and try not to bleed all over the seat."

He reached for her hand as he closed his eyes.

❧ *Chapter 17* ❧

Monday

On Monday afternoon, Emily was surprised how much she looked forward to her visit with Paulette Parker. She felt as if she were turning pages in an old diary, meeting her mother as a young woman.

When she got to the nursing home, she was told at the front desk that Paulette had been taken to Amarillo.

As Emily turned to leave, the girl who'd made them tea last week followed her to the door.

"She had a bad fall," the girl whispered. "I'm sorry Mrs. Parker will miss your visit. She was really excited about it."

"So was I," Emily said, reading the girl's name tag. "Thank you, Beth, for all you did last week. The tea made our visit special."

"You're welcome. You really made her happy. This morning all she could talk about was that you'd be back this afternoon. She insisted on walking around her room," the aide whispered. "The doctor left orders not to allow it, but we didn't see the need to restrain her." A tear drifted down Beth's face. "I feel like it was my fault she fell."

"Accidents happen. It wasn't your fault. Paulette

is a woman who lives life by her own rules."

"We found her just after breakfast. Her head hit the corner of the sink. It knocked her out, but most of the damage seemed be to her hip and leg. The doctor thinks the hip is broken."

"Does Tannon know?"

The aide nodded. "We called him. He said he'd meet the ambulance at the hospital. Mrs. Parker was so mad he wasn't here to go with her that the doctor had to give her something to calm her down for the ride. If she'd had ten kids, I don't think they could do all she wants her one son to do."

"I brought flowers for her." Emily held up the roses. It had taken the florist a half hour to weave brightly colored ribbons through the stems of the pale pink roses cut short to fit in a confetti-colored bowl. The effect was a Mardi Gras of color Emily thought Mrs. Parker would like. "I think I remember my mother saying Paulette had pink roses on her wedding dress."

"I could put them in her room, but she won't be back tonight. Maybe not for days."

"No, thanks, I'll take them home with me. I'd like her to see them fresh."

Emily drove home, trying to decide what to do. She didn't know what hospital. Even if she did get to Amarillo to see Paulette, it would probably only be for a few minutes.

Taking a day off to go see her mother's best

friend in the hospital didn't seem so bad, she told herself, knowing that she wouldn't do it.

As the afternoon aged, Emily couldn't stop thinking of the lonely old woman. Every time she passed the flowers on her bar, she wished she had some way to get them to Paulette. She needed to let her know that she was thinking of her.

Finally, at quarter to five, she got an idea. Tannon had said he was always working. He'd probably come back to his office tonight, even if it was just to pick up paperwork and clothes. If she took the flowers to his office, maybe he could take them to Amarillo.

Rushing, she made it to his office before the doors were locked. Though she'd seen the building before, she'd never thought about it being so big inside. The first floor was a bay of offices without walls except for the long glass one that obviously separated Tannon's office from a dozen employees. Inside everything seemed to be made of glass or steel. Even the desks and low shelves separating the work areas were made of metal. The only color in the room came from a massive brick fireplace that dominated one wall. The brickwork was beautiful and gas flames danced over rock logs designed to look like a campfire.

A long, polished desk stood guard at the entrance just off a simple lobby. The woman behind it looked more like a model than a receptionist. She stood as Emily walked in and smiled a perfect cold smile. "May I help you?"

Emily moved the flowers to one arm. "Is Tannon Parker in?"

"May I have your name, please?" Miss Perfect said.

"Emily Tomlinson. I'm delivering these. Just tell Tannon that they are for his mother. I promised I'd visit her today."

The girl wrote down Emily's words and studied her for a moment before deciding she was worth talking to. "He's not here, but he'll be back. He called, giving us a list of all the files he wants packed and ready. He may be staying up at the hospital for a few days with her, but he'll be working. Mr. Parker never stops working."

"How did he say his mother was?"

The girl looked blank. "I forgot to ask."

While the secretary wrote, Emily saw the room in a different light. Efficient, polished, very businesslike, but cold, sterile. There were no pictures of kids on desks, no coffee mugs with sayings on them, no personal touches.

"Will there be anything else?" The model looked like she needed to get back to work.

Emily set the flowers and her huge purse on the polished desk. "No, I'll leave him a note." She pulled out a notepad, borrowed a pen, and hastily scribbled: *Flowers for your mother. Hope she's doing better. I'm here if you need me, Emily.*

It crossed her mind that the last thing might be

a little too personal, but she had a feeling no one cared about Paulette, or Tannon. He was just the boss.

As she drove back to her apartment, she thought of how different the man Tannon was from the boy she'd known. They'd been friends in the kind of way people are who grow up around each other. They'd both been shy, so sometimes in school or at parties, they found themselves together, talking in spots away from the crowd. Once they were in high school, they'd share rides to events and talk about homework over the phone.

She'd always thought of him as her best boy friend. At least she had until "the accident," as her mother called it. Tannon had promised to be waiting out front of the school that night. He hadn't been there. She'd walked all the way to the back lot only to find his car locked.

Emily closed her eyes not wanting to remember what happened next. She'd been too frightened to even scream and so hurt she felt like her insides never healed even after all the bruises and cuts did. Being quiet and an A student didn't matter that night, for in five horrible minutes she became nothing more than a victim.

She'd told herself for fifteen years that it wasn't Tannon's fault. He wasn't the one who had assaulted her, but he hadn't been there to help either. He hadn't kept his promise and he'd never said he was sorry.

On nights when the memories came back, like tonight, Emily always took a long shower until the water turned cold, then zipped into her fuzzy robe. Pulling her moments journal from the drawer, she began to read. Favorite moments. Happy moments. Tender moments. They all calmed her mind.

When she folded the journal away, she knew she wouldn't sleep, so she popped popcorn and curled up on the couch to watch movies.

Halfway through the second movie, her doorbell rang.

Emily couldn't imagine who it could be. No one ever stopped by her place and the neighbors in the building just knocked. The widow lady across the hall even had a key to let herself in if she needed something.

Crawling out from the clutter, she tiptoed to the speaker against the bell and pushed. "Yes?" she said.

"Emily!" a man's voice shouted. "Can I come up? It's Tannon and it's freezing out here."

"Oh. Of course." She pushed the button to release the lock. By the time she'd carried her popcorn to the bar, he was knocking on her door.

When she opened it, he walked in without being asked. "I don't mean to bother you, but I need a favor and I've no one else to ask." She didn't miss his exhaustion in the slope of his shoulders or the nervousness in his voice.

"All right." She moved around him as he stood in the middle of her living room. "How can I help?" She knew that it had taken a lot for him to turn to her for help.

For a moment he didn't say anything. He just stared at her. "Did I wake you? I'm sorry. I saw your lights all on and thought you were up." He dug his fingers through his dark hair and sighed as if he'd made his hundredth mistake of the day.

"You didn't wake me. I was watching a movie." She added, "Would you like some popcorn?"

He shook his head. "You got any of those ribs left over? I don't think I've eaten today."

"No," she answered. "But I have stew. I'll warm some up while you tell me how your mother is and what I can do to help. I've been thinking about her all evening."

He stood on the other side of the bar and told her in detail what they'd gone through since this morning. His mother fought the doctors and nurses all the way, but they did their job. She had a break in her hip and hairline fractures just below the knee.

Emily warmed him up two slices of corn bread and a bowl of stew while he filled in details. As he ate, she poured another serving into the pan to warm and pulled out the last of the corn bread. He pulled off his coat, sat at her tiny table, and ate what she'd planned for four days' lunches.

"Thanks," he finally said when all the food was gone. "You're a good cook."

"Will you take the flowers to your mom?"

"I will, only I don't know if they'll let her have them. I don't know how long it will be until she's out of ICU. Maybe tomorrow." He looked down at his hands. "She wanted me to stay, but the doc said I'd only get to see her for fifteen minutes every two hours and she'd just be asleep. He told me to come on home."

Tannon stood. "I was wondering if you'd go over to my mother's house and pick out a few things she could use at the hospital. Maybe something she could wear once she's allowed something other than the hospital gowns and whatever things women pack in overnight bags." He pulled out a set of keys and handed them to her. "I don't know what to get and whatever I bring will be the wrong thing. She likes you. She'll like what you pick out."

"But you know where—"

"If I know Mom, everything will be in order. You'll know what to pick out. She loved the scarf you gave her. She wore it every day last week." His smile looked sad. "I've got to work at the office a few hours in the morning, but I could drop by the library after and pick up whatever you choose."

"Sure, I'll help," Emily said without further protest. "You look like you could use some rest."

"I guess I could. The doc told me not to come see her until tomorrow afternoon. She'll be having tests run and sleeping." Tannon laughed. "He said I wasn't a calming element for her. That's an understatement."

After a moment, Emily asked gently, "Want to watch the end of the movie with me? It's a comedy about two people who trade houses."

"Okay. It would be nice to relax. I feel like I've been in a dead run since five this morning." He waited until she sat, then took the other side of the couch.

She floated the blanket over them both and hit the play button. When she passed him the popcorn, he finished off the bowl.

"Want a root beer?"

"No, water is fine." He shoved the covers her way and stood. "I'll get it."

He went into her kitchen and brought back a bottle of water and a root beer as if he'd done so a hundred times. He opened hers before handing it to her, then crawled back beneath the quilt. "What'd I miss?" he asked as if he cared.

Emily laughed. "Nothing."

He leaned back and stretched his legs. Within ten minutes he was sound asleep.

She watched the rest of the movie, pretending she had company enjoying it with her. Afterward, she hated to wake him, so she covered him with the blanket and left him there.

The next morning, she dressed and was ready to leave for work before she set foot outside her bedroom. The blanket they'd shared last night was folded on the couch. Tannon was gone.

She drove over to the Parker home.

Everything belonging to Mrs. Parker was in perfect order. She picked out a few comfortable robes and a sweater with pants the same color, then pulled some makeup and hand lotion from the bathroom counter. As she walked out of the room, she noticed a small framed picture of Tannon at about ten years old and decided to take it also.

She left the suitcase in her car, thinking she'd walk out with Tannon when he came to pick it up. But the morning passed without him dropping by. She'd almost thought he'd forgotten when he showed up with a grocery bag in his hand.

"I brought lunch," he said. "Have you got a place where we could eat?"

Emily didn't want to take him to the small break table that was crammed into the storage room, and she wasn't sure there was enough room in her office for him to move around. No one was in the library except a homeless man pretending to read in the corner, Pamela Sue at her usual perch by the front desk, and Sam sleeping his lunch hour away in the back.

"How about we eat in the alcove?" Emily whispered.

"Sounds great."

As he followed her up the stairs, he whispered, "I called and checked on Mom. She's resting and doing much better today. They should have more to tell me by the time I go in this afternoon."

Emily walked into the sunny room where the writers' group had met a few days ago. "I'm glad she's better." She pulled what had been the cookie table closer to the windows while Tannon set up two chairs.

"Perfect," he said as he waited for her to sit. He pulled out sandwiches and added, "I didn't know what you liked, so I told my secretary to get one of every kind the deli at the grocery store made. Ham and cheese, turkey, chicken salad—"

"Chicken salad," she decided as she reached for the sandwich in his hand.

"Darn, that was the one I wanted."

"Oh, in that case—"

He laughed and she realized he was teasing her.

"In that case, Mr. Parker, you are out of luck."

He shrugged as if accepting defeat. "All right, but I get first choice on the chips and cookies."

"We'll negotiate." She laughed.

He pulled out a root beer and a bottle of water as he set the bag aside. They shared the chips and cookies as they finished off their sandwiches. The window offered a great view of the old downtown still covered in snow, and the sun warmed them while they talked.

When they finished, she put the trash in the

bag and he pushed the chairs back in place. "I enjoyed this," he said with his back to her.

"Me too," she answered. "I left my trunk unlocked, so you can pull your mother's suitcase out."

He moved a step closer to her and lowered his voice. "I like the way your hair curls as it dries."

She touched her head. "It does that when it's short. I've worn it this way for years." She'd almost said "since the accident."

"I noticed." He bent down, lightly brushed her curls and kissed her on the cheek. "Thanks for everything."

She was so surprised that for a moment she couldn't move. "You're welcome," she finally managed to reply. She had no idea whether to be mad or flattered about the kiss and the fact that he'd taken the time to notice her hair.

To her surprise, Tannon swore under his breath. "I didn't do that right. That wasn't meant to be a thank-you kiss."

Before she could ask any questions, he bent down again and pressed his lips to hers. He wasn't holding her or touching her anywhere else. All she had to do was move a breath away to break the kiss, but she didn't. She just stood there feeling his warm lips press against hers.

When he straightened, he stared at her as if trying to read her thoughts. "I'm out of practice," he said. "I'll get better."

Before she could come up with anything to say, he turned and walked out of the alcove. She heard his boots thumping down the stairs.

Tannon Parker must have lost his mind.

❧ *Chapter 18* ❧

Monday night

Tannon didn't let himself think about the little librarian until he left the hospital at midnight. While driving to Amarillo after their lunch, he'd spent his time on the phone dealing with problems at his company. His profits had tripled in the ten years he'd run the business. Unlike his father, Tannon was involved in every detail. He went over every report, every file, every log. He let nothing slide by, except maybe his life, but with any luck, that was about to change.

He'd almost fired the receptionist at the main desk in his office when she'd said, "Some candidate for a makeover left flowers for your mother." The only thing that stopped him was how he'd like to see the girl's face when he brought Emily through the office on the way to his apartment.

None of his staff, except the grocery delivery boy, had ever been in the elevator, much less his apartment. A few women had tried over the years, but Tannon never considered employees as possible dates. Since he rarely talked to anyone else, that pretty much ended his love life.

The beautiful women like his receptionist always seemed overly made up and reminded him of his mother with their constant talk about their clothes and shoes.

As he drove to the hotel on Interstate 40, he let his mind fill with Emily. She'd been so adorable in her snowball of a robe last night. He liked that her hair was wet from a shower and curled around in no order. She hadn't even tried to push it in place, and even better, she hadn't apologized. He'd made her nervous, but she'd still been kind, offering him food and a rest. He had no idea what movie they'd watched, but in her little apartment he felt comfortable, at ease.

Dear God, how he'd missed her over the years. When they were kids she was the one person who always took the time to talk to him. She always made him smile. She'd been loved and cherished by her parents and that made him feel good inside. He'd been ignored by his, but when the families got together, a bit of the Tomlinson family rubbed off onto his parents, at least for a while. When his mother insisted on overplanning a party, it never mattered to him as long as Emily was invited. He knew they'd find each other sometime during all the noise and talk, just talk. When they'd been in grade school, it had been under a table draped with a linen tablecloth. Later, it had been the backyard swing or the attic at her house.

He pulled up into the hotel parking lot and cut his lights. In the darkness, he let another memory float over him. He was sixteen and the football team had just made the state finals. All the newspaper staff at the school paper had worked late, long after the game was over and the crowds had left. He'd promised he'd hike across the parking lot to where he'd left his car by the stadium and drive up to the school door to pick up Emily that night after the newspaper was "put to bed," as their journalism teacher always said.

Only as he stepped out the side door, a girl stopped him with first one question, then another. He hadn't realized she was simply flirting for several minutes and he thought he would have to run to get away from her chatter. Finally, he'd said he had to go and ran for the stadium lot, knowing that Emily was probably already out front of the school waiting for him.

Only she hadn't been. She'd walked to his car. He was ten feet away from her when he saw her on the ground between two cars. She was making a sound like an animal in terrible pain. Blood and her ripped clothes were everywhere.

Tannon forced the memory aside and got out of his car. He hadn't thought of that night in years. He'd never spoken of it to anyone. Emily didn't know that he'd held her until the ambulance came, then ridden with her as they worked on her. He'd seen it all that night with the flashing light blinking horror. Her clothes in shreds, her face muddy and bruised, her body twisted in pain. "And the cuts," he whispered in the darkness. He'd never forget where they'd cut her.

The attack had changed her, made her even more shy and withdrawn. She'd never returned to school, instead opting to be schooled at home so she could graduate early and go away to college. His mother had tried to pull Emily's mother out, but Shelley withdrew after the attack. A world that would hurt her only child wasn't one she wanted to be seen in. It had taken her a year before she'd taken calls and another before Paulette had talked her into going out to lunch. His mother had her shortcomings, but being Shelley's friend wasn't one of them. Tannon would give her credit there.

He'd asked about Emily once when he saw her mother at the store. Shelley Tomlinson was always proud of her daughter. She told him all about how well Emily was doing in school. Mrs. Tomlinson had no idea that he'd ridden with Emily to the hospital or that he'd been the reason she'd been in the back parking lot alone. Emily must have closed what had happened away as he did. He'd heard she'd barely talked to the police about what had happened. The thugs who hurt her were never caught and the story faded as others took its place in headlines and conversations.

The attack of a shy girl few remembered from school was forgotten by most.

What had happened that night changed him also. He'd failed one more person in his life and the knowledge that he'd kept her secrets from that night didn't matter. He'd gone as far away to school as his parents would let him, but the memory of that night haunted him for months. For a long time all he wanted to do was to find a way to say he was sorry, but what good would that do? It wouldn't change the past. It wouldn't erase the scars.

Tannon unlocked the hotel door and stepped into his room. The man in the mirror greeted him. "So why'd you kiss her?" he asked himself.

But there was no answer back. It was simply something he'd been thinking about doing for years. Every woman he'd spent any time with since he was sixteen had been compared to her and none had quite measured up.

Tannon tugged off his boots and decided to text her. She was probably already asleep, but she'd get the message in the morning.

Mom is better. Doctor's optimistic about recovery. Moved her to private room. She loved the flowers. He pressed Send. The last thing he wanted to do was mention the kiss. His timing had been all wrong. The place was all wrong. He should have asked her if it was okay. Hell, the fifteen-year-old kid named Franky who hung out at the library was better at this game than he was.

Only, for Tannon, it wasn't a game, and if he had anything to do with it, it wouldn't be the last time he kissed the librarian.

His phone chimed. *I'm glad,* was her simple response.

He thought about it a while, then texted back, *I wish I were back in Harmony. What do you have for supper?*

The chime came back fast. *Nothing. You're too late. I ate it all.*

How about Wednesday night?

Spaghetti, she answered back.

Mind if I drop by?

He waited, wondering how long it would take for her to type a yes or no. Finally the phone chimed.

No. I don't mind. I'll make enough for two.

Tannon relaxed back against the mountain of pillows hotels feel obliged to provide. If he'd been a betting man, he would have laid odds that she wouldn't want to see him again. Maybe she didn't. Maybe she just felt sorry for him with his mother in the hospital. Or maybe she wanted to tell him off in person. Kissing her had been a dumb idea.

I'll be there at 7. I'll bring a couple of desserts and let you pick.

He waited, but there was no answer. She'd

probably gone to bed. Closing his eyes, he remembered her in her funny fluffy robe with her bare feet peeking out and her damp hair curling along her cheek and throat.

His last thought before he fell asleep was that he wished he were back in her crowded little apartment. Everything in the place seemed a part of her. If she'd only let him show up now and then, that would probably be all either one of them could handle.

"Good night, Emily," he whispered as he drifted off.

❧ *Chapter 19* ❧

February 14

Beau woke up on Tuesday morning determined to accomplish at least a few things on his list. He showered, dressed in clean clothes, then pulled the money from inside the lining of his shaving kit and headed out toward the bank. There was no need to take his car; the bank wasn't more than a few blocks away.

He made it to the front porch of the duplex before he lost his nerve. He'd never been in the Harmony State Bank. Not once. He wasn't even sure what to do. Maybe he would be wise to wait until Border was up and willing to go with him, but his partner probably didn't know any more about banking than he did. Big might know, being older, but Beau didn't want to ask him. Big had done so much for him, most without even knowing it.

"Morning, Beau." Ronny startled him as she stepped from her side of the duplex.

"Morning," he managed. "Where you headed so early?" He didn't really care where his next-door neighbor was going, but he had to say something.

She laughed. "You're never up this early so I guess you wouldn't know, but every morning I walk down to the Blue Moon Diner for coffee. I could make it here, but I like the routine of having coffee at the diner before heading into work."

"Mind if I walk along? I'm headed to the bank."

She laughed again, that sweet laugh that always made him smile. "Of course, but you might as well have coffee too. The bank doesn't open for an hour."

They walked along talking. Ronny wasn't old enough to be his mother, but that didn't stop her from mothering him. By the time they got to the diner, he'd asked enough questions that she was rattling on in detail about how to open a savings account.

To his surprise, Ronny picked a long table that would hold eight and took a seat.

Just after they ordered breakfast, two firemen came in and took a seat at Ronny and Beau's table without asking. At first he thought they might be flirting with Ronny, but pretty quickly Beau decided they were just friends of hers. She was a nice-looking woman, but from what he could see, she gave off no signals saying she was looking for a man.

By the time the food came, the table was crowded with single people, most in their late twenties and early thirties. They all seemed to be great friends. None were faces he recognized from the bar. These were the morning people, he thought, the kind he'd see rarely in his life, he figured. In an odd way, he'd stepped into another civilization.

Beau was thankful that no one insisted he join the conversation as it gave him time to quietly study the group of friends. Friendly, he assessed, but not as loud as the bar crowd. More polite to the waitress, less flirty. No profanity. No sexual comments. No off-colored jokes. They talked of what was happening in town and the weather.

Beau decided that if someone hadn't found a mate by thirty they all went back to being just friends. He was glad when Ronny stood and motioned that it was time to go. The group was nice, but they would never be his people. His people thrived in smoky air and bourbon breezes.

They paid out and she pointed him toward the bank. As he walked away from her, he smiled to himself. He'd always thought she was a lonely person, but Ronny had her share of morning friends. Too bad she didn't have a nighttime lover. Border swore she had once but Beau found that hard to believe.

Opening an account proved easier than he thought it might have been. Within ten minutes, his money was in the bank and he'd been given a card so if he ever needed cash he could just walk up to the ATM and pull money out.

As he was walking through the lobby, he thought he saw a blond ponytail. He could only see the back of a girl dressed in a western shirt, but the hair was the same as his dream girl's.

Beau dodged through the bank, but by the time he made it out the door she was gone. He spent a half hour walking the streets of Old Main, but he found nothing. No girl. No Mustang. Feeling like a fool for aching for someone he'd only known for a few hours, he walked back toward his duplex. Border would still be asleep, which meant that Beau couldn't play his music or even the TV, so he decided to stop off at the library and read for a while. The little librarian had introduced him to a collection of books about famous musicians.

"Morning, Miss Tomlinson," he said as he pulled off his hat and smiled at her. He'd always thought she had a quiet kind of beauty. Her curly brown hair that never stayed tied back made her look younger, but her clothes made her seem older.

"Morning, Beau. How's the career in music going? I promise one day I'll come see you."

"It's going great." He held out little hope that she'd come. Librarians and bars didn't seem to mix.

"I saved a few books that were donated for the book sale. I thought you might like to have them. One is called *San Antonio Rose* and the other is about the history of country-western music."

"I'd like that." He waited until she disappeared in her office and returned with the books.

She handed him several more than two books. "You might want to look through these as well. You're welcome to them if they interest you."

"How much do I owe you?"

She grinned. "An hour of volunteering at the book sale. Fair enough?"

"Fair enough."

He took the haul and looked around for a table where he could sit. The place was in shadow for a moment while his eyes adjusted, and then he saw her. The blonde with the ponytail. She was sitting in the center of the room absorbed in reading a book. A legal pad and several pencils were scattered in front of her.

"Miss Tomlinson, do you know who that girl over there is?"

"No, Beau," the librarian answered without looking up from her work.

"You do see her, don't you?" He had to ask. She couldn't just be something he'd needed so badly that he'd dreamed up her and the old classic car.

"Of course. She comes in here now and then to study, but as far as I know she's never applied for a card."

Beau walked over and sat down next to her as if it were the only seat open in the place.

For a while, she ignored him, but then she accidentally bumped his leg with her knee.

When she did it for the third time, he laughed out loud.

The girl glanced at him and winked. Beau swore his heart stopped. She was even prettier than he remembered.

Her knee slid along his leg as she whispered, "I have to study now, but can I meet you tonight if you have the time."

He didn't trust himself to say a word, so he just nodded.

"Where?"

He tugged the pen from her hand and jotted his address down on her paper.

"What time?" she whispered.

Anytime after dark, he wrote back. Then, before he did something crazy, he got up and walked out of the library.

The day seemed endless. Finally, Border started watching some movie on the old TV his brother had left and Beau moved to the porch despite the cold. He'd been playing for a while before the Ford convertible pulled up in front of the duplex.

He set the guitar down and walked out to the car. She moved over and he slid behind the wheel. Without a word, they headed for moonlight. He was in heaven again and he didn't care how or why it was happening.

He drove out beyond the lights of town or any farmhouse and stopped the car. Without hesitation, he pulled her close and kissed her full-out. She pulled the leather strap that held his hair back and dug her fingers in as if she were starving for the feel of his hair.

This was no first kiss of two kids just learning. This was full-grown passion and they both knew it. He'd been thinking about her all day. Thinking what he'd say and how he'd act, but now she was in his arms and he couldn't seem to think at all. As she opened her mouth to his kiss, he moved his hand inside her coat and covered her warm breast with his cold fingers. The feel of how perfectly his hand covered her made him light-headed.

She leaned back laughing softly as he took his time feeling of her small breast before kissing her again. She smelled of Ivory soap and starch, all fresh and clean, and she tasted of heaven. The air was near freezing around them, but all Beau felt was her against him.

He wasn't sure what would have happened next if a car hadn't blinked in the distance. By the time it neared, she'd moved back to the passenger's side of the car and he'd started driving again. After the car passed, he wasn't sure what to do so he just drove with the heater and the radio turned to full blast. She didn't move back over to his side and he wondered if he hadn't gone too far. She probably thought he was some kind of animal. After all, they knew next to nothing about each other.

Finally, he turned around and headed back to Harmony. When he parked in front of the duplex, he turned off the car and faced her. "W-what's your name?"

"My daddy calls me Trouble." She laughed. "What do you think?"

Closing his eyes, Beau thought about his dream of making it big in the music world. Out on that back road, he'd almost given it all up for a girl he didn't even know. Maybe she'd have been worth it, maybe not. "Trouble fits," he whispered.

He opened and closed his hand atop the steering wheel. Even now he wanted to touch her. No, he wanted more. The longing to feel her move under him was driving him mad. And what did he know about her? She had a daddy. She had money. The Ford was a cream restoration. She lived around here somewhere. That's it.

"You feel it too," she whispered. "That pull. That need. Like we're addicts within reach of a drug whenever we're near each other."

"Y-yeah," he answered without looking at her. "I-I felt it the m-moment I-I saw you." No memory would ever be so pure in his brain.

"All I know about you is you play and sing beautifully, and you stutter. The stuttering doesn't bother me, by the way. Doesn't dilute the attraction."

She took a deep breath. "How about we just take a drive now and then? No touching. Not even any talking if you like. Just driving for a while, until we get used to each other. Right now I feel like if we get too close for too long we might both spontaneously combust."

"I-I don't know if I'd care but y-you're p-probably right." He stepped out of the car. "I-I'm at the bar Saturday night."

"I know. Look for me when you walk out. If I'm there, I'm there."

He watched her until the taillights of the old Ford vanished, then turned and headed toward the duplex. On the porch, the guitar stopped him and he found himself picking out a haunting tune. For once, the words didn't come, only the music danced in his head. Finally, he grinned thinking he knew one more thing about her. She had more sense than he did. She'd stopped.

As always, he reached into his music for comfort. The beat pounded against his heart making him not feel so lonely. He played letting the melody drift out over the wind and blend with the sound of the evening train rolling through Harmony and the hoot of a night owl in the hundred-year-old elm. All the sounds around him, all the feelings, all the words he'd never be brave enough to say moved with his fingers across the strings of his music and he knew with no doubt that a part of him would love Trouble for the rest of his life.

❧ *Chapter 20* ❧

Wednesday afternoon

Rick Matheson was flirting with one of his nurses when his cousin-in-law, the sheriff, walked in with Trace Adams. The cute little nurse was pretty, but she couldn't hold a candle to the two tall women who stood before him now. Trace and Alex carried strength and power with grace. In the three days the doctor and Alex had insisted on him staying under guard while at the hospital, Rick caught himself listening for Trace's voice and looking for her when he woke.

She'd gone with the sheriff to check out a break-in at his office. They'd claimed someone had trashed the place but except for a few open file cabinets, it sounded pretty much like he'd left it. Besides, whatever file they were looking for was probably stuffed away between his bed and the wall at Winter's Inn Bed-and-Breakfast.

Alex didn't want him going back to the bed-and-breakfast before the window was replaced and the alarm system was fully operational.

He'd been trapped in the hospital room since Sunday and was starting to get cabin fever. No one except a few of the staff and the sheriff's office knew about what had happened Sunday when the window at the bed-and-breakfast had shattered. The fall he'd taken when Trace plowed into him to save his life had cost him more stitches and bruises, but at least he was alive. Glass from the window had also rained down on him adding another layer of scrapes and cuts over his already battered body.

But the real pain for Rick was his pride. He'd stood there, a target, while someone had tried to kill him again. He felt like the tackle dummy on a practice field waiting for the next hit.

"Evening, Sheriff," he said as he tried his best to smile at Alex. "Little late for a visit, isn't it, or are you taking the night watch over me?"

The sheriff waited until the nurse closed the door. "You ready to get out of here?"

"Sure. I've been telling you that for two days." He suspected a trap. "I've also made it plain that I'm not going to a safe house or another town or jail. Whoever is trying to kill me is a coward and I've no intention of running."

"I know." She shrugged. "I've thought about it and until we find whoever it is, you're probably as safe at Winter's Inn as you are anywhere. At least in Harmony we can keep an eye on you. If you ran, the guy might follow and we'd be on unfamiliar ground."

Rick wondered why he didn't feel any happier. He wanted to go back to the bed-and-breakfast. He'd won the argument. At least for now. But no one, including him, seemed to be happy about it. The waiting, the being constantly on guard was beginning to wear on everyone. "I don't like the idea that someone is trying to murder me, but I've got a job to do." He'd hoped his words convinced Trace of how important he was, but he doubted it. In fact, he was surprised she'd hung around. He figured she'd have been on the road again as soon as the snow cleared.

Alex opened the closet and pulled out his jeans. "The shirt you had on was ruined with all the blood. Put on your pants and keep the hospital gown. Hank will have the truck warmed up by the time you get around back and it should be dark enough for you to slip out."

"I'm leaving now?" Rick didn't reach for his jeans.

"You wanted to leave and now is as good a time to transport you as any." Alex stepped to the door. "I'll wait outside and let you know when the hall is clear."

Rick grabbed his jeans as she disappeared. He felt like a prisoner being relocated.

Trace Adams didn't say a word as she dropped his shoes by the bed.

"Aren't you going to leave while I put on my jeans?" he snapped, even though none of this was her fault.

"Why? I'm the one who stripped them off you when you came in here." She had the nerve to wink at him. "You ain't got nothing I haven't seen, cowboy."

He swore as he stood and pulled on his jeans and shoved his feet into his loafers. "Any chance you'd strip for me so we could call it even?"

"Not a chance." She laughed. "Sometimes the world's not fair."

"You could have told me that before I fell through missing steps or had my car burned or almost got killed by a garden gnome."

She handed him a jacket she'd walked in carrying.

He tugged it on and pulled up the hood. "Whose is this?"

"Hank's. He found it in the back of his truck."

"Figures. It smells like smoke."

"Look at the bright side, Matheson, I'm going to stay a few days longer and keep you company."

"Why?"

"Curiosity." She grinned. "This is more excitement than I've had in months. Who knows, with any luck, I'll have a chance to knock you out of harm's way and send you in for stitches again."

He studied her wishing he could make sense of this strange woman. "Glad I could be of service, but I don't need a babysitter."

"I'm not applying for the job. Just hanging around until my aunt gets back. Any objections?"

"Not a single one, beautiful." He zipped the jacket closed. "You're the most interesting lady in my life right now and you don't even like me."

"You got that right. I've always thought lawyers were like ticks. Nobody knows how many there are around and they suck the blood out of anyone they get near." She faced him with her warrior princess stance, complete with fists on her hips. "And don't call me beautiful or any other name but Trace."

He moved toward the exit. "Where'd you get a name like that anyway?"

"My dad was a cop who loved his work. He named me after trace evidence." She smiled in an odd way that left him wondering if she were kidding him.

Rick leaned against the door waiting for Alex's signal to leave. "So, Trace Adams, you hate lawyers, how about just thinking of me as a man?"

"I'm not fond of many of them either."

He wasn't surprised. "So, you like women?"

"Not particularly. Most I know play way too many games."

He laughed. "You know in some strange way I'm starting to feel better. Tell me, Adams, who *do* you like?"

"I like people who are strong and do what is right. I like people who are honest."

He grinned knowing he'd finally caught her. "So, tell me honestly who asked you to stay on and keep an eye on me."

To her credit, she looked him straight on without trying to dodge the question. "The sheriff," she answered. "And her husband, Hank. He said he was asking on behalf of the whole Matheson family. Your mother called in to thank me for saving your life when one of the nurses let her know you were back in the hospital. She asked me to watch over her little boy. The doc asked twice, hoping she didn't have to see you again." Trace smiled when he looked shocked, then she added, "Oh, and your partner in the other law office and her husband Gabe stopped by yesterday and offered me a Land Rover to drive if I'd stay on for a few days."

Rick banged the back of his head against the wall and closed his eyes. "Do they all think I'm so helpless?"

"No," Trace answered. "They all care about you and they think your life is in danger. You've turned down help from the law and your family. I seem the only option left."

He started to ask what good she'd be, but he'd

seen her in action firsthand. "Want to tell me what you do for a living?"

"No. I'm on leave. Helping you figure out who is trying to bump you off just seemed like something to do for fun while I'm on vacation."

"Great, I'm the cabin puzzle." He didn't know which bothered him more, that folks had asked her to watch over him or that she didn't see it as any big deal. "One last question."

She looked bothered.

"Are you armed?"

The door opened. As the sheriff waved them out, Trace passed him and whispered, "Always."

"Great. A woman carrying a weapon, my favorite kind of date."

❧ *Chapter 21* ❧

Wednesday night

At exactly seven o'clock, Tannon rang the doorbell to Emily's apartment building.

"Yes?" Her voice sounded hesitant as it crackled through the intercom.

"It's me." He waited for the lock to click. Finally, it did. He bolted in with a bakery box in one hand and a bottle of wine in the other.

When he got to the fourth floor, he noticed her door slightly ajar, so he walked in feeling more like a kid on his first date than a man over thirty visiting a woman he'd known all his life.

"Evening," he said when he saw her standing in the kitchen. "Is it all right if I come in?"

Emily frowned. "I don't know. That depends on what's in the box."

"Red velvet cake and a strawberry pie. I called Three Sisters' and had them deliver what they thought would be your favorite to my office. Since it's the day after Valentine's, I got the feeling they sent over the leftovers."

"They don't usually make deliveries. The sisters have a strict rule about that."

"I don't think they would have for me, but when I said it was a surprise for you, they gave in." He lifted the pie out first. It had been decorated with candy hearts on top. Next came the cake with BE MINE scrolled in thick icing. "I forgot about it being Valentine's Day yesterday when I placed the order. It's not a holiday I've ever had to remember."

Emily laughed. "Now you've started something. They'll never believe I'm just feeding a stray."

"Why tell them? Let the three old ladies guess if they like." He raised an eyebrow. "Unless, of course, you already had a delivery from them yesterday?"

She lifted her chin. "Actually, I did. Sam, our janitor, bought cookies for everyone. It was so not like him we were all in shock."

"I guess I'll have to watch out for him." Tannon took the time to look around. He wouldn't have been surprised to see a vase of flowers. He'd always thought Emily pretty and couldn't believe some single guy in Harmony hadn't noticed by now, but not once in the years he'd dropped by the library on Friday night had a date been waiting for her. He'd told himself that they probably stopped by on the many nights he wasn't in town, but now he started to wonder. "Maybe I should drop by and tell the sisters to watch out for my interests."

She served up one plate of spaghetti, seemingly unaware that he might not be kidding. "Did anyone ever tell you you're a wicked man?"

"Yeah, half my staff."

Emily filled another plate as she commented, "Your secretary is very beautiful. She could be on the cover of a fashion magazine."

"Maybe, but she didn't look half as adorable as you did in the fuzzy robe. Tell me, do you wear that thing every night, or was it a company outfit?"

"What's wrong with my pink robe? It's warm." They sat down at the table, and as he had before, he walked to the kitchen and grabbed two glasses.

"Nothing's wrong with it, Emily. I've just never seen you in anything but black, white, or navy blue. If you didn't wear scarves, I'd think you were color-blind."

"Black works for the library. I think of it as professional."

He looked down at his starched jeans and white shirt. "I guess I'm the same way. Jeans, boots, and any shirt from the cleaners. I did go wild once and bought a Hawaiian shirt to wear to a theme party. That was a waste of money."

"How many times did you wear it?" she asked.

"Once," he admitted. "Felt like a fool. It didn't go with a Stetson and the boys at the feedlot would have shot me on sight if I even wore it to work."

She laughed. "I'd love to see you in it."

"Not likely, but feel free to borrow it anytime." He loved the easy way they were talking. He reached for the wine bottle, wishing the meal could go on for hours.

"I don't usually drink wine," she admitted. "I don't even have an opener."

He tugged one from his pocket. "I picked this up with the wine. Wild guess I might need it."

He opened the bottle and poured her a glass as he told her all about what had happened at the hospital. His mother might be hurting, but she was still running the show. She'd even started a list of what had to be changed before she'd consider herself comfortable.

When they moved to have dessert on the couch, he poured the last of the wine and they watched the news as they ate.

"Can I stay here tonight?" he asked before thinking about it.

"No," she laughed. "You can see your place from here. I think you're sober enough to make it home. You could walk through the center of town and be there in ten minutes."

"I'm not drunk, Emily, I just like it here." He hit the couch pillow between them as if puffing it up. "I slept great here a few nights ago."

"Well, I'm not subletting the living room out to you, so forget it." She stood and straightened, telling him it was time for him to go.

He pulled on his coat. "All right. Kick me out, but kiss me good-bye first."

"Why?" Her one word made it plain that they were not lovers, nor would they ever be.

"Maybe I need the practice," he said as he walked to the door.

She laughed, obviously remembering a time when they were kids and she'd asked if she could practice on him. "All right. One kiss for practice."

His hand was already on the doorknob when she stepped up beside him, leaned forward, and waited for him to brush her lips with his.

Tannon watched her. If he was going to get only one kiss, he might as well give it his best shot. He put his arm gently around her waist and tugged her to him as his mouth lowered. He felt her lip tremble slightly and her heart pounded against his chest, but she didn't turn away.

He wished he could believe that she kissed him back, but that wasn't quite it. She didn't stop him, but he felt no encouragement to continue.

Slowly, he straightened. "That wasn't so bad," he whispered.

"No." She looked at the buttons on his shirt.

"Emily, do you think we could be friends? Real friends. Honest friends. I could use one right now."

"I think we are friends, Tannon. Maybe not close, but friends would be an all right place to be."

He moved a few inches away and opened the door. "I agree. It would be nice to have someone to eat a meal with now and then or watch a movie late some night."

"But no more sleeping over or kissing," she added.

"I'll agree to the sleeping over, but I insist on a good-night kiss now and then. If for no other reason than to keep me from getting rusty at it."

She grinned. "Okay. One good-night kiss now and then, but no more Valentine desserts."

He nodded when he slipped out the door. He didn't look back as he walked to the elevator. He knew she was watching him. She was probably wondering the same thing he was.

What were they doing?

❧ *Chapter 22* ❧

Thursday

Rick slept until ten the next morning. For a moment after he woke, he smiled a groggy smile, thinking all was fine with his world. Then he remembered. The pain came back along with the depressing facts.

For a while he just lay on his stomach, wondering where he'd be right now if he'd decided to go into coaching and not law. Being a lawyer wasn't working out like he planned. It's pretty bad when you hang out with so many lowlifes you can't figure out which one is trying to kill you.

When the door opened, he didn't move.

"You awake, Matheson?" Trace asked without bothering to whisper.

"Yeah."

"Don't move. I'll check your stitches. I promised the doc I'd make sure you're not bleeding again."

"The torture begins even before I get breakfast," he mumbled as her hand moved over the flesh of his left shoulder.

"That's not the hurt one," he added.

"I know." She moved slowly closer to the bandages. "Just testing to see how warm your skin is." Her knuckles moved gently along his spine. "I kind of like touching you—or at least the few places on you that aren't hurt."

He thought of telling her that he was warming all over if she wanted to do more testing, but then she might stop. He also thought it odd that such a cold woman would admit wanting to touch anyone. She was about as far from one of those touchy-feely women who wanted to give back rubs and hold hands as he'd ever seen.

"You missed breakfast." Her finger tugged at the tape covering his other shoulder. "Eggs Benedict like I've never had, with sage sausage cooked—"

"Save me the details."

"All right. Just wanted you to know what you missed."

He let her work without complaining. He was tired of complaining. He was tired of sitting around wondering when the next elf would fly through the window. "How about we get out of here today?" he said as she patted his arm letting him know she was finished. "I could show you around Harmony and then drop by my office."

Rick was already planning his defense when she said, "All right."

"Seriously?"

"Sure. I've figured that whoever is after you isn't too bright. Maybe we can flush him out. I think it's unlikely he'll try a hit when other people are around; after all, he picked a back staircase after dark and a snowy day when you were the only one he saw in the window. He may have had no idea I was only a few feet away."

Suddenly Rick's idea of going out didn't sound so grand. If the stalker was dumb, somewhere in public might be his next try since catching his prey alone hadn't worked. "So if we go out, I'm the bait."

She grinned. "Sounds like a good plan."

Rick slowly lifted himself out of bed and walked over to the pile of clothes Mrs. Biggs had washed for him. He figured since Trace had already seen him nude she wouldn't mind seeing his underwear.

Trace smiled as if she'd read his mind. "You do have a great body, Matheson. Tell me, how do you keep from getting fat and flabby with a desk job?"

"Before I took to getting beat up regularly, I swam a few times a week. Ran some on week-ends." He pulled on a clean pair of jeans. "Maybe just good genes. All Mathesons are tall. How about your family?"

"I'll get my coat." She was on the move. Walking away from both him and the question.

"Meet me in the kitchen," he called after her. "I'm starving."

An hour later, after downing a half dozen scrambled eggs and the leftover sausage, Rick felt like he was strong enough to leave the house.

Trace pulled the Land Rover Gabe Leary had

loaned them up to the porch and Rick climbed in slowly. She left the car running as she ran back in for blankets and pillows.

A rolled pillow at the small of his back and a fluffy blanket over the seat made the ride far more comfortable. His injured shoulder barely touched the back of the seat. He could take a little pain. The cool air smelled so good.

As they drove around Harmony, he explained every part of the town, even telling her what used to be in a few spots. She said it wasn't as pretty as small towns she'd seen in New England or on the shores of California, but Harmony had its charm. The two dried-up creekbeds that cut through the center of town made for curving streets and side-walks along tree-lined trails.

Most of the snow had disappeared except on lawns. Almost everyone who saw them waved as if they were the world's shortest parade.

Rick tried to talk her into walking the mall, but she wasn't interested. He suggested a show, but she didn't think a dark public place would be a good idea. Finally, because he didn't want to go home, he talked her into driving out to the old Matheson ranch. Hank owned the place now and ran cattle as well as horses on the land.

To his surprise, Trace knew nothing about ranching. "You act like you've never stepped foot out of a city." He laughed when she stopped at the first cattle guard.

"I haven't except over highways. For me, the world is cities separated by miles of nothing but gas stations."

"Your dad never took you camping?"

"Nope. He wasn't around."

Rick let the answer settle in. He had a feeling if he asked another question she'd close up again. Finally, he sighed. "My dad died before I was grown, but he used to take me camping. My mom loves to tell the story that I was barely potty trained once when they took all the kids and a pop-up to Yellowstone. I wouldn't squat in the woods, so he had me go in a big can he hauled coal in for the fire. When we got back home, I spent the rest of the spring running out to the garden to sit on the cans around new tomato plants."

Trace laughed, really laughed for the first time.

Rick smiled. "You think that's funny?"

"No," she said. "I think it's funny that you think it's funny. You got any more stories like that?"

"Hundreds, unfortunately." They pulled up to the Matheson ranch house. "Don't suggest my two great-aunts tell any or we'll never get out of here. Hank calls this the women's house because his mother and her two old aunts live here. His sisters used to live here after they got divorced, but Liz married Gabe, the guy who loaned you this vehicle, and his other sister, Claire, moved to Dallas. Her daughter is going through treatments there and may have to have more operations on her legs."

He stared at her. "By the way, why did Gabe loan you this? Do you know him?"

Trace shook her head. "Nope, but I know a friend of his."

Rick grinned. "Then you know Denver Sims. Only friend Gabe claims. He's a U.S. Marshal." Rick didn't say more, but pieces of a puzzle were beginning to fit together. She'd moved too fast in danger not to have been trained, and he guessed she hadn't been lying about having a gun. If she knew a U.S. Marshal, she might just be in law enforcement.

He decided to wait before jumping into a theory that might send Trace away forever. If her dad had been a cop, like she said, maybe the reason he was never around to take her camping was that he died in the line of duty.

"Why are we stopping here?" she asked as she climbed out of the car stretching her long legs like a cat. The house in front of them looked like it had grown up from the land. It had walls the color of the earth and wildflowers along the walks.

"They'll have tea and cookies. After being laughed at over my camping story, I've worked up an appetite. Plus, my cousin, Claire, is a world-class artist. She stores her latest works up in a studio on the third floor. If you promise to be nice,

I'll give you the tour. You're not going to believe what she paints."

Ten minutes later they were settled into the aunts' sitting room at the back of the huge rambling home. As Aunt Pat handed Trace a cup of tea, Trace asked about family stories as if she could wait no longer to hear more.

Rick groaned and leaned back into the soft overstuffed chair by the window. The afternoon sun warmed him as he drifted off.

It was twilight when Trace touched his arm and told him it was time to go.

He apologized to the aunts, but they didn't seem the least upset. They both hugged Trace good-bye as if she'd become a part of the family in one afternoon.

"I'll show you the art collection some other time," he said as he led her to the front door, doubting there would ever be another time.

When Trace started the car, Rick asked, "Want to stop for some food?"

"You hungry again?"

He shrugged. "It's a habit I got into and am having trouble breaking. Yes, I'm hungry and I know just where to stop. Best barbecue wings in the state."

Ten minutes later they walked into Buffalo's.

"The place isn't usually this crowded on a Thursday night," Rick said, as if apologizing. "The Partners must be playing."

"Who?"

Rick lightly touched her back as he guided her to a table. "They're a local band. Kid named Beau who's probably not old enough to be in the place and his partner, Border Biggs. He's Mrs. Biggs's grandson. Nice boy." Rick grinned. "Looks just like her."

Trace didn't look like she wanted to be in the bar. He raised an eyebrow and leaned close to her. "It's all right. I'll protect you." When she frowned, he added, "I thought biker chicks thrived on bar air."

"I'm not a biker chick. I just happen to ride a motorcycle, and no one could last long on this air. The smell of beer is so heavy the owner should charge to breathe in here. Maybe we should leave."

Before he could answer, a couple stopped by the table to ask how Rick was feeling. Then a gang of men about Rick's age moved over to say hello and ask if he wanted to play pool. When he declined, they hung around waiting to be introduced to Trace.

She had the feel of the place by then and before he could say more than her name, she'd excused herself and said she had to order. The guys wandered off once she left and Rick sat alone watching her stand in line to order. She hadn't asked what he wanted, but from the limited menu written above the pass-through window to the kitchen, it couldn't have been hard to figure out.

He noticed the way she studied the crowd and how her gaze kept scanning back to him. The music had started by the time she made it back with two beers and a basket of wings. Before she sat, she pulled her chair beside his. He would have been flattered, but he guessed she wanted her back to the wall.

To his surprise, the music drew her. Trace Adams was a complicated woman. She climbed out on rooftops at night, rode a Harley, said she knew Gabe's friend, the U.S. Marshal, and carried a weapon. And, he added one more fact, liked country-western music. In some states, people could be declared brain-damaged for that.

When the wings were gone, he asked, "You want to dance?"

"No, but that kid behind the chicken wire cage can play. I could listen to him all night." She leaned her elbows on the table. "He's got a voice as rich as Vince Gill's and plays with Keith Urban skills. Most of his songs are oldies, but I haven't recognized a few."

"Those are his songs."

She didn't glance at Rick. "They're straight from the heart. Hope you're his friend, because he's going to need a good lawyer when Nashville comes calling."

"You think I'm a good lawyer?"

She looked at him finally. "I don't know, but if

some outlaw's trying to kill you, he must think so. If you were bad, he'd just bribe you to leave and save time." She glanced down at his old T-shirt and jeans. "From the looks of you, I'd say you've never taken a bribe."

Rick leaned back in his chair, trying to decode her message enough to tell if she'd been complimenting him or insulting him.

They listened for a while. Finally, between songs, Rick whispered, "You know, if you don't start at least acting like you're with me, half the guys in this place are going to be headed over here soon."

Trace laughed. "Pathetic line, Matheson."

"No line. The wolves are circling."

He watched her scan the room then nod slightly. Without another word, she leaned over and kissed him on the mouth. It was a quick, hard, closed-mouth kiss that was over before it could start any fire, but he liked the feel of her lips.

"That's not going to fool anyone," Rick whispered.

She tried again.

The kiss lasted longer and she put her hand on his chest as she leaned close. She was doing all the right things, but there was no passion in her action. When she pulled an inch away, she whispered, "Convincing?"

"Good enough." He smiled down at her, realizing he'd just learned something no one knew about Trace Adams. She knew nothing about kissing. He touched her hand. "Come on. I'll introduce you to the band, and then let's get out of here."

She nodded. "Good idea. The crowd's getting louder and drunker."

They made their way to the stage just as the last song in the first set ended. Rick introduced Beau Yates, but he only nodded when she told him how much she loved his music. Border, on the other hand, couldn't stop talking.

To Trace's credit, she didn't even blink when she said, "You must be Mrs. Biggs's grandson."

The tattooed kid nodded and replied, "You must be the woman who owns the bike in Martha Q's garage." Border Biggs made a low whistling sound.

A bottle hit the cage before Trace answered.

Border laughed. "Time to get back to playing before the first fight of the night breaks out."

Rick took her hand and they moved across the now-empty dance floor. Two guys were yelling at each other over by the pool table and several friends of each seemed to want to join in for a fight.

"We'd better hurry," Rick whispered as she pulled free of his hand.

He turned to yell as all hell broke loose around him. Suddenly, she was shoving him toward the front door as everyone in the place seemed to be rushing for the pool table area. He felt something sharp stab into his arm. Then they were through the rushing river of people and Trace was pulling him outside.

On the porch, Rick planted his feet and stopped. She continued to tug him until he said, "My arm."

Trace turned back, and in the one light over the door, he saw her face turn white. Holding his elbow close to his side, he looked down to see two darts sticking out of his arm.

"Pull them out."

Trace just stared at the two darts.

"Pull them out!"

She circled her fingers around the darts and jerked.

They'd been planted deep. Blood rushed out the open holes left in his skin.

"I'll get you to the hospital."

"No." He'd had enough of emergency rooms. "The fire station is just down the street. Whoever is there tonight can bandage me up. It's nothing."

They walked through the darkness toward the lights of the fire station. Rick didn't want to talk about it. The darts were just an accident. Someone in the crowd had simply had them in his hand when he moved toward the pool tables and accidentally stabbed them into his arm. It was a mishap. It crossed Rick's mind that if he yelled it, his words still wouldn't sound convincing.

Willie Davis, one of the volunteers at the firehouse, patched him up and offered Rick a cup of coffee. Since he'd already had his tetanus shot, there was no need to go to the hospital unless the bleeding refused to stop. Willie had been studying first aid, so he entertained Rick with stories about what could go wrong with even a small cut if it wasn't doctored properly.

Trace watched and listened. When two more firemen came in, she mumbled something about going after the car and disappeared about the time the men began teasing Rick about being mistaken for a dartboard.

Rick watched her go, knowing that she could take care of herself and that it would be a while before she returned. For the second time, it struck him as odd that a woman who carried a gun would hate the sight of blood.

❧ Chapter 23 ❧

Thursday night

Trace walked slowly back to the bar, her mind piecing together all the facts. She'd thought she'd had the situation totally under control. All evening no one had stepped within three feet of Rick without her being aware of it, but then, suddenly in a blink, he was hurt. Not bad, not dangerously, but almost as if someone was passing along a warning. Someone was telling the lawyer that he could get to him. Either this someone was dumber than any criminal she'd ever worked with, or he was toying with Rick. But why?

On a hunch, she pulled her cell and snapped a shot of every license plate in the parking lot. Then she walked back into the bar. Rick had been right about one thing—this wasn't the kind of place where a woman could have a drink alone without having half the drunks in the place bothering her. Trace had one choice and she knew exactly who to turn to for help.

She walked to the cage Rick had called a stage and asked Border if he'd like to have a drink with her.

He almost dropped his guitar as he hurried out of the cage. Beau continued to play, but Trace didn't miss the way he winked at his partner.

"I need a bodyguard. I need someone I can trust," she said as they walked across the dance floor. "Rick was stabbed with two darts, and I'd like you to help me look around for who might have done it."

"I'll guard your body all night," Border whispered. "My grandmother showed me your bike Sunday when you were at the hospital with Rick. Any woman who can handle a hog can ask any favor she likes."

"I don't want to be bothered while I look around, so just stay close." She patted his arm. "And when this is over, I'll let you take the bike for a ride."

"I'll be stuck to you like glue, lady."

Trace looked at the kid. Something about his over two hundred pounds of tattoos made him downright adorable. "Just keep the drunks away from me as I move around the room. The darts were royal blue, custom-made. I'm just looking for the rest of the set tonight."

He pushed a few cowboys aside as if they were the swinging doors to the bar and said, "If I hadn't made it with the band, I was thinking about being a PI or maybe a bounty hunter."

"I could tell from the first you were very observant. You'd make a great PI." She fought the urge to pat his head.

They walked the bar, moving from table to table as they talked. No royal blue darts. The two pool players who'd started all the excitement were now sharing a pitcher. Most of the couples were settling into slow dancing. "Foreplay on your feet," Border called it, and Trace had to laugh.

When they passed the bar for the third time, a drunk fell off one of the stools and almost bumped her. Border's arm blocked him. He was doing his job, which was more than she'd done with Rick earlier.

"Nothing," she said as she walked out the front door.

Border followed. "Sorry."

She shook his hand. "Don't say anything to anyone about this, would you?"

"You got it. I'll just say you wanted to take me home, but I wasn't interested. No one will believe it, but it'll stop any more questions. Because they'll figure I'm delusional."

"Thanks. You did a good job."

He grinned. "I'll be happy to watch your body anytime."

She stepped into the darkness and headed toward the Land Rover. In a strange way, Rick had been right. Border Biggs was just like his grandma. Willing to help.

A few minutes later, when she picked up Rick at the fire station, she almost wished she were back with the tattooed kid. Rick's mood had gone from being bothered to being enraged.

"Want to talk about it?" she asked after he'd sat silent most of the way home.

"No," he answered.

"What's the matter?" She'd never been able to let a sleeping dog lie.

"You mean other than being stalked by the village idiot?"

"Yeah, other than that." She parked the Land Rover in the garage and waited for his answer.

Finally, as she knew he would, he exploded. "For starters, I have no money and hate my job. Someone trashed my apartment and torched my car. Then, as if my life's not bad enough, someone tried to kill me . . . *again!*"

Trace stared directly in front of her. "Look on

the bright side, Matheson, the wings were good tonight."

He shot out of the car and was halfway to the porch before she caught up. Her long legs had no problem matching his stride. "I'm glad you find my life so funny, Marshal."

"Marshal?"

"Don't waste your breath denying it. Gabe told Alex, and she told Hank you weren't just friends with his buddy Denver—you worked with him. You're a federal marshal."

"I'm on vacation," she answered, knowing it was a weak response. She should have been up front with him from the first, but he was so set against having anyone watching over him. Trace had thought it would be easier to lie, and now Rick would probably never trust her again. "I'm sorry." She had to try to clear this mess up or he'd be yelling at her from now on. "I screwed up. I should have told you." When he still didn't look at her, she continued, "You might as well know it all. I'm not on vacation. I'm on leave after a shooting."

"And you're not Martha Q's niece?"

She shook her head. "I met her once when I came through here on my way to Dallas. She's a hoot. I wouldn't mind having her in my family, but no, I'm not related to her. It was just a way to set me up in the house so I could keep an eye on you."

Some of the anger flowed out of him with one long frosty breath.

They were on the porch. He turned his back to her to unlock the door. As they stepped into the hallway, he finally looked at her. "No, I'm the one who's messed up. I'm the one who has the hots for a woman who's being paid to watch over me. You, Marshal Adams, are a liar, but I'm the fool. At this rate, even an idiot should be able to put me out of my misery. What I don't understand is why someone like me isn't easy to bump off."

"You've got the hots for me?"

Rick swore. "Is that the only part of the conversation you heard?" He moved down the hallway. "Well, don't worry about it. Something about knowing you're probably wearing a badge on your underwear calms me down considerably. Maybe if I just take a few thousand aspirin and go to bed, I'll wake up in a few weeks and find out this nightmare is over."

"I'm not," she answered as she followed him down the hall.

"You're not what?"

"I'm not wearing a badge on my underwear. I don't wear underwear."

Rick turned the knob to his room and used his head to knock it open. "Kill me now."

She laughed but didn't step in behind him. "Get some sleep, Matheson. I'll see you in the morning."

❧ *Chapter 24* ❧

Friday

Emily sat at her desk in the back of the library staring out at the long line of elms winding their way along the back of the property. She'd texted Tannon several times yesterday asking about his mother, and he'd finally answered back this morning that he was heading to Amarillo as soon as he could get out of the office. He said he'd gotten back to Harmony too late yesterday to call.

The note hadn't been friendly. Maybe he really was busy. Maybe he was having second thoughts about being friends. Neither one of them was really the friend type.

Emily stood and walked the library. She was nervous about the town council meeting this afternoon. Thinking about what Tannon was doing helped distract her from work. He must have driven home late last night and then was planning to leave as soon as he could to return to the hospital. Maybe his mother was worse, maybe even dying, and he didn't want to worry her with what he must think of as his problem.

"You're missing your ten o'clock break," the children's librarian said as she passed. "Too cold to go out even to run over to the bakery, I guess?"

For Darla, the world under eighty degrees was always too cold. She'd been the librarian in the children's section for so long she'd seen generations pass through. Now and then she'd call a little boy by his father's name. She could read every book in the youth section without even glancing at the words and must have dated Dr. Suess for all she knew about the man.

"I was just leaving," Emily said as she hurried toward her coat. She didn't want to go to the bakery. The sisters would have far too many questions about Tannon buying her desserts on Wednesday. So, instead, she climbed in her car and drove over to Tannon's office. His big pickup was still in the first parking slot, telling Emily that he hadn't left town yet.

On impulse, she pulled into the visitor's parking space beside him and grabbed the book she'd been reading from her bag. If he didn't have time to talk to her, he'd have to tell her to her face; otherwise, she planned to at least check on his mother's condition.

The same sharply dressed receptionist was at the long front desk. This time she didn't stand when Emily walked in, she just stared.

"May I help you?" Her voice was professional, but not friendly.

Emily suddenly felt out of place. "I thought . . . I thought . . ."

She took a deep breath while the receptionist

looked bored. "I'd like to see Tannon for a moment, if it's not a problem."

The receptionist folded her thin arms over the flat chest. "I'm sorry, but Mr. Parker is very busy just now."

"Oh." Emily hadn't thought she'd have to fight to see Tannon. She'd only meant to wish him well with his mother.

The phone on the long desk buzzed.

"Yes, Mr. Parker." The receptionist turned away, ignoring Emily. "Yes, Mr. Parker. I'll have the file loaded." She listened for several seconds before adding, "I'll see that it's taken care of." As she turned to reach for her pen, she noticed Emily. "Oh, there is a woman here who wanted to speak to you. I told her you were busy, but I'll set up a tentative time with her for the first of next week."

The receptionist raised her gaze as she covered the receiver. "Your name, miss?"

"Emily," she whispered, wondering if she shouldn't have given an alias. This situation was probably only embarrassing Tannon.

The receptionist repeated the name, then stared for a moment before lowering the phone. "He'll be right down, miss. He asked me to tell you to meet him at the elevator." She looked like a woman repeating government secrets.

With one long manicured finger, the model pointed at the steel door in the small lobby just beyond the office's glass wall.

Emily made it three steps before the door opened and Tannon stepped out. With his long legs, he was at her side before she thought to move. He took her arm gently and tugged her toward the elevator, but his stare and words were for the receptionist. "Don't ever keep Miss Tomlinson waiting again."

Emily was surprised at the hard edge to his tone. She'd never seen this side of Tannon.

He must have sensed it too, because he added, "She's an old friend. If she comes to see me, send her straight through to wherever I am."

"Yes, Mr. Parker," the receptionist answered.

Without a word they stepped on the elevator. When Emily turned, the entire office staff was staring at her as the doors closed.

"I came to—" she started just as Tannon said, "I'm glad you—"

They both laughed shattering the tension.

"You first," she said.

"I heard from the hospital. Mom has an infection. She's back in ICU. I'm glad you came. You can help me pack. It looks like I'm going to have to stay a few days." He nodded once. "Now you."

"I thought I'd bring her a book. I knew you'd be on your way soon." She held the book up as if for proof. "But I guess now she won't be needing it today."

The elevator opened into his living room. "Oh

my," she said staring into the big room with glass walls and a high ceiling. "This is where you live?"

"You like it?" He tugged her into the mass of leather furniture and stainless steel. Everywhere there was color, he'd used earthy browns and deep greens just as she had in her apartment.

"It's beautiful." She smiled guessing that her opinion mattered. "It's like something I've seen pictures of in magazines." To the right, a six-foot-high glass flower arrangement adorned with tiny white lights sat in the center of a table big enough to seat ten, and to the left a kitchen, which looked like it should belong in a restaurant, framed one corner of the big room.

Tannon smiled. "That's how I planned it. I saw this picture and told the builder to make it look like the picture. I can see in every direction, but the glass is tinted so no one can see in. I don't like the feeling of being closed in."

"Everyone must love coming up here." Emily turned in a circle. "So much space."

"No one, including my mom, has ever been up here before now."

She stopped. "Really?"

"Really." He lowered his head. "I must sound pretty pathetic, but I've never invited anyone here. The cleaning staff comes in once a week to change the sheets and dust. That's it."

Emily wasn't sure she wanted to think too

much about why he'd asked her up. "And I'm here," she announced, "to help you pack."

"Right," he agreed, and pointed her toward the bedroom. "I don't know how long I'll be there this time. I may be sleeping in the waiting room if she gets any worse. I know it won't help but I need to be near."

She walked into a bedroom that exactly matched the color scheme of the rest of the apartment. In an odd way, the room felt welcoming to her, almost as if she'd helped to design it.

Clothes were tossed across the bed where he'd pitched them toward the open suitcase in a hurry.

As if she were working a puzzle, she walked around the bed, looking at his clothes. So far the only things in his bag were white socks and white underwear. The clothes hanging in his open closet looked exactly like the ones on the bed. Pressed long-sleeved shirts with his initials on the cuff, creased boot-cut jeans and tan dress slacks, western-cut sports jackets and leather coats.

"I see the problem," she said as he watched her. "What you need is something casual and you don't have anything casual. Nothing for sitting around the hospital."

"I'm not wearing the Hawaiian shirt."

She spotted it in the very back of the closet.

"What about short sleeves?"

"I don't wear short sleeves. If it gets hot, I just roll the sleeves up."

"What do you wear on your day off or at night relaxing? Old jeans, jogging pants, a jersey?"

"I don't take days off and most nights I work until time to go to bed. The little time I spend watching the news is hardly worth a wardrobe change."

"What do you sleep in?"

"Nothing," he answered with a slow smile. "What do you sleep in, Emily?"

She couldn't believe she blushed as if they were seventeen again, learning that special kind of teasing that pushes the line.

"While you help me, how about a drink?" His smile said he loved teasing her, but his words let her off the hook.

"No, thanks, unless you have diet root beer?"

He disappeared and came back with a cold bottle. "I just happened to have one," he said as he handed it to her.

She'd picked out a few things and after one sip, went back to folding clothes. "I figured out you could take off your shirts if you have to sleep at the hospital and just sleep in a T-shirt."

He stuffed a shaving kit into his suitcase as she asked, "Don't you ever wear any color of underwear besides white?"

He opened his mouth, but before he could say anything, she added, "Never mind. Forget I asked."

They were both laughing a few minutes later

when they stepped out of the elevator. He carried his suitcase and coat. She held her root beer.

The receptionist didn't say a word as she handed him his briefcase, but her nod to Emily was polite and questioning.

Tannon looped his coat over Emily's arm and took the case. "Walk with me to my car, would you, Emily?"

"Of course." She had no doubt the entire office staff watched her leave the building.

After Tannon dropped his bags in his truck, he turned around and opened her car door. "Thanks for the help. I'll call when I can, but you've got a busy day what with the town council meeting this afternoon and the writers' group tonight."

She'd almost forgotten about both. "I'll tell you all about them after you let me know how your mother is." She moved around to step into her car, but his hand covered hers atop the car door.

When she looked up, he met her stare. "I wish I could be here with you tonight. We could go over to the diner and talk after your meeting. I'm needed here in case your volunteer escapes."

"And I wish I could go with you," she answered honestly. "If your mom's not better tomorrow, I'll drive up after work and sit with her a while."

He nodded but didn't let go of her hand. "I wish this were one of those times I could kiss you good-bye," he whispered, glancing at the busy street behind them and the wall of glass in front of them.

She understood. He must be feeling very much alone. He might be a powerful man, but inside he was still an only son whose mother might be dying. "I'll be there tomorrow," she whispered. She made a mental note to find someone to cover her hours.

"I'll be waiting," he answered, and stepped away.

Emily almost laughed aloud when she was safe inside her car. They sounded like a knight and his lady saying good-bye before battle, not two people standing in a busy parking lot. Tannon and she were barely friends. She was obviously reading far too much into what he said.

As she drove back to the library, she decided that had been her problem. She lived her own life in her head as if it were fiction finding plots and quests. All her days were ordinary days with little of matter ever happening, yet she thought of them as adventures. Tonight, in her moment journal, she might write more than a few words. She might try a scene, a love scene with passionate kisses and touches that set fire to her thoughts as well as her skin.

By the time she made it back to her office, she'd pushed her wild thoughts aside so she could concentrate on the writers' meeting at seven. Martha Q Patterson was out of town, so there wouldn't be as many in attendance tonight, and

Tannon wouldn't be waiting downstairs for her when it was over.

Arranging the chairs in the alcove, she walked back to her office depressed. The writers' group wouldn't be nearly so much fun knowing she'd have no one to share the stories with later. She wanted to be with Tannon, not just writing about him in her journal. For the first time, she wanted a real moment and not just one in her thoughts.

The phone rang.

"Hello, Harmony County Library." She tried to push her cloud aside.

"Emily." Tannon's low voice drew her. "I forgot to ask if I could call you at nine thirty tonight. That'll give you time to get home and put on that sexy fuzzy pink robe and set out your supper. I want to hear all about the writers' meeting. We'll talk while you eat. It won't be as good as chili fries at the diner, but it'll do."

"It's a date." She smiled, wondering if he was thinking the same thing she'd been thinking.

"And, honey, don't worry about the town council. They can't eat you."

"Thanks for pointing out the bright side." She laughed, realizing she'd forgotten about that.

He took a long breath and added, "Got to go. Talk to you tonight."

He was gone before she had a chance to say good-bye.

For a few minutes, she just stared at the phone.

She and Tannon Parker might just be becoming real friends again. He'd even called her honey, like they were close. In an odd way, it felt good to have him for a friend again after all these years. Anger has a way of fading and forgiveness felt right. They'd never talked about it. He'd never explained where he'd been, but Emily knew deep down that if he'd been there, he would have helped.

It felt right to have him in her life.

Maybe she was just letting her imagination run away again. After all, he probably called every woman he knew "friend." No, she decided. He wasn't the type. He was probably just kidding her; after all he'd called her fuzzy robe "sexy."

She shrugged. She was no more his honey than her robe was sexy, but it did feel good to have someone kid her.

❧ *Chapter 25* ❧

Trace Adams paced back and forth in front of the long windows overlooking the courthouse. Rick Matheson's office was far too small, but the long wall of windows almost made the little space bearable. "This place is nothing but a fishbowl. How do you stand it here?"

"You know," Rick said, looking up from his desk for the tenth time, "it's hard to concentrate with you always moving and mumbling. Not that I'm complaining about the way you move. It's just hard to think of anything else, that's all. You've got the kind of body I spent my adolescence dreaming about."

"Why are we here again?" She didn't bother to look his direction. Watching the town square reminded her of watching an ant bed. It really wasn't all that interesting, but she couldn't look away. "Anyone can walk by and see you from here. I can think of a dozen places where a sniper could take you out and vanish before the bullet hit the window."

"I told you that I've got a couple, Minnie and Eldon Peters, coming in to ask questions about getting a divorce. It's easy money I can't afford to turn down. So stop suggesting future ways to kill me and let me do my job."

"What kind of money?" She wasn't really interested, just bored.

"If I were in a big city like Lubbock, I could probably get three hundred an hour just for talking to them. Here I charge one hundred and fifty for the first visit and pray the check doesn't bounce. In her phone call, the wife said they want to do a collaborative divorce. That means they agree on how everything is split and I do the paperwork."

"You ever do this kind of divorce before?" She sat on the corner of his desk and ignored the way he watched her.

Rick nodded. "Once, for a couple who didn't own anything except a car and a dog. He got the Chevy along with the payments and she got a hundred dollars for dog food along with the dog. He paid her in cash and me with a check."

Trace smiled. "Let me guess, the check bounced."

He shrugged. "I'm not too bright, but I learn. I told this couple I wouldn't even see them until the check cleared. That was over a week ago. I've already spent the money. I have to keep this appointment."

She watched the window. "I'll check them out when they come in. If I don't see any weapons, I'll go out in the hall and wait. Fair enough?"

"Believe me, divorcing couples are more likely to kill each other than the lawyer. Drug dealers are easier to calm down than a man about to lose half of everything or a woman who thinks she's been wronged."

Leaning against the glass, she whispered, "How old is this couple you're seeing?"

"Don't know. I've never met them before. Their address was a route number over by Clifton Creek. They initially e-mailed, asking if I'd take the case, and then they mailed in the check. Only talked to the wife once. She didn't sound young."

He stood slowly and walked to her side. Two white heads moved up the front stairs.

"You think that could be them? They've got to be in their seventies."

"No way," Rick whispered from just behind her.

Five minutes later they made it into Rick's office. Trace managed to keep a straight face as she said good-bye and headed downstairs. The husband was hard of hearing so Rick would have to yell anything he said. It might prove to be a very interesting hour, but she didn't plan to stay around.

On the steps, she realized what a great view of all the small businesses she had. This building would make the perfect place to hang surveillance cameras. It crossed her thoughts that Rick could see any crime committed from the bank to the Blue Moon Diner.

Or . . . someone could think he saw something. The robbery of the Blue Moon's cash drawer crossed her mind.

A criminal might try to frighten him into keeping quiet. Or better yet, run him out of town. Was there any way that was plausible? It was a long shot, but maybe she'd mention it to Alex the next time she saw the sheriff.

Trace walked into the bookstore putting possibilities together in her head. Maybe Rick shouldn't be looking for men he'd defended but for criminals still out there. Someone who did something illegal and thought Rick might have witnessed it. Or thought Rick might defend them. He'd never won a case. They might consider running him out of town before they got caught hoping it would improve their odds if they did have to go to trial. She grinned at the wild angle her thoughts were taking.

Trace jumped when two middle-aged men greeted her from just behind a cluttered wall of books. One she knew, the bookstore owner named George Hatcher. The other man looked like a homeless person.

Hatcher introduced her as Rick's friend, probably because he couldn't remember her name. He told her the tattered little man at his side was a yet unpublished, but no less grand, mystery writer. "Zack Hunter and I are working on our chapters to read for the writers' group tonight at the library. We're founding members of the group."

Trace didn't know anything about a writers' group, nor did she much care, but she smiled politely. "Sorry to bother you creative gentlemen."

"Oh no, miss, no bother," both insisted.

"I'll get you a cup of coffee." George reached for one worn cup off a rack above a coffeepot. "We were just about to take a break."

"Good," she said. "I have a mystery to discuss with experts like yourselves." They weren't much in the way of authorities, but they were locals and might be able to add something to her theory.

Neither argued with her. After all, Zack was writing a mystery and George had read a thousand, so they qualified as experts. As quickly as she could, she outlined the mystery of Rick's injuries and asked for their advice. She didn't really expect anything useful but thought talking to them might help organize her own thoughts.

Zack pulled out what looked like a new pipe and began trying to fill the bowl. "Well," he said, drawing out the word to ensure no one tried to cut into his thoughts. "I'd say it has to be the bookstore owner below the lawyer's office who is our felon. After all, he's been making a killing with the curious coming in here."

"Or better yet," George piped in, bouncing in his chair like a fourth-grader, "it's the bookstore ghost who's been waiting around for years. In fact, I think that would make a fine title for a mystery. *The Bookstore Ghost.*"

"A ghost?" Zack frowned.

"Sure. No one has seen anyone nearby when the crimes happen. A shadow in the alley, maybe, but no other proof. Maybe he died because of a crooked lawyer and haunts around bumping off everyone who passes the bar that he sees." George's eyes were twinkling. "Just think about it, a serial ghost killer. Maybe he picked on Matheson because he read his name somewhere. When he runs out of young lawyers, he'll head for the older ones."

Zack shook his head. "What if the killer wants the lawyer dead because he wants his office? No, no, no. He doesn't just want the office—he *has* to get to it. He buried his wife in the walls years ago and he's afraid Rick might remodel."

"I like my ghost better. The story has more potential. Never think of a book, Mr. Hunter, think of a series. How many dead wives can you have in walls, but a homicidal lawyer killer, now that has the promise of a series."

Zack wasn't buying it. "No sex in your plot," he said. "Every big book has sex. Ghosts don't have any, but a wife killer might. Maybe he caught her with another man? Maybe he kept her body so he could hold her at night? His obsession made him forget to pay the bills and one day he was evicted without having time to take her along. She's up there"—he glanced at the ceiling—"just waiting for him to come back and get her."

George frowned. "You're creeping me out."

"Well, you're spooking me out."

Trace slipped away with them arguing. As she walked back up the stairs, she realized she wasn't any closer to solving the mystery than she'd been ten minutes ago. Mental note to self: Never ask a writer about reality.

Rick's door was closed, but she could hear him talking. He was explaining all that had to be done to get the divorce. If the couple said anything, she didn't hear them. Maybe they both died of heart attacks when he told them what it cost.

She walked over to an empty space beside the stairs where someone had left an old wicker chair in an effort to decorate. It was dusty but comfortable. Trace sat and propped her long legs against the top of the stair railing.

With a smile, she remembered what Rick had said about her having the build of his dream girl. In her line of work, she usually wore black suits and sometimes a bulletproof vest. No one ever admired her body, or maybe no one had ever been brave enough to comment.

In the warm hallway, she stopped trying to listen to Rick's lecture and relaxed. Two weeks ago she'd been on a team heading in to break up a drug ring. She'd been doing her job just as she had for five years. All she'd ever wanted to be was a marshal like her father and grandfather. The Adamses had been U.S. Marshals all the way back to the Wild West days.

As the team moved in, Trace remembered thinking that the day was brighter than usual. The thought crossed her mind that if something went wrong and she died today, it was a good last day. The team moved from the light into the shadows of an abandoned warehouse.

Within seconds, something went terribly wrong. Bullets exploded around her as if she were in the middle of a fireworks explosion. Trace held her weapon tightly as she spun in a circle, but she could see no one to aim at. Smoke, yelling, screams filled the morning air. One of the cops fell into her. He'd been shot in the face. Blood was everywhere as he trapped her down with his bulky body.

For a moment she was paralyzed with indecision. Should she fight to save him or go after the shooters? He was screaming and losing blood so fast she knew he wouldn't last long, but his body weighed heavy across her shoulders.

Another officer's body toppled over them like a pileup of football players on the field. She struggled to move, but the officer's bleeding arm dripped blood into her face. She couldn't get free. She couldn't breathe.

Then it was over with a sudden explosion. Lightning flashed. Her world went dark.

The noise had stopped when she came to. People were pulling the bodies off her as they worked hastily to stop the bleeding. A hand helped her up, checked to see if any of the blood she'd been lying in was hers.

She didn't know the medic. Had never seen him before. But she saw the relief in his face when he found no wound.

"You okay, Marshal?" His hands cupped her face as he stared into her eyes.

Trace nodded. She didn't feel all right, but no part of her body was hurting with the fire of a bullet.

The medic sat her down out of the way and covered her shoulders with a blanket. Without a word, he went back to help others. Trace had no idea how long she sat there, maybe ten minutes, maybe two hours. People were moving around her, talking, shouting, running. All she saw was the blood pooling across the floor toward a drain.

Her captain told her to go with one of the detectives back to the station. He ordered her to clean up, but when she got to the showers, she couldn't seem to get the blood off. No matter how long she scrubbed it wouldn't come off. It was in her hair and on her face. It dripped over her body as if the roof were leaking crimson rain.

One of the cleaning ladies at the station found her passed out with the shower running cold over her. They'd taken her to the hospital. Three days later she checked herself out of the hospital and pulled her bike out of storage. She needed to ride. She needed to outrun the nightmare.

She'd made it as far south as Kansas City when Denver Sims called. He'd worked a few cases with her in Chicago, and he must have heard she was on leave. He had probably been filled in on how she'd cracked up, because he asked a favor. "Just drop by and make sure the kid is okay," Denver had said. "It shouldn't take more than a day or two, and I'll owe you one, Adams."

"Drinks and a steak," she said.

"Drinks and a steak," he agreed, and hung up the phone.

Trace wasn't sure why she'd said yes. Maybe because Denver called the twenty-eight-year-old lawyer a kid. She was the same age, but she'd lived a lifetime already and felt older. She also found it interesting that the whole town seemed to care about Rick Matheson. She couldn't name three people outside the marshal's office who cared whether she lived or died.

Her father had been a hero, but he'd been killed in action before he'd had time to take her camping. In truth, all she knew about him was his legend. Since she could remember, she'd wanted to be hard like him. She was the best at what she did. But, for once, the best in that warehouse hadn't been good enough. If she hadn't been trapped under the wounded, she would have died in the explosion. All those around her had carried weapons. They'd fired, but they hadn't stopped the explosion. They'd all died and she'd walked away without a scratch. She told herself she was good at what she did . . .

Or she had been. Now she wasn't sure she could protect one lawyer, but she knew if she didn't, her mind just might finish the job of splintering in two.

Finally, Rick's door opened and Mr. and Mrs. Peters walked out, too lost in their own world to notice Trace.

Once they were out of sight, Rick handed Trace a square envelope. "Eldon Peters brought this in. He said the lady from the cleaners handed it to him since he was going up. She claimed it must have been dropped in her box by mistake."

Trace took the corner of the letter. Rick's name was printed in black across the front. "You open it?" she said as she looked for any detail, any clue.

"Yeah. Just like the first note. One word. *Leave.* I'm betting there's not a fingerprint on it except the downstairs lady's, Peters's, mine, yours."

"You're worried."

He shook his head. "After the darts, I'm about ready to climb the clock tower and yell, 'Bring it on!' I'm not too happy about having a pen pal, but how much harm can a letter do? I'll start worrying when he comes at me with a weapon bigger than a garden decoration."

She laughed. "If it comes, I'll be right beside you, Matheson. You know, for a lawyer, you've got grit."

"Thanks. I just hope none of it leaks out the next time I'm hit."

❧ *Chapter 26* ❧

Friday night
Harmony Library

At quarter to seven Emily watched Geraldine Edison walk across the street with a plate of cookies and what had to be her next chapter to read to the group stuffed into her huge red purse. Zack Hunter was right behind her and offered to carry the cookies, but Geraldine didn't look like she quite trusted him.

The pair reminded Emily of a plus-size Little Red Ridinghood and an aging, slightly hunched-over Big Bad Wolf.

She tried to keep from laughing as she welcomed them and followed them upstairs where Rick Matheson sat with his legal pad, ready to take notes for Martha Q. A tall, thin woman with black hair stood near the windows as if on guard. Snow White, Emily thought, hoping the seven dwarfs didn't show up because there wouldn't be enough chairs.

"What's the lawyer doing here?" Sam whispered from just behind Emily. He held his broom at the ready as if it were a weapon. She'd often thought the janitor would consider it a good day if no one came into the library.

He wasn't smiling, but then he never smiled, Emily thought, as she whispered back, "He's taking notes for Martha Q Patterson. They're good friends. I think he's staying at her place while she's gone."

"I don't like it." Sam, who usually did his best to not get involved with anything except spills in the library, surprised her. "Meetings like this shouldn't allow drop-ins, and I'm not sure Martha Q should trust him. Just 'cause his name is Matheson don't make him honest or reliable."

Before she could comment, Rick waved at her.

As she moved toward him, she glanced back to Sam, but as always he'd vanished. "Yes, Rick?"

The lawyer smiled a grin that was downright adorable. Prince Charming, Emily thought. He was a few years behind her in school, but Emily couldn't remember a time when she didn't know who Rick Matheson was.

"Got any idea how long this meeting will last?" He didn't look like he was looking forward to the evening.

"The library closes at nine. They have to be finished by then." Like everyone in town, she'd heard he'd been hurt, but with his jacket on she couldn't see any bandages. "You all right?"

He flashed her a not-so-bright smile and shrugged. "Sure. Thanks."

Emily tried her best to act relaxed as the others came in, but it was almost seven and she hadn't heard a word from the town council. They'd never been so late. Something had to be wrong. Maybe she'd have to face budget cuts or, worse, lose her job. Part of her wanted to run as fast as she could over to the town hall and tell them that she had nowhere to go if they closed the library, but that wouldn't be professional.

George Hatcher arrived with two closet writers he'd discovered. One was a man in his late forties named Simon Bishop. He had the hint of a British accent and told everyone he wanted to write suspense. The other looked like she might have spent too much time in outer space. She had wild red hair and mismatched socks. Even at first glance Lily Anne Loving had that "phone home" look about her. When Emily asked her what she wrote, she said she was working on a memoir about her motherland before she was abducted and sent to earth.

Peter was the last to arrive and asked to go first. He passed out one page of poetry he said he'd been working on all week. He rushed around the room with willow-in-the-wind kind of movements.

George Hatcher told him that poets starve.

Peter answered that to write poetry is to live. He pulled his pipe from his pocket and held it in one hand as he read. The group was polite. Lily Anne said she loved it. George said it had a nice beat.

Geraldine agreed with George and passed around the cookies.

Peter deflated in the chair next to Rick. The lawyer handed back the poem with *Grand!* written two inches high at the top. Peter nodded his silent thank-you and straightened a bit in the chair.

Emily sat back and smiled. She was already thinking of how she'd tell Tannon all about the Friday night writers' meeting. She had to fight to keep from taking notes. Martha Q might not be in attendance, but all the others were raring to go.

Geraldine read the second chapter of her historical romance. The Southern belle had lost her major due to old battle wounds and she was now making love in one of the abandoned underground railroad hideouts. Her new lover was a spy, a Yankee in a tattered Confederate uniform, but the heroine didn't notice until they were in the mindless bliss of mating. It seemed he dropped his accent about the same time she dropped her drawers.

Everyone loved the chapter except Peter, who told her that there were so many legs and breasts flying around he thought he was at a Baptist fried chicken cook-off.

The girl George Hatcher brought read a two-page scene about learning to walk with only two legs. Lily Anne said her real last name translated to something close to Star, but she had been forced by her earthly captors to go by the name of Lily Anne Loving.

When she finished reading, no one said a word. Emily jumped in and claimed she couldn't wait to hear more and everyone quickly agreed. Apparently, alien abductees were temperamental.

The last to read was Zack. He reread the first chapter of his mystery, only he'd added in clues to the murder. The work was still disjointed and choppy, but he'd improved so much everyone gave him a round of applause. Even Rick acted as if he'd enjoyed the chapter, but since he was in the middle of his own mystery, he didn't seem to step into fiction too quickly.

At nine o'clock, they all hurried out talking. Emily stepped in her office and pulled on her coat suddenly in a hurry to go home. It had been a long day.

Pamela Sue was waiting at the door so they could walk out together. They were halfway to the cars when she said, "Oh, I almost forgot, the chairman of the town council called and told me to tell you that the library budget has been increased by five percent with a three percent raise for you."

"Really?"

Pamela Sue shrugged. "They must have looked out the window and saw the crowd of cars parked in the lot tonight." She veered off to her car. "See you next week. Good night."

Emily felt like dancing and squealing with joy, but she simply smiled and said, "Yes, it is a very good night."

Thirty minutes later, she was wrapped in her robe with a bowl of soup when the phone rang. Within minutes, she'd told Tannon all about her night. All the writers and what they read and then the best news about the council giving her a raise.

Finally, she realized he was being very quiet.

"What's wrong?" she asked.

"Nothing the doctor didn't expect. There's no

change with Mom and that is not good." He let out a long breath as though the tiredness inside of him would take much longer than a night to heal. "On a good day I'm not much in the way of company and this hasn't been a good day."

"I'm sorry I rattled on and on about the group and the library."

"No. I enjoyed it. It felt good to have someone talk to me about something besides vital signs. I only wish I could have been there to take you out tonight. This hospital makes the day seem endless. I think they pipe something in the air that makes you feel tired from the moment you walk in the place."

"You want me to come tomorrow?"

"Yes," he answered without hesitation.

"I'll be there before noon." She had an idea of just how much it cost him to admit he needed someone. "I'll try to get someone to cover my Saturday hours."

"Pack a bag, Emily, would you? I'll get you a room if you can stay until Sunday. It would be great to have someone to talk to for a change."

"All right. I'll come."

"Thanks," he said, "and one more thing, I wish like hell I'd kissed you this morning."

Emily was silent for a few heartbeats, then she answered, "I wish you had too." There was nothing more to say, and she hung up the phone.

❧ *Chapter 27* ❧

Buffalo Bar and Grill

Harley had already turned off the bar lights by the time Beau finished loading up his equipment. The place had been packed tonight. Even Ronny and a few of her friends from the breakfast club came. Beau liked seeing what he called his new daytime friends and he liked seeing Ronny laugh. She was a nice woman who didn't seem to get in her share of laughter.

Border reminded him that she had loved once, even if it was for a short time, but Beau wasn't sure he believed his partner. What kind of man would leave a woman like her? She was nice-looking in the take-home-to-Mom kind of way. Ronny could cook and said she made all A's in college classes, and best of all, she was kind. People who are truly kind are rare.

The guy who left her must have been a real bum.

Maybe it was that kindness that made her invite Border to join the others for pizza when closing time rolled around. She'd also invited Beau, but he said no. At the time, he was too interested in why pretty women like Ronny and Reagan Truman always tried to feed Border Biggs.

Beau was still smiling as he walked out of the bar, thinking of how Border tried to convince him once that because Border shaved his head, women always figured he was cold and hungry. Since they couldn't do anything about his hair, they fed him.

Halfway to his car Beau noticed the red Ford convertible parked in the shadows. It looked like something out of the past come to call. Beau didn't care. If the girl and her car were simply ghosts, he was still going for the ride.

This time he dropped his guitar in the backseat of the Mustang and climbed in the passenger's side. "Drive," he said as he leaned back and pulled his hat low.

She did what he knew she would and pulled away from the bar and headed for moonlight.

His body relaxed into the seat as she turned the radio to a country music station. Beau decided he'd died and gone to heaven. No Pearly Gates, no streets of gold, just one angel beside him and "Thunder Road" flowing through the wind.

After a half hour, she stopped the car in the center of a back road. "Want to drive?"

"Not tonight."

"Want to move closer and keep me warm while I drive?"

He slid closer and put his arm around her shoulders. As he leaned his head against her hair, he whispered, "You smell great."

She laughed. "You smell like smoke and barbecue and beer."

He kissed the side of her throat. "Drive," he whispered against her ear as he slid his hand inside her coat. "I'll keep you warm."

She kept both hands on the wheel as he moved his cold fingers over her petite body. Through the layers of clothes, he dreamed of how she'd feel without anything on. She was slim but definitely more woman than girl. Smiling to himself, Beau realized that if he removed anything she had on, all she'd feel was cold, so he settled back enjoying the night and the nearness of passion just beyond his reach.

All the town seemed asleep when she finally pulled back into the parking lot of Buffalo's. Without a word, he kissed her on the cheek and climbed out of the car.

He turned to her after lifting his guitar out of the back. She smiled at him, pulled the ribbon from her ponytail, and handed it to him.

She was gone before he could think of anything to say. He decided she was his drug and tonight she'd given him all he really needed to keep going. She wasn't like any girl he'd ever met. She didn't want to talk and she didn't mind where his hands roamed. All she offered was company and a ride in the wind.

Once he was alone in the duplex, he wrapped the ribbon around the neck of his guitar and began to play. She was his walk on the wild side, his inspiration for dreams.

No one passed the house except Ronny's mom, spying on a daughter she'd disowned. Beau tipped his hat at Dallas Logan and smiled when she gunned her car and drove away. He thought about this little duplex tucked away between businesses and storage buildings. It seemed a place for those without a home. Ronny, Border and he weren't runaways; they were more like tossed-aways, like old furniture put on the street next to the trash.

Beau felt his mood dance on his fingers over the strings. The people he lived with had little-used hearts waiting for a chance at love. Waiting for a chance to live and matter to someone. They had homeless hearts.

❧ *Chapter 28* ❧

Saturday afternoon
Blue Moon Diner

The afternoon sun against the front windows warmed them as they sat in the deserted diner eating lunch. Rick had complained of being hungry since noon, but Trace wanted to miss the crowds. She'd had enough of them Thursday night at the bar. He'd teased her about wanting him all to herself, but the fewer people around, the safer he was.

"Now tell me one more time why that old couple, the Peterses, want a divorce?" Trace asked as she tried to hold the biggest hamburger she'd ever ordered in her hands.

Rick laughed. "First, you've got to realize there are two reasons why people want divorces. There's the one they tell everyone, and then there's the real one. As far as divorces go, it's rarely what it seems."

Trace put down her hamburger. "And you know this, O wise one, how?"

"Observation. As a lawyer, I've trained myself to study people until I can read what they are not saying as well as analyze what they say."

"You are so full of it, Matheson."

"Do you want to hear the real reason or not?"

"All right. Why is a couple married over forty years divorcing?"

He winked at her. "He says it's because she spends all their money on the grandkids and she says it's because he never wants to go anywhere, but in truth, the real reason is the opposite reason as to why they got married."

Trace frowned and took a bite of her hamburger.

"Stay with me on this, Marshal. They married because he wanted sex and she wouldn't without the ring. Now they're divorcing because she wants it and he doesn't, and apparently he thinks he's paid enough for the services he got in bed."

"You're nuts."

"No, it's the truth, I swear. Men from twenty on are rushing downhill. Women, on the other hand, are moving up. If couples are very lucky, they meet with equal drives somewhere close to thirty. You might want to note that, since the matching age for you and me seems to be about where we are right now." He used his napkin to wipe mustard off the corner of her mouth.

Trace swatted him away. "So, Matheson, is this some pathetic way of telling me that I should sleep with you before your shelf-life is expired?"

"Something like that." He smiled until his dimple showed. "Is it working?"

"No. But I have wondered what that hot body of yours looks like when it's not bandaged. Of course, at the rate you're going, I may never find out."

"The way I see it is whoever wanted me dead is long gone or given up. The dart stabbing was just misfortune. Some drunk probably realized what he did and disappeared." He shrugged. "Though I like the attention, I'm not worth a federal marshal following me, and I've probably caused enough excitement around town. This is one of those things that will die down fast and become another one of George Hatcher's ghost stories to entertain tourists."

"You get tourists here?" Trace wasn't buying into his theory.

"Well, no. We mostly get visiting relatives of residents. The closest we ever get to having a tourist season is when there's a big funeral and out-of-town relatives fill the hotels for a few days."

Trace played with one of her French fries. "You make this town sound really boring."

"Not at all. Harmony's a great place. We just keep it a secret from outsiders. I'd tell you all about the wonders of Harmony, but then I'd have to marry you to keep you here. I'd have to have sex with you until I gave out and you divorced me so you could find someone younger." He leaned close and whispered, "You going to eat the rest of that hamburger?"

"I'm saving myself for pie." She watched him steal her food. "So what is the reason our white-haired couple *said* they are getting a divorce again? Surely the grandkids can't be splitting them up."

"I shouldn't be telling you anything."

"It's part of an investigation." She bribed him by moving her plate to the middle of the table so he could share her fries. "Besides, you already said they were just talking to you. No case, right?"

"Not so far. Right now they both seem happy to pay me a hundred and fifty just to referee." Rick took the bribe and pulled her plate toward him.

"He claims he's wasted years living with her controlling ways. If he answers the phone, she has to know who it is. If he draws out ten dollars in cash, she has to have an accounting of what he spends it on. He claims if he flushes twice, she's knocking on the bathroom door wanting to know what's wrong."

"Why does she hate him?"

Rick finished chewing and finally answered. "She said he keeps calling her by the wrong name and she's had enough. Her name is Minnie and he's called her Wanda since they married. He claims it fits her."

"So they are getting a divorce over that?"

"No." Rick reached toward Trace's drink and she slapped his hand. He sat back, defeated. They hadn't seen the waitress since she brought the food. Refills were too much bother with only two customers in the place. "I told them what it cost. They both agreed it was too much money."

"What happened then?"

"Nothing. They just stood up, thanked me. He took her hand and said, 'Come on, Wanda, let's go home.' When they were in the hall, I heard her tell him to stop by the Dollar Store so she could bring the kids back a surprise from town."

Trace couldn't keep a straight face. She laughed, a giggle at first and then a full, all-out body-shaking laugh.

Rick smiled, obviously loving watching her relax.

She was still laughing when Rick heard a car engine. Out of the corner of his eye, he saw something blue racing toward them.

On instinct, he moved to block. One arm flew across the table and circled Trace's waist as he ran away from the window.

They were almost to the counter when a car hit the six-inch concrete block in the handicapped parking spot and was airborne when it slammed into the window and across the table where they'd been eating.

Rick just watched wood splinter, but Trace pulled her weapon from her boot and ran toward the driver's side of the car. Before the dirt and smoke cleared, she was pulling on the door and yelling orders.

Rick leaned against the counter, watching and trying to make sense of a car parked inside the diner.

The now-familiar roar of the fire alarm sounded from a few blocks away. People outside were running toward them. Cass stormed from the kitchen, cussing.

Rick watched it all as if it were the remains of a stunt in a movie. This time his heart wasn't racing. This time he didn't feel terrified that he was almost killed.

He closed his eyes. Was it possible that calamity had become the norm in his life?

"The car's empty!" Trace yelled as Alex and

her deputies stormed through the door as if it hadn't occurred to them to enter through the ten-foot hole in the wall.

"Are you two all right?" Alex demanded.

Trace nodded.

Rick felt like he'd lost his script in this drama that had become his life. He just stared at the old blue Audi parked where his lunch had been a few minutes ago. Steam was coming from under the car's hood, and glass still tinkled down from above where pieces of window clung to the molding.

Alex stepped closer. "First, Rick, are you hurt again?"

"No," he said without looking at the sheriff. "I'm fine."

The deputy yelled that the accelerator had been tied down.

Trace walked away from the wreck. She looked straight at Alex. "Forget the others. This was attempted murder, Sheriff."

Rick had a feeling there would be no more talk of accidents that he'd just been unlucky enough to fall into. He watched as Trace leaned down and slid her Glock into the side of her boot. Their table had become a crime scene, and if he hadn't moved quickly, his body would now be beneath the rubble.

Cass was still cussing, but no one was listening. Alex was on the phone, listing all the help she wanted. Deputies were roping off the area with tape.

Rick waited. He wasn't even sure for what. He just waited.

❧ *Chapter 29* ❧

Northwest Texas Hospital
Amarillo

Tannon paced the waiting room of ICU. He'd asked himself a dozen times if this latest crisis with his mother had somehow driven him to push Emily into more than she wanted with him. Until a few weeks ago, he'd been happy just checking on his mother a couple times a month. As long as he knew she was all right, the world seemed in balance no matter what was happening at work or with his ever-demanding mother.

He wasn't sure why he'd asked her the favor of checking on his mother, but somehow that first visit had changed everything. He'd had a lifetime habit of closing himself off from people. She'd been the only one he'd really ever let in, and when she disappeared from his life, he'd nailed the door shut. He had friends he played cards with. Business colleagues. But no one he let close. No one he was completely honest with.

Every time the waiting room doors opened,

Tannon glanced up, even knowing that it was too early for Emily to arrive. She'd probably have to call someone to cover for her at the library, maybe have to go in and open up like she did every morning. He tried to remember Emily's exact words: *I'll be there before noon.*

After the ten o'clock visit to his mother's side, Tannon calmed. Emily would be with him before the next visit. She'd spent yesterday measuring out the day two hours at a time. He could wait. He almost laughed aloud. Everyone who worked for him, from the truck drivers to his staff, would be shocked if they knew how much he needed the little librarian. He was a man who needed nothing.

He paced, watched the weather on TV, tried to read, stared at the clock.

At five minutes to twelve, the nurse stepped out to tell family that they would have ten minutes of visitation.

Tannon walked to the door and waited his turn to pass through. Two guests to a room were all that was allowed.

Just as he walked past the nurse, he felt a cold hand slip into his.

He didn't turn around. He knew Emily had made it. As they walked to his mother's room, he held her fingers tightly, knowing now that no matter what happened he could handle it.

"You're freezing," he said.

"It's cold out and I had to park a mile away."

He finally looked at her. Emily was wrapped in a puffy coat that went past her knees. She looked more like she belonged in the North Pole than in West Texas. "Where are your gloves?"

"I couldn't find them. How is your mother?"

"The same." He reminded himself that she was here to see Paulette, not be questioned by him. "This is her room."

They walked through the open sliding glass door into a room where machines surrounded his frail mother. Emily wrapped her other hand around his arm and moved closer. He could feel her against him but he remained stone.

A nurse looked up from a chart. "The doctor will be in soon, Mr. Parker."

"Any change?" Tannon barely recognized his own voice.

The nurse shook her head.

Emily moved to the far side of the bed. She rubbed her hands together before she took Paulette's hand. She talked softly as if believing his mother could hear her.

The doctor came in to say that he was hopeful and that the next few hours would be very important. Tannon had heard it all before. Logic told him that this wouldn't go on forever, nothing did, but part of him believed that this time in his life would never end. This—taking care of family, putting his life on hold for them and the company—seemed all he'd ever known, but he couldn't, wouldn't, turn away from his responsibility.

His mother didn't wake up, didn't make a move. He got through the visit by watching Emily. He'd always thought there was something frail about her. Maybe it was her slender frame or maybe her big eyes. But it was more than that. She had a way about her that seemed to calm his world like a gentle rain on a warm night.

When they went back to the waiting room, he thanked Emily for coming to be with his mother. He knew his words were cold and formal but he didn't know how to say more.

To his surprise, she shook her head. "No, Tannon, I came to be with you. Your mother's got a staff of doctors and nurses to watch over her. I came to be with you."

He bent and kissed her then, no longer caring who might be watching. The kiss was soft and tender, but when it ended the hug continued. For a long time, he just held her against him.

When she finally pulled away, she said, "I'm starving. We've got over an hour to find something to eat."

He wasn't hungry, but he put his arm around her shoulder and they walked to the cafeteria. While they ate, he begged her to tell him every detail of the writers' meeting one more time. When she couldn't remember every line of Peter's poem, he complained and she threatened to make him join.

They walked back for the short two o'clock visit, then took a nap cuddled beneath her big coat until the four o'clock visit.

As the day aged, they talked in the corner of the waiting room. He told her about his business and she told him of her days in college. They avoided talking about the time when she'd left high school after "the accident" and the car wreck that had killed her parents. No mention of the month she'd been in the hospital, after which she'd gone home to recover and to be homeschooled. She'd missed the spring trip, the prom, and graduation because as soon as she could leave Harmony she'd moved into a dorm and started college a semester early.

Tannon couldn't help but wonder what would have happened if there had been no attack in the parking lot that night she was sixteen. Would he have asked her to the prom? Maybe they would have gone to the same college, started dating, married young, and had a couple of kids by now.

He stopped himself. Thinking of what might have been was too painful. Stick to the facts. They were friends, he decided, as he watched her reading beside him. That would have to be enough for now.

The north wind rattled the windows, and she tugged off her shoes and tucked her feet beneath his leg for warmth. Time passed so quickly the nurse was announcing the six o'clock visitation before either of them realized it was time.

After the visit, they found vending machines with cans of soup and week-old rolls. She claimed it was the worst food she'd ever had and he said it was about par with the dinners he usually had on the road.

At the last visit at eight, the doctor announced all looked stable. "Doctor's orders. Go home and get some sleep. We'll call if there is any change."

Tannon drove her to her car, and then she followed him to the hotel. He'd already checked her in next door to him so they didn't bother stopping at the desk.

When he set her suitcase inside her room, he hugged her one last time and kissed the top of her head. "Thanks for coming up," he whispered.

She smiled and said good night.

He stepped inside his own room, missing the nearness of her he'd felt all day. For a while, he tried to watch the news as he read through business papers that needed signing, but the loneliness didn't leave. She was one wall away.

When he clicked off his set, he could hear hers through the wall. For a half hour he tried to sleep, but there seemed no hope. He blamed it on the muffled sound from her room, but he knew that wasn't it.

Finally, he could stand it no longer. He went to the connecting door and knocked.

An eternity passed. He was about to knock again when she turned the lock.

"Yes," she asked. "Is something wrong, Tannon?"

"Something is very wrong," he said. "I can't sleep in my room. Can I sleep in yours?"

She peeked around him. "Your room is exactly like mine."

"No, it's not."

"Yes, it is. Trading rooms won't help you sleep."

Tannon frowned. "I don't want to trade rooms. I want to sleep in your room."

"Are you teasing me, Tannon, because if you are it's not funny."

"I just want to sleep in the same room as you. I don't want to be alone tonight. No other motive, I swear." He knew a half dozen women who'd gladly share his room and his bed, but they weren't Emily. He felt like a nut for asking, but he had to try. "Look, this isn't some kind of line or come-on." He had no idea how to explain himself. The idea was starting to sound stupid even to him. "Forget I—"

"Well, all right, but you keep your jeans and T-shirt on."

Tannon closed his eyes. He was a grown man who'd slept with his share of women during his college days and none of the time had been spent sleeping, but with Emily, he knew she was serious.

Her hand slipped in his. "Well, come on. I

couldn't sleep either because it's so cold in here. I should have brought my fuzzy robe."

He looked down at her nightshirt, which said BOOK WORM, and laughed. "I'll even keep my socks on, honey. I am starting to wonder where you buy your nightgowns."

"I got this at the last Texas Library Association convention. It glows in the dark."

"Great."

They climbed into bed. For a while, both lay on their backs.

He finally shifted enough to look at her. "If you're cold, don't you think it might be better if we cuddle?"

"All right." She moved closer to him and he rolled to his side, almost touching her.

She laughed suddenly. "Remember when we were about five or six and I wanted you to sleep over at my house?"

He smiled in the darkness. "Yeah, our parents wouldn't let us. I guess they thought it might become a habit."

"You were my best friend, Tannon. It seemed right at the time."

"It still does," he answered as he tugged the covers over her shoulder.

Once she stopped shivering, he laid his arm around her waist and tugged her close, and only then did they both sleep soundly.

When he awoke a little before dawn, she was

sleeping on her stomach and his hand was resting on her hip. Part of him wanted more from her, but he didn't want to risk what they were building. He was a man playing blackjack blindfolded. They might both be adults, but it seemed they had to go all the way back to start over. It might be twenty-five years late, but they'd finally had that sleepover she wanted.

He watched her until she finally raised her head. Hair curtained her face and she tried blowing it away as she looked his direction.

"Who are you and why are you in my bed?"

He laughed and pushed her hair back with his hand. "I hope you don't always wake up saying that. You're beautiful in the morning, you know."

"Oh, I know." She propped her chin up. "You, on the other hand, look terrible." She ran her finger over two days' growth of beard. "Get out of my bed."

He sat up. "All right. Thanks for sleeping with me." He patted her on the bottom, something he never would have done before.

"Anytime," she answered as she searched for her glasses. "What time is it anyway?"

He stood and looked back at her trying to read the clock. "How about we get dressed and I'll buy you breakfast?"

"All right, but give me time. I don't wake up easily." She fought with the covers as she rolled from the bed. When she emerged, her nightshirt was bunched around her waist and her powder blue bikini panties were on full display.

Before she tugged the shirt down, Tannon saw a glimpse of the scars running from her belly button down. Red jagged scars.

He looked up as she found her glasses, but before she could face him, he turned and ran from the room. "Breakfast in fifteen," he managed to say before he closed the door between their rooms.

For a long time, he stood in the shower fighting for control. That night in high school came flooding back to him, washing over him with wave after wave of pain. She'd been shaking with cold and crying when he'd found her between two parked cars.

He'd covered her with his jacket and yelled for someone to call 911. A man answered that he would make the call, but he didn't seem to want to come close enough to help. Tannon knelt beside her, pulling her into his lap as he tried to hold her. Her mouth and nose were bleeding where it looked like someone had used her face as a punching bag. Both eyes were so swollen he wasn't sure she could see at all. When he'd glanced down, he saw dirt and bruises along her arms and across her chest, but from her waist down, blood was everywhere.

She'd been cut! Sliced as if someone wanted to torture her before they killed her.

The medics arrived, asking if he found her like

this. When he nodded, another asked if he'd seen who hurt her. Tannon shook his head. As they unloaded the stretcher, the first guy told Tannon that the sheriff would be out here when he had time and if he knew anything that might help he should hang around and talk to him.

They'd lifted her away from him, but they hadn't commented when he climbed in the ambulance. He'd held her hand as tightly as he could while they worked on keeping her alive. Tannon hadn't looked down again at the cuts that night. He'd stared at her face and moved her long bloody hair back. When they'd taken her into the hospital, he'd stayed behind in the dark of the emergency room's driveway. The waiting room was packed, and a sheriff's deputy stood in the center as if directing traffic. No one saw Tannon walk away. Even the EMTs had been so busy trying to help Emily, they didn't seem to notice him tagging along.

His letter jacket that he'd been so proud of was tossed into a Dumpster as he walked back to the school. The town seemed all shadows, blacks and grays, empty as he sliced through the sleeping streets. The roar of the crowds during the game earlier had vanished, but the echoes of Emily crying still filled his mind. He wished he'd been five minutes earlier, but he couldn't even help with a clue to who might have hurt her.

The parking lot near the stadium was dark

and empty. Yellow tape marked the spot where she'd been hurt. He had no idea how long he stared at it before he finally got in his car and drove home. It was dawn when he walked in the kitchen door.

"Coming in a little late," his father commented behind his newspaper. Ted Parker had seemed an old man all of Tannon's life, but he'd never looked as old as he did that morning.

"Emily was hurt last night." Tannon waited for them to look up, but neither did. His mom said something about calling Shelley later and his father changed the subject. As always, they were in their own world and he only lived on the fringes. They didn't care enough to ask questions. They'd probably been arguing about something and he'd interrupted them.

He walked to his room and closed the door. It didn't bother him that they hadn't looked at him. What killed Tannon was the fact they hadn't cared enough about Emily to ask questions.

The next morning the news was all about how a power plant between Clifton Creek and Harmony had almost exploded. A dozen men had been hospitalized, two in critical condition. There were pictures and a story about the big game, shots of brides with wedding details, and accounts of car wrecks between two drunks, but no mention of a girl being beat up in the parking lot.

Tannon told himself that her parents might

have kept it out of the paper. It seemed like something they would have done to protect her. He didn't want to think that her story might not have been important enough to print.

❦ Chapter 30 ❦

Sunday morning

"You awake?" Trace whispered as she poked her head around the door to Rick's room.

"Yeah, come on in." Rick didn't look like he'd slept at all. Papers and books were scattered around his bed as if he'd searched for something all night.

When they'd finally made it back to the bed-and-breakfast, neither wanted supper. They'd sat in his room watching a basketball game and talking about nothing. Both had said everything they'd wanted to about the car crashing into the diner. She'd thanked him for saving her life. He'd only seemed to half listen to all the facts once Alex returned from the scene and filled them in.

Rick Matheson was changing. Looking at him now, Trace decided Denver Sims would no longer call him "that kid of a lawyer," like he had when he'd asked Trace to stop by Harmony and check on him.

The sheriff reported that the old blue Audi

belonged to the county clerk at the courthouse. He'd parked it in the same parking spot across the street from the diner for nineteen years. Whoever planned the crime had wired the car and locked down the accelerator. Once it was rolling, the Audi sat in a direct line to the diner. If there had been other cars parked in front, if someone had been driving down the street a minute earlier or later, they might have had a collision with the Audi. If anyone had been on the sidewalk, they could have been killed.

Trace listened to all the what-ifs and tried to put the pieces together in her brain. Rick had told the waitress he wanted to sit by the sunny windows. He'd picked the center booth. She'd picked the time of day. An hour later and the county clerk might have been getting off work at the courthouse and seen someone messing with his Audi. An hour earlier and more traffic would have been on the street picking up kids from school two blocks away. Whoever did this was either very good or very lucky.

Or, Trace thought, Rick Matheson was the most unlucky man she'd ever met, and from the looks of him now, he wasn't happy about winning the title.

She sat on the edge of his bed. Absently, she brushed her hand over his bare shoulder. Cute, but still unlucky; she revised her view of him.

It bothered her far more that he might have

been killed than that she was in danger. Danger was part of her job, maybe the part that had drawn her to the service. But not him. He didn't crave danger. "You all right?" she said, her voice low and caring.

"Yeah. I feel like one of those ducks in the shooting gallery just circling around waiting for the next person to pay a dollar and take a shot at me."

"Why'd you pick that table?"

He didn't look at her. "I always sit there. In fact, I work through lunch most of the time and catch a bite in the afternoon when the diner is quiet. I like sitting in the sun and thinking over what I'm going to say in court. Cass doesn't seem to care how long I stay when he's not busy and I refill my own coffee."

The pieces were starting to fit together. Whoever was doing this knew Rick very well. "What else do you do routinely out of habit?"

He rolled over and studied her as if reading her thoughts. "I usually work until after dark and go down the back stairs. I park my car behind the bookstore every day. I try to make it in to Buffalo's one night during the weekend for wings. I eat at the Blue Moon a couple of times a week."

"What else?"

"I sit in the same pew in the First United Methodist Church on Sundays with Mathesons surrounding me. I run around the park a little after dawn when it's warm enough. I visit my mother most Wednesday nights for supper. I worked on my car, when I had one. I go out with friends. I used to date now and then, but I've given that up lately. I read. I watch sports on TV. I buy most of my groceries where I buy my gas. Any other questions?"

She leaned back on the pillow beside him. "You live a very exciting life, Matheson."

"What do you do, Marshal? It's only fair you tell me. After all, for all we know you were the target at the diner and not me."

"Okay, fair enough. I work out every morning between six and seven, shower at the gym and head into headquarters. I have a thirty-minute drive, always trying to make it in before eight. I rarely leave the office before seven because the paperwork never seems to be done. By the time I make the drive back home, it's usually dark. I eat something that's frozen four minutes before it hits my plate. Watch reality TV or the History Channel and go to bed by ten. On weekends, I like to ski alone in the winter, hike in the summer. Since I travel with my job, I usually try to avoid people whenever I'm off work. I have no pets. No houseplants. And would rather clean my service weapon than do my nails."

"You're not exactly telling me anything I didn't know or couldn't have guessed, except the part about reality TV. Just thinking of you watching

256

bikini-clad girls fishing for alligators in the gold mines of Alaska freaks me out."

She swung at his shoulder and he didn't even try to block the blow. Laughing she asked, "Seriously, Matheson, what do you do for fun in this town?"

His eyes met hers. "This is pretty high up on the list." He caught her hand and held it for a moment. "All I could think about when I saw that car coming toward us was that you might be hurt."

Before she could react, he rolled toward her and kissed her. She went with the kiss and was surprised how fast it turned hot with need.

When he finally pulled away, she tried to make light of what had happened between them. "You're not going to tell me we could both die any minute so we might as well make love now."

"No." His hand moved along her side. "I was going to tell you I could get used to kisses like that."

He leaned near again and kissed her with enough fire to warm her blood. He wasn't pinning her down, wasn't even holding her, but she didn't turn away. He drew her. There was something good and clean about him, even wounded. He might be intelligent and funny, but the little boy still flickered inside the man. His kiss had an honesty about it that made her want more and to test the depths of his passion.

When he straightened, both of them were out of breath.

She sat up. "We shouldn't be doing this."

"Why? Because you don't want to or because you want to too much?"

"First, tell me why you kissed me." Trace didn't look up at him. She guessed he'd read more in her eyes than she wanted to give away.

Rick leaned back away from her. "I don't know. It just seemed something to do. Don't tell me you haven't been thinking about doing the same thing."

"All right," she answered. "I've been thinking about it, but it shouldn't have happened. I'm here to protect you."

He didn't move for a long moment, then he rolled from the bed and walked to the door. "In other words, I'm just a job, nothing more. Right, Marshal?"

"Right," she answered.

"Today is exactly why I didn't want anyone getting involved. I know you think you're help-ing, but all you're doing is getting in the way."

"I'm not leaving." She could see the anger building in him and understood it, but she couldn't let how he felt, or even what he said, interfere with her job.

"Fine," he said as he walked out the door.

She didn't see him for over an hour. He walked into the parlor where she'd been reading and watching the street.

When he returned in a well-fitting suit with a crisp white shirt and conservative tie, Rick

Matheson looked completely different. He looked like a successful lawyer. No bandages showed, and with his already wide shoulders padded by the suit, he appeared in the prime of health.

"Where'd you get the suit?" she asked. All she'd ever seen him in was old shirts and jeans.

"I had a few in the cleaners. Thanks to Martha Q, I had enough money to bail them out. They delivered them yesterday while we were busy dodging an Audi served at lunch."

She knew he was angry, he probably had a right to be, but she didn't want him hostile. "Want to tell me where you're going?"

He didn't look up. "You should be able to figure it out. I told you my entire route yesterday. It's Sunday morning. I'm going to church. I plan to walk unless you want to offer me a ride."

"It's dangerous."

"Well, then, I guess you'll have to do your job, Marshal."

She wanted to run over him herself. She thought he might have been disappointed about the turndown after the kiss, but it never occurred to her that the easygoing, lighthearted guy might actually be mad.

He was a half block away when she caught up with him in the Land Rover.

"Get in," she shouted. "I'll drive you."

He didn't argue. The walk had taken a toll on him. He was in pain.

"I'm not going in, but I'll be outside waiting."

"Fair enough. Pull in there. I'll go in and come out the side door." He didn't look at her when he climbed slowly out.

The hour Rick was inside, Trace tried to decide if she should call Denver Sims and tell him to find someone else for the job. She hadn't known what she was getting into and now that her cover was blown, she might not be as effective.

The only problem was she knew she was one of the best at what she did and she also realized that she cared about the idiot lawyer. She cared if he lived or died. This wasn't just a job, a favor for a friend. Somehow it had turned into far more.

Turning off all emotions, she thought logically. The criminal they were looking for wasn't likely to be in church. She'd bet most of the people in the small building had known one another all their lives and they'd recognize a stranger. So, if he wasn't inside, the culprit was outside with her, maybe even watching her now.

She needed to move somewhere where she could scan the area without him seeing her. She slipped from the car and headed toward the side door. Music was playing as she opened the door and disappeared. To anyone who might be watching, it looked like she'd stepped inside, but Trace slipped around the door and vanished behind the church between a garden wall and the drainpipe.

Within seconds she was on the roof and

heading up the shady side where the shadows of hundred-year-old trees shielded her from view.

At the top she lay in the dark lines of barren elm branches and looked at the street below. She could see all entrances except the front one, the least likely someone causing trouble might go to.

When the organ played she could not only hear it, but feel the music through the roof. The Methodists were certainly raising their voices to heaven. After a few minutes, she climbed to the shadow of the steeple and did her job.

She watched over Rick Matheson.

❧ *Chapter 31* ❧

Sunday afternoon

Emily made an evening visit at six to Paulette Parker's ICU room, then walked out with Tannon. Somehow, after spending the night close together, there didn't seem to be a need to talk. It was almost like they were close again, knowing they were thinking each other's thoughts.

They made it to a quiet spot along a hospital corridor before he stopped her with a touch. She turned into him for one last long hug.

"I hate leaving you here," she whispered.

"I'll be all right. Thanks for coming. Thanks for letting me sleep over."

Emily smiled. "Sounds strange. Maybe we shouldn't tell anyone."

"I don't care what it sounds like. It felt good to hold you all night long." He kissed the top of her head. "Call me when you make it home."

She nodded, almost afraid to say too much. They'd been polite friends all day, careful not to step too far, careful not to presume too much. The old friendship that had lasted through their childhood was there, solid as ever. Two shy, only children who'd found each other and lost each other had found their way back.

Only this adult friendship was too new. It hadn't been tested. It might not last.

"Tannon, you have to let me go if I'm ever going to start home."

He laughed and pulled her tighter. "All right. Promise you won't have sleepovers with anyone else and I'll let you go."

"I promise."

She was still laughing when his mouth covered hers. She was ready and willing for a tender kiss, but this was more. He lifted her off the ground and kissed her. She told herself he just needed to connect with someone during this terrible time of waiting. She'd be a fool to read too much into a kiss.

When he lowered her back to the ground, he whispered, "You didn't kiss me back."

"Didn't I?"

"It's all right. I stepped out of line. It's been a long time since I kissed anyone I cared about."

She looked up at him trying to read him. He hadn't stepped out of line. They'd agreed to a good-bye kiss. Was he trying to tell her he cared about her? Or just out of practice kissing? Emily decided to deal with the easiest misunderstanding first. "I did kiss you back."

"No, you didn't."

"Yes, I did. Or at least I thought I did." She needed time to think. "Oh, forget it. I need to drive home."

He nodded. "We'll talk about it when I make it back to Harmony."

He held her hand as he walked her to her car, but he made no move to kiss her again. The polite Tannon was back.

When she climbed in the car, he knelt down beside her open door but didn't say anything.

She put on her seat belt, adjusted the steering wheel, and turned on her engine, but he didn't move. Finally, she turned to him. "Are we reaching the point of being more than friends?"

"I think we are, honey. How do you feel about that?" He frowned as if he'd just been told they both had the same terminal illness.

"As long as it's with you, I think I can handle it."

"I'll never hurt you, Emily."

She smiled. "I know. That's why I let you sleep over."

He touched her shoulder lightly and closed the door. When she drove away from the hospital, she could still see him standing by the front door watching her.

❦ *Chapter 32* ❦

Monday

Rick didn't even ask the marshal following him around if he should leave the house; he just dressed and walked to work as if it were an ordinary day in his life, even if it might be the last.

Trace Adams followed him quietly for a half block, but he knew it wouldn't last. When she caught up to him at the first busy corner she whispered, "Idiot."

"Good morning to you too." He waited, but she didn't take the bait. "You know," he said as he started across the street, "most women don't crawl out on the roof every night. Though watching you play Bat Woman is sexy as hell, I can't figure out if you're howling at the moon or maybe part reindeer."

She stayed in step with him but didn't speak, so Rick grinned and continued. "Tell me, when did you start climbing out windows? Maybe one night when you were about five or six and grew tired of loading and unloading your guns? I hate to be the one to point it out to you, but sitting on the roof isn't something most girls do. I'll bet you were cute though in your little rompers made of leather. Could you get those boots in toddler sizes?"

"Shut up, Matheson."

"She talks. That's great. Since you'll be following me around all day, don't you think it would help if you would stop being mad at me?"

"I'm not mad at you."

"You've been mad at me, Marshal, since I kissed you yesterday morning." He smiled and nodded at an old man sitting in front of the florist shop. When they were ten feet down the walk, he added, "If I remember correctly, you kissed me back, so don't lay the crime at my door."

"Lapse in judgment," she replied.

"Yeah, right. If you ever want to relapse, just let me know."

She wasn't looking at him when he turned to her hoping for an answer. Her gaze was fixed on a couple standing outside the used bookstore. "Did you know the two white heads were coming back?"

"No, but I think you should frisk them this time. It's bound to be a plot against my life."

When he reached the elderly couple, Rick smiled warmly as if they were old friends. "How may I help you this morning, Mr. and Mrs. Peters?"

Minnie looked at her husband, Eldon. "We're here to buy another hour of your time."

"All right. Let's go upstairs." As they walked slowly up, Rick introduced the Peterses to Marshal Trace Adams again and said she was with him on official business.

When they finally reached Rick's office, Minnie pointed at Trace and asked, "Is she staying?"

Rick saw the worry in the old woman's eyes. "No," he said quickly. "Not unless you'd like her to."

"Will it cost extra?"

"No," both Rick and Trace said at once.

"Then I'd like it if she stays." Minnie moved to the chair she'd sat in Friday. "You may have a criminal case on your hands, Mr. Matheson, so it wouldn't hurt to have the marshal here to testify to all that is said this morning." When no one, including Eldon, moved, she continued, "I've reason to believe Eldon is trying to kill me."

Minnie's tall, aging husband lowered slowly into the chair next to her. "Now, Wanda, you know that's not true. It was an accident."

The old woman rummaged in her purse and pulled out three fifty-dollar bills. "Our hour starts now. If we go over, I've got more cash."

Rick nodded. Trace moved closer.

"Maybe you should start at the beginning, Mrs. Peters." Rick tried his best to keep from thinking how much he was making and how important every detail would be if he had to build a case.

"I haven't got enough money to start at the beginning," Minnie retorted with a shrug. "I just need to know if I need to hire a lawyer or talk to the police."

"If we talk to the police, you'll be sitting in the cell next to me." Eldon took off his worn Stetson and lowered his head. "With my luck I wouldn't even get any peace in prison. Hell, for all I know they went co-ed like all the damn dorms in colleges did. I got four grandkids in college and they got people of the opposite sex living right next door. In my day, we didn't even eat in the same dining hall. Hell, I wouldn't have lasted a year with girls on campus."

Minnie shook her head. "You didn't last a year."

"It just didn't take me long to figure out I'd rather farm than study. I told my folks that when they sent me off, but my dad never heard a word I said."

"What happened that brought you two here today?" Rick was tempted to let them ramble, but he couldn't wait to hear the details of the attempted murder. This might prove to be his best file ever.

Minnie pressed her thin lips together so hard they disappeared. "I'm not talking until I get some assurance from you, Mr. Matheson, that you'll be my lawyer and not his. We searched a hundred miles around and you're the cheapest on your hourly rate. I'm the one who found you and I'm keeping you."

"Now, Wanda, he's got a right to make up his own mind. This ain't no Easter egg hunt. You can't just say you get to keep him 'cause you found him. Maybe he'd rather go with the more logical one of us or, better yet, the innocent one."

Rick glanced at the clock and smiled. They'd been in his office fifteen minutes and hadn't even told him the problem yet. He'd be making money today.

As soon as the thought registered, he felt guilty. What kind of lawyer thinks of money at a time like this? He mentally slapped the smile off his face and swore he'd do his best, whatever came next.

He frowned, wondering if any of the lawyers within a hundred miles had people like this dropping by. Probably all of them. But what did he know? He was the cheapest around, and none of them probably wanted to talk to him. That didn't set well.

"Look, Mr. and Mrs. Peters, I don't want to waste your money. If we could just get to the facts, maybe I could help you."

"I can tell you what her problem is." Eldon leaned back in his chair, causing Trace to jump for fear he might not be able to balance, but he just teetered as he launched into his version of events. "She thought she wanted a divorce until she found out she'd only get half our money. Once we got home, she figured out the only way to get it all was to kill me. Two nights ago she started salting my food and yesterday she bought me a box of cigars." He let the front two legs of his chair drop and added, "This morning, she started baking sweets like she hasn't baked in twenty years. She knows I'm diabetic."

"I forget," Minnie said quickly. "A woman's memory goes about the same time her husband's sex drive drops. I've committed no crime, right, Mr. Matheson? He's the one who put the car in gear while I had one foot still on the ground. He's the one who could have killed me."

"It's no crime to be in a hurry. If you didn't think you had to open and read the mail before you get back in the car, I might not be dying of old age waiting for you all the time."

Rick glanced at Trace. Her only answer was a shrug so he decided to change directions. "How long has this fight been going on between the two of you?"

Neither one of them answered.

Rick leaned halfway across the desk. "Look, I'm not a marriage counselor. If you want a divorce, I can help you, but if you just came here for a referee, you're out of luck. Marshal Adams and I are going to go downstairs and get some coffee.

When I come back, I'd like you two to have come to a decision."

He motioned Trace to follow him. "And by the way," he said from the door, "you're both still on my clock, so don't take too long to decide or you'll owe me another hundred and fifty dollars."

They were halfway down the stairs when Trace smiled. "You think they might kill each other?"

"If they do, it's your problem, not mine," Rick said as he turned into the bookstore.

George Hatcher wasn't at his usual station at the front. Rick felt the hair rise on the back of his neck and saw Trace had tensed like a trained soldier ready to fight. They moved slowly through the empty store.

Nothing looked out of place except the back door was open. He'd seen George leave the door open on summer days but never when it was this cold.

They moved toward the back.

The door creaked open in the breeze and both saw George Hatcher's body lying facedown on the steps.

Trace's actions were lightning fast. She pulled a gun from her boot and stepped in front of Rick before he could move. "Stay here," she ordered as she leaned low and took a step outside.

George raised his head and moaned. Blood dripped from a scrape on his cheek.

Rick couldn't just stand there watching and no weapon appeared to be handy. Besides if anyone was out there, the marshal could handle them. Hell, she could probably handle a gang.

"Rick? That you?" Hatcher mumbled. "Help me up."

Without another thought of self-preservation, Rick walked outside and knelt beside the bookstore owner. "What happened? Are you all right?"

Trace was several feet away, her weapon still at the ready as she surveyed the parking area and alley beyond.

"I'm fine." George took Rick's arm and stood slowly like a man unsure which limbs might hold. "I fell. Must have not been watching where I was going."

Rick heard someone talking and realized his office back window was just above and for once, it was open. Eldon Peters was complaining about his wife's driving. It didn't take a detective to figure out that George might have been eavesdropping.

Rick made a mental note to keep his window closed.

Fighting down a smile, he asked, "You think you might have broken anything?"

Hatcher took a hesitant step as if testing his bones. "I don't think so." He brushed his cheek. "I must have scraped my face on the corner of those old stairs when I fell. Don't know how it could have happened. I've made that trip to the trash a hundred times."

George must have gone to the alley and heard something upstairs on his way back. Then he must have tried to balance on the uneven steps while he was listening.

Trace walked back to them. "You all right, Mr. H?" she said in her relaxed tone as if she hadn't been a warrior only seconds ago.

"Yeah, I'm fine. Just an old fool for not paying attention."

Trace took his arm. "It wasn't your fault. Things like this happen. Who knows, it might have even been that ghost you say you hear around the place."

George brightened. "That's a possibility. The sheriff doesn't have one clue as to who sawed the steps. Maybe the ghost doesn't want any of us around the place. I need to call and get an expert to come in and investigate."

Rick wasn't sure Alex would have time to help George. She'd probably send Phil Gentry, her deputy. As long as he was near a coffeepot, he'd entertain any possible crime theory.

"Don't you think we should doctor that scrape on your face, George? It could get infected." Trace tried to pull him toward his chair, but he would have none of it.

"I got to reach Mrs. Weatherbee before she

leaves for Wichita Falls. She reads palms over there on Monday afternoons, but this is far more important." He patted his cheek with a napkin as he punched in the call. "We're doing break-through work here."

Rick finally caught Trace's gaze and motioned they leave. She nodded. While George gave details to the town's only fortune-teller, Trace and Rick walked out front.

"So, do we stay with the ghost serial killer or with the dueling murderers upstairs?" she asked as if she were being serious. "Who knew small towns could be so interesting?"

They started up the stairs. "It's me," Rick said. "Interesting things always happen around interesting people."

She frowned at him.

He grinned. "You were sexy back there, going all U.S. Marshal on me."

"Don't go there, Matheson. I'm just watching over you." Before he could think of anything to say, she asked, "Wonder how the senior citizens are doing in your office. I sure hope we don't find the blood and white hair flying."

Rick checked his watch. "This looks like it could be a long morning. I'll buy lunch."

When he made it back to his office Mr. and Mrs. Peters were not talking to each other and three fresh fifty-dollar bills lay on his desk. Rick took the money and sat down. "I'll respect your time-out for as long as you wish to sit in my office, and then we'll talk."

Minnie lifted her eyebrow as if guessing he was just passing time, but her lips had disappeared into that thin line again. It was obvious she didn't plan to be the first one to break the silence.

Rick glanced at Eldon and he looked just as stubborn.

Trace stood behind them rolling her eyes. It took her about three minutes to get bored and disappear.

Rick waited.

When the second hour was up, Minnie stood and thanked him for his time. Eldon followed her out, saying that they'd be back.

Rick liked the money, but this had to be the most boring case he'd had to date. He gave them time to get downstairs, then grabbed his jacket and bolted for the door.

As he swung the office door open and ran to find Trace, she collided with him in a full body slam. Both stepped back and complained.

"What are you doing?" she snapped.

"I was going to find you for lunch, Wanda."

To his surprise, the serious federal marshal burst out laughing.

❧ Chapter 33 ❧

Emily walked around the second floor of the library, making sure everything was in place. She loved the smell of books.

All was quiet. Everyone had run over to the used bookstore to deliver all the books on ghosts that they could find. Pamela Sue even picked up a few children's books. George Hatcher was calling in the writers' group as well as everyone he could think of who believed in ghosts.

Emily thought it strange that Pamela Sue thought the moon landing was a hoax but believed spirits roamed the earth pestering humans. She'd even talked the children's librarian into going along to see what was happening at the used bookstore. Apparently, the expert palm reader, Mrs. Weatherbee, was going to give a talk as soon as she arrived.

Walking down the steps, Emily smiled. Thankfully, she was going to miss it. Memories already haunted her, she didn't need ghosts as well.

She stopped at the set of mysteries called The Secrets of Comeback Bay. She checked to see if there had been another entry, but there was none. Maybe one of the two people passing notes in the old books had moved away, or died. She might never know the truth. It had been so long since they'd written in the book.

As she held the mystery in the center of the silent library, Emily thought she could almost feel Tannon's arms around her. It felt so right to be with him, but she knew she was doing what she always did with men. She was starting to push him away.

The friendship they'd rebuilt was great, but when he kissed her she knew that at some point he'd want more. She wanted his touch, his kiss, even that taste of his passion, but she wasn't sure she could handle more.

How could she say that she didn't want intimacy? No, that wasn't true. She wanted it. She just didn't want him to see her nude. She'd gotten over the attack all those years ago. Except for a few quirks, she thought she'd walked away healthy. Only, she'd been scared, and in order to be truly with a man, he'd have to see those scars.

Emily made up her mind. She'd take what Tannon offered. The friendship. The kissing. The caring. Then, when it finally stepped too far, she'd walk away as she'd done before. She'd run before he saw the scars.

This time, though, it would hurt her far more than the attack had. This time when she left a man standing there wondering what happened, she'd also leave her heart. Tannon wasn't a man she could leave easily, but this one time she would kiss him back.

None of the guys she'd dated in college had even noticed her holding back, but he had. He'd noticed because it mattered to him.

Emily closed the book and walked downstairs as Sam bumped his way out of the back with a vacuum cleaner in one hand and the hose in the other. "I know we don't do this during open hours, but there's a mess of sunflower seeds over by the computers. I thought since no one was here, I might clean them up."

"All right," Emily said, realizing it was almost two hours before Sam was supposed to be at work. "How long have you been here?"

"I came in right after you opened. Couldn't sleep so decided to come to work early."

She'd never known him to come in five minutes early, much less the whole morning. Except for Fridays, he always stayed an hour after the library closed.

"So you were here when George Hatcher called about the bookstore ghost?" Emily didn't understand why, but she didn't quite believe the janitor.

"Yeah, I heard them talking but didn't see no reason for running over there to see something that's invisible in the first place."

"Do you believe men landed on the moon?"

Sam, as usual, looked bothered when asked to stop and talk. "Of course. Can I go clean up the sunflower seeds before another pile drops on them and we end up with stalactites coming up off the floor."

"Stalagmites," she corrected, as if it mattered.

Sam moved away mumbling something about the whole town going crazy lately.

Emily's office phone sounded and she ran to catch the call. "Hello," she answered out of breath.

Tannon's low laughter came from the other end. "Been running in the library again, honey?"

She laughed. "Of course."

"Too bad. I was hoping it was me."

She held the phone so tightly the tips of her fingers turned white. "Is your mom all right? She didn't take a turn for the worse after I left yesterday, did she?"

"No, she's actually doing a little better this morning. I called to tell you I wish I'd kissed you good-bye one more time."

"You're always saying that." She laughed.

"I know. I guess I can't get enough. Do you mind terribly, Emily? Could you handle a few more kisses in your life?"

She took a deep breath. "I could handle a few more."

"I'll be home as soon as I can. I miss you."

She thought of all the things she could say, that she'd miss him, that she'd kiss him back when he came home, that she was falling for her best friend, but all she could get out was "Good-bye."

She hung up the phone and noticed her hand

was shaking. How could she tell him that she'd never gone beyond a few kisses with any guy before? She was more than thirty years old—women her age counted their lovers in double digits. His words whispered back to her as she stood very still, *Can you handle a little more?*

This time, she vowed. This time she could.

❧ *Chapter 34* ❧

Tuesday night

Beau had set his guitar down a half hour ago and moved down to the last porch step. Wrapped up in his coat and an old blanket, he planned to spend a few minutes studying the stars. The night was still and quiet like it gets just before a storm. He thought he could feel a bit of spring in the wind. His grandpa used to tell him to live by the seasons, not the clock. Beau was starting to realize what the old man meant.

As always, he felt lonely, but he knew Trouble wouldn't be by to pick him up tonight. Wherever she lived, whatever she did, she only drove the red Mustang on weekends. He'd walked by the library a dozen times hoping to run into her again. He'd even made it to breakfast with Ronny in hopes of catching her, but his almost girlfriend was never around and there was no sign of the car.

A few days ago he asked the breakfast club if anyone knew of a smoking hot red '65 Ford in town. None of them remembered seeing one. Apparently his midnight date was as much a ghost as George Hatcher's bookstore spirit everyone was talking about. Each time George told the story, it got bigger. He wore the scrape on his cheek like a battle wound.

The lights were out in both apartments so he could see the stars and the sliver of a moon. Man, tonight would have been a perfect time for a midnight ride.

Beau thought he heard a door open behind him, but it was too dark on the porch to see anything. Then the hair on the back of his neck stood on end as footsteps headed toward him.

"Ronny?" he said. "Is that you?"

"Beau," she whispered. "I didn't see you there."

"Sorry I frightened you. I just couldn't sleep and thought I'd watch the stars."

She didn't say anything for a minute. He could feel her close more than see her. Finally, she whispered, "Beau, we're friends, right?"

"Right," he answered, trying to make out her face in the dark.

"I need a favor, a promise." She moved closer as the flash of car light turned on their street a few blocks away.

"Name it." Beau knew her well enough to guess that whatever she asked wouldn't be illegal.

The car slowed as it moved closer.

She leaned so close she was almost touching his ear when she whispered, "Forget you saw me tonight. Promise."

"I never saw you."

The car stopped in front of the duplex. A long expensive Lincoln looking fresh off the assembly line.

"I never saw you leave with a midnight lover," he whispered.

She stepped away and whispered so low it carried light on the breeze. "It's not what it looks like, Beau, and I can't explain."

As the door opened, Ronny ran toward it. Beau heard her thrill of laughter as she climbed in, then almost without a sound, the car pulled away picking up speed.

Beau smiled. He'd wasted his time feeling sorry for Ronny, obviously she had something very private going on. He picked up his guitar and began to play.

An hour later the sheriff's cruiser pulled up and two deputies climbed out. Beau must have dozed off for he'd thought the lights were falling stars for a minute before he realized what they were. He didn't move as one of the deputies stepped onto the porch and shined his flashlight across Beau's boots.

"That you, Beau Yates?" Deputy Gentry said in his official voice.

Beau acted like they'd woke him up. "Yeah, was I snoring too loud?"

The other deputy pounded on Ronny's door as Gentry explained, "No, you can sleep on the porch if you want to, kid. We're here to talk to Ronny Logan. Her mother had a dream that she was kidnapped tonight, maybe raped and killed. She won't settle down, so we finally agreed to come check on her. Dallas Logan swore she'd stand outside the office and yell till dawn if we didn't do something."

"Why didn't you just put her in jail? That old bag is crazy. She drives by here all the time, trying to spy on Ronny."

"I know, but if we arrested her we might have to strip-search her and none of us was willing to do that. Waking up the daughter seemed like the only other plan."

The other deputy continued to pound.

Gentry flashed the light in Beau's face. "You know where she is?"

"N-no," Beau lied.

The deputy went around to the back of the house and pounded again. Lights came on in Border's room, and a minute later Border stormed out, wearing only his underwear and tattoos.

In the daylight, with his clothes on, Border was frightening. Now, raging like a bear woke in the middle of winter, he was downright terrifying.

He slammed the screen open so fast and hard he almost knocked Gentry off the porch. The young deputy came around the corner and thought Border had attacked Gentry. He pulled his flashlight up and swung it like a club at Border's head. Beau jumped to block the blow, and they all ended up rolling around on the porch with Border and the deputy swinging while Beau and Gentry tried to stay out of the way.

Thirty minutes later, Beau would have laughed at the entire scene if he hadn't been handcuffed in the back of the cruiser and on his way to jail. Gentry was in the front seat taking turns yelling, first at the young deputy for being an idiot and then at Border for waking up swinging.

Beau guessed Gentry felt bad because he was talking to people who had been minding their own business an hour ago and now they were on their way to spend the night in jail all because some crazy lady had a dream.

When Beau walked in he spotted Dallas Logan dressed in the ugliest bathrobe ever made. The hem was once trimmed with rubber duckies, but after a thousand washings, they had begun to flake off, leaving headless ducks marching along the bottom of the robe.

She rushed toward him, her fists on her hips. "One of them did it!" she yelled. "Right now my daughter's body is buried in a shallow grave after they did who-knows-what with her. I've known all along these two were up to no good. They just waited for their chance, and tonight they must have found it."

If Gentry hadn't blocked her way, Beau had no doubt Dallas and her mutilated duck robe would have come flying into him.

"Your daughter's not dead," he said before he thought.

Gentry glared at him. "You know this for certain?"

"N-no. B-but the last time I saw her she was fine."

"And when was that?"

"I-I don't remember." He lied again. Since midnight, lying had become a habit.

Gentry nodded toward the deputy behind the desk. "Maybe we better wake the judge up and get a warrant to search her apartment. Something doesn't feel right. Lock these two up until I get some answers."

Border bumped against Beau and whispered, "Tell them you're not talking until you see your lawyer."

"B-but I didn't do anything." All he was doing was trying to keep a promise to Ronny. "I-I don't even know a lawyer."

Border took over. "We're not talking until we talk to our lawyer!"

"What do you think you did?" Gentry asked Border.

"I don't know, I guess I'm being charged with guilt by association."

"B-but I didn't do anything," Beau tried again.

Border glared at Gentry. "And I was with him when it didn't happen."

❧ *Chapter 35* ❧

Wednesday

The phone woke Rick before daylight. He fumbled around the nightstand and finally caught the cell phone. "Matheson," he said as he sat up.

"Rick, it's Alex. Can you come down to the sheriff's office? Beau Yates was brought in last night."

"What charge?"

"None so far, but he won't talk to us. Says he wants to see a lawyer."

Rick scrubbed his face. "That doesn't sound good." Usually, innocent people couldn't stop talking about how innocent they were.

"That's not the worst part. The deputies brought Border Biggs in with Yates."

Rick was fully awake now. "What'd he do?"

"Got in a fight with one of deputies, but I think we can straighten it out if the guys will just talk to us. Don't tell Mrs. Biggs about her grandson. I don't want her upset."

"Okay. I'll get dressed and be right down. Have either of them said anything?"

Alex laughed. "Yeah, Border's asked twice what time breakfast is. Could you pick up a dozen doughnuts as an appetizer? I don't know if he'll make it until eight without food."

"Sure, I'm on my way."

When he ended the call, Rick wasn't surprised to hear footsteps on the stairs. "Come on in, Marshal," he yelled as he headed for the shower.

Trace stood on the other side of the open bathroom door and asked questions as he stripped. When he turned on the water she yelled, "I'll be ready in five. Don't open the front door until I'm with you."

He stepped under the warm water and said, "Why not just climb in here with me now? The water's already hot."

He guessed she was gone or he would have heard some snappy comeback. She hadn't been friendly to him since he'd made the mistake of kissing her. In hindsight, it was probably a stupid thing to do, but she looked so hot. Hell, even mad at him she still looked hot.

When he dressed and stepped into the hallway, she was waiting by the door. She didn't say a word as they walked out and climbed into the Land Rover Hank had loaned them. It didn't even have time to warm up before they reached the bakery. Rick ordered three dozen doughnuts and chatted with Geraldine while her sister filled the order.

When they pulled away, Trace finally spoke. "I don't see why this town needs a paper or radio station. If we'd been there five more minutes, we'd have known everything going on in town."

Rick smiled. "It wasn't what she said that was important. It was what she didn't say. She didn't know about Beau Yates. The word's not out yet."

Trace faced him. "And do we know anything?"

"Nope, but we will by the time these doughnuts are gone."

To Rick's surprise, Trace completely engaged in the problem as soon as she stepped into the office. She was now in her element. She passed out doughnuts to the staff, asking questions, acting interested in everything as he walked back to talk to the boys.

Border had watched one too many cop shows. He kept making up things he thought were going on. Beau, on the other hand, was quiet. Rick was near enough to their age that he didn't seem a threat so they talked to him as they downed the doughnuts.

When Rick stood, saying he was going to go try and get them out as soon as possible, Beau caught him by the arm before he could leave. "Would you ask if I can have my guitar? I don't mind being locked up for a few days, but I have to have the Gibson."

"Sure," Rick said, feeling sorry for the shy,

talented kid. "I'll go over to your place and get it myself."

"Thanks." Beau moved away from the bars.

Rick found Alex and Trace in Alex's office. He poured himself a cup of coffee and sat down. The sun was barely up and he felt like he'd already worked the day.

"What did you learn, providing you can share?" Alex said. "All I've been able to discover is that Ronny Logan keeps a clean house. Not much of a crime scene."

"I didn't get much info either. Beau was asleep on the porch. Border woke and thought someone was breaking into their house." Rick decided if this were an episode in a crime series, it could play out during a commercial.

Trace nodded. "That's what Gentry said. He admits that the fight on the porch was just a mistake. No one even got bloody, so it couldn't have been much of a fight."

Alex leaned back in her chair. "So they know nothing, and Ronny Logan is still missing. Of course, she's old enough to spend a night away from home without being investigated."

Rick wasn't sure exactly what he should say. He'd asked about Ronny, and Border had yelled that he knew nothing, but Beau had been quiet, too quiet. Maybe he was just shy or tired, but something didn't fit.

"Sheriff?" The dispatcher poked his head into

the office. "Ronny Logan just called, asking if we wanted a special delivery made early. I told her how we were all looking for her and she said she'd worked last night, trying to catch up. Her mother was here all night screaming that Ronny was dead and she'd been three blocks away, sorting mail in a back room without windows."

All three in the office let out their breath at the same time.

"Why didn't she answer her cell phone?"

"I asked her that." The dispatcher smiled. "She said her mother is always calling in the middle of the night and hanging up, so she left it back at her apartment turned off."

Alex stood as the dispatcher added, "You want me to call her mom and tell her?"

"No, I think I'll drive over and have a talk with Dallas Logan myself." Alex turned to Rick. "Thanks for coming in. You want to go tell your almost clients that they are free to go?"

"Sure. I'll even give them a ride."

When they walked out to the car, Rick didn't even bother to look surprised when he pulled another note from his windshield. Same square envelope. Same wide magic marker print of his name on the front.

Trace leaned close as he unfolded his latest fan mail. The other two had simply said, *Leave*. This one was far more creative. The letters, large and bold, were cut from what might have been a book. The note read, *Leave or Die.*

Trace reached in her back pocket, pulled out a plastic bag, and dropped it inside. As if nothing were unusual about her actions, she turned to Border and Beau. "Would you guys do me a big favor? Would you drive this car back to the B&B and then stop in and eat the breakfast Mrs. Biggs has waiting? I'm sure your grandmother will be happy to let you two take our places this morning. We need to spend a little time with Alex."

"Another threat?" Beau didn't bother to play dumb. He might not know the details, but everyone in town knew that someone was stalking Matheson.

Trace nodded once. "Any leads, boys? I'm fresh out."

"Yeah, look for a cut-up picture book," Beau offered.

❦ *Chapter 36* ❦

Wednesday night

Tannon didn't make it back to Harmony until Wednesday night. His mother was finally moved out of ICU and he'd hired a nurse who was far better at putting up with Paulette's moods than he was. As soon as he knew his mother was stable, he headed for home and the mountain of work piling up on his office desk.

He'd talked to Emily every day and it almost killed him to tell her he couldn't see her Wednesday night. "It'll be after midnight when I finish and by then I wouldn't be fit company, but we're still on for Friday night. I'll be waiting for you when the writers' group wraps up." He wanted nothing more than to hold her, but his father had drilled into him that the business was his responsibility. When the old man left, he'd dumped a world of problems on Tannon along with lectures reminding him that if he didn't do his job everyone in the company would suffer. So, tonight, only Tannon would suffer by not seeing Emily.

She'd said she understood, but as he worked he thought of calling her and asking if he could come over for a few minutes. Only it wouldn't be a few minutes. Since he'd kissed her, their friendship had shifted. He'd slept alone all his life, yet after one night with her in his arms, he'd reached for her in the darkness as if her not being in his bed was the exception, not the rule. His body wanted her near, but his mind told him that as long as she didn't want him he'd never step over the line.

With the river of memories between them, she wasn't likely to want him for anything more than a friend and he could live with that. It made him sad remembering how she let him kiss her yet hadn't kissed him back, even though she said she had. Maybe it wasn't him. Maybe something had died inside of her that night fifteen years ago in the dark parking lot. Maybe when they'd cut her, they'd cut away passion for any man from her life. He'd never heard anyone mention Emily even flirting much less having a date.

Tannon forced himself to go back to work. He couldn't, wouldn't, think of Emily as damaged.

By ten, he'd buried himself so deeply into work that he didn't hear the buzzer the first time it sounded. When the noise finally did register, he almost didn't answer. Who in their right mind would be calling at this hour?

Glancing out the window, he saw Emily's car parked next to his and didn't bother with the elevator. He ran down the stairs.

She was all bundled up, and when he opened the main door, she handed him a pot. While he stood without shoes and held the door, she ran back to her car for another bag of what looked like groceries. She was laughing and shivering when she returned.

"What are you doing here?" He smiled thinking she was wearing the perfect burglar disguise. Every part of her body was covered in wool.

"Did you eat dinner?" she asked, rushing into the elevator and pushing the up button while still dancing to keep warm.

"No."

"Then I brought you food." She hurried into his apartment as if nervous. "I couldn't sleep, so I decided to start cooking."

He unpacked the bag while she pulled off her coat. "I didn't want to bother you, but I worried that you didn't eat."

The nerves were still there, like a frightened rabbit.

"Don't mother me, Emily. I'm not in the mood." The words were out before he could stop them.

When he looked at her, she seemed to have turned to stone. He'd frightened her completely still.

"I'm sorry." He'd given orders and spoken so frankly about everything for so many years that now Tannon didn't know if he knew how to have a normal conversation. "I'm tired and worried about Mom and hungry. Thanks for worrying about me. It's not something I'm used to anyone doing." He fought the urge to grab her and hold her so tight words wouldn't stand between them, but he guessed that would only frighten her more.

"You look tired." Her voice was kind telling him silently that she'd forgiven him. "I'm here to help, if you'll let me." Her cold hand touched his jaw.

"You already are," he admitted. Just having her with him calmed his world; it always had. "And you are so right. I'm starving to death. I don't think I've had anything but coffee all day. I'm glad you came."

He piled the food on the coffee table and they talked while he ate. She'd made a chili soup and a meat loaf that tasted better than he'd ever had in a restaurant. He laughed at her little pies but ate three before she told him one was considered a serving.

"I know," he explained as he reached for another, "but I didn't like the apple or peach, so I had to eat the pecan." He winked. "Maybe I should give the apple another try."

She watched him eat the last little pie. "I'll make more next time."

Next time. He liked the sound of that.

When they took the trash to the kitchen, she said, "I know you're working, so I won't take up any more of your time." She reached for her coat. "If you'll just walk me to my car, I'll—"

"Stay," he said stopping her. "Sleep over with me."

Emily didn't look at him. He knew asking her to stay here was different than it had been in the hotel. They were in Harmony now.

"Stay," he asked again.

She shook her head. "I didn't bring—"

"You can sleep in one of my shirts. I'll wake you before any of the staff comes in downstairs." When she didn't answer, he added, "I've never had anyone up here. I've never minded being alone, but I don't want to be alone tonight. I don't want to be without you." He wished he'd kissed her when she'd come in, but there hadn't been a time that seemed right, and now she might leave without him even touching her.

"I could stay a while but only if I don't keep you from finishing your work. I didn't come to bother you."

"Make yourself at home. I've got a collection of books on the Southwest you might find interesting. You can read or rummage through my movies, though I doubt I've got much you'd like. Just knowing you're here relaxes me." He knew he was rattling, but he couldn't seem to stop. "Stay as long as you want, Emily. I promise I'll keep working." He thought of standing in front of the door and blocking her way out, but more than he wanted her near, he wanted her to stay because she wanted to.

Though he moved over to his work spread out on the dining table, he was very much aware of where she was, what she was doing. She took off her coat and set about cleaning up the kitchen. Because she didn't want to keep asking where things belonged, she simply opened cabinets until she found the right place. When she finished there, she went into his bedroom and he heard the bookcase cabinets creak as she opened them. He'd collected western novels set in Texas since he was in college and knew she'd find the old Louis L'Amour and Zane Grey early editions fascinating.

She was gone so long he decided she probably went through every drawer in his closet and he didn't care. When she finally walked out of his bedroom, he looked up and felt like someone had shocked his heart.

Emily was wearing his Hawaiian shirt and nothing else as far as he could see.

"I decided to sleep over and I guessed this would be the only shirt in your closet you wouldn't miss."

"You look great in that shirt," he said when he could draw enough breath. "Maybe I should buy a dozen. I'm almost finished here."

"Oh, okay. I think I'll go on to bed. Left or right?"

"What?"

"Which side do you sleep on?"

"Left."

"Well, good night."

After she disappeared, Tannon couldn't concentrate on work. He forced himself to wait fifteen minutes before going to his bathroom and pulling on an old pair of sweatpants he kept on the back of the door. They were faded, but they were the closest thing he had to pajamas.

When he slipped into bed, Emily was curled in the center sound asleep. He tugged away one of the pillows she was holding and pulled her against him. Kissing the top of her head he whispered, "Thanks for sleeping over." He couldn't hold back the rumble of a chuckle. If anyone in town knew what they were doing, the word *crazy* would probably come to mind. "Good night," he said as he closed his eyes and breathed her in as if she were the first fresh air he'd had in years.

She didn't answer, but the warmth of her breath brushed his cheek lulling him to sleep.

Even in sleep, he reached for her, needing to know she was close. Just before dawn, he woke as he always did. First light was just beginning to spread across the eastern horizon. His bedroom had blackout curtains, which he could pull to preserve their darkness, but he had to face the day.

For a while, he watched the town shift from night to day. He loved the way the first beams always seemed to catch the clock tower and the church steeples. At seven, all the streetlights stopped blinking yellow and began to work in earnest. Slowly, like a rumble of far away thunder nearing, cars and trucks moved below.

"Emily," he whispered, brushing his hand along her back, "wake up."

She raised her head and looked at him. As before, her hair had gone completely wild while she slept and he thought it adorable.

"You're beautiful in the morning," he said.

"Who are you and what are you doing in my bed?"

"It's my bed and I'm the same guy you slept with last week."

She let out a sigh. "I have to quit doing this. Now, who are you again?"

She acted like she couldn't place him, so he tried again. "I'm the man who plans to feed you breakfast if you can get dressed in fifteen minutes."

She rolled away from him and froze when she saw the floor-to-ceiling windows. "Are you sure the whole town can't see us?"

"I'm sure," he said as she ran to the bathroom and slammed the door behind her. "But," he added to no one, "I wouldn't give a damn if they could."

Fifteen minutes later, she was standing at the door ready to go. "I'm starving. I hope you meant that about buying me breakfast."

"I did. What time do you have to be at the library?"

"I open at nine, but I like to get there by a quarter till."

"Then we've got plenty of time." He took her hand and pulled her into the elevator. As the doors closed, he whispered, "Thanks for staying over." He bent and brushed her lips with his. "I love sleeping with you."

She smiled. "I feel the same. When I'm with

you, I'm always safe and warm, but you know, Tannon, people don't just go around sleeping together. We can't do this again."

"They don't?" He acted surprised. "We can't?"

"No. You know what I mean."

The elevator door opened and they rushed out. They were at the outside door before he stopped to ask, "Where are we going?"

"I don't know," she answered.

"I don't care. The diner is closed for remodeling. Every other place in town will be packed this time of morning."

"People will see us together," she whispered.

"Does it matter? People saw us out the other night together."

"I know, but eating breakfast seems somehow different." The shy Emily had returned.

He wanted to scream that he didn't care what people thought, but he forced himself to smile. "Where can I get coffee? I can't think without coffee."

"My house," she offered with a smile. "I'll cook you breakfast." She jumped in her car. "Last one there has to do dishes."

Tannon let her pull onto the street first and followed her to her place. When she disappeared into the underground parking, he circled the block and parked on the street. By the time he made it up to her place, she'd already pulled off her coat and had the coffee on.

They cooked breakfast together and ate at the little table by the windows. The space was so small his knees bumped hers as they ate, but he didn't complain.

As soon as she took her last bite, she stood. "I have to get to work."

She was halfway to the door, pulling on her coat as she ran when he caught up with her. "No," he said as he stopped her. "Kiss me good-bye before you go."

Laughing, she put her hands on the sides of his whiskery face and kissed him quickly on the mouth. "Good-bye and don't forget to do the dishes."

She was gone before he thought to react. If he had, he could have held her tightly and kissed her until she kissed him back. Really kissed him. He stood in her cluttered little apartment for a long time, letting one fact settle into his logical mind.

Tannon Parker was in love with Emily. He always had been and he always would be. There was not one thing he could do about it. The only problem was getting her to love him, not as a friend, but as a lover.

But would she allow herself to love him once she found out what he'd never told her or anyone else about the night she'd been hurt?

What if she turned away?

Could he let her go? Would he?

❧ *Chapter 37* ❧

Thursday

Rick Matheson walked out on the porch of Winter's Inn. The morning was gray, with huge boiling clouds hanging so low he felt like he could throw a rock and hit one.

For the first time since he'd fallen through the steps almost three weeks ago, he felt whole. The wounds were healing, but it was more than that. Maybe because of the threat on his life, he'd known fear for the first time. Real fear. Not just for himself but for someone else as well. He and Trace could have been killed when the car blazed into the diner. She'd been laughing and for once not watching every movement. He'd seen the car coming and reacted, not with his brain but with his gut. Somehow that one second he'd lived through had made him stronger. He'd discovered some-thing inside himself. A warrior, maybe. Or maybe a bit of the pioneer blood that made his great-great-grandparents leave settled lives and come to Texas where they had to fight to survive.

"You shouldn't be out here in the open," Trace said from just behind him.

"I was thinking about how every time I think this guy has given up on stalking me, something happens. I've checked my files and gone through every memory since birth and I still can't come up with one reason why someone wants to kill me."

"Me neither." He heard the frustration in her tone. "You're a nice guy, Matheson."

"That's the first compliment you've ever given me. I'm touched."

"Don't be. Things would be so much simpler if you'd cheated a man or ruined his life or stole his girlfriend. Then, at least, we'd have a suspect."

Rick leaned against the railing like he always did. He liked being half in the shadow of the porch and half in the day. "If we had a suspect, you could go back home or ride off on your bike and forget about this town."

"I'll never forget this place. There's an odd kind of peace here. I can see why people live in small towns."

"What about me, Marshal? Will you remember me?"

"You saved my life. That's the second time lately that I've come a breath away from death. I'm starting to think my number's up."

"Oh, great. You think the Grim Reaper's trailing you, so you come hang out with the Matheson most likely to die in this town."

"Sounded logical at the time, but now I see your point."

He studied her while she watched the world

beyond the porch, and he couldn't help but wonder if she ever relaxed. "If I make it through this and come up to Chicago sometime, is there a chance you might go out with me, like on a date?"

Trace shook her head. "Don't complicate this, Matheson. You're not my type. Nice guys never have been."

Her gaze met his for the first time. He saw it in her eyes. She was lying. For a second, he thought she might move toward him, but she stiffened. Maybe what he'd gone through the past few weeks made him reckless, but he spoke his mind. "When this is over, Trace, I'm climbing the stairs. We can climb on the roof or in bed, but for a few hours we're going to be together, just me and you."

She shook her head. "When this is over, I'll be gone. I don't do roots or relationships. Never have. In my line of work, it doesn't pay."

Before he could answer, his cell rang. "What's up, Alex?"

After listening for a minute, he turned off the phone and said, "The sheriff wants to meet us at the library. Says she's got something interesting to show us. It better be important if we're missing one of Mrs. Biggs's breakfast."

Trace reached inside for her coat. "I'll tell Mrs. Biggs to keep it warm and maybe we can eat it tonight."

"There won't be anything to keep warm. Border and Beau will have finished it off."

Ten minutes later they were all in the children's section of the Harmony County Library looking at a children's book.

"It appears," Alex said as she pointed, "all the words were cut from this one book. Whoever did it shoved the book to the back of the shelf and must have thought that no one would find it. But one of the volunteers was checking it out yesterday and noticed one of the pages sticking out. Emily thought it was just a prank until she heard about the note you got. She called me."

"Anyone could have done it." Emily looked over the desk at the book. Tears were in her eyes. "Not anyone," she corrected herself. "A monster. Who else would cut up a children's book? This wasn't a page a child accidentally tore. This was done on purpose."

"Do you keep a record of who comes in here? I don't think we'd have to go back more than a few weeks." Alex waited.

Emily shook her head. "We do a count, but we don't take names."

Trace's voice was cold and matter-of-fact as she said, "Did Beau Yates come in here within the past few weeks?"

"Yes," Emily answered as if she were on the stand and being forced to testify.

"Why Beau?" Alex snapped, trying to follow some invisible thread Trace had tossed out.

"Because when we found the note on the car

yesterday morning, Beau Yates and Border Biggs were with us. Both saw Rick open the note. When I commented that I didn't know where to look for the next clue, he suggested looking for a cut-up children's book."

No one wanted to believe Beau could be involved. Rick told himself it had to be just a coincidence, but Beau had been in the bar the night he'd been stabbed with the darts and he could have easily slipped through the dried-up creek bed behind the office. It was almost a direct path from his duplex. Of course, the creek bed was the most direct path to half the old homes in the original part of town.

Sam had stopped sweeping the aisle a few feet away. He took advantage of their silence to add his two cents. "That Yates boy's got long hair. That's always a sign folks should be concerned. I've seen him circling by the library the past few days as if he's looking for something, or maybe he's just afraid someone would find that book. He don't work all day. There's no telling what kind of trouble he's getting into. No wonder everyone thought he kidnapped Ronny Logan. His type is always the kind who do strange things."

Emily opened her mouth to correct Sam, but Alex got words out first. "No one thinks Beau kidnapped Ronny. If you have facts, I'd love to hear them, Sam. If not, please keep your opinions to yourself."

Sam huffed and moved on. Rick had the feeling that women sheriffs ranked right down there next to long-haired men.

Alex asked Emily to make a list of every person who walked into the library that she could remember. She also wanted to check every name who checked out a book. Whoever did this had to have time to cut the letters out, then put the book back on the shelf. With someone always at the front desk, it wouldn't have been an easy chore. Even Darla, the children's librarian, would need to be questioned again just in case she saw something, anything that might help.

She doubted the stalker had checked out the book or even hung around the children's section. More than likely, he walked by and picked up the book, then moved to another part of the library. There were corners and boxed windows where anyone could disappear for a while.

Rick walked up the stairs and stood in the little alcove where the writers met. The realization that he could have been in the library at the same time as the person trying to kill him bothered him. It had taken him a long time but Rick was finally mad. No, not mad, furious.

In a few days, Martha Q would be back and his job of watching over Winter's Inn would be over. Trace would probably leave. After all, she'd reminded him this morning that she wasn't attracted to nice guys. But she was attracted to him, he thought—he'd seen it in her eyes, and the one time he'd kissed her, she'd taken her time pulling away.

Rick heard the janitor rattling his way up the stairs before he saw Sam appear in the doorway. He looked bothered to find Rick taking up space, but he set his broom down and asked, "Heard any word of Martha Q Patterson coming back to town?" He cleared his throat and added, "Some of the writers' group asked about her."

"She's due in tomorrow, I think."

Sam nodded like he didn't care one way or the other. "You gonna move out when she gets back?"

This was one of the times Rick wished he lived in a bigger town. Everyone, even the library janitor apparently, kept up with him.

"Yeah," he answered, wondering just where he would go.

Thanks to Martha Q's hundred dollars a day and the Peterses' long visit, he now had enough money to rent a decent apartment. His mother told him he could come home, but Rick knew that if he did she'd make it hard to leave. He knew her— she'd nail the way out shut, one good deed after another. She'd do his laundry, cook his favorite meals, change his sheets. Before long, he'd be forty and still living with his mother. By then, she'd be so old people would look at him as thoughtless and ungrateful if he moved out.

Rick noticed Trace standing just behind Sam. He hadn't seen her come up.

"You know, Matheson, I think you're taking advantage of Martha Q. It ain't right, you staying there free while she's gone and it sure ain't right if you stay once she gets back."

"Thanks for the judgment." Rick tried to keep his voice calm, but the old man was butting in where he didn't belong. "I'll be sure to keep that in mind."

"Rick." Trace made the old man jump. "We'd better get going."

He walked past Sam before he said something he'd regret.

Halfway down the stairs, Sam called, "I don't guess you'll be coming to the writers' group anymore since she's coming back."

"I'll be there," Rick answered without slowing. Until that moment he hadn't thought he'd come, but something about the old guy bothered him just enough to change his plans.

Trace dropped him off at his office and said she wanted to talk to Alex. He didn't ask about what. He needed to be alone. The cut-up note, the possibility that Beau was involved, the nosy janitor—all were winds making the storm of his bad mood worsen.

He was halfway up the front stairs to his office when George Hatcher came running out of the bookstore.

Rick wasn't up for another ghost theory. He thought of bolting up the steps before the chubby little man could stop him, but he didn't; after all, he was a nice guy. "Morning, George."

"Don't have time to talk. Got three customers. Just wanted to hand you these notes. I wrote down the names of folks who dropped by your office." He shoved several cards toward Rick and headed back to his store.

Rick carried them into his office and tossed them on his desk. As they scattered, he was relieved to see that no square envelope was among them.

After pulling his drapes open so he could see the town and locking his door, Rick gave the notes his full attention. Two were from people who wanted him to do their wills, one was from a man who wanted him to look over contracts, and one was from a woman who wanted to file divorce papers on a husband she hadn't seen in six months but who was still using her credit card. All had numbers and names on the back.

It wasn't exactly the legal-eagle kind of work he'd hoped for, but it was work. Rick smiled. It was also a way to step out of his problems for a while and climb into someone else's.

Trace called twice to check on him and promised to be back by noon. Whatever she and the sheriff were up to didn't include informing him. Which was fine. He was tired of talking about the stalker.

He called all his future clients back and set up times they could come in. It felt good to be working.

At about eleven o'clock, a woman dressed in what looked like scarves tapped on his door. She introduced herself as Mrs. Weatherbee and said she was a friend of George's downstairs.

Rick offered her a seat. "How can I help you, Mrs. Weatherbee?"

She smiled. "I'm not here to ask for help, Mr. Matheson. I'm here to offer it. I've seen your future."

"How much do I owe you, Mrs. Weatherbee?"

"But, sir, I haven't told you it yet."

Rick pulled out a ten. "It doesn't matter, just the fact that you saw one makes my day."

She giggled. "You're one of those 'fly by the seat of their pants' people who wants to turn the pages of life one at a time to see what happens."

"That's me."

The strange lady stood. "Then I'll leave you to your adventure."

❧ *Chapter 38* ❧

Thursday afternoon

Border Biggs had pulled his Harley into the front yard to work on it when the sun finally showed itself. Beau leaned against the window off Ronny's little kitchen and smiled. "Sun's out," he said to no one.

Ronny nodded as she cleaned her counter. Beau had always thought she was a pretty lady, but lately he swore she had a glow about her. If she'd been eight or ten years younger, she would have made him nervous, but somehow over the months she'd become a member of his new family. The knowledge that she had a secret that made her smile made Beau happy.

"Thanks for teaching me to make French toast. It wasn't near as hard as I thought it might be."

She smiled. "You're welcome. How about I teach you something new to cook every Thursday afternoon? It's my only early day off and I'm usually studying at night. I'll leave the post office about two, pick up whatever we need, and we can be cooking by three. That too early for you?" She laughed.

"I'll try to make it up by then." Beau moved

closer. "About the other night. It's none of my business but how'd—"

She stopped him. "I went for a ride with an old friend. Nothing else. When I got back and saw a cop parked out front, I figured my mother had done something crazy. I panicked and went to the office. I thought I'd just work an hour or two, but the fear of what I'd find back here kept me working." Ronny patted his hand. "I'm sorry, Beau, that she got you and Border involved."

"It didn't matter. Gave me some jailhouse experience I'll write a song about one day."

"You might get your chance to add another chapter," Border yelled through the open window. "Looks like the sheriff pulling up."

Beau watched the sheriff and Martha Q's niece he'd met at Winter's Inn climb out of the cruiser. Border already had his hands in the air, but they walked right past him.

"Beau," Alex called as her boots tapped across the porch. "You home?"

"I'm over here," he said as he opened Ronny's apartment door. "We're making French toast." It crossed his mind that he'd just said the dumbest thing anyone about to be arrested ever said. The only good news was that neither woman was pointing a gun at him.

"Could we talk to you in private?" the sheriff asked.

"I'm with friends," Beau said, forcing himself not to back away. "We can talk."

"Someone accused you of writing the note Rick Matheson found on his car," she said point-blank.

"Not again." Border puffed up like a bear.

To Beau's surprise, Alex smiled. "Calm down, Border. I know he didn't do it. How could he have when he was in my jail? Only why'd you guess the letters came from a picture book?"

Beau shrugged. "I don't know. The library was the only place my old man would let me go alone. I must have read every book in the children's section by the time I was ten."

"Fair enough. Makes sense. Now, do you know someone who hates you enough to try and pin what's happening to Rick Matheson on you?"

Beau shrugged. "No. Right now my dad hates me, but having a son play in a bar is not as bad as having one in jail."

"Maybe it's someone who hates our music," Border offered.

No one acted as if they were listening to him.

"Watch your back, Beau," the sheriff said. "Call me if anything strange happens."

Beau had the feeling she wasn't talking about midnight rides with a girl named Trouble.

❦ *Chapter 39* ❦

Friday morning

Tannon walked in the county sheriff's office and removed his hat. "I'd like to see Sheriff McAllen," he said to the first person he saw.

"I'm Deputy Phil Gentry, Mr. Parker, I've met you a few times at fund-raisers for the fire department. Thanks for supplying the beef for that last cookout. Your support went a long way to making us one of the best volunteer fire departments in the state."

When Tannon didn't say anything, the deputy continued, "Maybe I can help you. I'd be happy to if I can."

Tannon thanked the man with a handshake and said again that he'd like to see Sheriff Alex McAllen.

"This way." Gentry began walking toward the back of the building. "But you might want to call her Matheson now—she's been married a few years to Hank."

"Right." Tannon knew about Hank and Alex. The whole town did. For a month, the women at his office talked about the way they got married. With half the town kin planning a big wedding, they ran off to tie the knot. Word was some of Hank's aunts didn't speak to him for a year.

Alex stepped to her open door when she saw Tannon and the deputy coming. She offered her hand. "Tannon," she said with a smile. "Tannon Parker."

"Alex." He'd known her since she first ran for sheriff and walked in his office to ask if she could put up a sign. They spoke whenever they saw each other, and she'd worked a few wrecks over the years that his rigs had been involved in. Both had always been professional and friendly enough to be on a first-name basis. He hoped that paid off for him now.

He knew two facts about her that were important: She was honest and she didn't gossip.

The deputy walked off and Alex invited him in. "How may I be of service?" she asked, knowing that he wasn't a man who would just drop by to visit.

"I have a favor to ask. A big favor."

"All right." Her intelligent eyes studied him. "I'll do what I can to help."

Tannon shifted, knowing he was about to tell her something he'd never told anyone. "Fifteen years ago when I was in high school, I found Emily Tomlinson beat up in the parking lot by the stadium. She almost died from a random beating and never returned to school. I don't think she knows it was me who found her and held her until the ambulance came."

Alex leaned back in her chair. "I remember looking over that case once. They never found the boys who attacked her. Notes at the time suggested it might have been one of several groups of boys who attended the game and then got drunk in the parking lot. If I remember right, she could give very few details. First she was fighting for her life and later the doctors didn't think it would be good for her to try to make her relive the attack. The sheriff back then was good, but had his hands full with a murder trial that had been moved to Lubbock, and the deputies left here were running shorthanded."

Alex paused and took a deep breath. "You didn't have anything to do with that did you, Tannon? You didn't see anything that is not in the records?"

"I wasn't there when it happened, if that's what you're thinking, but it was my fault." Slowly Tannon began to tell her every detail. The end of the big game. The newspaper staff working late. A girl asking him questions and slowing him down when he went for his car. The run across blacktop to stadium parking.

"I remember hearing a few people standing around drinking after the game, but I didn't see anyone, not even one car I could ID. All I was thinking about at the time was Emily waiting on the front steps of the school a half mile away."

He was silent for a while before he told of hearing her wild, haunting cry. He'd parked on the last row and he'd found her between other parked cars and an old wire fence. He'd held her until the ambulance arrived, trying to keep her warm, trying to wipe away blood, trying to calm her, but she never heard him. She was beyond listening.

His words were choppy, but he got every detail out, including throwing his letter jacket in the trash on the walk home.

"Your statement wasn't in the file." It was more of a statement than a question.

"I didn't see anything that would help catch the guys, and that night while the EMTs were working on her, they barely noticed me. One of them kept yelling that she had to hang on until they got to the hospital. They didn't even ask me my name. I was sixteen. She was my best friend. I thought if I didn't talk about it I wouldn't think about it, but months passed before I could get the memory out of my head."

He looked down at his hands thinking about how he should have come forward. Even not knowing anything, maybe he could have helped. But then he'd have to tell some stranger how he'd seen Emily like that all hurt and beaten. Somehow by not talking he thought he'd given her some small amount of privacy. He'd been wrong.

"I thought it might have been you in the ambulance that night when I read the report." Alex stood and walked to the window.

"What?" He looked up, seeing only her outline against the sunshine.

"The report from one of the groundskeepers at the stadium said a kid found her and yelled for someone to call 911. The man also said he saw the kid holding someone, but he couldn't tell in the dark if it was a man or woman from where he stood. The groundskeeper couldn't give us any information about you because he said he didn't want to get involved with fights in the parking lot. Apparently some drunk minors were doing damage to the locker rooms and the groundskeeper saw that as his territory. At least he took the time to call 911."

"Why'd you think it was me?"

"I don't know. I'm a little older than you and Emily, but I remembered your mom and Emily's mom were always helping out with school dances and parties. I remembered seeing the two of you talking at the parties, and I guess I thought you were friends. In the 911 caller's statement, he said the kid holding her was crying."

"I don't remember that," Tannon finally answered. "But you're right, we were friends, we are still."

"I guessed so. I've seen the city council minutes. You're certainly a friend of the county library."

He waved his hand as if brushing her comment aside because it wasn't important here.

She nodded her agreement. "So, Tannon, why

are you here fifteen years after the attack, wanting to talk to me?"

"I'm not here to tell you anything. When it happened, I didn't see Emily again until years later when her parents were killed in a car wreck. I don't think she even noticed me at the funeral. Both my parents were in the hospital, so I only slipped away for a few minutes that day to make it to the gravesite." He straightened as if making up his mind. "When the attack on Emily happened, I ran. I tried to block it from my mind as if I could forget it, but that never worked."

When the sheriff simply waited, he finished, "I'm here to stop running. I'd like you to let me read the file. Every page. Every detail."

"That's highly irregular, Tannon. Why would you want to examine something you've been trying to put behind you for years?"

"Because Emily matters to me. She's always mattered to me."

The sheriff smiled. "You're falling in love with her."

"No." Tannon felt like he was being tortured. "I've never been out of love with her, but if I'm going to be the kind of man she needs, I have to know what she went through. I was there holding her. I saw it all that night, but I blocked out what happened afterward. I know she was in the hospital for a long time, that's all. I'm not sure it wouldn't break us both for her to have to talk about it, but I need to know and this seems the only other way."

Alex stood and walked to the file. "I'm probably breaking all kinds of laws, but I'll leave the file on my desk for a few minutes if you promise you'll never tell anyone, including Emily, that you saw it."

"No." Tannon stood as she pulled the file. "I want you to lock me in a cell for an hour with the file. There will be no running this time. Maybe she's put this behind her and I need to do the same. If she hasn't, I'll need an hour to know the nightmare completely so I'll know how to help her fight it."

She looked at him as if trying to understand why he'd ask such a thing. "It haunts you, doesn't it?"

"Not after today. When I walk out of that cell, what happened in the parking lot will be the past. I don't think I can move on with the future until I put this to rest."

"All right. We've got a back cell we use for juveniles when we're waiting for them to be picked up. I'll lock you in for an hour." She tucked the file under her arm and walked out of her office.

Tannon followed, knowing he was about to face his demons and praying he was strong enough to walk away leaving them behind.

He stepped into the cell and didn't turn around

when he heard the lock clank closed. After a few minutes, he heard the sheriff tell everyone to go to lunch, that she would man the office for the next hour. If anyone objected, Tannon didn't hear.

In the silence, he sat down at a steel table and slowly opened Emily's police file. One by one, he read each account. The EMTs who'd found her. The emergency room nurse. The night watchman at the school who claimed he'd been on break. Finally, Emily's statement. She hadn't seen them at first. She only remembered being hit in the head from behind. She thought there were three, maybe four. When her head cleared from the blow, it was too dark where they dragged her to see anything. She saw no faces. One boy was behind her, holding her mouth. Every time she made a sound, his grip tightened until she couldn't breathe. When she stopped trying to scream, he let go of her mouth and pinned her arms behind her. Another boy started slapping her, daring her to make a sound. When she finally did, he hit her so hard she saw stars. She fell to her knees and she thought she heard a laugh before a foot slammed into the side of her face.

"That will keep her quiet," a voice said.

Tannon forced himself to keep reading. She told how one was angry and kept calling her names as he hit her while two others pulled on her arms. She kept falling to her knees and they kept jerking her up by her long hair. They held her so she couldn't get away from the blows until she could no longer stand. She finally stopped struggling and crumbled. When she didn't move, one started trying to pull off her clothes. When she tried to roll into a ball, they kicked at her and held her arms in the dirt with their boots. Finally, she stopped fighting and they spread her out on the ground.

Tannon stopped. Stood. Walked to the toilet and threw up. He paced the small cell as if it were a cage. He didn't know if he could read more. Slamming his fist against the concrete wall, he held the roar of anger inside him. He had to face the rest. He had to finish. He had to be as brave as she had been.

By the time the sheriff walked back down the hallway to his cell, he was standing at the bars waiting. The file was folded on the steel table, looking as if it hadn't been touched.

"Are you ready, Tannon?"

"I'm ready," he said almost calmly as she unlocked the door.

They walked out side by side into the bay of desks. The sheriff didn't say a word until they were on the front steps. "Did you find what you were looking for?"

He nodded, not trusting words. He'd found what he'd needed to know, even though the pain of it would never leave. Yet somehow the truth was easier to deal with than not knowing.

They stood for a moment as if neither had any idea what to say. He was glad she didn't try to make him believe that the case would ever be closed. After fifteen years, there was little chance.

"Tannon," she finally said, "your hand is bleeding. You might want to head over to the hospital and have it checked."

He looked down. He hadn't even noticed that blood slowly dripped off his fingers. "I'll do that," he said, and turned to his truck.

He knew the sheriff knew what had happened when he'd been alone in the cell. He'd thank her later for not bothering him with questions. He'd fix his hand and—he almost swore this aloud — he'd fix the pain in his heart. He'd carried an open wound there for far too long.

❧ *Chapter 40* ❧

Friday evening

Emily was surprised when Tannon stormed into the library at a quarter to seven. Though tall, there was a grace about his movements. He was a man comfortable with his build and he might even be thought of as handsome if he ever smiled. She knew, without asking, that he could probably work on the huge trucks he owned as well as drive them. She wouldn't have been surprised if he climbed in the saddle from time to time to help load cattle.

"Evening," he said with a nod. "I thought I'd come early to cover any emergencies." Tannon glanced at Pamela Sue, then turned back to Emily with raised eyebrows.

She almost giggled. Pamela Sue had wrapped and sprayed her hair in a dozen ringlets with tiny ribbons braided into each. The shiny ribbon was far too stiff to curl into the ringlets, so as her hair relaxed its curl in the humid air, a spiky bristle of ribbons seemed to form.

"Does she get reception from that mess?" Tannon whispered.

Emily motioned for him to follow her to her office before he got them both in trouble.

As soon as they were behind a closed door, Emily laughed even as she scolded. "Now, don't pick on my volunteer; you already frighten her. She told me so."

"Me frighten her?" Tannon moved almost nose to nose with Emily and did his best to whisper, but he wasn't a man in the habit of lowering his voice. "That lady scares me to death. Last time you left me downstairs with her, she told me she knew how to make handcuffs out of yarn." He pressed against Emily, feeling her laughter against his chest. "I wouldn't be surprised to find human bones in her basement. Now and then I swear she clicks her needles together just to irritate me."

"She does not." Emily smiled up at him, happy to see him relaxed and happy for a change. There was something different in his eyes, almost as if he'd weathered a storm and was enjoying letting his heart slow to normal.

"She does too." He grinned. "Even asked if I'd try on one of the torture sweaters for size. Until I met her, I never dreamed S&M would have knitting groups."

Looping her arm over his shoulder, she closed the few inches between them and touched her lips to his. He took her advance without complaint. This was the first time she'd been so bold and she felt great knowing that Tannon would welcome her boldness.

"Be nice while I'm at the meeting," she whispered, loving the warmth of his mouth barely touching hers. "Try your best not to run her off."

His hand moved across her back, pulling her gently to him and she knew the knitter on the other side of the door was no longer in his thoughts. "Let me hold you, really hold you for a minute, Emily." He pressed his lips against her hair and breathed deeply, taking her not only into his lungs but into his heart as well.

"Kiss me again like you just did. That was the best moment of my day." He could have lowered his mouth to her, but he waited for her.

Standing on her toes, she kissed him again.

She'd meant to give him another light touch, but he wanted more. The kiss turned tender. He had a way of making her feel like kissing him was the most important thing he had to do in his life. He made her feel special, cherished. His strong arms wrapped around her cocooning her in warmth.

When she finally pushed him away, they were both smiling.

"I'll see you at nine," she promised. "And I'll be hungry, so I hope you brought money."

He put his hand up to block the door as he moved in for one last light kiss against her throat. "I'm hungry right now."

His mouth had almost reached hers when Emily saw the bandage across his hand and stepped out of his reach. "Tannon, you're hurt. What happened?"

"Nothing," he whispered too fast for it to be true. "Just a scrape. Doc said no bones were broken and it wasn't that many stitches."

This time it was he who opened the door. "You'd better get up to the meeting. I didn't mean to make you late." His words were kind, but he'd lost the gentle smile.

"But—"

"Emily, it's nothing. I just scraped my hand on a piece of concrete. Stop worrying about me." His last words sounded more like an order than a request. A hardness had returned. The boss was back, she thought, and the gentle man she'd always loved had been shoved aside.

He was almost pushing her out into the main library. It was time to make a stand. She wanted her Tannon back, not the cold man everyone thought him to be. "I will not stop. Someone needs to worry about you. When the meeting is over, I want to have a look at that hand and make sure it's not bleeding."

She saw anger fire in his eyes and added, "In fact, I plan to check it several times during the night to make sure—"

All the anger melted. "You're sleeping over again?"

She gave a shrug. She knew she'd made it plain that she didn't think it was what normal people did who were just friends, but somehow they were shifting. "I think I should, considering your condition," she answered, not ready to admit the direction they both knew they were heading.

A slow grin spread over his face. "Absolutely."

She ran up the stairs, suddenly in a hurry for the meeting to be over. Emily had no idea where she was going in this relationship, but she was having more fun than she ever dreamed. Funny how days run on forever the same, and then one day it isn't the same old day and you're not sure what moment the world changed, you just know it did. Tannon was slowly becoming more than a friend, and once she'd seen behind the armor, she'd found the boy she'd always cared about inside the man.

All the writers were assembled by the time she made it upstairs.

Peter stood in the center of the alcove, waiting to go first.

The strange alien girl, Lily Anne Loving, was dressed in what looked like her pajamas. Fuzzy slippers completed her outfit. She tapped her fingernails on pages on her lap as if she were listening to a concert.

Zack, wearing what looked like the same clothes he'd worn every meeting, was eating a cookie while he talked to George about all he'd found on the Internet. Apparently ghosts were never serial killers. They might have the first, right here in Harmony.

Emily smiled. All was right with the world, she thought as she took her seat.

Rick Matheson and his silent friend were missing, but Martha Q Patterson came rushing in as though she'd planned an entrance. Her face looked a little puffy, but everyone greeted her warmly and tried not to stare.

"I'm sorry I'm late," she said dusting off her chair with her scarf, "but I've been keeping up with everyone and can hardly wait to begin. I've solved my writer's block and am ready to read." She pulled out papers from her huge bag. "When it's my turn, of course."

Emily, like all the others, looked the dear woman up and down trying to figure out where she'd had plastic surgery. When Martha Q sat down very gingerly, Emily knew what her first guess would be.

At exactly five minutes after seven, Emily started the meeting.

Peter read his poem, explaining how brilliant it was before and after the reading. Everyone agreed with him.

Geraldine read the next chapter of her romance set in Washington, D.C. Her heroine had turned in the spy she'd slept with in the last chapter and watched him shot at midnight by a firing squad on the mall. Then, in her grief and shame, she slept with two privates she'd met on the way home from the execution. One to soothe her grief and the other her shame. Neither helped, so she decided she'd have to leave the capital and go back to her plantation. She traveled across the Mason–Dixon line, handing out her cards to any man in uniform she met. When she crossed from the North to the South, both checkpoints searched her completely. The sergeant on the Southern side was too rough so she hit him with her umbrella and demanded he do it over again more gently. Of course, as men do, he asked to marry her and she, of course, turned him down.

When Geraldine finished, Zack said her character gave "supporting the troops" a whole new meaning. He then mentioned that he'd served in the National Guard for six years, and if she needed any research help, he was available.

Only Martha Q had the nerve to giggle.

George Hatcher said he was losing interest in the story and maybe she should come by his bookstore and pick up a few books on the post–Civil War period. He also commented that he doubted women of that era were quite as frisky. Taking all those clothes off and putting them back on must have been exhausting.

Everyone else said the story was moving along fine and a change of location would probably work as a new twist in the plot.

Simon, the shy closet writer whom George had brought in last week, read the opening of his suspense novel about door-to-door salesmen who were zombies. Peter thought the plot was a little far-fetched, but Lily Anne Loving swore she'd once seen an Avon lady who was a zombie. She explained that that was why, now and then, you see one who has on way too much makeup. They have to get color into their pale faces somehow.

The group took a break and Emily went downstairs to check on the library. Pamela Sue was at the desk fighting with a knot in her yarn. Tannon stood by the door, talking with Rick Matheson. Sam leaned on his broom a few feet away, listening in.

"Joining our group again, Rick?" she asked as she moved close to Tannon's side.

"Nope. Martha Q can handle it from here."

"Where you moving to now that your job is over at the B&B?" Tannon asked.

"I don't know. I'm looking for a place, but Martha Q offered me a room for as long as I want to stay."

Everyone heard Sam mumbling as he almost brushed the broom over their shoes.

Emily fought down a laugh. "If I didn't know better, I'd think he's sweet on her," she whispered when Sam had moved several feet away.

"I'd better watch my back," Rick added. "I could get swept away. Only, I doubt your theory, Miss Tomlinson. Mrs. Biggs says he comes over now and then to fix stuff for the B&B, and all he does is complain that the old place is too much for Martha Q. When he helped with replacing the window glass last week, he told Mrs. Biggs she shouldn't let Trace and me stay at the place with Martha Q gone."

"Speaking of that, where's your shadow?"

Rick looked around. "I don't know. She was here a minute ago. Might check the roof."

Emily laughed, but she had the feeling Rick wasn't kidding.

They talked on for a few minutes. Tannon let his left hand brush hers a few times, letting her know he was near. He must want to touch her as dearly as she wanted to touch him. After all these years, they couldn't seem to be close enough to each other.

When Emily hurried back to the group, her cheeks were red. As she'd turned toward the stairs, Tannon had let his fingers brush across her back. It was only a light touch no one could have noticed, but Emily knew it was a promise, a whispered *later*.

She stepped to the center of the circle and called the group back to order. "Lily Anne Loving, would you like to read next?"

The girl's skin was so white it was almost transparent. She stood slowly, wide-eyed and frightened. Her "yes" was so low that everyone leaned forward to listen.

She began her story slowly, almost hesitantly. Her words circled the small area as if haunting the room before settling not in the listeners' ears but in the dark corners of their minds. She wrote of a stormy night in Las Vegas, New Mexico. An old hotel draped in cobwebs and neglect. She described a rainy midnight where the wind howled like an animal in pain and a fortune-teller wearing black lace sat in the shabby lobby.

"Your future for a dollar," the old Gypsy *whispered as every guest passed. "Your future for a pound."*

No one spoke to the old woman. A few didn't even seem to see her as they rushed out of the rain and up to the front desk in search of a room for the night.

One young mother, weighed down with a sleeping child and bags, slowed, glancing at the strange cards on the table as she followed her husband.

The old woman looked up and whispered, "I'll read yours for free if I can feel the beat of your heart, little mother. It's been a long time since I've felt that rhythm."

The young mother clutched her baby closer as she felt as if she were being pulled toward the table. Pulled by a hook deep in her chest. She swore she could hear the urgent click of a blade being sharpened.

Lily Anne stopped reading and lowered her head as she dropped the hand that held her story.

Everyone in the room told her to go on as they waited on the edge of their chairs.

"That's all I've written so far. I only had an hour today to work on it."

"Well, it scared me plumb to death already," Geraldine announced. "If you'd written more, I'd be the one having a heart attack and not that poor young mother. That old witch is trying to steal her heart. I've heard stories about those who try such things."

"What makes you think that's what would happen?" George shouted. "Maybe she's a serial killer and she keeps the heart as her trophy."

"I'm sure I've heard of such a thing in Greek mythology," Peter chimed in, as if he were the voice of reason in the box of nuts.

Emily watched the room explode. Everyone was talking at once, even Simon. She looked at the landing and saw Tannon rushing up the stairs.

When he saw her, he asked simply, "Riot?"

She nodded and, to her surprise, he turned and went back down. Obviously, a riot was something he thought she could handle.

When the world of writing finally settled, Martha Q began her story about a widow who owned a bed-and-breakfast. Most of it was a description of the house and the still-beautiful innkeeper who solved the problems of everyone in town.

The group was kind and encouraging, except for Zack, who fell asleep during the reading. As always, each person had suggestions for the plot and no two ran in the same direction.

The group was still talking and arguing when they left. Apparently taking over someone's story wasn't off-limits.

Emily cleaned up, put the chairs back in order, and went downstairs.

Pamela Sue had already left, but Tannon was waiting for Emily when she rushed down the stairs.

He looked out of place behind the desk and she

wondered if he threatened anyone who dared check out a book.

"Let's go home," she said as she neared. "I've had all the zombies and witches I can handle for one night."

"Sounds perfect. I've got supper already cooked and the heater turned up at my place. The temperature's been dropping since dark, so I thought you might like to stay in tonight and eat."

He followed her out, locked the door, and pulled her close to him as they ran for her car. Once she was settled in, he closed her door and crossed to his truck.

On the short drive to his office building, she thought of how quickly they'd become comfortable with one another and how good it felt to have a close friend. She had the feeling that, like her, he rarely let people close. He'd built a shell and she'd hidden away in her books. They both knew hundreds of people and called many "friend"—but not the kind of friends they were and always had been to each other.

The bridge between them had shattered once. Emily blamed the accident at first, thinking it must have been hard for him too. He might have even thought that it was his fault. Later, in college, she went in one direction and he in another. She guessed he thought of her as often as she thought of him, almost like a family member who'd moved far away. There had been a hundred times she'd almost called him. She wanted to ask where he'd been that night, why he had never visited her in the hospital. Later, in college, she'd just wanted to talk, but the bridge had fallen from their own neglect.

As she parked beside him in front of his office building, she wished they hadn't waited so many years. For years they'd been within a few blocks of one another and hadn't connected.

He opened her car door and took her hand with his left as they ran for the elevator. It was after nine, and the building looked abandoned without lights or people.

Emily laughed, thinking the memory of Lily Anne's story was coloring her view of the night.

She found supper waiting. Ham, coleslaw, potato salad, and cherry pie. All looking very much like they'd been picked up at the deli counter in the grocery store. She warmed by the fireplace as he set everything on the table. He'd shoved his work to one side and put out place mats that looked new and napkins made from folded paper towels.

"Ready," he said, and motioned her into the dining area.

"It's wonderful," she said, almost laughing at how proud he was of himself.

He held her chair for her. They were halfway through the meal when she said, "Want to tell me about how you hurt your hand?"

"No," he said. "It was just an accident. I hit a wall."

She knew there was more to the story because he didn't meet her eyes when he told her. "Accidents happen," she said, letting him off the hook.

"Accidents happen," he echoed, and then changed the subject to the writing group.

When they finished cleaning up, she put on his Hawaiian shirt and sat cross-legged on the bed while he let her change the bandage. The hand was swollen and the skin broken around the knuckles. He didn't say a word or make a sound as she pulled away the bloody gauze where the doctor had stitched up a few places. His fingers were bruised and scabbed. Without much thought, she leaned down and kissed the injury, wishing one kiss could make things better the way it always had for her when she'd been little.

She felt, more than saw, his body stiffen, but he didn't pull away.

It was almost eleven by the time he went into the bathroom to change. Emily curled up on the pillows and watched the lights of the town beyond the windows. Part of her wondered how it could feel so right to be here with him. She'd known girls in college who'd sleep over at different boys' rooms every night on the weekends, but she never had. She'd tried going out a few times to meet guys, but she was always the one who didn't get picked up and had to drive the car home. Or, with boys in class, they seemed to want to study together and weren't all that attracted to her. They'd call her names like buddy and pal, as if she were just one of the guys.

Not that she'd truly wanted to stay with any one of them. It had never felt like the right time.

With Tannon, it was different. She knew he was attracted to her. He'd insisted they kiss good night. Emily doubted men did that who weren't attracted, but he was never pushy. Maybe he was happy with the way it was now. They couldn't go on sleeping over at each other's houses, but for now, it seemed right. More than friends, less than lovers.

When he came to bed, she pretended to be asleep. He tugged her to him and pulled the covers over her shoulder.

After several minutes, she whispered, "You asleep?"

"No," he admitted.

"Good." She rolled closer. Her mouth brushed his before her one word was out. The kiss wasn't a good-night kiss. If she was going to kiss him, really kiss him, she didn't want to make a half-hearted effort. If they were truly more than friends it was time they set a few new rules.

For a moment, he didn't react to her advance, but then his hand plowed into her hair and pulled her close against him.

She opened her mouth and deepened the kiss as her hand brushed lightly over the bare skin of his shoulder, needing the feel of him.

After a few seconds, he jerked away so fast Emily let out a little cry.

"Do you mean this?" He studied her in the soft light from the streets below. "Do you want me to kiss you like that? Because what you just did was a hell of a lot more than a friendly good-night kiss."

"I'm the one who started it, so of course I mean it, but if it's too much for you, I'll understand." She giggled, knowing that she'd surprised him with her advance almost as much as she'd surprised herself. "You told me once that you wanted me to kiss you back and I thought now might be a good time to start."

"Start what?" He rolled above her, pressing his chest over hers. "I think I can handle whatever you want, only you have to tell me where the line is."

She felt like a child being asked what she wanted for Christmas and knowing there was no limit. "How about a few long, slow kisses to start and we'll feel our way from there." She moved her hand from his shoulder to his chest laughing at the way his hair tickled against her fingers. "I kind of missed out on that time when couples spend hours just kissing. By the time I started dating in college people were skipping the kissing part and just asking 'your place or mine.' I'd kind of like one of those 'curl my toes' kind of kisses girls used to talk about in high school. You think we could go back that far and play around with it for a while?"

He smiled down at her. "You do know the kissing comes with touching?"

She nodded. "I believe I've already started that addition. I wouldn't want to leave anything out so, if you don't mind—"

There was no more time or need for words. He lifted her, blanket and all, off the bed and headed toward the living room.

"What are you doing?" she squealed.

"If we're going parking, we'd better do it on the couch. I don't trust you in bed."

When she giggled, he added, "You're already ahead of me on the touching part, but I'll catch up."

He sat down with her in his lap and began kissing her with a warmth and passion she'd never known. All their clothes remained on, but when he finally carried her back to bed she knew she'd been kissed and touched and held lovingly just as she'd always dreamed of.

"If we're going no farther tonight, honey, we'd better go to sleep."

She was too relaxed and too tired to do anything but moan her agreement.

"You all right, Emily?" he whispered as he

kissed just below her ear when she cuddled closer.

"Yes," she mumbled. "I was just wondering how good I'd feel if you'd had two hands to work with."

He laughed and pulled her back against him. "Hang around and you'll find out."

She breathed in the smell of him and the warmth of him. "I plan to do that."

The soft sound of his slow breathing was her only answer.

❧ *Chapter 41* ❧

Saturday night

Rick pulled on his best jacket and stepped out of the downstairs bedroom of Winter's Inn. Martha Q and Trace had been chatting in the drawing room for an hour as if they really were related. He'd listened to them while he'd dressed. Martha Q was all about the writers' group and Trace's questions about each member just egged her on. What Martha Q didn't know for fact, she pulled from fiction, making each member of the group far more interesting than they probably were. She even included the librarian and the janitor in her tale, claiming Emily was probably frigid after being attacked in high school. She didn't know the details, no one really did, but Martha Q was sure it was terrible.

As for Sam the janitor, he'd been in love with Martha Q, according to Martha Q, most of his life. "Of course," she explained, "half the men in Harmony were in love with me at one time or another. I teased some, married some, and ignored some, but I never used a man."

She glanced up as Rick walked into the room and giggled when he winked at her.

"Don't you look nice." Martha Q whistled. "You've put on some weight, boy, and you look good enough to eat. If I were ten years younger, I'd give you a whirl. There's nothing that looks finer than a tall man in jeans and a starched shirt."

Rick laughed, thinking if she was ten years younger she'd still be old enough to be his mother. "Thanks," he managed. "I thought I'd go over to Buffalo's and have a drink." It was the only place he was sure that the man stalking him had been.

Trace stood slowly as if debating with herself whether to argue or give in. "That's not a good idea," she finally said in a tone that hinted his plan might be the worst idea ever.

Her eyes challenged him, but it would take more than a look to stop him. "I'm through with hiding, waiting for some guy to come find me. I'm going hunting for him."

"You're using yourself as bait." He had no doubt Trace Adams would handcuff him to the house if she thought she could get away with it, but unless she pulled a gun, he planned to walk out the door.

"I'm going," he said simply. "Would one of you ladies like to join me?"

Martha Q laughed. "My lord, boy, it's after ten. I haven't gone out that late in years."

"Marshal?" he said, knowing she'd consider it part of her job to go along. They'd looked for a safe apartment for him today, and she'd probably talked to Alex about watching out for him after she left. He could feel her leaving, even though she hadn't packed her bag. Her vacation was up. She had no reason to stay except because of his problem, and he had a feeling no one but a Matheson would consider it worth a U.S. Marshal's time to babysit him.

"Give me five," she said, heading up the stairs. "If you're going to get yourself killed, I might as well go along to arrest the son-of-a-bitch who murders you."

Martha Q waited for the footsteps to reach the top of the stairs before she said, "The girl's crazy about you."

"Yeah, I can tell."

Martha Q leaned toward him. "That woman drinks adrenaline for breakfast. She lives on excitement. Give her passion, wild and full-out, or walk away. Some women you got to court with words and flowers; others, you got to show them what you want." Martha Q leaned back, crossed her arms over her round little body and added, "Don't give her time to think. Just act."

"Thanks for the advice, but her type isn't going to fall for a small-town lawyer. She's big city, drug busts and gang wars. She wouldn't have stayed around for as long as she has if someone wasn't trying to kill me, and I can't draw that out forever. Eventually the stalker will get bored or he'll get me. Either way, I don't see me ending up with her."

"What you don't know about women would fill the Palo Duro canyon to the brim. Men don't always have to give a woman what she wants; they need to give her what she needs. If you take the time to know her, really know her, you'll find the one thing she needs more than anything else."

"That's just it. We're out of time."

He heard footsteps tumbling down the stairs and knew that his time was up in more ways than one.

Trace walked past him, opened the door and said simply, "Let's get this over with, Matheson."

Martha Q stood on the porch and waved them good-bye like they were kids on a first date.

They were halfway to the bar when Trace said, "You're an idiot."

"I've heard that before. Why don't you get a new line?"

"Why don't you get a brain? After putting up with that stubborn streak of yours, I'm surprised more than one person isn't trying to kill you."

Rick pulled into the packed parking lot. "Don't act like you care, Marshal." He pulled into an illegal spot and climbed out of the car. He was around to her side before she opened her door.

"I do care," she said as she stood inches away. "Your idiotic behavior is starting to rub off on me, I guess."

He had the feeling she wanted to say more, maybe even something nice, but they were both mad, and for the life of him he couldn't think what had started this argument. Without warning, he reached for her. He pushed her a few inches until her back bumped against the car and then he leaned into her, full body, full contact. "Kiss me," he ordered. "If you're right and I'm going to die tonight, I want the taste of you with me when I fall."

The kiss was hard and primal. Nothing like he'd ever kissed a woman before. His hands held her shoulders as he leaned her head back and opened his mouth against hers. When she dug her fingers in his hair and took his advance with a hunger of her own, his knees almost buckled. Without breaking the kiss, he shoved her leather jacket aside and felt of her body in long possessive strokes. He wanted her like he'd never wanted any woman or any thing in his life. The leather, the gun, the anger didn't matter. He wanted Trace. He broke the kiss and moved to her throat, tasting his way down her neck as he unbuttoned her shirt. As his hand spread over her skin, he returned to her mouth for a kiss that was almost violent with need.

Far in the back of his brain, he prepared for the kick or punch she'd deliver at any moment to stop him, but it never came. She didn't go soft and loving in his arms, but her hunger matched his and he felt her fingers clawing their way down his back as she moved against him.

A group of drunks walked by in the shadows yelling things like "Get a room." Rick sobered enough to pull his mouth away slowly and allow himself to breathe. Trace remained against him as she gulped for air. The world settled.

"I'm not apologizing," he whispered against her hair.

"I'm not asking you to," she answered. "I've never felt like—" She didn't finish.

He pushed his forehead against hers and laughed. "I know, me neither."

He held her for a while, feeling her body breathe against his, feeling her hands lightly move over him as if she were learning the feel of him. There were no words. No words either could say for what had happened. But they'd both felt it. They both felt it still. This strong beautiful woman was rocking his world and somehow he'd managed to do the same to hers. At some point they'd have to talk about it, but right now they both just wanted to feel pure passion settling, waiting until the time would be right to fire again.

"Come on," he finally said, taking her hand. "I'll buy you a drink."

For once, she didn't argue, but she turned loose of his hand as they neared the bar, and he knew without looking that she was touching her weapon, making sure all was in place and ready. He could have changed his mind and gone back to the bed-and-breakfast, but right now nowhere was safe.

❧ *Chapter 42* ❧

Beau watched the crowd as he played. As always, he looked for his mystery girl, hoping she'd drop by, hoping she'd be waiting when he finished for the night. Once in a while, he thought of what he should talk to her about. Maybe if she came by this week he could tell her about almost being arrested. He could tell her his dream.

As he ended one song and started another, he knew he wouldn't tell her anything. Just like, if he were honest with himself, he didn't want to know all the facts about her. If they talked, he might discover she wasn't as bright as he thought she was or as funny or even as sexy.

He wanted to see her parked in that great old

car out in the back parking lot after midnight tonight. If she wasn't there, she would be in his dreams. He was dying to hit the blacktop on back roads that had never known a stripe other than moon-beams. He wanted to lean back and feel the wind in his hair and the warmth of her next to him. He wanted to reach over and hold her breast, knowing that it would make her smile.

A song began to form in his head about dodging reality and chasing the dream. Words drifted through his mind about how sometimes the dreams he had when he was alone became more real than life and how he'd slipped between one world and another until he didn't know which was which.

He knew that regardless of whether she showed up tonight, he wouldn't sleep. The girl or the song would fill his mind till dawn.

Border leaned in his line of vision and pointed with his head toward the back booth nearest the cage Harley called the stage.

Beau watched a couple sit down. It took a few turns of the lights for him to see who they were.

He couldn't believe Miss Tomlinson, the librarian, had come to listen to him play. Over the years, they'd become friends. She always asked how he was doing. When he was about fourteen, he'd told her that he was playing the guitar. Now and then she'd order a book about country music for the library and hand it to him first. Until he left home, she'd been the only person who'd encouraged him. Though she'd only said a few words now and then, her caring mattered to him.

And now she was sitting in the booth nearest to the band. Some guy Beau had never seen was at her side. He was big, in a strong, powerful kind of way. Big enough to take care of Emily Tomlinson if anyone bothered her in a place like this. Beau figured if someone even tried, he'd come out of the cage to help if necessary.

Another couple walked in and took the seat on the other side of the booth. Beau smiled, suddenly impressed with the crowd. His lawyer had come to hear him and he'd brought that good-looking biker chick Border drooled over every time he saw her.

Beau straightened. Maybe Rick Matheson had only been his lawyer for about a minute, but he'd come to offer help and that mattered. He was classing the place up tonight. In a few years, they'd pay a hundred bucks a ticket to see him on a real stage.

He motioned for Border to take a ride as Beau began to play guitar for the crowd. Border set his bass down and just listened. A yell went up, and then everyone settled down knowing they were listening to a master perform. Even the drunks at the bar stilled. No one moved, except Harley, who continued to make drinks, because the minute Beau stopped playing the orders would come in.

When he finished, a roar shook the rafters and

Beau smiled at one table, letting them know that he'd played just for them. Miss Tomlinson was smiling as she clapped and Rick stood up to shout with the others.

"Way to go," Border whispered.

In the stillness between the applause and Beau striking another chord, one shot rang out across the dance floor.

Then there was silence for a fraction of a second while everyone in the room sucked in air at the same time.

The second shot was almost drowned out by the noise as it registered on the crowd that a gun had just been fired. Even Beau knew what gunfire sounded like, but he hesitated, not knowing what to do.

Border pushed him to the floor of the cage. Beau saw Trace Adams fly out of the booth and push Rick backward. He also saw the man with the librarian swing her under his wing like some giant bird of prey.

Another shot pinged off the tin ceiling.

For one heartbeat, all was silent once more, and then people started screaming and running. Beau pulled the plug to the stage lights, and the cage went dark. He and Border lay flat as they watched the place go crazy.

"This is what I call excitement," Border yelled. "If we don't get shot, that is. I've never been in a gunfight."

"We're not in it, we're witnesses." Beau figured for once the corner was probably the safest place to be. With the lights out, no one in the room could see them.

"What? We're witnesses?" Border swore. "You know what they do with witnesses. If the bad guys win, we're dead."

"I don't see anybody shooting and the only one with a gun is Harley standing on the bar."

Border turned his head and yelled, "Harley, get off the bar. What do you think you are, a target?"

"Shut up, Border," Harley yelled over all the noise. "You boys stay down. Nobody fires a gun in my place. I won't stand for it." He raised his voice and his shotgun. "Come on out, you bastard, so I can shoot you. You want to hear gunfire? Well, it'll be the last thing you hear."

Beau looked over at the booth. Rick was still standing, and the woman in leather had pulled a gun and looked like she was on guard. The man with Emily Tomlinson was still covering her with his arm, but blood was spreading out over the sleeve of his shirt just below the elbow. Everyone else in the room seemed to be running around in circles, screaming. Boots on the wooden dance floor sounded like a hundred head of cattle crossing.

About the time the crowd cleared, the sheriff and two deputies came in, guns drawn.

"Man," Border whispered. "This is the OK

Corral. But where are the bad guys?" Whoever had done the shooting must have rushed out with the crowd.

The noise from before made the sudden silence seem deafening. Beau watched as Harley stood, his shotgun on ready as the sheriff and her deputies spread out. They found a woman under one of the tables. She kept crying as she hurried out saying she had to come back for her new purse. One of the deputies woke a drunk up and told him it was closing time. He'd missed the excitement completely.

"All clear here," one deputy yelled from the hallway leading to the bathrooms.

"All clear here," echoed the other from the kitchen entrance.

"Flip on all the lights, Harley," the sheriff ordered.

To Beau's shock, real light that didn't twinkle, blink, or rotate came on. He'd always thought the place was a dump, but in the bright light it was worse. Stains from who knew what on the walls. Rips in the booth padding. Dead flies along the back ledges. Walls he'd thought were painted tan now showed themselves as raw boards that must have been nailed together by drunks.

Beau stood, forcing himself not to look too closely at the floor he'd just been lying on.

"All clear," Alex said. "Did anyone see the shooter?"

No one spoke.

"Beau, you and Border all right?" she asked.

"Yeah, we took cover," Border answered as if this were a nightly happening and they knew the drill. "Can we come out of this cage?"

"Come on out. The bar's closed for the night." She looked at her deputies. "Go see if anyone outside is sober enough to have seen anything like someone holding a gun or maybe from what direction the shots were fired."

She walked over to the booth. "Everyone all right?"

Beau noticed the big guy still had his arm around Emily. He whispered something to her, then kissed her on the head. Whoever this guy was, he wasn't just some man talking to the librarian. She mattered to him, and obviously from the way she cuddled into him, he mattered to her too.

The biker chick with Matheson was pacing off the room as if looking for clues. She was the only one in the room who had not holstered her weapon. She handled it with the ease of a warrior long used to holding iron.

Alex leaned across the booth and said as calmly as if she were simply passing time, "I hate to tell you this again, Tannon, but you're bleeding."

He looked down at his arm. Blood was dripping off his shirt at the elbow. "I was worried about Emily. It's just a scratch."

Alex grinned. "It's evidence. We're on our way to the hospital."

Emily looked so white Beau thought she might pass out. If she did, the only injured person in the room would probably be the one who'd insist on carrying her out. He talked softly to her as Alex wrapped his arm with one of the bar towels.

The big guy, someone said his name was Tannon Parker, helped Emily out of the booth. "Breathe, Emily, breathe. It's all over and I'm not hurt bad. Honest, it doesn't even hurt."

She looked up at him with those big eyes Beau had always thought were her best feature. "Your arm was across me. If you hadn't covered me, the bullet might have hit me. Tannon, you saved my life."

Her words were so simple, but the meaning flooded the room. Until that moment, it had all been about the excitement. Her words made it real. Someone could have been killed!

Alex faced Rick. "I know you think this is your stalker, but we don't know that. It might have been an argument between drunks or a husband and wife fighting."

"He was here, probably waiting for me to come to him. He was here." Rick studied the room as if the shadow of someone trying to kill him might still be there. "I sensed him. The shooter was trying to kill me and I don't even know why. Each time he gets a little more determined, his efforts are more dangerous. It won't take long before one of us runs out of luck."

Harley yelled, "He could have been after me. I pissed off half the crowd tonight when I ran out of wings. Hell, he could have been after Border Biggs. The kid misses every other note he plays. Maybe there was a true music lover in here tonight who couldn't take anymore."

"Me?" Border paled beneath all his tattoos.

Beau shook his head, surprised at how calm he was after his first shoot-out. "Well, at least I know he wasn't after me. I'm just an innocent bystander in the dangerous midnight crowd where bullets fly and blood spills."

Harley glared at him. "You're starting to talk like a country-western song, kid. Why don't you go back to stuttering?"

Alex motioned Tannon and Emily toward the door. "I'll want all of you in my office tomorrow morning to give statements. Harley, lock the place up. I'll send a man to go over everything tomorrow, but I don't think we'll discover any clues." She glanced at Rick's friend. "You agree, Marshal?"

"I'm afraid you're right." The biker girl shook her head. "There are a dozen places he could have hidden and fired from and every one of them will have layers of fingerprints. We'll be lucky to find a shell casing."

"We'll look tomorrow." Alex took charge. "Right now, get Rick back to the B&B. I'll call you from the hospital if we dig a bullet out."

"I don't like the sound of that," Tannon complained as he followed the sheriff toward the door.

Just before everyone left, Border asked, "What do we do?"

Rick smiled. "I've had threats and attempts on my life for no reason, and the band looks confused. How about you boys come on home with me? We'll rob Martha Q's refrigerator. Nothing works up an appetite like being shot at."

They didn't wait to be asked twice. By the time Rick was on the porch, both of them were trailing inches behind. A deputy met them at the steps and walked with them to Rick's car. Beau couldn't help but wonder what good he'd be if the shooter were hiding somewhere in the dark parking lot. Phil Gentry seemed nice enough, but he didn't look like the type who'd take a bullet for a lawyer much less a country-western singer.

As soon as Beau climbed in the backseat, he scrunched down, removing his head from any target line.

Border, on the other hand, leaned forward. If a bullet flew from any direction it had a good chance at hitting him, but Border had questions and he didn't plan to wait for an answer. "Did I hear the sheriff call you a marshal?" he asked the girl with Rick.

"Deputy U.S. Marshal Trace Adams at your service."

Border started bouncing on the seat like he

weighed fifty, not two hundred and fifty, pounds. "That must be an exciting job. You been shot at before?"

"Yes," Trace answered as she drove. "A few weeks before I came here."

"I bet that was so exciting," Border said. "What happened? That is, if you can tell me. I bet it was wild."

In a bland tone, as if she were talking to a child, she answered, "My team walked into a trap at an old warehouse we thought was empty. We were caught in cross-fire. Everyone died except me. I walked away without a scratch."

No one in the car said a word until they were inside the bed-and-breakfast. Even then when they ate from plastic leftover cartons, no one mentioned anything about a shooting, past or present.

❦ *Chapter 43* ❦

After the band left Martha Q's place, Rick wasn't surprised to find Trace in the dark drawing room studying the movements beyond the window. He could tell by her stance that she was on guard, watching, protecting, even though the doors were locked and the security system was on.

"You all right?" he asked as he moved to her side.

"I'm thinking when he comes again, he'll hit somewhere quiet, someplace where you're alone and he'll have no distractions. Tonight wasn't planned out. He probably saw us come in and went out to his car or truck for the gun. He wasn't thinking about the people, only you." She watched one of the sheriff's cruisers pass slowly in front of the house. "He knows he made a mistake tonight. His next hit will be planned. When he comes again, he'll be better prepared."

"Don't you mean 'if' he comes again? Maybe tonight's failure will turn him off and he'll give up."

"You're dreaming, Matheson."

He leaned very near her ear. "If I were," he whispered, "you'd be naked."

She pushed away. "Get serious. Whoever's out there isn't stopping until you're dead. He proved that tonight by risking firing at you in a crowd. He's insane, and each attempt drives him a little farther over the edge."

Rick leaned against the frame of the window. The night was so still it could have been a Thomas Kinkade painting just beyond the porch. "I've been around guns all my life and I'm guessing you have too. What are the chances of someone firing three shots in a crowded bar and *not* hitting anyone?"

"He hit Tannon Parker."

"I heard the third bullet ricochet off the roof. I

think that hit was an accident. The shooter was aiming at the roof."

She moved closer, keeping her voice low. "So you're saying the gunfire was meant to frighten you, not kill you?"

He nodded very slowly as if letting the idea sink in.

"What about the car through the diner window? I was there. It was no accident."

"Yeah, but we were the only ones there. Think about it, Trace. I was sitting facing the direction the car came from. I would have had to be asleep not to see it coming."

Trace thought for a moment, then nodded. "So you think someone is *not* trying to kill you, that they just want to scare you to death."

Rick bumped his shoulder against hers. "I think whoever is out there is trying to scare me into changing my behavior. All I can't figure out is what they want me to do or not do. Maybe my moving out of town would make them happy. If I had a case, I'd think they'd want me to abandon it and run. If I were dating anyone they'd be sending a message for me to get lost."

"So, since you're not dating and you don't have any clients except the Peterses, the only choice left is *get out of town*."

"You offering to take me in?"

She laughed. "I can't even keep a plant alive. You could always consider the possibility that someone just picked your name out of the phone book or the school annual. Maybe it's not you but just a random target he's selected."

Rick moved his hand along her back. "Nope, it's personal. He picked me. I just don't know why, but the guy had to have studied my habits." Rick leaned in close and touched his body to hers. "How about kissing me like you did before we went into the bar?"

She started to answer, but his mouth covered hers and they were both lost. He loved the feel of her against him, and he knew she felt the same way. She'd be gone in a few days and he'd either be dead or moving on with his life, but either way Rick knew he'd be missing her all the way to cell memory level.

With one hot kiss, she'd become the benchmark of what he wanted. Since the eighth grade, he'd probably kissed a hundred or more girls, but not one could measure up to the way she reacted to him.

He pushed her toward the couch and leaned down over her body as she relaxed against the dozen pillows.

"We can't be doing this," she said as she pulled his shirt open. "We have to stop."

"Yeah, right," he laughed as he tugged her boots off.

She bit into his shoulder as he moved his hand down her back until he cupped her bottom. With one tug, he straightened her flat on the couch and lowered himself above her. Loving her was a battle of passion with both giving and taking. Both holding back before surrendering. Both demanding all that the other could give.

He felt like he was touching flames. No, not just touching, diving into the fire. Being here, touching her was a hundred times better than any fantasy he could have imagined. Her body fit against his. Her breathing matched his. Her passion exploded against him. Making love to her was like riding the rapids down the Grand Canyon or skiing a few feet ahead of an avalanche. There was no stopping, no slowing down, no time to think. The knowledge that she was running full speed with him made his heart pound so hard it threatened to crack his ribs from the inside.

When it was over, clothes and shattered minds lay around them. For a few minutes, Rick simply fought to breathe, then he rolled to his feet.

She lay among the pillows, her long body beautiful in the moonlight. For the first time since he'd known Trace, she was still, completely still, totally relaxed. He moved his hand along her body, damp with sweat, and a spark of fire began to burn atop the coals of the last blaze. She opened her eyes and in the green depths he saw a fire building also.

"Come on," he whispered as he leaned over and lifted her up. "We're taking a shower. I'm not sleeping with you while we're both sweaty."

"No," she complained, but her body was limp as a rag doll. "I'm not sleeping with you."

He pulled her into the warm shower and began washing her, allowing his hands to move slowly over her.

She took turns moaning her pleasure and swearing she would not sleep with him.

They were still arguing when they moved out of the shower, but he was laughing as he tossed her on the bed. Something about knowing that a woman could easily kill you a half dozen painful ways if she wanted to makes a man completely secure in bullying her.

"I'm not staying," she said as she sat up.

"Yes, you are," he answered as he laid his arm across her and pulled the covers up. "So shut up and go to sleep."

"Why?" she challenged, without fighting back.

"Because, Trace Adams, I'm crazy about you, and unless you plan to shoot me, you might as well get used to having me around." He laughed as she rolled against him. "I tell you what, how about you sleep and I'll watch over you for a change?"

He patted her bottom. "Now stop moving around. Forget about leaving and go to sleep."

To his surprise that was exactly what she did.

❧ *Chapter 44* ❧

Saturday midnight

Tannon didn't like the way Dr. Addison Spencer looked at him when he walked into the emergency room. He decided she probably had him marked as a troublemaker since this was his second wound in two days.

When he told her it happened in a bar, he didn't do much to improve her opinion. While she worked, he tried asking about Tinch Turner. Everyone knew it was just a matter of time before the two of them tied the knot. She might be a big-city girl used to living with a boyfriend, but Tinch was small town. He'd want a ring on her finger.

The doc looked up from the bloody arm. "Looks like the bullet just grazed across your skin. It's deep. Probably leave a scar but not deep enough to require stitches. You're a very lucky man, Mr. Parker."

So much for small talk, Tannon thought. "The sheriff will be disappointed that you don't have to dig a bullet out of me."

Addison finally smiled. "We gave up digging bullets out a hundred years ago. It's called surgery if needed, which you don't. I'd send a few prescriptions home with you, but I'm sure you're not halfway through the bottles I gave you yesterday."

As she cleaned and bandaged his arm, she finally answered his question. "Tinch is fine, by the way. He's probably sleeping in his pickup out back waiting for me to finish my shift, which was over two hours ago."

"I'm holding you up."

"You and a dozen others. This must be a full moon—you wouldn't believe the crazy things going on tonight."

"Yes, I would." Tannon leaned back and closed his eyes. "Tinch and I are friends, or at least we were when we were kids. I'm real glad to see him happy again. I'm glad he found a woman like you, Addison."

"A woman like me?" Addison frowned, and he wouldn't have been surprised if she told him to call her Dr. Spencer.

Several compliments came to mind. Addison was beautiful and obviously very bright, but he had a feeling that wouldn't be something she'd care to hear, so he said the only thing that matters: "a loving woman."

She accepted the compliment as she finished taping his arm. When they walked out into the lobby, she saw Emily rushing toward them and said, "It appears, Mr. Parker, you've found the same kind of woman."

Tannon grinned. "I have and I plan to do my best to keep her, but she doesn't know it yet."

Emily hugged him tightly, asking one question after another without giving Tannon any time to answer.

Dr. Spencer stepped back and smiled. Her words were soft, but he heard them. She said simply, "I think she knows."

Tannon answered all Emily's questions as they drove back to his place. It had been her idea to go to the bar to hear Beau play and now she kept blaming herself for his wound.

They didn't touch as they rode up the elevator. When the door opened he said, "You're staying with me tonight." It was a statement. He couldn't let her leave after coming so close to losing her.

"All right." She fumbled for the pain pills the doctor had handed her in case Tannon needed them.

"I don't want those," he answered before she asked.

"All right," she said, and set them on the counter. "Can I get you—"

"Emily, stop mothering me."

"All right."

"And stop saying all right. Everything is not all right. You were frightened and I'm mad." He hadn't meant to yell, but even he could hear the words bouncing off the wall and back at him.

She stood there looking adorable in her wool coat and wool gloves and wool scarf. He hadn't even thought of the jacket he'd left in the bar. If a snow slide rolled off the Rockies and smothered the whole town, she'd be the only one in Harmony prepared.

"Are you mad at me, Tannon?" She moved her hands as if winding invisible yarn.

He forced the muscles in his jaw to relax but he couldn't manage a smile. "No. I'm not mad at you, honey. I'm mad at whoever fired those shots. I almost lost you. Oh, God, if I'd lost you again . . ." He couldn't finish.

She raised her hand and brushed her glove along his cheek. As always she understood him far better than he'd ever understand her.

Pulling her to him, he lifted her off the floor and just held her as tight as he dared. "If I lost you, I think I might go mad." He was afraid if he told her just how much she meant to him that he'd frighten her even more than the shots in the bar had. She'd always been his normal, his balance in a world that didn't make sense. Even when they'd been apart at college, he'd known she was there and once they were both back in Harmony, just knowing she was safe a few blocks away in the library had balanced his days.

He lowered her slowly. "Can we go to bed? It's been a long day."

"All . . . of course. You're probably exhausted."

She disappeared into the bathroom and he slowly stripped his clothes off and crawled into what was now his side of the bed. Between his hand and his arm, a slow ache thumbed against his right side. Taking a few aspirin, he washed them down with bourbon and water. He took his time letting his muscles relax. He'd spent his entire adult life learning to be hard and cold and all business. Now he was going to have to learn to be kind. It wasn't enough that he protected her, that he'd die for her. He needed not to frighten her with his dark moods.

He waited for an eternity for her to step out of the bathroom, and finally she emerged wearing his shirt. He knew they needed to talk. They needed to get out all the unsaid words they'd both held back for years. He had to tell her he was sorry he hadn't been there for her fifteen years ago. He had to know that she'd forgiven him before he could let his heart completely go.

Part of him wouldn't blame her for walking away when she learned that he'd been the one who'd found her that night and walked away without ever talking to her. He'd left her at the hospital. He should have been there to stop the fight. He should have been there as she recovered. He should have always been there for her. If he had, maybe she wouldn't be so shy now. Maybe she wouldn't be afraid of relationships. Maybe she wouldn't be afraid of the dark.

But right now, with her standing in the glow of the streetlights in his shadowy bedroom, all he could think about was holding her. Reason told him he couldn't silently wash away all the pain she'd suffered, but reason wasn't his strong suit right now. He'd been there for her tonight and maybe that could be a place where loving could start.

"You want to sit on the couch tonight or in bed when I take my time kissing you good night?"

"In bed, but don't close the drapes. I like it when I can see you. I don't like the dark."

He knew why. He remembered her screams in the back parking lot by the stadium. The night had been so dark between the car and the back fence he couldn't tell where she'd been hurt until car lights flashed over them. "There's nothing in the dark but me. You're not afraid of me, are you, Emily?"

"No, I've never been afraid of you." She moved toward the bed.

"Then what are you afraid of now? The shooting is over. The doors are locked and I flipped the switch on the elevator. We're alone and safe."

"I just don't like the dark." She puffed up her pillows.

He remembered her apartment. The lights in every room were on when he'd entered.

"Emily, tell me about the night you were attacked. Tell me about the time your mother always called 'the accident,' even though every-one in town knew it was no accident."

"I don't want to talk about it. Mom said if I

never talked about it I'd forget all about it in time. I'd heal. It was only a few minutes of my life, but somehow everything seems measured in the before and after of that one slice of time."

He sat down on the bed and brushed his hand over her hair. "And did you heal?"

She turned away. "I don't want to talk about it. Let's go to sleep."

When he reached for her arm, she pulled away. "I don't want to be touched tonight. I'm tired. I'll kiss you good night in the morning."

Tannon knew he'd lost the battle, and if he wasn't careful, he'd lose her too. "If that's the way you want it."

"That's the way I want it."

"Then good night." He forced any anger or frustration from his voice and hoped she didn't hear how mad at the world he felt. She was so gentle, so kind. Nothing or no one should ever hurt her.

She was here in his bed, wasn't that enough for a while? He didn't have to force her to talk. He didn't have to push her into being more than they were now. Now was good. Hell, now was the best time in his life. Work was still demanding more hours than were in a day. His mother wouldn't be out of the hospital for at least another week, but she was well enough to complain. But Emily was safe beside him and that mattered all the way to his core.

He had no idea how long he lay watching the lights of town. An hour, two. Finally, he felt the bed shift and she rolled toward him.

"Hold me," she whispered. "I don't want to talk. I just want to feel safe."

He gently wrapped her in his arms and they both fell asleep. Holding her was all he wanted, and if feeling safe was all she wanted, he decided he could live with that. As he drifted off, he swore there would never be another time when he wasn't there to protect her from harm. He'd been there tonight and he'd be there again. Maybe one day he'd get up enough courage to tell her she was the best part of him, she always had been.

A little after dawn he awoke with her kissing his neck and her hand brushing his chest.

"Morning," he mumbled. "You the new alarm clock?"

She continued kissing him, moving up to his cheek. "Your beard tickles."

"I could go shave and be back in five minutes."

She laughed against his ear. "No. We have to get up." She rolled from the bed. "Mind if I take a shower here? Then all I'll have to do is change clothes when I get back to my place."

"Help yourself." He yelled as she disappeared into the bathroom. "You could move a few things over. My closet has got plenty of room. That way you wouldn't have to make a run to your place every time you sleep over."

"No," she answered. "That would be too much like we were living together."

She closed the door before he had time to answer. Tannon buried his face in her pillow and took a deep breath of the honeysuckle scent left by her hair. Of course they couldn't look like they were living together; after all, they were only sleeping over at each other's place. They were just friends.

He listened to the shower, wishing he'd offered to share rather than let her go first. When the water stopped and she walked out wrapped in one of his big towels, he thought this just-friends arrangement would surely put him in an early grave. If she hadn't disappeared into the kitchen to make coffee, he might have lost what little reason he had left. This sleeping-over arrangement was a thorny heaven.

After a quick shower with his arm wrapped in a towel to keep the bandage dry, he managed to pull on a pair of jeans by the time she pattered back into his bedroom on bare feet. She handed him a cup of coffee before curling into the covers and complaining about how cold it was.

He walked over to her and pulled the covers over her shoulders. "Morning, darlin'," he said as he pushed her hair back and kissed her lightly. "How about I warm you up while you give me that kiss you promised?" Maybe it was time to let her know they could be far more than friends.

After all, she was walking around his apartment wearing a towel and complaining of being cold. What more encouragement did he need?

Cradling her against him, he moved his left hand beneath the blanket and brushed his fingers over her cold shoulder as he kissed her. The frightened child had disappeared with the light and the woman in his arms responded willingly to his advance.

Slowly, she warmed and his touch grew bolder. His hands pushed the damp towel away from her as he moved over her body hidden beneath the blanket. He kept his touch light, brushing across areas he hoped to spend a great deal of time exploring later. The advance hadn't been planned; he simply moved with the natural flow of loving her.

"I like morning kisses better than good-bye kisses. They make me think about kissing you all day long."

When she pulled her arms out from beneath the covers to circle his neck, he tugged the blanket lower as the kiss deepened and he felt her bare breasts press against his chest. He pulled the covers over them both and kept the kiss tender.

Finally, out of breath, she pulled away and the covers slipped to her waist.

He met her eyes, wide and filled with passion, and he knew nothing that had just happened had been an accident. "You're beautiful." His voice sounded low and hesitant. "And you want this."

She smiled. "Yes," she answered simply as if the question needed no more explanation.

"You amaze me." He leaned over and kissed her softly as he moved his hand over her breast. "People who just sleep over don't do this, you know." He kissed his way to her ear and back. "And I'm guessing women who only want to be friends don't walk around in a towel."

"I know," she laughed. "But I had a feeling you wouldn't mind if I did."

"I wouldn't mind at all." He didn't want to think about what was happening, he just wanted to feel and taste and smell her close like this. Sometime in the near future he'd probably have an argument about how this dream couldn't possibly have really happened so he'd need many details for proof to convince himself.

He shifted above her, his chest lightly touching her breasts as he dug his unbandaged hand into her wild hair and kissed her with more tenderness and passion than he'd known lived within him. This wasn't some one-night stand after one too many beers. This was Emily and he wanted it to be just right.

Her breath shortened and her fingers moved over his back, pulling him to her. "One more kiss like this," she whispered.

He lowered his weight over her, feeling the give of her body beneath him. His heart beat against hers. His breaths balanced with hers. His lips pressed gently against hers.

She made a little sound like a yelp. "Your hand. I forgot about you being shot." She tried to pull away. "Stop, Tannon, stop. We might hurt you."

Tannon laughed, pulling up the last bit of sanity left in his brain. "You won't hurt me. But I'm afraid I have to get dressed. I have a few employees coming in this morning to catch up on the work I've missed lately. Much as I'd like to do this all day, unless you want the town to know you slept over, maybe we should think about leaving."

She squealed and jumped up from the bed, taking the blanket with her as she ran to the closet for her clothes. Then she hurried into the bathroom to dress.

"You don't have to close the door," he said more to himself than her. "I already know what you look like."

The door slammed.

He climbed out of bed and managed to be dressed when she came out. "I have to head out for Amarillo soon," he said as he handed her a now cold cup of coffee. "But we're sleeping at your place tonight. I'll probably give my staff a heart attack, but from now on, no one works on Sunday. That way, neither one of us will have to get up early, and your place will be more private than here. I want to work on perfecting those morning kisses you like so much, so we'll need time to work. It might not be a bad idea to start early and work all night."

He walked to the elevator with her, holding her purse and coat as she pinned the side of her hair up. "I've got to go see Mom, but I'll be back by dark. Wait dinner on me." He leaned into her as the elevator moved down, loving the way her body melted into his.

"I haven't invited you over yet," she whispered with a shy smile.

"Yes, you have. You just didn't use words."

The door opened and he straightened, glad to see that the office was still dark. If they played this game long enough, someone coming in early was bound to notice. Tannon didn't care, but he figured Emily would, so he reminded himself that they needed to be more careful.

"You coming over for a quick breakfast?"

"No, I've got too much work to do before I head out." He winked at her. "But it's going to take a pot of coffee to get rid of the taste of you and I don't know if my mind has any chance of clearing."

She laughed. "I started something, didn't I?"

"Yes, you did. Something I plan on finishing."

He stood watching her drive away and feeling newborn, raw with need and happy for the first time in years.

Lifting his coffee cup, he whispered, "See you tonight, my love."

❧ *Chapter 45* ❧

Trace could never remember sleeping as soundly as she did Saturday night after the shooting. She'd been running on adrenaline for an hour, trying to think about how to best protect Rick. The lawyer had a death wish, she decided. What kind of man goes out looking for trouble like he did?

Then he'd tossed her against the car and kissed her in the parking lot like no other man would have dared kiss her. If she hadn't liked it so much, she might have shot him herself.

When they were finally home and talking about the shooting, he'd started touching her and before she knew how it had happened, he was kissing her again. There had been nothing gentle about the way Rick made love to her. In fact, she was pretty sure she had a few bruises and had given a few as well.

The polite, frightened failure of a lawyer she'd met two weeks ago was gone. The man she'd slept with last night would never be called "boy" by anyone.

She slipped from his bed and tiptoed up the stairs, hoping Martha Q wouldn't hear her leaving Rick's room. In the shower, she checked for bruises and bites. Had he bitten her? No, that was her biting him. In the moment, it seemed like the right thing to do.

By the time it was first light, she'd dressed and climbed out the third-floor window. Somewhere close was the stalker. All she had to do was find him. He was close. He had been all along. Close enough to saw the steps and start a fire. Close enough for darts and gunfire. Close enough to cut up a children's book in a county library without anyone suspecting.

Staying in the morning shadows, she slipped behind the house and made her way along a cottonwood trail to the sheriff's office. If the stalker was watching the bed-and-breakfast, he'd think she was still there.

With luck, Rick would sleep another few hours at least. Trace wanted to do as much work as she could without him being aware. If Rick knew, he'd want to get involved and that could only mean trouble, because if he came along, the stalker might not be far behind.

A tired deputy coming off the night shift agreed to take her over to Buffalo's so she could start looking around. Harley had handed the deputy a key last night, claiming Sunday was his only day off and he didn't want to be bothered.

The deputy reached in his pocket and handed her a piece of paper along with the keys. "Harley told me that the sheriff asked him to make a list of all his customers who play darts on a regular basis. It took him a while, but he came up with those who'd probably have custom-made darts."

When Trace looked at the list, he leaned over her shoulder and added, "The only girl on the list is my cousin Betty. She's beat most of the regulars so many times they won't play with her."

"Know what color her darts are?"

"Red," the deputy said. "Bright red."

Trace thanked him and walked into the bar alone. After a few minutes of searching, she turned on the lights. She'd done a dozen crime scenes worse than this one so the dirt and spilled beer didn't bother her. Though she'd look for shells and fresh bullet holes on the walls, what she'd really come in for was to get the feel of the place. To be very still and let her mind think like the stalker's.

She moved along the walls and into corners, each time stopping to see what the view would be. After a half hour she'd found only two places where she could see the booth by the cage clearly and where any bullet wouldn't have to cross the dance floor. One spot was against the wall near the kitchen. It would have been too busy a place with people walking by placing orders. The other was by the front door in a space that once might have served as a coatrack. Here a three-by-four square was closed in on three sides by a wall about five feet high. Anyone standing in the space with only twinkling lights around would be almost invisible.

And there, in the space by the door, Trace found three shells. Carefully, she bagged them, realizing Rick had been right. There were better places to fire from, but any others would increase the chances that someone besides Rick would be hurt. The shooter either wanted to hit only Rick, or he'd wanted to frighten everyone.

Walking directly across to the wall behind the booth, she found two small bullet holes in the wall about six feet up. The shooter was aiming at Rick's head. A harder target to hit but a sure kill.

Trace closed her eyes, trying to relive the moments before the shots. Rick had been standing, yelling, cheering. He wouldn't be easy to hit. After the first shot, she'd moved in front of Rick, making the shooter's second shot even harder. She was up beside him, watching the crowd before the third shot. Maybe the shooter was distracted and the shot went wild, or maybe he pulled the trigger in frustration, knowing the shot would frighten the crowd and cause a stampede. The perfect time to escape.

Whoever fired last night wanted to hurt only Rick, no one else.

She walked slowly back to the sheriff's office piecing together what she knew, what she'd been trained to organize, until answers formed. The shooter would come again, more deadly next time and in a place where he could have more control.

When she got to the station, Phil Gentry was

signing in. He smiled at her. "How's our lawyer this morning? I heard what happened last night."

"He's still asleep. I left Martha Q and Mrs. Biggs to watch over him."

"What can I do for you, Marshal?"

"Could I see the names of all the people in the county who have registered .22 pistols?" She handed him the bag of shells.

"Sure, but it's not many. Most folks don't register guns unless they buy something new. Even if they were registered once, the owner may not still have them."

"But you know they have them?"

"Of course. If we demanded every Texan to register every gun, half of them would claim all the guns they owned fell in the lake." He smiled at her frustration. "If you want to know who has a .22 here in town, go over to the gun range next to the golf course. Bill Ottoson can tell you. He not only runs the range, but he also works on any weapon that needs fixing."

An hour later, Bill had talked her into letting him fire her service weapon while he rattled off names.

By the time Trace made it back to Winter's Inn, it was afternoon. She found Rick working at the desk in the second-floor sitting room. He looked up when she walked in and smiled.

She had no trouble reading his mind. "I don't want to talk about it."

"All right. How about we talk about the shooting. Maybe it'll turn you on like it did last night."

She scowled and he nodded once as if in apology.

"I've been studying all the lists we have here." He showed her all the yellow pads he'd collected. "Clients I've worked with. All in jail but the Peterses and Martha Q, who thinks she's a client. People who have visited the library in the past few weeks. No one stands out."

He lifted a new list. "People who can walk around downtown without being noticed. I've named them the invisible people. I'm guessing my stalker is close all the time. He either lives or works around the square."

"People who own .22 pistols." She added another list to his stack. "And"—she pulled the deputy's list out—"people who play darts at Buffalo's and probably have their own darts."

Trace sat on the arm of one of the leather chairs and studied the lists. "We know whoever he is goes to the library, hangs out and plays darts at the bar, knows the town well enough to set your car on fire and not be noticed leaving."

Rick frowned at the gun list. He recognized almost every name. After a long while, he looked up. "You do realize that half the men in the writers' group own guns."

He stood. "I need to walk. I think best on my feet."

She didn't bother arguing. "We drive out of town. Make sure we aren't being followed. Then we walk."

"Fine." He sounded bothered by her restrictions, but he agreed.

Before they made it downstairs, Rick took a call from his mother. She'd heard about the shooting at church and was upset. She wanted him to come over for supper and talk. Which, in Matheson language, meant that half of the clan would be there.

He tried to get out of it but finally admitted to Trace that he'd put them off long enough. They were worried. The whole town was worried. He needed to let his family know that he was all right. They'd all give him advice and they'd feel better.

Trace said she wanted to check a few more ideas out. "If you'll call Alex and Hank to pick you up, I'll let you go," she said.

Rick raised an eyebrow. "Oh, you'll *let* me go."

He was standing, moving around the desk before she realized her mistake.

The game was on. He chased her through half the house before he caught her in the third-floor bathroom and kissed her. Another one of those all-out, knock-your-socks-off kisses that left her shaking with need and about to lose control.

When they were both out of breath, she pushed

him away. "Did you ever think of asking instead of just attacking?"

"Nope," he answered. "You ever think of offering?"

"Nope."

"You want me to back off?" he asked, already knowing the answer.

She smiled. "When I do, I'll pull a weapon."

"Fair enough. Until then, I'll keep coming."

They walked out of the tiny bathroom and saw Martha Q standing at the bottom of the stairs. Her arms were folded over her chest and her smile reached from ear to ear. "I guess you guys finally figured it out, did you? It's about time. All I ask is that you try not to break the furniture."

Rick recovered first and hurried down the stairs. He kissed Martha Q on the cheek and said, "I have no idea what you are talking about, Martha Q. We were simply having a discussion about dinner." He winked. "I have to call my cousin and go over to my mother's house. Your niece is staying here for the Sunday night dinner with the Biggs boys."

Martha Q rolled her eyes. "I forgot it was Sunday. I'll go check and see if Mrs. Biggs needs me to run to the store. I swear those boys can eat more than I've ever seen."

Thirty minutes later, Trace stood on the porch as Rick walked out with a loaf of banana bread tucked under his arm like a football.

He looked straight at her. "You will be here when I get back?"

She nodded. "When I leave, Matheson, I promise I'll say good-bye."

"Fair enough."

A truck honked and he was gone before she had time to tell him to be careful. He'd be with his family. One was a sheriff. Rick would be safer there than with her.

Trace had seen one name on the list that drew her attention. Rick hadn't caught it because the name wasn't listed on the library list or the gun list, but he'd been near them every day.

❦ *Chapter 46* ❦

Sunday night

Tannon drove ninety miles an hour through the night. The afternoon with his mother had been worse than usual. As she recovered, she grew more and more demanding and everything he did was wrong. She'd told him once that every time she looked at him, she missed his father more. You'd think two people who had one child would smother him with attention and care, but it had never happened, and it was about time he stopped waiting for any love to flow over him. His mother loved herself more than she could ever love Tannon or his father.

Paulette Parker had gotten her way all her life. She'd been spoiled as a child; her one friend, Shelley, Emily's mother, had always given in to her plans; and her husband had worshipped her. Only age stood up against Paulette and wouldn't give in to her tantrums.

The only bright spot in the visit had been when Tannon mentioned Emily. His mother had gone on a rage about how he should have married her, but now it was too late. She'd never take a hard man like him. Not sweet little Emily.

Tannon hadn't said a word, but inside he smiled, remembering how he'd held her at dawn and thinking about how he'd hold her tonight.

He rested his bandaged hand on the steering wheel and forced all the anger from his thoughts. He wanted Emily tonight. He needed to feel her against him. The thought of what tonight might promise had kept him sane all day and now he was late getting back to Harmony, the one place in the world he wanted to be.

He parked the truck and ran up the steps to her building, pressed the code and was in. Emily had probably had dinner ready for two hours. He almost ran when the elevator opened. He pounded on the door of her apartment, but no one answered. He pounded again. He even tried the door, but found it locked.

Maybe she'd fallen asleep waiting. Maybe she was in the shower. Maybe she'd gone to bed without him.

"Hey, mister," a woman in a nightgown said from down the hallway.

"Sorry." Tannon turned toward her, not feeling sorry at all. "I didn't mean to disturb you."

The woman stepped out into the hallway. "You must be the guy I'm supposed to give this note to. Emily said you'd be banging the door down if she wasn't back and she was right. She said to tell you she forgot to charge her phone so she couldn't call you."

Tannon took the note and nodded his thanks. Before the woman was back in her apartment, he'd ripped it open.

I'll be back as soon as I can. The marshal called and asked me to open the library so she could look around.

He read the note again, then folded it and put it in his coat pocket. It made no sense. The shooting happened in the bar. Why would anyone want to look around the library? Whatever they wanted could surely wait until Monday.

He ran down the stairs, not caring that his boots were probably waking up people on every floor. Something wasn't right.

❦ *Chapter 47* ❦

Emily sat at the main desk feeling very alone. Trace Adams and one of the deputies were wandering around somewhere in the back. She'd followed them for a while, but they made her nervous touching things, moving things. Libraries had an order about them and the public didn't belong in the back.

She jumped when she saw a shadow cross the door. Even knowing the door was locked, for a moment she couldn't make herself look.

Then she heard a tapping and Tannon's voice calling her name.

Emily ran to let him in. Suddenly nothing about the night seemed frightening.

He didn't kiss her, but his arm held her tight as he walked her away from the doors. She'd expected him to start firing questions, but he didn't. She was safe and that was all that seemed to matter.

Before she could explain that she had no idea why the marshal would want to search the library, Trace stepped out of the back with the deputy at her side. The marshal carried a plastic bag with two darts inside.

"Emily," she said calmly. "Would you happen to have Sam Perkins's address?"

Emily went to her office and returned with a slip of paper. "This is it, or at least it was when he applied for the job a few years ago. Before that, I think he hung around town doing odd jobs and staying wherever was cheap. Is something wrong?"

"No," the marshal said. "We'd just like to ask him a few questions. Thank you for allowing us to look around." She took a step, then looked back. "Does anyone go into the staff area besides staff?"

"No."

"Thanks."

Emily wanted to ask more questions, but she doubted she'd learn more. With Tannon's fingers wrapped around her hand all she could think about was getting someplace where they could be alone.

They walked out just behind the marshal and Tannon followed her back to her apartment. They didn't kiss when they were back at her place. He was polite, asking about her day, wondering why the marshal would want to talk to the janitor, complimenting her on the meal she'd left warming in the oven, helping her with the dishes.

Finally, they were standing in her living room. Only a few feet remained between them, but neither knew how to cross it.

"Do you want to watch a movie?" she asked, feeling her shyness all the way to her bones.

They'd touched and kissed before, but each time they were separated it seemed they had to start all over again in knowing how to love.

"No, I'm not interested in a movie," he said before straightening and pulling in his breath as though the task before him might be difficult. "I want to go to bed with you. I'm not interested in a sleepover. I'm interested in sleeping with you every night for the rest of my life if you're agreeable to the idea."

He frowned. "We can be friends if that's all you want, Emily, but I think it's only fair I tell you straight out how I feel. I can't fall in love with you, honey, because I've been in love with you all my life."

When she didn't say anything, he continued his side of a debate she hadn't prepared for. "I know I'm not good enough for you. My mother reminded me of that fact today. I'm not sure I know how to be gentle and patient, but I'd like to try. I yell when I'm angry and I know that frightens you, so I'll try to keep it down. All the way home, I've been thinking of what to say, what I need to say to make you love me, and now it doesn't seem to be coming out right. I've got money enough to buy you a house if that's what you want. I should have bought a ring, but I wasn't sure you'd let me get that far."

"Tannon," she said softly, but he was lost in his speech.

"I work about sixty hours a week, but I can cut that down. I'd be home for supper most nights. I'd—"

Emily had heard enough. "Tannon. Stop talking and come to bed."

He looked at her a moment before her words sank into his tired brain, and then he smiled a slow smile.

She offered her hand and he took it. When they were in the bedroom, she let him turn off a few of the lights. She stood on her side of the bed and he stood on his. Slowly, they began to take their clothes off. There was no alluring strip, just two people preparing to climb into bed as if they'd done so in front of each other a thousand times.

When she pulled her slacks off, she held her breath and turned, letting him see the scars crossing over her stomach. No one, not even her roommates in college, had ever seen the scars.

He looked down at them, then back up at her eyes. For years, she'd feared what a man would say when he saw the scars. She'd promised she'd never take a lover because of that fear, but Tannon wasn't a lover—he was her best friend.

He moved slowly to her and kissed her gently before kneeling down on one knee. His big hand moved over the red jagged lines dug into her flesh years ago. "Do they bother you?"

"No. They're just the remains of one bad time. Are they ugly to you?"

"Yes, not because of the way they look, but because they are a reminder of when you were hurt." He stared at them a moment, then looked up. "I don't care about them. The you inside is so beautiful I barely see them."

Without a word, he leaned and kissed her damaged body. "Only you matter, Emily, but I have to tell you: I've always known about them. I'm the one who found you that night. I'm the one who held you until the medics came. I saw what they did to you that night."

She felt the cold of the room against her bare skin. "Why didn't you stay with me? Why didn't you visit? I don't remember much of the attack. The doctor said I passed out during it either from head trauma or loss of blood. When I woke up hours later, I felt very alone. Why didn't you come?"

"Because it was all my fault. I was late getting to my car. I was late picking you up. Afterward, I thought you'd hate me for not being there, and if you knew I found you and held you, then you'd hate that I'd seen you like that. Either way, I figured I'd be the last person you wanted to show up for a visit."

"No," she corrected, tears flowing for the first time in a long time. "You told me to wait in the front. I'm the one who went to the lot. I'm the one who didn't listen."

He stood and pulled her against him, wrapping her in his warmth as he always did. "At the time,

I thought I'd wait a while and then we'd talk, but you never came back to school."

She cried, holding on to him, letting all the anger and grief go as he kissed the top of her hair and whispered, "Don't cry, honey. Don't cry. I wish it had been me who got hurt. I would have taken the beating gladly if I'd known you were safe. I love you. I always have."

Without a word, he lifted her and put her in bed, then climbed in beside her and pulled her close. At first his touch was comforting, then caring.

"Do you think you could learn to love me, Emily?"

"No," she answered, and rose to her elbow so she could see his face. "I already do."

Rain tapped on the windows as they began to make love. They were in no hurry, they had a lifetime and both knew it.

He'd been wrong about not thinking he was gentle. His big hands moved over her with tender strokes even when he was sound asleep. Sometimes he'd pass over the scars on his journey of exploring every curve and she'd remember that she'd once been afraid to show them to anyone. She couldn't erase them or change what had happened to her, but as she felt his love surround her she no longer thought of herself as being scarred. Slowly, as the night aged, she realized that the scars didn't matter to him. He would love her no less.

They'd have a life together.

The two lovers who wrote out their feelings in the margins of The Secrets of Comeback Bay series drifted through her mind. Like her and Tannon, they'd lived in the same town, each dreaming of the other. Only they'd never been brave enough to say how they felt out loud.

❧ *Chapter 48* ❧

Monday

Rick walked into his office feeling like he'd played an all-night football game in the mud. Trace hadn't been home when he'd gotten back from the Matheson family dinner last night. He'd waited around reading until twelve, then gone up to her room.

The relief that her things were still there offered him little joy. He didn't know where she was. If she was safe. If he was safe without her. He tried her cell and heard it ring upstairs. Wherever she'd gone, she hadn't taken it.

When the rain started, he knew she had to be somewhere out in it. She was close, he decided, but not safe, and the thought drove him insane.

By three a.m. he was wide awake, questioning how he'd acted. Maybe he'd come on too strong and she'd simply relocated. The few things she'd left would be easy to replace. No, he reasoned, she would have told Martha Q or Mrs. Biggs. He'd already woken them both up once to ask questions and didn't want to think about what they'd say if he did it again.

By seven, he'd given up all hope of sleep and dressed for work. Several of his new clients would be dropping by the office today and he thought he'd go over and make sure the place looked presentable. Or at least as presentable as an old office with used furniture, a worn rug and chipped paint could look.

Hank offered to pick him up since it was still raining. He didn't ask about Trace when he helped Rick carry files up to the office.

"Will you be all right here alone?" Hank asked as if Rick were a first-grader.

"Yeah. I've got work to do and I'll lock the office door."

Hank nodded. "Alex said she'd be by to check on you. Just call 911 if you suspect anything. We'll both be on our way when we see the ID. You won't have to say a thing."

Rick laughed. "George will be just below soon. I think he hears everything that goes on in my office, plus half the town is probably watching over me."

"Where's the marshal?"

Rick shrugged. "I'm sure she's around. After all,

it would look bad on her record if I died during her watch."

Hank raised an eyebrow as if he knew there was more in what Rick wasn't saying, but he didn't have time to ask. He set the box down and left.

Rick opened the curtains to a rainy day world and sat down behind his desk. After the shooting Saturday night, everyone was very serious about the threats on his life. No more jokes. Sometimes he even got the creepy feeling folks were looking at him as if they were staring at the pre-dead walking. They'd stretch their neck for one more look like it might be their last.

Glancing at his watch, he frowned. His first client, a couple wanting to write a will, wouldn't be in for another hour. If it had been a normal day and there weren't some nut somewhere out there wanting to kill him, Rick might have walked over to the diner for coffee.

Oh yeah, the diner wasn't open now, thanks to him. Rick never thought he'd miss the place. Maybe he just missed the coffee.

He couldn't even go down to the used book-store. Hatcher never opened until about nine.

So here he was, tired, worried about Trace, even though she'd be mad if she knew anyone worried about her, and stuck in his office without any coffee. Could the day get any worse?

He heard the back door in the hallway open.

Apparently, the day was about to get worse.

Someone would have had to climb over two missing steps to enter from that direction and that didn't seem like a positive. Trace might have thought of coming in that direction, but she'd have no reason to. Besides, he could hear footsteps and Trace was like a cat, she never made a sound.

Rick pulled his phone from his pocket and dialed 911. Hank probably hadn't had time to get back to the fire station, but the sheriff's office would pick up. If this was a false alarm, maybe Hank would bring him coffee. If the threat was real, this might be the only time he'd be able to call.

As he heard footsteps move to his door, he slipped the phone in his top drawer and stood, crossing the room so that his back was against the windows.

The knob turned. The lock held. Rick froze, waiting.

He heard the rattle of keys then the lock turned.

With the rain, Rick knew he'd have the advantage if someone stepped in. They'd be in the bright light, he'd be in the shadows.

To his surprise, Sam Perkins shuffled through the door. For a moment Rick felt relieved to see the library janitor. He did odd jobs around town. It made sense that he'd have keys to some of the buildings he worked on.

Rick straightened. No one had called a handyman, and even if they had, why would he come up the broken back stairs? Another thought crossed his mind. Sam Perkins had been around for years. He was one of those invisible people moving in the shadows. Of the office buildings. Of the library. Of the bed-and-breakfast. No one noticed him.

Rick glanced at the square envelope in his left hand. "Come to leave another note?"

Sam's wet coat shifted as he now revealed his right hand.

Rick saw the gun in his grip. "Or this time have you decided to face me when you try to kill me?"

Sam smiled. "Nothing against you, Matheson. You just got in my way. If you'd been smart enough to leave town, I wouldn't be here now."

Rick made his body relax as he lowered his shoulders and opened his hands. He didn't want to appear threatening. The man was better than twice his age, but the gun gave him quite the advantage. "Since it's finally just me and you, Sam, would you mind telling me why it's so important that I leave town?"

Sam hesitated as if thinking about answering.

Rick studied the man. His clothes were wet and wrinkled. The cuffs of his pants were muddy, and he obviously hadn't shaved or bathed in a while. He had the look of a drifter who lived beneath a bridge. Rick had heard rumors that before Sam got the job at the library he'd been intermittently homeless. He had neither family nor friends in Harmony, at least not that Rick knew of.

"I'll tell you if you want to know. I was standing just outside when I heard you tell Hank you'd have a while to work before anyone came in, so I guess we got time."

"Fine, want to have a seat?" Rick would love to get a desk between him and Sam.

"No." Sam widened his stance. "You take one twitch toward me, Matheson, and you'll die not knowing why."

Rick lifted his hands in surrender. "Fine. I won't move. Just tell me what I ever did to you that makes you so angry."

Sam's laughter was hard, choppy. "I ain't mad at you. You're just in my way. I seen the way you wormed your way close to the woman I've loved for years. You two start by going to lunch, and then you move into her place to watch over it while she's gone, only when she comes back you don't leave."

Ideas popped like popcorn in Rick's tired brain. "You think I've come between you and"—he couldn't even imagine it being true, but he gave it a shot—"and Martha Q?"

"She even went off to get all prettied up for you. I've been around over the years when she married older men and younger men, bums who mistreated her and rich guys who cheated on her, but this time you've gone too far. I don't have nothing against you, but this time I'm not standing by and watching her make another mistake."

Rick wanted to laugh out loud, but he knew he'd be shot. How many times in the past year had he said he loved Martha Q? When she took him to lunch his first week? When she offered him a place to stay? When she told him how to treat Trace? The night he'd come to the library to take notes at the meeting, he'd even told the writers' group that he was sitting in for her because he just loved her.

"Sam, I—"

"Don't try to deny it," he said, raising the gun. "She's the only dream I have left and you're not taking her from me. I loved her for a time when I was a kid. I loved her then, but we moved away, and when I made it back she'd already married. I spent a few years drunk, a while roughnecking all over the state, a few years in jail. Every time I made it back to her, she was married to some other jerk."

Rick almost said that with a résumé like that he couldn't understand why Martha Q overlooked him in the lineup of possible husbands. The janitor didn't look like the laughing kind. He looked more like the murdering kind. Rick had to think.

"I don't blame you for loving her, but you're in my way, Matheson." Sam nodded as if he'd finally made up his mind about what had to be done. "It's time for you to disappear."

Hank and someone from the sheriff's department were probably on their way, but footsteps might startle Sam and he'd fire. If Trace picked this moment to appear, she wouldn't be expecting an ambush. She might only add to the body count.

He had to act, and act fast.

"Sam, you're right. I do love Martha Q." Not the brightest thing to say, but all he could come up with.

The old janitor relaxed an inch as if he'd been waiting for Rick to call him crazy or wrong.

"I've been wild about her, just like half the men in this town." Rick had heard the stories about Martha Q's younger days. He thought of adding that most of the half were dead by now, but he didn't think that would help his case.

"I've tried every way I know how to get her to fall for me." Rick tried to look miserable.

Sam frowned and aimed the gun.

Rick rushed on. "Only, I can't get anywhere with that woman. It appears she's thinking of someone else." Rick knew he was gambling, but the stakes were counted in minutes he had left to live. "There's someone in her past she cared for years ago and she can't get him out of her mind. He's the one she's prettying up for. He's the one she thinks will someday knock on her door."

"I told her I wouldn't come until I was rich or famous," Sam said.

"That doesn't matter to her, Sam. She's waiting

for you. You don't have to step over me or even around me. I'm invisible to her. I'm no more than a homeless puppy she's taken in."

Sam nodded. "I've never known her to go out with a Matheson. She told me once she didn't like men who were too tall. Said they were hard to kiss." The gun lowered a few inches.

Rick was no longer in the line of fire. His brain went manic as he tried to put the pieces together. "She told me she had a secret reason for going to the writers' meetings. She might not want to write, Sam. She must have wanted to see you. That's why she came those nights. That's why she got all dolled up. It was in hopes of seeing you." Rick was surprised his nose wasn't growing, he was lying so completely. If Sam Perkins had been on a woman like Martha Q's radar, he would have been hog-tied and branded by now.

"I did see her looking around," Sam agreed. "And one night I think she smiled at me when she walked by. It might have been a twitch, though."

"She's waiting." Rick took a step toward the janitor. "If you kill me, you'll only make trouble for her. Think about it. She'll have to go all the way to Bailee to find another lawyer."

Sam agreed with a nod. "If you're just a stray dog to her, I'd probably make her mad killing you. She's got a kind heart."

"You've got to go talk to her." Rick took another step, knowing he wouldn't let Sam out of the office to go anywhere. "You have to tell her how you feel."

"I can't. I never made nothing of myself like I told her I would. Besides, she knows how I feel. I wrote it down years ago in a set of books we both read. I promised I'd come back when I could take care of her."

"That won't matter to her. Go ahead, write her a note and ask her. She needs you living at Winter's Inn. Mrs. Biggs told me you fix things around there and things always need fixing." Rick pushed a legal pad across the desk as he stepped to Sam's side and took the gun.

A heartbeat later, what seemed like half the town rushed into his office. Rick kept his hand on Sam's shoulder as he faced them.

Alex listened to Rick's low statement, hand-cuffed Sam, and said he could finish the letter to Martha Q over a warm cup of coffee in a dry cell. Sam didn't put up any fight. He even apologized to Rick on his way out.

As the room cleared, Trace slipped through the door.

"About time you got here." Rick stood and walked toward her. "Some bodyguard you turned out to be. I had to save myself."

"How'd you do that, Matheson?"

"I talked my way out of it."

She grinned. "Maybe you're not as bad a lawyer as you think you are?"

"Maybe not." He mentally patted himself on the back. "Where have you been? I was worried about you."

"I found the darts in Sam's locker at the library, but that wasn't enough proof, so I went to his place. I watched the house for an hour, then saw him leave about midnight. He walked over to the B&B, but I think the alarm system kept him from stepping foot on the property. He slept in the arbor out back until dawn. When he saw you leave the house with Hank, he crossed through the trees and made it here before you did."

"You knew he was coming after me. You knew he was armed, but you didn't stop him."

"We didn't have enough on him to make anything stick, so arresting him would only make him madder."

Rick frowned. "So your plan was to hang around and watch until he killed me so you'd have evidence."

"Something like that." She pulled her hand from her pocket and let bullets roll from her fingers onto the desk. "I hated the thought of more damage to that great body of yours, so I took these out of his gun while he was asleep. He even made it easy for me by leaving the gun next to him while he snored away."

"Nice of you to tell me. I almost had a heart attack."

"I couldn't tell you. You had to be convincing. I

was ten feet away, listening the whole time. Alex and I talked it over. Sam was like the town mole. If he knew we were chasing him, he'd go underground and we'd never find him."

Rick took a deep breath. "It's over. It's finally over."

"Yeah, but don't think things will go back to normal. People are already waiting for you downstairs. You're going to be busy, Counselor."

He nodded. "Tell Alex I'll be over as soon as I can to talk to Sam. I'll do what I can for him."

"I'm going to go back to the B&B to tell Martha Q a man was willing to kill for her. That should make her day."

Rick touched her shoulder, surprised at how cold she was. The knowledge registered. If Sam had stayed out all night, so had she. "How about a real date tonight? I'll take you out to eat and we can spend the night discussing the case while I warm you up."

She shook her head. "It's time I moved on. My leave is up. I've got enough paperwork to keep me busy for a few hours, but I'll drop by afterward to say good-bye, Rick."

He fought down his answer. She'd kept her word—she said she'd say good-bye before she left him—but she was leaving him. In truth, he didn't know what they would talk about now that Sam was caught. He ached to hold her, to feel that long, lean body wrapped around him, but they needed time to get to know one another and the clock had run out. "I'll meet you back at the house when you finish. I'll help you pack." He could think of nothing else to say.

"Fair enough. I'll call when I leave the sheriff's office."

He watched her leave, knowing that she'd probably be in every sexy dream he would have until he was eighty. They'd never talked of love or caring. It seemed out of place to talk of it now.

❧ *Chapter 49* ❧

It was a little after ten when Emily got the call from Alex telling her that Sam Perkins had been arrested. When she told her staff, everyone cried. Emily, because she felt sorry for Sam. The rest of the staff, because it all seemed so sad, and Pamela Sue, because they no longer had a janitor.

The mood in the library was so down that Emily considered taking her first sick day, but she didn't want to go home alone. Tannon told her he had work at his office and then planned to make the drive back to visit his mother. She thought of calling him, but she knew he was busy.

A few minutes later, the library phone rang. Pamela Sue, as always, jumped for it.

Emily moved away from the desk, picking up books that had been left on the study tables.

"Emily," Pam shouted. "It's a woman from Parker Trucking. She says she wants to talk to the librarian."

Rushing over, she took the phone. "Yes, this is Miss Tomlinson. How may I help you?"

"Miss Tomlinson, I'm sorry to bother you and I may get fired for this, but Mr. Parker is upstairs and isn't answering his phone. He's missed two meetings. We're afraid something is very wrong. He took a call on his cell phone an hour ago and walked out of his office looking very upset."

"I'll be right there." Emily dropped the phone, grabbed her keys and ran.

Five minutes later, she was standing in front of the secretary's desk. Half the staff were close enough to listen. They all looked worried, reminding Emily of soldiers without a leader.

The pretty secretary began. "Mr. Parker never misses a meeting, and he always answers his cell phone. In fact, he's been known to fire people who didn't make him aware of a problem with the company as soon as possible." She looked around at the others. "When he didn't come down or answer his phone, we decided to call you."

"Why?" Emily said.

"You're the only person he's ever let in," she answered simply.

Emily wasn't sure if she meant into his living area or into his life, but it didn't matter. She agreed—something was wrong. "Thank you for your concern. I'll be right back." Without another word, she walked to the elevator and pushed the button. It didn't respond. Tannon had turned it off like he did every time they'd gone upstairs together.

She tried the door to the stairs leading up to his apartment. It was locked. She turned to the crowd she knew would be watching. "Do any of you have the key to this door?"

"I know where one is." A man stepped forward. "I saw Mr. Parker put one here in case there was ever a fire." He reached above the fire extinguisher and handed it to Emily.

Without hesitation, she opened the door and climbed the stairs.

Her relief when she saw Tannon standing by the window of his living area hit her like a tidal wave. "Tannon," she whispered.

He looked over and smiled. "Hi, honey." No *What are you doing here?* No anger.

As she walked to him, she saw a deep sadness in his eyes. "Are you all right?"

"I am now." He leaned down and kissed her tenderly as if he'd been waiting all day just for her kiss.

She hugged him and whispered as the kiss ended, "I love you so much."

He kissed the top of her head. "I know. I love you double that."

She smiled. "Want to tell me what the call

was about that sent you up here hiding?"

He pulled her closer. "I'm not hiding. I'm thinking. The call was from my mom's doctor. We thought she was doing better, but she's fighting with the doctors again, saying she's not going to cooperate."

"Tannon, what can I do to help?"

He shrugged. "Nothing, just ride out her moods with everyone else. It's a lot to deal with. I didn't want to lay my problem at your door. I have to take care of her. It's not fair to get you mixed up in the drama of my mother."

Emily knew it was time to make up her mind. "Your problem is my problem, Tannon. Let me be there for you. Don't push me away like you do everyone else."

He smiled down at her. "I've been thinking about doing just that. After the call I thought about pushing you into a safe place and out of this mess of a life, but I can't. I need you too much. Without you, I'm not whole. I never have been. I know it's not fair, but I can't walk away and leave my duty and I can't live without you in my life."

She smiled. "I feel the same. Life can't always be perfect. In fact, maybe it never is, but we can make it through." She pulled away. "I'll call the library and take a few days off. You go pack."

"You bossing me around again?"

"Either you pack or I'll pack for you, and if I do, I'm packing the Hawaiian shirt for you."

He smiled. "I'll pack and I'm taking the shirt, but not for me, for you. We won't be getting two rooms this time. You're sleeping over in my room."

Ten minutes later, they rode down in the elevator. Tannon slipped his arm around her shoulder as the door opened. All the staff was standing as if at attention.

He frowned, then forced a smile. "I'm leaving for a few days," he said. "I know you all can handle things. My wife and I will be back soon."

"Your wife?" The man who'd found the key to the stairs seemed to be the only member able to speak.

Tannon nodded once. "She will be as soon as I get her to the courthouse."

His staff was too shocked to react. Tannon pulled Emily out of the office and ran for his truck.

Once they were driving away, she said, "You bossing me around, Tannon?"

"Nope, just stating a fact. I can't live without you. You can't live without me. We might as well get married."

She laughed. "The office would never believe what a romantic you are." Her mind drifted to the night when he'd held her so tenderly. "Say one romantic thing to me, Tannon."

He reached for her hand and kissed it. "You hold my heart, honey. You always have."

She sighed and moved beneath his shoulder.

❧ *Chapter 50* ❧

Rick worked most of the day, letting all the tension slowly leave his body. The horror was over, and somehow he'd come through stronger. He almost wanted to thank Sam Perkins.

When he finally made it home, he found a cheery Martha Q waiting to talk. She told him how upset she'd been that the trouble he'd suffered was because of her. She wanted to hear every detail of what had happened in his office. When he finished, she told him that she felt it was her duty to write Sam; after all, she'd obviously broken his heart and driven him mad.

"I've had that effect on men before but never to this point. The thought of him pointing a gun at you and even thinking about firing frightens me."

"At his age, Sam might never get out of jail." When Martha Q looked like she might cry, Rick added, "Your letters will mean a great deal to him, I'm sure."

Martha Q wanted to know if they allowed conjugal visits for pen pals.

Rick faked a cough and almost killed himself falling over furniture as he ran from the room.

When he made it to the kitchen, Mrs. Biggs was waiting with a glass of water.

"Thanks," he managed.

"I'm sure she forgot to tell you, Mr. Matheson, that Trace Adams left about an hour ago. She said to tell you she couldn't wait any longer to say good-bye."

Rick took her words like a blow. He knew the marshal was leaving, but he'd thought he'd see her one last time.

Mrs. Biggs seemed to understand. "She said she was stopping by my grandson's place. Said she promised him a ride on her bike." Mrs. Biggs giggled. "I called my Border and told him to take his time on the bike. I'm guessing your girl is still waiting for him to come back."

"She's not my girl," Rick answered as he handed her the glass and headed out.

"You'll need these." Mrs. Biggs handed him the keys to the Land Rover. "I'd go out the back if I were you. I don't think Martha Q will be finished telling her thoughts for another decade."

Rick walked out the back door and drove to the old duplex near the town square. When he pulled up, he saw Trace sitting on the porch listening to Beau play his guitar.

As he walked up, the kid quit playing. Rick nodded at him but his words were for Trace.

"I thought you were going to say good-bye."

"I got tired of waiting. It's time I leave. As soon as Border comes back, I'm on the road, Matheson. There's no reason for me to stay."

He could see their wild night together still

burning in her green eyes. "We need to talk in private. Beau, you mind if we borrow your place?"

"Fine," Beau said as they walked past him. "If you break anything, you buy it."

"Keep playing. We'll only be a minute."

He followed Trace into the apartment and slammed the door. A hundred things he wanted to say filled his mind, but the need to hold her was too great. He grabbed her arm, twirled her toward him and caught her with both arms.

"Rick," she began.

"So you do know my first name." He smiled down at her. "When I finish kissing you good-bye, I hope you can still remember it." He lowered his mouth before she had time to say anything and kissed her as if he were dying for the taste of her.

As he knew she would, Trace kissed him back. For a while they were lost in the passion. Finally, the kiss turned tender as did his touch. When he finally broke the kiss, he whispered, "I'm coming to Chicago in a month and we're going to have that real date."

"I won't answer the door." She moved her hand over his hip.

"Yes, you will. You'll be starving for me by then. You'll answer the door and you'll be wearing a dress. We'll go out to dinner and then come back to your place."

He kissed her again. "Promise me you'll be there."

She nodded. "I'll be there, but this between us will never work. I've never been half of a couple before."

He smiled. "I'm bringing food and water. We'll give it three or four days before we decide."

She smiled. "What will we do for three or four days?"

"Talk, among other things." He pushed her a few inches away as he heard the motorcycle returning. "Now kiss me good-bye again."

Ten minutes later, they finally walked out of the apartment. Border and Beau were both trying to act like nothing was going on.

Trace hugged them both and told them how good it was to meet them. When she hugged Rick, she whispered, "One month."

As she drove away Rick realized all they had was possibilities, but for now that was enough.

❦ *Chapter 51* ❦

Beau played his songs as the night grew late. He couldn't stop smiling at the way he'd seen Rick Matheson and Trace Adams look at each other. He'd heard her whisper, "One month," but he doubted either of them would last that long apart. They were the lucky ones. They'd found something that came along once in a lifetime.

A song came to him about lovers driven by passion into a loving that lasted forever.

Near midnight, he stopped singing and just played a few of the old tunes he loved. He wasn't sure how it happened, but sometime in his learning to play the music started skipping his brain and going straight from his ears to his fingers. He could play almost anything he heard. It was like the music had come into him and now would live within him as long as he breathed.

Maybe he didn't need hard times to play. Maybe just life with its good and bad was all he needed. The prize wasn't to live a perfect life but only to survive the times between the perfect moments that come along just often enough to keep him going.

As his fingers moved, an old classic Ford pulled up in front of the duplex. "Write me a ticket, Red," he whispered as he set his guitar down and walked out.

"Evening, Trouble." He tipped his hat.

"Want to go for a ride?" She smiled. "I know an old part of Route 66 that no one's been on for years."

He spread his arms out along the top of her car door and leaned down to kiss her before walking around to the other side to climb in.

With his hat low and his head back he said simply, "Drive."

She shot off into the night, heading for moonlight along a blacktop road.

Center Point Large Print
600 Brooks Road / PO Box 1
Thorndike ME 04986-0001 USA

(207) 568-3717

US & Canada:
1 800 929-9108
www.centerpointlargeprint.com